After losing a big corporate job, Karen Quinn helped found Smart City Kids, a New York-based company that helps families survive the application process to Manhattan's most competitive public and private schools. Now a full-time writer, she lives in New York. *The Ivy Chronicles* is her first novel. Visit her website at www.karenquinn.net

The Ivy Chronicles

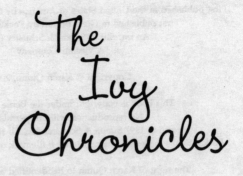

A NOVEL

Karen Quinn

**POCKET
BOOKS**

LONDON • NEW YORK • SYDNEY • TORONTO

First published in the United States of America by the Penguin Group, 2005
First published in Great Britain by Pocket Books, 2005
An imprint of Simon & Schuster UK Ltd
A Viacom Company

3   5   7   9   10   8   6   4   2

Simon & Schuster UK Ltd
Africa House
64–78 Kingsway
London WC2B 6AH

www.simonsays.co.uk

Simon & Schuster Australia
Sydney

A CIP catalogue record for this book is available from
the British Library

ISBN 0743492161
EAN 9780743492164

Typeset by Palimpsest Book Production Limited,
Polmont, Stirlingshire
Printed and bound in Great Britain by
Cox & Wyman Ltd, Reading, Berkshire

To my mother, Shari Nedler, who can do anything,
and who taught me to believe that I can do the same.

To my father, Sonny Nedler, who is my guardian angel.
Never have I felt so heavenly blessed.

Acknowledgments

The Ivy Chronicles would never have been published if not for the help of a great many generous people. I wish to thank Pam Dorman, who saw the potential in my manuscript and then showed me how to make it better. Special gratitude to Clare Ferraro, Rakia Clark, Carolyn Coleburn, Alex Gigante, Mindy Im, Judi Powers, Nancy Sheppard, Julie Shiroishi, and all the talented people at Viking who brought this book to life. A heartfelt thanks to Suzanne Baboneau and Kate Lyall Grant for publishing *The Ivy Chronicles* abroad. Much appreciation to Sarah Nundy at Andrew Nurnberg Associates and Shari Smiley and Sally Willcox at CAA. *Merci beaucoup* to my Renaissance friend, Stuart Calderwood, who copyedited this book not once but twice. I am forever indebted to Robin Straus, agent extraordinaire, for taking me on. And God bless Beverly Knowles, our babysitter and member of the Jamaican branch of the Quinn family, for finding me an agent. Is there *nothing* Bev can't do?

Every day, I thank my lucky stars for Mark Quinn, my amazing husband, who never once suggested that I get a real job. I owe a huge debt to my children, Schuyler and

viii   *The Ivy Chronicles*

Sam Quinn, without whose tuition bills this book would never have been written. Special acknowledgment to Sam Quinn for all the funny things he said that found their way into these pages. And no, Sam, I will *not* pay you a commission. I want to express my deep-felt appreciation to Shari Nedler and Judith Levy, whose laughter and encouragement in the very beginning kept me writing. I am profoundly grateful to a few extraordinary people whose insightful comments and personal support will always be remembered: Don Nedler, Michael Nedler, Candice Olson, Judith Kahn, Eva Okada, and Kathleen Stowers.

To Roxana Reid, my former partner and co-founder of Smart City Kids, who is the quintessential admissions adviser – patient, knowledgeable, ethical, sympathetic, and hysterically funny. If I ever need to get one of my children into school, you're the one I'll call. To my fabulous clients, especially those who had just graduated from Pull-Ups when first we met – I'm still rooting for you. Thanks to Drayton Bird, who so graciously lent me his name for my baddie. (To set the record straight, the real Drayton is as good a man as they come.) Thanks also to all my other friends who allowed me to use their names in the story for smaller but no less important roles. To Om Dutta Sharma, the selfless New York City cab driver who did indeed start a school for girls in Doobher Kishanpur, India: If true generosity begins with sacrifice, then you are the real thing. For more information about Mr. Sharma's school, write to: Pt. Sitaram Balkishan Charitable Trust, 6115 Broadway, Woodside, New York 11377.

And finally, while space prevents me from acknowledging everyone's specific contribution to *The Ivy Chronicles*,

I want to thank the following people who walked with me for part of this journey: Jerry Bauer, Meris Blumstein, Claire Chasnoff, Margaret Cooper, Stacy Creamer, Robin Daas, Jennifer Deare, David and Lisa Drapkin, my e-group, Keith Fisher, Victoria Goldman, Ken Gomez, Pat Hurlock, Carole Hyatt, Marla Isackson, Stephen Jones, Barbara Kanter, Gail Kenowitz, Susan Kleinberg, Monica Langley, Chivaun Mahoney, Francesca Marc-Antonio, Jeff Miller, Murray Miller, Peter Olson, Jodi Paulovich, Beth Phoenix, Marvys Pou, Avi Portal, Lynne, Wendy, Janet, and Ted Quinn, Nancy Schulman, the staff at Sonny's Fine Jewelry in Denver, Linda Spector, Christian and Victoria Tse, John and Barbara White, and Jennifer Wilen.

www.karenquinn.net

A Note to Readers

The author worked as a consultant, helping hundreds of New York City families through the private, public, and nursery-school admissions process, and this story was inspired by that experience. *The Ivy Chronicles*, however, is a work of fiction. Names, characters, organizations, places, events, incidents, and the schools portrayed in the story are products of the author's imagination. Any resemblance to actual names, people, organizations, places, events, incidents, and schools is coincidental. In addition, certain public figures make brief appearances in the story. They have been included without their knowledge or cooperation. Their interaction with the fictional characters is a product of the author's imagination and is not intended to be understood as negatively reflecting on anyone or having actually taken place. Although some real New York City institutions and people are mentioned, all are used fictitiously.

PART 1

The Limo Doesn't Stop Here Anymore

1. The Girl from Park Avenue

Konrad insisted that everyone be at his desk by 7:45 A.M. No exceptions. It would be sexist, he said, to cut the mothers on the team any slack. Easy for him to say. He had a stay-at-home wife and two full-time nannies to handle his family's morning drill. You know, we each have one. In my case – walk the dog, dress the kids, make breakfast, rinse the dishes, supervise brushing, flossing, and bed-making, look for lost homework, load up backpacks, while at the same time getting myself out of bed, showered, dressed, made up, and out the door.

The race continues on the street: grab a cab, drop Sir Elton at doggie day care, and deliver the girls to their overpriced early-bird program. If I've gotten this far by seven, I'll have just enough time to sprint to the subway at 86th and Lex and shoot down to Fulton Street. Finally, jump off the train, drop a dollar into the PLEASE FEED ME I'M HUNGRY lady's cup, zip into the building, dash toward my elevator bank after a quick stop at Starbucks for coffee light, two Sweet'n Lows, and a bagel to go, and declare victory if my butt hits the chair and the clock hasn't struck 7:45.

Technically, my unemployed husband could have

handled the morning routine. What I mean is, it would have been *physically possible* for him to manage it if he didn't insist on sleeping until 9:00. Yeah, I know. I should have been tougher. But trust me, it was easier to handle it myself than fight the battle. Cad had been unemployed for eight months. A derivatives trader at Bear Stearns, he was fired after betting wrong on Russian government debt. Still he persisted in living like nothing had changed. He would have hired someone for the A.M. job, but given our financial state and the fact that neither of us spends enough time with the girls, I couldn't agree. Plus, let's face it, what man takes charge of the morning marathon? Yes, of course, there are exceptions, perhaps in a parallel universe, but not in my world.

On this particular day, I *just* wanted to snuggle back into my warm Duxiana bed with its heavenly feather duster and yummy down quilt, the bedding I'd acquired at ABC Carpet and Home for the price of a small car. Mmmm, that would feel delicious. Already I'd completed the usual routine while also swinging by Duane Reade for the glitter hairspray Skyler and Kate wanted for Chanukah. It was 7:47 when I arrived at the twenty-first-floor offices of Myoki Bank, where I was a vice president of some stature. It felt like I'd already put in a day.

The lights turned on automatically when I walked into the office. Hanging my coat on the hook inside the door, I recalled the sacrifices I'd made to earn the privilege of a door instead of a mere cubicle. For the past six months, I'd been assigned a critical project, code name 'Bull Chip' – which had me working until 9:00 or 10:00 P.M. through the week and several hours a day on weekends. I skipped my six-year-old's birthday party to supervise systems testing.

I spent half my vacation solving Bull Chip problems that no one else could handle. I missed my fifteen-year business-school reunion because two team members quit suddenly and Konrad insisted I stay in town to hire replacements. But this project would turbocharge my career and land me the promotion I deserved, so it would all be worth it.

As I took the buttered bagel out of its brown paper bag, a flash of white and pale yellow centered squarely on my chair caught my eye. It was a memo with a Post-it attached, placed where it was sure to get my attention:

SEE ME ASAP — KONRAD.

Konrad was my profoundly ambitious, chemically depressed boss. One of those golden corporate boys with a professionally choreographed smile, a speaking coach, a driver, and an assistant for his assistant's assistant — all paid for by the company because Konrad's time was so valuable. Unlike his peers, who were merely soap-opera-star handsome, Konrad was so stunning he took your breath away. Just imagine the best features of Brad Pitt, Pierce Brosnan, and Robert Redford combined into one perfect package, punctuated with a trademark Brioni bow tie. That was Konrad, the blond-haired, blue-eyed Adonis who had graced the covers of Myoki's annual report for the last seven years. Behind his back, his direct reports called him the Face. We were sure he had 'posed' his way to the top.

The note was giving me the willies. This was irregular. When Konrad wanted me, his songwriter-secretary just called with a summons. 'Ivy, Konrad wants to see you right away. Can you drop eeevvverything and fly up to sixty?'

'Has he taken his meds?' I would ask. None of his direct reports dared to face him until he'd had his daily Wellbutrin. It paid to know what you were up against.

'I'm not sure, but Ed left in tears.'

Hearing this, I would postpone. Today, however, there was merely the note, attached to a memo from whom? My eye scanned the heading:

MEMO TO: Konrad Kavaler
FR: Drayton Bird
RE: Reengineering recommendation

Konrad, it occurs to me that with the $5MM we've each been charged with saving, we could help each other by cutting Ivy Ames's department and merging it into mine, creating a 'Center of Marketing Excellence.' My team is handling the same function as hers, but on an international basis, so they are up to speed. You could eliminate her position plus two direct reports, saving $700M in salary, benefits, T&E, real estate, etc. We could replace her Iowa call center with telemarketers in India, saving another $2.5MM. We've dissolved my acquisition group, so I'm down 26 heads and $7MM in expenses. I've got the talent to manage the combined function and the budget capacity to absorb the cost. It would be a win-win for both of us.

Let me know your thoughts.

Oh, shit, I thought.

I sat, swiveled around, and took in the spectacular view of New York Harbor that I hadn't noticed in months. My face burned and my heart beat so hard it hurt. Nonchalantly, I placed the brown paper bag on my face and hyperventilated, hoping no one saw. *Breathe. Breathe. Breathe.* I chanted silently, trying not to cough as I inhaled the airborne Sweet'n Low particles floating in the sack.

The phone rang. My stomach lurched, settling somewhere between the upper chest and throat. I turned to answer, noting on caller ID that it was songwriter-secretary. 'Konrad wants to see you now,' he emoted. 'He says you should bring the memo.'

'I'll be there. Has he taken his pills?'

'I dispensed them myself. He's very upbeat today.' He pronounced 'very' so it sounded like 'varrry.'

Five minutes and two elevator banks later, I was in Konrad's office. He ushered me over to the living-room area and gestured to the artificially weathered brown leather chair reserved for visitors. Damn. If I'd known I was going to see Konrad, I would have dressed better. Juxtaposed against his pinstriped Hugo Boss suit and red bow tie, the Persian rugs and the original Chagall, I was hopelessly outmatched.

'Look,' he said, wasting no time on small talk, 'I got that note from Drayton this morning and I want your input before I action it. What are your thoughts?'

Think quickly. Think quickly. Say something smart.

'It's a ridiculous idea,' I started.

Too defensive. Re-laaaax.

'The international practices are completely different from

the domestic ones. Just because we both run "marketing" functions doesn't mean we "market" the same way.' I made quotation marks in the air with my fingers each time I said 'market.' What a nimrod.

'Plus,' I continued, 'he hires trainees who don't know their ass from their elbow. My staff are experienced professionals. If anything, we should merge *his* department into *mine*, let *me* run the show, and we'd save just as much for Myoki.'

'I'm not sure what the answer is,' Konrad said, 'but he has the beginning of a good idea. Cascade your objections to Drayton and see what the pushback is. Recommend who should run the show and how we can downsize. I have to save five million and you could be a hero by serving up some heads.'

Just what I've always wanted to be, I thought miserably. *An unemployed hero.*

Drayton's landgrab threatened my very existence at Myoki, but I had to pretend to cooperate. That's the first rule of survival in a big corporation: Always act like you support your enemy's proposals, while behind his back do everything you can to kill his plans and, if possible, him. 'That sounds great, Konrad. I'll call Drayton right away,' I said in a faux-enthusiastic voice.

By the time I got back to 21, my heart was beating normally again. I was thinking about the fourteen months of severance I'd get if they fired me. I could take time off, lose twenty pounds, learn to program TiVo, maybe take some classes at the Kabbala Center.

I dialed Drayton's extension and he picked up, always a surprise with caller ID. 'Drayton,' I asked, 'how's Bea?'

Bea was his seven-year-old daughter, who played regularly with my Skyler. They both attended Balmoral, the holy grail of girl's schools in Manhattan. I would never have taken Drayton for such a slippery fish. Just last spring, Cadmon and I had attended the birthday party he threw for his high-maintenance wife, Sassy, at the Palace Hotel. He'd arranged for the grand ballroom to be transformed into Times Square on New Year's Eve. There were neon signs, subway turnstiles, caricature artists, actors playing homeless people. Sassy dropped the ball at midnight. Michael Crawford performed Broadway hits. Instead of forty candles, Drayton commissioned forty birthday cakes baked by Manhattan's most celebrated pastry chefs. Cad and I had reciprocated a few weeks ago by taking Drayton and Sassy to dinner at Le Bernardin. At the time, I thought the four of us had really clicked.

'Oh, Bea's brilliant. Thank you for asking,' Drayton said. He was English. 'She's looking forward to her birthday party next month. Will Skyler come?'

'Of course,' I answered. 'Sassy said you're having a dance party, right? It sounds fun.'

'It will be,' Drayton said. 'We just booked Clay Aiken.'

'Clay Aiken does birthday parties for eight-year-olds?'

'Normally not. But Beatrice's godfather is the president of his record label, so he arranged it. Nothing's too good for our little angels, now is it?'

'No, no, nothing's too good . . . hey, I uh saw the memo you wrote Konrad. I like your idea. But I think there may be ways to consolidate without eliminating any senior positions. Anyway, Konrad suggested we get together and game-plan a merger of our departments.'

'Ab-so-LUTE-ly,' Drayton said in that annoying insincere way English people speak. 'I want to sort this out straight-away. The problem is, I'm lit-rally walking out the door for a three-day off-site. Then on Thuuursday, I'm off to London for the week*end* to visit my father. He was just diagnosed with heart disease.'

'Oh, my God! That's awful,' I said, pretending to care. 'My mother had heart disease, too. She died last year.'

'Yes, well, thank you,' Drayton said. 'I'll be back in a week. Let's tackle the issue at 1:00 on the fourteenth and we'll winkle out a solution that aligns both our visions.'

'Right,' I said. *Whatever that means.* 'But do me a favor and don't work on it till we get together. This should come from both of us.'

'Ab-so-LUTE-ly,' Drayton promised. 'Next week then. Cheerio.' Cheerio my ass. Drayton hadn't lived in England for the last twenty years. We say 'goodbye' in America, Drayton, in case you hadn't noticed.

With their 'finest place to work' initiatives, diversity councils, on-site gyms, and touted (but rarely used) sabbat-ical programs, large corporations might give one the impression that they're bastions of fairness and compas-sion. They're not. Asking an employee to come up with a reorganization plan that includes his own demise happens every day. Once you become a vice president in a big company, they expect you to be a grown-up. I hate that.

'Bonnie,' I said to my assistant as I put my coat on, 'I've got a meeting with the agency uptown. I'll see you this afternoon, or maybe tomorrow, depending on how long this takes.'

I went to Barneys.

∾

The next morning, I felt strangely calm about my predica-
ment. Cadmon, a former master politician in the corporate
arena, convinced me that I could turn this thing around.
I came up with an ingenious scheme to do an end run
around Drayton. While he was in London caring for his
sick father, I would jockey for control of his department.
Everyone knew Drayton was a lightweight, while I was the
acknowledged powerhouse. This was just the turn of events
I needed to get a bigger department than ever, a raise, an
office on 60. I was optimistic, almost giddy with the
thought.

Walking to my desk, I noticed, once again, white paper
with a yellow sticky on my chair.

SEE ME ASAP – KONRAD.

The attachment appeared to be some sort of report.
Damn.

I sat at my desk and began to read:

MEMO TO: Konrad Kavaler
FR: Drayton Bird
RE: Reengineering Recommendation

Glad to hear you support my recommendation
regarding merging your marketing function into
mine. Spoke with Ivy Ames yesterday and she
thinks it's a brilliant idea. I took the liberty of
developing a roll-out plan – outlined below.

Also attached are proposed new org charts as well as P&Ls showing the savings to be derived from the merger. Finally, I met with HR, and severance packages for Ivy and her direct reports will be forwarded to you by 10:00 A.M.

If you're in agreement, let me know. I'd suggest we announce ASAP so we can hit the ground running after the new year, but of course, it's your call.

2. Once Upon a Pink Slip

I leafed through Drayton's report and its attachments, which had been prepared with such excruciating detail that I knew my fate was sealed. I understood now that this was a setup. I'd been badly outmaneuvered. How could I not have seen it coming? Konrad only wanted my input so that when he let me go, I couldn't say I wasn't involved in the decision.

I hated my job; that was true. I'd been bored with the assignment from the beginning and going through the motions for years. But that didn't mean I wanted to leave.

Quick, quick, think. How could I save my job? I looked around for my tattered copy of *The Art of War*. There had to be a strategy to cover this. Maybe I could make a last stand. Like Custer. Shit, it was too late. I knew it. I'd witnessed this scenario often enough to understand that my career at Myoki was over. I'd caused it to happen to my own rivals plenty of times. Once Human Resources prints the severance package with your name on it, there's no turning back.

Could this *really* be happening? Just last year, Cadmon and I made almost two million dollars between us. We had a magnificent apartment on Park Avenue, nannies seven days a week, a rental in the estate section of Southampton. Then, in March, Cadmon was fired. I became the bread-winner. We were so addicted to the good life that we hadn't lowered our standards, certain that Cadmon's new job would materialize any day. It hadn't.

I went to the computer and pulled up our budget spread-sheet, looking for places to save. Let's see . . . mortgage ($120,000), two tuitions ($50,000), charitable donations ($25,000), tutors ($15,000), birthday parties ($22,000), summer camp ($14,000), private lessons ($20,000), Hamptons rental ($60,000), ski vacation ($15,000), cars and garage ($35,000), clothes, dry cleaning, tailoring ($50,000), personal trainers, yoga, nutritionist ($28,000), entertain-ment, flowers and catering ($60,000), doggie day care, massage therapy, grooming and poochie sushi for Sir Elton ($24,000), my hair ($12,000), my nails ($5,200), my analyst ($24,000), my life-energy coach ($18,000), car service ($4,000), nannies and maid ($74,000), Botox, collagen, and laser resurfacing ($18,000), tips and staff gifts ($4,000), and a slew of other expenses like food, insurance, electricity, tele-phone, cable, doctor bills – all the boring but necessary stuff that adds up to a big number. Stricken with an overwhelm-ing sense of loss, I knew we could no longer afford our life. Making it worse, Cad and I had always failed miser-ably at sacrifice. I couldn't imagine what to cut from our budget.

I sat at my desk and stared, numb. Tears welled in my eyes and began sploshing down my face while a golf-ball-sized lump filled my throat. *Stop crying. Stop crying. Be a grown-up.*

The phone rang, breaking the spell. I took a deep breath and answered.

It was songwriter-secretary. 'Konrad wants to see you. Can you be here in five?'

'Sure,' I answered. 'Meds?'

'Two hours ago,' he said.

I stopped in the restroom on my way upstairs. Gaaah. Tammy Faye Bakker Messner under-eyes. Can't let anyone see me like this. Breathing deeply and splashing water on my face, I did what I could to pull myself together.

On 60, Konrad kept me waiting for half an hour. I pretended to be fascinated by an article on comparative interest rates in *Municipal Bond News*. Another EVP stuck his head in the door and Konrad waved him in. Forty-five minutes later, Konrad buzzed for me. I almost expected songwriter-secretary to chant 'Dead man walking' as I did the slow march to his office.

'So, I see you're supporting the merger of your department with Drayton's,' Konrad began. 'My compliments to you for stepping up to the plate, being a team player, making the sacrifice.' Baseball references were common among Myoki executives.

'Well, not exactly, Konrad. Drayton asked me to wait a week to work on the proposal and I . . .'

'Are you saying you *didn't* tell Drayton you thought it was a good idea?' Konrad asked.

'No, I said I *liked* the idea, but I wanted to sit down and discuss it with him, only he couldn't because he was going to an off-site . . .'

'What are you talking about? I met with him last night. Get your facts straight, Ames. Anyway, the point is, I need to get some heads off my books to get to the five-million-dollar save and this is a smart way to do it, don't you agree?'

'Well, of course, it's smart for you to cut *somewhere*, but my staff are heavy hitters. Drayton wants to draft rookies who barely speak English,' I said, using analogies I thought might sway him.

'Ivy, we're lowering quality all over the bank to save money. None of us is indispensable. Times are tough. We need to invent new paradigms, smash old boundaries, think outside the box, pick low-hanging fruit, make elegant decisions, walk the talk, fall on our swords, and so on and so forth.'

'Right,' I mumbled. I'd forgotten what a deep thinker Konrad could be.

'If you need a reference,' Konrad continued, 'call me. And you know what I'd say? I'd say you were a winner. Not many employees would put the interests of the bank, the bank we all love, above their own. You're a rare bird, Ivy Ames.'

'Well, gee, thank you, Konrad.' I hesitated, then said what was on my mind. What could he do, fire me? 'Can I ask you something?'

'Of course,' he said, making his concerned-boss face.

'My guess is you've been planning to lay me off for some time,' I ventured.

His silence confirmed my suspicions.

'If that was the case, how could you let me work day and night on Bull Chip knowing you were gonna ax me before Christmas?' I asked. 'Now I won't get a bonus. Two-thirds of my compensation is bonus. My family *depends* on that money.'

'Ivy, Ivy, Ivy,' he said, 'if I'd told you six months ago I was thinking about laying you off, you never would have worked so hard on Bull Chip, now would you have?' The 'duh-uh' at the end of the sentence was implied.

'And your conscience didn't bother you, doing that to me?' I asked.

'Conscience?' For a moment, Konrad seemed confused. 'Ivy, this is business. Besides, you may have done the heavy lifting on the project, but it was *my* vision that conceived the idea. That was the *real* accomplishment. That's what should *and will* be rewarded. And while you won't be getting a bonus for your efforts, if anyone calls for a recommendation, I'll tell them what a fine job you did. Your work saved the bank at least a hundred million dollars. You should put that on your résumé,' he suggested helpfully.

Hot tears began spilling down my cheeks again. I couldn't stop them. Rejection has always made me sad, not angry.

Konrad offered me the monogrammed handkerchief from his jacket pocket. I blew my nose, making a loud honking sound. I continued to blow and wipe, giving his linen hankie a thorough soaking. 'Thanks,' I said, putting it back in his hand. It grossed him out, but he kept his face straight, not daring to reveal any sign of weakness.

Konrad handed me a schedule for the rest of the day.

10:00 A.M. – meet with Sharon and Young Mi and
                    announce they've been downsized.
                    Send them to Human Resources.
11:00 A.M. – meet with Human Resources to go over
                    your package.
  1:00 P.M. – meet with remainder of your team,
                    Drayton, Konrad, to announce transition.

2:00 P.M. – car will take you home. Your things
will be shipped tomorrow.

I looked up at Konrad, who avoided my eyes.

'This isn't personal, you know,' Konrad said. 'When you
play ball in the majors, you have to make tough calls. Put
yourself in my place, Ivy. Think how hard this has been
for me. And look, *I'm* keeping it together.' Konrad leaned
forward and lowered his voice. 'Frankly, I don't think it's
professional of you to cry. Men hate that, you know. Now
me, I can handle tears. I'm evolved. But if you're ever in
this position again, try to avoid the waterworks.'

I glared at him. It took every ounce of willpower I
possessed not to say what I was thinking at that moment.

'Hey, it'll probably happen to me soon, too,' he joked
in a clumsy attempt toward camaraderie.

I hope so, I thought but didn't say.

'Well, I'll see you at one o' clock.' Konrad pulled at his
collar like Rodney Dangerfield. It was the first time I'd
seen the guy sweat.

The next few hours were a blur. As their boss, I was
expected to fire my two directors, Sharon and Young Mi.
I was white. Sharon was African American. Young Mi was
Chinese American. If you ignored the fact that we were all
girls, this had been an equal-opportunity firing. Making me
sack them was cruel and unusual punishment. I wept. They
cried. We hugged.

Human Resources was equally delightful. My payout
would only be fourteen weeks – 'New rules,' the drone
explained. 'We reengineered the severance policy. You
have to be a *senior* vice president to get a month for every

year. You're only entitled to a week for each twelve months served. Didn't you get the memo? Also, you need to sign this agreement not to sue us for wrongful termination before you can receive your lump-sum settlement.'

For about five seconds I contemplated suing them. Surely they'd pay more than fourteen weeks' salary just to make me go away. But litigation drags on forever. And lawyers cost a fortune. Shit. I had so many bills to pay. I signed the damn thing and pocketed the check.

Smarmy Drayton was at the one o'clock hand-over meeting. To suppress my tears, I concentrated on counting his oily pores from across the table. His lips kept curling into a smirk that he'd attempt to hide with his hand and a cough.

Konrad told my people that there would be a reorganization and they would report to Drayton now. He explained his vision for my department, providing them with more direction than he'd given me for the last four years. Drayton nodded knowingly as Konrad spoke, as though he were listening to the Dalai Lama or Tony Robbins.

Drayton thanked Konrad in his kiss-ass way, stopping just short of giving him a blowjob for his courage to make the hard decision to let me go. Then, he welcomed my people to his team and yammered on and on about what good personal friends we were, how I was the consummate professional for whom he had the utmost respect, and what a loss my leaving would be for the company, blah, blah, blah. He led the group in a polite round of applause honoring my contribution to the bank. Finally, he mentioned what great things I'd told him about each of them and how he looked forward to working with such talented players. The guy could not have unloaded more crap if he'd taken a dump in the middle of the conference-room table.

When Konrad asked if I wanted to say anything to my team, I could only eke out a few words, 'I've enjoyed working with you.' At that point, the swelling in my throat made talking impossible, so I smiled like I thought the restructuring was just a super idea.

Konrad remembered that he'd forgotten to confiscate my office key, security badge, BlackBerry, and corporate Visa card. He asked for them. With my former direct reports on hand to witness the final humiliation, I handed each item over. This was beginning to feel more and more like a court-martial.

Konrad dismissed the group and called Drayton in for a private chat. I hugged each person tightly. Saying good-bye to Bonnie, my faithful assistant, was particularly wrenching. She'd made sure the office ran smoothly when my mother was dying last year. Because of her, I was at Mom's side for her last days. I wasn't surprised that the company held on to Bonnie. Loyal assistants working at Myoki were as common as Paris Hilton shopping at Fashion Barn, and management knew it. I hugged her and we promised to stay in touch. The security guard, who was waiting to escort me out, kept looking at his watch.

Walking to the elevator, I ran into Drayton.

'No hard feelings, I hope,' he said with an exaggeratedly sympathetic smile, extending his hand. 'Sassy and I so enjoyed our evening out with you, and we want to do it again.'

Oh, yes, Drayton, I'll be calling you for a dinner date real soon.

'Hey, not at all,' I said, smiling, shaking his moist but well-manicured hand. *Eeeuw!* He was wearing clear nail polish. 'I'm looking forward to some time at home with my kids. You did me a favor, Drayton.' I pressed the elevator button.

'Ah yes . . . splendid . . . splendid. I must say, Ivy, well done. I raaather admire the way you've handled this. But *do* call me if you need anything, *anything at all,*' he said with fake concern.

What I ached to do at that moment was hurt the man. Knee him in the balls. Punch him in the face. Stick my le grand de Montblanc fountain pen up his nose, piercing his brainstem, rendering him paralyzed, condemning him to life as a vegetable. But the security guard was watching, and resorting to violence would defy the cardinal rule of getting fired – don't burn your bridges. So I didn't.

༄

A black Lincoln Town Car that smelled of stale cigarettes and sweat was waiting downstairs. Regrettably, it was the last time Myoki would send me home in classic Manhattan midlevel executive style. We drove up Church and cut over to Greene in SoHo. The streets were filled with chunky-haired people dressed in black who obviously spent their workdays outside the corporate world. *What do they do to support themselves?* I wondered. The last fourteen years of my life had been spent in the hermetically sealed offices of Myoki Bank. For the first time, it dawned on me that there was this whole other world where people could be outside at 2:00 P.M. on a weekday. *Maybe I could become one of these people,* I thought. *They seem so free.*

'Near corner or far,' the driver asked when we aproached my building. 'Near,' I replied. He asked for my voucher. I wrote in a $500 tip and told him to have a nice day.

Walking through my lobby, I felt the nervous stares of the doorman and concierge. It must be written all over my face that I was fired.

Stepping into the elevator was a relief. Then, remembering that doormen were watching through hidden cameras, I held my head high. I longed for the sympathetic hug I knew Cadmon would offer when I told him the news.

'Cadmon,' I called as I walked in. 'Cad . . . ?' I looked around but couldn't find him. He wasn't at his computer. *Must be at the gym.* Sir Elton, our pug, came running to greet me. He chased his tail enthusiastically when he saw me. I walked right past him. From the kitchen, I could hear Rosie, our nanny, and Elva, our maid, jabbering away to each other in Spanish. I couldn't face them. What would they think? Me, home in the middle of the day. Fired. By tomorrow, every maid and nanny on Park Avenue would know. The next day, their bosses would hear. Ugh, the shame!

Stripping off my jacket, I suddenly felt exhausted. Should I crawl into bed or work out? Bed. Definitely bed. Too bad it hadn't been made yet. Pee. I needed to pee. Then sleeping or crying, whichever came first.

The bathroom smelled like orange blossoms when I walked in. Like a delicious bubble bath was already drawn and waiting for me. Then I noticed Cadmon in his robe sitting on the toilet rubbing soap on a naked woman in my bathtub. The naked woman was Sassy, Drayton's wife. Sweet mother of God, those tits!

I *hated* her. Incredibly, my first thought was, *how does she* do *it – plastic surgery or workouts?* My second thought was to pummel that perfect face with a can of deodorant.

Like deer caught in the headlights, Sassy and Cadmon looked at me.

I stopped in my tracks, stunned.

'You're fucking Sassy?' I asked Cad quietly, already knowing the answer.

'Let me explain,' Cadmon said, resorting to the reasonable tone he used when he felt he needed to quote-unquote handle me. 'Nothing happened. I know this looks bad, but . . .'

'Stop,' I blurted. 'You can't possibly think I'm that stupid. Out. I want you both out of here.' By then, Sassy was hugging herself to cover her nakedness and trying to disappear beneath the bubbles.

Instead of tears, I was angry. That felt right. The two lying shits deserved my rage.

I looked at Sassy. 'Out,' I demanded, pointing toward the door. 'Get out now.'

'Okay, could you hand me the towel . . . please,' came her mortified reply.

'Oh, you want to dry off? *You want to dry off?*' I grabbed the blow-dryer that we always left plugged in by the sink, turned it on high, and screamed, 'If you don't get your tight little ass out of my house this instant, you can dry off with this.' I held it over the water. 'One . . . two . . .' Sassy bounded out of the tub and sprinted through the apartment like Jackie Joyner-Kersey, hurdling furniture and racing out the door tracking bubbles and water in her wake. Rosie and Elva must have been spying. I distinctly heard gasps and the words 'Ay, chihuahua!' followed by urgent Spanish whispering outside the bedroom door.

What was I thinking? The cheating scumbags weren't worth going to jail for. *Is adultery a defense for manslaughter anymore?* I wondered. Nah, not in New York. Maybe in Arkansas.

At least the doormen would get a thrill as Sassy rode downstairs. There's one security tape that wouldn't get erased.

For the first time in my life, I had an out-of-body experience. Floating to the ceiling, I surveyed the scene below. *This cannot be happening. I've been fired. My husband is screwing another woman – the wife of the asshole responsible for getting me canned, no less. My entire life is falling apart on the same day. What are the odds? What do I do? Do I let Cadmon explain and forgive him? Do I kick him out? If I kick him out, I won't have a husband. I'll be an unemployed single mother, and that would suck. I've gotten fat. How can I date anyone looking like this? Dammit, I'll have to start grooming my crotch again. Why didn't I get a tummy tuck when we could afford it? Why? Why? How'll Sassy get home naked? Would a cabdriver pick up a nude woman? Probably. But how would she pay the fare?* All these thoughts flashed through my mind in one second, the way people's lives do when they're about to die.

I came back to earth. 'Cad, I'm going to pick up the kids. Pack some things and leave. I don't want you here when I get back.'

He looked pitiful standing by the toilet in his Ritz

Carlton terrycloth robe with the torn pocket. There would be no hug to comfort me for getting fired tonight. I turned and left, hiding the tears that were streaming down my face. Cadmon had ripped my heart out, but I'd sooner dance the samba bare-ass naked down Madison Avenue than let him know it.

3. Misery Is a Choice

Cadmon packed his clothes and computer and moved into the Perry Street Towers in the Far West Village with his brother, Don, the successful one. Later, he left a voice mail asking me to put his golf clubs in the Porsche, which he'd pick up when he could. *Oh, sure, no problem*, I thought. *Be happy to schlep fifty pounds of iron five blocks to our parking garage.* Have *you* ever tried to cram a set of clubs into a Porsche? Trust me, it's impossible. Eventually, I ditched the bag and stuffed the sticks in the front seat. Just as I was about to leave, an irresistible urge to dance came over me. So I put on his spikes and did the twist all over the hood of the car, bawling like a baby.

In the weeks that followed, I barely managed to drag myself out of bed to take the girls to and from school. The rest of the time, I hid under the covers, intermittently sobbing, reading self-help books, and listening to old Joni Mitchell tunes. I wasn't depressed exactly, but there was this unfillable emptiness and feeling of doom that I couldn't shake.

My only pleasure was lying in bed with Sir Elton and

my daughters watching *Radical Reinvention,* a reality TV show where people who were even worse off than I was were rescued through plastic-surgery makeovers. I wondered if I'd sunk low enough to qualify for that show. One morning, after I'd been weeping on and off for twenty-four hours straight, my seven-year-old called 911 for help. That's when it hit me that I'd probably sunk as low as I could, so I slapped myself in the face (metaphorically, of course) and snapped out of it. With two little girls to support, I didn't have the luxury of a nervous breakdown. At least that's what I told the paramedics when they arrived.

I needed my mother and was furious with her for dying last year. Talk about bad timing. We'd always been unnaturally close, and had phoned each other several times a day. Secretly I'd hoped to go before her because I didn't think I could live in a world where she didn't exist. Now I needed her to hold me, kiss my cheek, and promise this would all work out. Praying to Mom for one of those spirit visits the death-and-dying books are always touting, the only response I got was silence. More silence. Still more silence.

The irony of losing everything at thirty-nine wasn't lost on me. That had been Mom's age when she discovered that Daddy was cheating on her after he promised it would *never* happen again. This time it was with an Hispanic dancer from *West Side Story.* We were living in Brooklyn Heights then, in an elegantly restored townhouse paid for by Dad's thriving manufacturing business – Schechter's Fine Schmattas. He was the first ragman to knock off Parisian couture dresses for Middle America. Daddy's polyester fakes fed our family well and made him a very rich man. Designers were always harassing him, calling him a thief and a liar. But he was a wily one, Dad was. He'd change the patterns just enough to stay one step ahead of the law. Daddy used to say, 'I have no conscience and I need the cash.' He said it like a joke, but I'm still not sure it was.

One afternoon, I came home from school to discover that my bags were packed and a taxi was waiting. Without so much as a 'Ta-ta' to Daddy, Mom and I hopped in the cab and headed for Manhattan. Mom had finally had enough of Dad's tomcatting around. She wouldn't let me look back as we drove off, but instead insisted that I look forward to our better future. I was devastated, not because my family was falling apart, but because I was up for a perfect-attendance award at school, and now I wouldn't win.

Unfortunately, Mom had never worked and wasn't qualified to do much. Eventually, she secured a position as social secretary for Olivia de Campo, who was Mayor Lindsay's first cousin's father-in-law's great-niece. The two of us lived in a tiny, windowless servant's room in the basement of their limestone mansion just off Fifth Avenue. The house was across the street from a public school so fine that even the de Campos sent their daughter, Ondrea. I attended classes with children of means, all of whom treated me like a flea-ridden stray cat once Ondrea told them I was her servant's kid.

Junior Miss de Campo entertained frequently at the manse, and she made a point of telling me I wasn't welcome. Senior Mrs. de Campo, however, believed one should treat the garbageman the same as the Queen of England, so she invited me to Ondrea's Valentine's Day party. Thrilled by my good fortune, Mom worked tirelessly to make me a fake cowhide skirt for the occasion. I could barely hide my happiness, convinced that this was the break I needed to make friends. When I walked into the party, Ondrea announced to her posse of popular kids that 'Jewgirl' had arrived. 'Jewgirl, Jewgirl, Jewgirl,' they chanted, laughing at me. I took refuge in my mother's arms, but she was powerless to do anything.

To make it all worse, I was a short, chubby kid with blue winged glasses and a big nose we could no longer afford to have fixed. The better future that Mom had promised as we fled Brooklyn never materialized.

With no friends to speak of, I studied like my life depended on it, and earned a full scholarship to Yale for both undergraduate and business school. That opened the door to my fine career at Myoki, which led me to being fired by Konrad Kavaler and ultimately to my current sea of woes. But the years in between were good. I got green contact lenses and grew into my nose, and I turned out taller and prettier than anyone would have thought possible. I married Cadmon, who was as charismatic and dapper as I always imagined Dad had been. With his derivatives-trading career, it wasn't long before the two of us were raking in buttloads of cash like junior aristocrats. We had no desire to join high society. No, we just wanted the swanky apartment, the private schools, the home in the Hamptons, the help, the vacations, the designer clothes, the friendships with celebs – all the meaningless, pretentious perks that go along with having money. Truth be told, it was everything we'd ever dreamed of and more. We had two daughters and rode the gravy train of happiness like every other well-paid Manhattan professional couple. Given my history, I was just waiting for the day we'd lose everything, so it came as no surprise to me when we did.

Okay, I thought, *enough with the despair.* It was time to drag my sorry ass out of bed and start over. In my diminished state, I wore jeans and no makeup when I took the girls to class. This caused a minor scandal among the mothers and nannies at our private school, where drop-off and pick-up featured ninety-eight-pound classically elegant moms straight from the pages of the *Times* 'Sunday Styles' section. I kid you not. Some days, the paparazzi camped outside the school snapping pictures of our very own trophy wives striking poses as they commiserated among themselves over servant problems and insatiable husbands. I dyed my hair blond. I'd always wanted to do that, but it would have been a career-breaker at Myoki. I started lifting weights and working out to my *Abs of Steel* video, determined to get back to the old pretty me.

I economized. For $9.99 instead of $399, I colored my own hair. Fingers and toes were self-polished. I cleaned my house and taught the girls to pitch in. Doggie day care, nutritionists, and personal trainers were out of the question, so I walked Sir Elton regularly. Vacations were scrapped. My car was sold. Dry cleaning was history. I dismissed my analyst, dermatologist, plastic surgeon, and life-energy coach. All extracurricular activities for the girls were eliminated, including the dance lessons they loved so much at the Alvin Ailey studio. In perfect Myoki style, I reengineered my life and cut expenses by 85 percent.

As the weeks went by, I adapted to a life of genteel poverty. Mom and I had done it when we left Dad and

Easy Street behind in Brooklyn. I could do it again. To my surprise, I didn't miss Cadmon. What I missed was the fearlessness that came with being half of a couple. I wondered if I would ever again have the bravado I used to possess as Cadmon's wife. For added confidence, I took to carrying around a tissue-wrapped sweater in a Barneys shopping bag. When one can't *be* a winner, one can *look* like a winner. It wasn't as powerful a moxie-builder as a husband, but it was something.

My best friend, Faith, suggested that I see her psychic to gain insight into the future. I went. What a mistake. The psychic, Madame Lala, an old Czech woman with gnarly fingers and one eye that looked like a scrambled egg, shuffled her well-worn deck of tarot cards and asked me to select one.

I meditated real hard, intent on choosing the perfect card. She turned it over. It was The Tower. I don't know much about tarot, but this was one badass card. It was a horrifying image of lightning striking a stone prison. As the structure crashes and burns, a volcano erupts in the background, releasing a sea of lava. People are fleeing for their lives. I was unnerved when I saw the card, pretty sure that it didn't foretell good times ahead.

Madame Lala looked agitated. 'I see chaos, upheaval, and destruction in your life.'

'Yes, but can you tell me something I don't already know?'

'Your life is in a state of unrest. Energies are out of balance. This card predicts disaster, catastrophe, a crisis in your future. I see your world collapsing around you. You must take action before it is too late.'

'Can you be a little more specific, Madame Lala?' I had the feeling her information was out of date. Hadn't this already happened?

'Let me consult the spirits. Ahhh. Now it is clear. The spirits are telling me that you're going to be hit by a bus.'

'What!' I said. 'Oh, that's just swell. My life keeps getting better and better.'

'Wait, maybe I spoke too soon. Let me look at your chart.' Frowning, she examined my personal computer-generated horoscope. 'It may not be an actual bus. The bus may be a metaphor for a penis. Yes, that's it. I see a male. Perhaps you are about to meet a man. Or, maybe I'm confused and you *will* be hit by a physical bus. I cannot enlighten you more. The spirits are not allowing me to look beyond the veil.'

Tears began to drip down my face. I couldn't help it. I had so hoped that she would bring news of better times to come. Madam Lala offered me the soiled handkerchief that had been tucked into her bra. I politely declined. Then I thanked her for the reading and then willed myself to forget it had ever happened.

4. This Little Piggy Went to Private School

While Kate and Skyler were in school, I shopped for a smaller apartment. Our Classic Seven on Park Avenue had been bought in the headier times. It was everything I'd ever wanted in a home. There were distressed-maple plank floors, sunlight galore from twenty-four windows, an eat-in chef's kitchen, and a simply furnished master bedroom that was my spiritual sanctuary. Each girl had her own room with custom-designed canopy bunk beds. Master Li, the top feng shui man on the East Coast, helped me place our furniture to create harmony and ensure happiness, prosperity, and luck. He'd planted red envelopes with Chinese coins in my orange tree, blessing the space and pronouncing it sacred.

After my world collapsed, I reported Master Li to the Better Business Bureau. He reluctantly returned $1,500 of his $10,000 fee, but not before accusing me of killing the orange tree where the envelopes were buried. I explained that it wasn't me who killed it. He'd placed the damn tree in a corner that got no light.

I had no idea how I would pull myself up and reclaim the gracious life I'd worked so hard to attain, but I vowed to try. With Cadmon and me both unemployed and divorce the next logical step, the apartment had to go. Meris, my real-estate agent, showed me some places in Brooklyn, Chinatown, and the Lower East Side, where rents were only half as exorbitant as they were uptown.

The most terrifying change was caring for the girls myself. Cash-flow constraints (as in no cash flowing *in*) had forced me to let our nannies go. Like most of my friends, I had never been a mother without professional help. My daily interaction with the girls had been during our rushed morning marathon. In the evenings, they were delivered to me fed, clean, and dressed for bed. Before, I was Mommy once removed. Now I bathed them, cooked for them, arranged playdates, calmed fears, kissed boo-boos, helped with homework, volunteered at school. To my surprise and delight, caring for the children was a joy. I'd been missing out on so much by delegating my mommy responsibilities. Too bad I had to lose my job and husband to figure that out.

I learned how to be a real mother the hard way. I should have known to say no when Kate begged me to let her take care of Romeo, the class guinea pig, over the holidays. 'I'll feed him and play with him. You won't even know he's here.' Reluctantly, I agreed, knowing what an honor it was to be asked to care for the class pet during school break.

'It's unusual for us to board our animals with families who'll be home over Christmas,' Mrs. Leyde explained. 'We like to see our snakes and guinea pigs travel to Europe or Africa with top-tier families during vacation. It's important for class pets to experience life beyond the cage, don't you think?'

'Absolutely,' I said.

'But since Kate's father left, she's become so attached to Romeo. We'll make an exception in this case.'

'Thank you, Mrs. Leyde. You won't regret this.'

When Romeo came home, Kate was ecstatic, giving him a tour around our apartment, with introductions to Kate's other pets ('This is Sir Elton, our pug; this is my fish, Beverly . . . the reason she looks so good is because I have her on a strict exercise program'). Next, they visited the girls' bathroom, where Romeo had a strawberry bubble bath and a blow-dry. Later, Kate tried to dress him in Barbie clothes, but nothing fit. Instead, she strapped him into a doll stroller for a walk around the apartment, with a quick stop in the kitchen for tea and cookies. Both child and guinea pig were exhausted when they sat down to watch *Arthur*. Kate passed out in front of the TV, as did Romeo.

Are guinea pigs supposed to be so quiet? I wondered. *He's just sleeping,* I told myself. To be sure, I felt for a pulse. There was none. Within two hours of his arrival, Romeo was dead as a stone.

5. One Sick Fish

O h fuck. Oh fuck. Oh fuck. We killed the guinea pig. Mrs. Leyde went out on a limb for us and look what we've gone and done. I massaged Romeo's little heart and attempted mouth-to-mouth to no avail.

I called Mrs. Leyde and told her exactly what had happened. *Well, sort of.* 'Mrs. Leyde, you aren't going to believe this. Romeo just died. He was eating pellets in his cage when he clutched his chest and keeled over. We didn't do anything out of the ordinary with him,' I lied. Mrs. Leyde took it way better than I expected, surmising that the walk from school to our apartment must have been too much for him. 'He was old,' she said, 'in guinea-pig years.'

'What should I do with the body?' I said. Mrs. Leyde asked that we keep it in the freezer until after the holidays. Some of the children might want to see his remains before burial.

When Kate woke up, she was inconsolable. 'How could this have happened?' I couldn't bring myself to tell her she'd killed the damn rodent. 'Apparently, Romeo had a heart murmur and it . . . exploded,' I improvised. Being new to hands-on motherhood, I wasn't sure if lying was the right strategy, but I went with it.

The freezer became a temporary morgue, where Romeo was interred in a Ziploc bag and lay in state next to the Perdue chicken nuggets and Ore-Ida french fries. The next day, I heard a horrific scream from my kitchen. Skyler, my older daughter, had come face-to-face with the lifeless open eyes of a frozen Romeo while looking for an Eskimo Pie. I had hoped to keep his passing a secret from her – why traumatize both children? Oh, well.

Kate felt rotten that Romeo had died on her watch. She tried to avoid her friends after vacation. 'Mommy, I feel sick tomorrow. I can't go to school,' she whimpered. 'You must go,' I said. At circle-time, the children were told of Romeo's passing. There were tears and hugs and wacky guinea-pig stories exchanged. A memorial service was held in the school yard. Mrs. Leyde delivered the eulogy. The children kissed Romeo's stiff, cold body before he was gently consigned to the earth under the slide in the backyard next to Slick, the garter snake who choked to death on a Lego. The children sang their 'goodbye' song, and many cried. Mrs. Leyde asked for a moment of silence in Romeo's honor, but none of the kids could hold still. 'I'm so sorry,' Kate said over and over. 'You should be, you guinea-pig murderer,' her friend Gaby said, while the other kids insisted it wasn't her fault. But even at the tender age of six, and despite my attempts to shield her, Kate knew it was.

❧

Following Romeo's death, Kate became obsessed with her goldfish, Beverly. She was determined to become a brilliant pet-master and see her charge into old age. I urged her to refrain from playing with the fish directly.

We added some new marbles and a mermaid to the bottom of the bowl. Every day, after school, she gently spoke to her pet. I wondered what inspired her attachment – Romeo's death or Cadmon's departure. Whichever it was, the fish seemed to provide a comforting kind of therapy.

A few weeks after Kate became so bewitched by Beverly's charm, we returned from school to find the fish swimming erratically in her bowl. What could have happened? Yesterday she was fine – gliding perfectly back and forth, making regular bowel movements. Today, she appeared drunk. Maybe it was something she ate. Maybe it was a fish virus. Kate screamed so loud and for so long upon discovering Beverly's malady that the neighbors complained and the head of the co-op board marched over, threatening me with a fine if I couldn't control my child.

'Look,' I said desperately, 'there's probably not a lot to be done, but let me call the vet. Maybe she can be fixed.' I knew there was no hope, but what could I say? The kid was heartbroken.

'Yes, yes, call the vet, *please*,' Kate begged.

I phoned Sir Elton's pet hospital for advice. They referred us to Dr. Heller, the top fish surgeon on the Upper East Side. Who knew there was such a specialty? Kate listened on the bedroom extension while Dr. Heller explained that Beverly probably developed an obstruction that limited her ability to regulate air, leaving her improperly buoyant.

'Is there anything to be done?' *Please say no. Please say no. Please say no*, I chanted silently. If I had to guess, a Park Avenue fish surgeon would not come cheap.

'We can operate,' Dr. Heller said.

Oh, dear God, say it's not so! 'Really?'

'There's a delicate procedure where we surgically insert a tiny stone in her abdomen to weigh it down. It's her only hope.'

'We're on our way, Doctor,' Kate said.

'WAIT!' I interrupted. 'How much will this cost?'

'Fifteen hundred dollars.'

'*Fifteen hundred!* The fish was only ten dollars!'

'I can understand your not wanting to make the investment. Most people would just flush her down the toilet and get a new one,' the doctor explained.

'*NOOOOOO!*' Kate screamed. Her wailing began again, this time with a vengeance.

'Kate, stop, hush. Nobody's getting flushed down the toilet. Doctor, give us your address. We're on our way.'

The next day, Beverly was tired from the anesthesia, but swimming right-side-up and in mostly straight lines. I was $1,500 poorer. Luckily, the refund check from Master Li had arrived. I endorsed it over to Dr. Heller. There were a hundred more sensible ways to spend that money, but Beverly meant a lot to Kate and Kate meant everything to me. So there you have it.

I will say this once and then forever hold my peace. Being a senior executive at a multinational corporation is a piece of cake next to being a full-time mom. I'd like to see Konrad Kavaler handle a dead guinea pig and a goldfish with a buoyancy disorder.

6. Desperate Times, Desperate Measures

My plight was becoming more untenable by the day. I could approach it like *The Little Engine That Could*, or like *Aladdin*. I preferred *Aladdin* because I'm from America and we are not a patient people. With a camera set up on Skyler's dresser, wearing no makeup and a three-piece kelly-green pants suit by Jaclyn Smith for Kmart, I filmed my video application for *Radical Reinvention*. Aaand . . . *action*.

'Please . . . I uh hope . . . no, I *beg* you to choose me for a radical makeover because I . . .' – sad sigh – 'just got fired, my pet died, and I caught my husband taking a bath with another woman . . . and they were naked. Now, I'm gonna have to start dating again *and look at me*. Who would want . . . *this?*' I gestured dramatically at my lumpy, puffy body and the lifeless hair I'd sprayed with vegetable oil for a stringier presentation. 'Plus, my mother died, I'm about to lose my home, I had to fire my nanny, my maid, and my kids' tutors. I have to color my *own* hair and do my *own* nails. My psychic says I'm gonna get hit by a bus. And have you ever seen a frown line this deep?' I pointed to the canyon that subdivided my forehead. 'I need . . . no, I'm *desperate* for Botox.'

I stopped the camera and watched the footage. When did I start looking so . . . old? And my voice, did it sound like I was abusing helium to everyone else? I needed to sell myself as a world-class loser if I was to have any chance of getting picked. So far, I know I was convinced. On to the next question. Aaand . . . *action*.

'If I'm selected for *Radical Reinvention*, here's what I'd want done. A complete facelift, breast implants, an upper and lower eye job, Botox or some permanent solution to my frown line, and lip implants. A tummy tuck, liposuction on my hips, ankles, back, and upper arms, buttock augmentation, LASIK surgery for my eyes, braces, bleaching, and those da Vinci porcelain veneers for my teeth. Also, I'd like to have that toe-shortening operation so my feet look better in heels. Oh, and laser hair-removal everywhere except my head and eyes. That's everything. Well, of course, it goes without saying that a top Beverly Hills salon would do my hair and makeup, and obviously you'd send me to Versace for a new wardrobe. And a trainer, naturally. But everyone gets that. Oh, and I'd love it if my "reveal" could be at the Water Club. They have the perfect great stairway for a dramatic entrance. That's it. Thank you.' I made a defeated world-weary face for the parting shot.

After reviewing the tape, I was initially pleased with how badly I'd come off. Then I realized I wouldn't have a speck of dignity left if I let anyone see me like that. It was a wrenching decision. The upside was enormous. Submitting the tape was the only way to get a team of deep-pocketed professionals to come to my rescue. But what about that thing called self-respect? Did I hate myself so much that I'd risk death, allow doctors to slice me open, endure excruciating pain and public ridicule to become a different person? Yes, I think maybe I did. I reminded myself that if they didn't pick me, no one would ever have to know. And if they did pick me, I'd be radically reinvented. Men would find me attractive. I'd be confident again. Someone might marry me. *Dignity, schmignity,* I thought as I mailed the application.

7. Snubbed

Skyler came home from school in tears.

'What's the matter?' I asked her. 'Why are you crying?'

'Bea's having a dance party with Clay Aiken and all the girls are going but I'm not invited.'

'Of course you're invited. I used to work with her daddy and he told me you'd be invited. Besides, you're not allowed to have a birthday party at your school if you don't include the whole class. I'm sure you're mistaken,' I said to my baby.

'No, Bea was talking about the party today and she told everyone I wasn't invited. Her mommy says we're not in the same class as Bea's family and she can't play with me anymore. I don't get it, Mommy. I *am* in Bea's class.'

'Of course you are, sweetheart. Bea's mother is confused. Don't worry, I'll straighten her out.' *Okay, Sassy, you wanna fight? Fight with me, you trollop. Don't go messing with my little girl.*

Skyler continued to weep, and I held her and stroked her hair. It was soft and curly as only a child's locks can be. 'It's not fair, it's not fair,' she kept repeating. *Welcome to the real world,* I thought.

Later that evening, I arranged for my neighbor to watch the girls. Walking by Park Avenue Synagogue, I spotted six abandoned flower arrangements on the sidewalk, there for the taking. Removing the YOU'LL ALWAYS LIVE IN OUR HEARTS, MANNY banner, I made off with the sparsest one.

'Flowers for Mrs. Bird,' I told the doorman. He announced the delivery and I was buzzed up.

The uniformed housekeeper answered and I handed her the flowers. 'Is Mrs. Bird in?' I inquired, peering inside the door.

'They're having dinner right now,' she said, blocking my view.

I bolted past her and headed straight for the smell of savory roast chicken and haricots verts. Sitting around the table were Sassy, Drayton, Bea, and three-year-old Max. There were fresh flowers on their Chinese Chippendale table, linen placemats with matching napkins, and crystal glasses – including a Waterford sippy cup for Max. Sassy was ringing a delicate silver bell, signaling that the next course should be served. She was wearing one of those chin girdles they prescribe after a mini neck-lift. Her hair had been recently cut and professionally flat-ironed, her nails were perfectly French-manicured, and she had on a dress from the current Max Mara line. Seeing her all dolled up like that stung. God, I missed my old life. The only consolation was knowing that Sassy was married to a girly-man who painted his nails.

'Sassy, I have to talk to you,' I said.

'What an unexpected surprise! How *are* you, Ivy? You look raaather well and blond hair becomes you, doesn't it.' The way Drayton said this, you'd think he actually meant it. I considered reciprocating by complimenting his latest field of hair plugs, but I thought better of it.

'Sorry to interrupt your dinner, but I need to speak with Sassy.'

'Why don't you join us?' Drayton suggested as Sassy rose quickly to whisk me off to the next room.

'Sassy, you've invited all the girls in Bea's class to her birthday party except Skyler. She's crushed. I'm here to ask you to include her.'

'Ivy, it's not that we don't want to include Skyler, of course we do. But the party's for children *and* parents, and Dray and I didn't think *you'd* feel comfortable with the crowd we've invited.'

'Of course I'd feel comfortable. I go to school events with these families all the time.'

'Yes, but we're also having some "special" children and their parents,' she said making quotation marks with her fingers when she said 'special.' 'You know, Michael J. Fox's twins, Connie Chung and Maury Povich's son, Kelly Ripa's boy – you'd feel like a fish out of water what with the downturn you've suffered. It would be cruel of us to put you in that position.'

'Look, Sassy, I don't give a shit about coming to your daughter's party. But Skyler's hurt because she's been excluded. She doesn't understand why. And I'm certainly not gonna tell her it's because I caught you fucking her daddy.' As soon as the words were out of my mouth, I noticed Drayton standing in the doorway. He had heard everything. Oops.

8. You Gotta Have Friends

W ith Drayton lurking in the background, Sassy let loose with a low blow. 'Ivy, I know you lost your job and your husband dumped you and you're being forced to sell your home, but that's no excuse for making up vicious lies about me and my family. Under the circumstances, it would be better if Bea didn't play with Skyler, and I would appreciate it if you would leave my house right now.'

Drayton sidled up to his wife. 'I think you owe Sassy an apology,' he added in that snarky patronizing tone he used at the office. 'We've been nothing but kind to you and your family. Why would you *say* such an ugly thing to her?'

Well, let's see. You stole my job. Sassy fucked my husband, ruined my marriage, and dissed my daughter. That's what I wanted to say, but didn't. Instead, I looked at the two of them standing in solidarity and shook my head. This was not going well. I needed to make it right for Skyler.

I took a deep breath. 'Yes, I must be losing it. It's just that . . . it's hard for me not to be jealous of you two. You have everything I've lost – a good marriage, a beautiful home, a secure job. I'm really, really sorry.'

Resisting the urge to vomit, I continued. 'Would you do me one favor? And I'm *only* asking you this because I'm so down on my luck. Would you tell Bea that Skyler *is* invited to her party, but that she can't come? Would you do that to spare Skyler's feelings?'

'Of couuurse, we will,' Drayton said, his tone dripping with insincerity. 'Now, you take care of yourself and if there's anything we can do to help you, anything at all, just ring me at work.' Sassy stood there, arms folded, eyes narrowed.

'Thanks, Drayton,' I said. 'I appreciate your support.' I was burning inside, humiliated that my life had come to this.

'By the way,' Drayton added casually as we approached the door, 'what are you asking for your apartment?'

I stared at him.

'We'd be interested in having a look,' he said, oblivious. 'We love our place, but you've got the better address. So, this may be the perfect time for a change. When would be a good time for us to stop by?'

'Why don't you call my agent, Meris Blumstein? She's with Corcoran,' I told him.

Once home, I explained to Skyler that she was welcome to go to Bea's party, but gosh darn it, we would be out of town that weekend. The next day, I got busy making travel plans.

∞

I needed a career. And I needed one fast.

Radical Reinvention hadn't called. My savings were depleted. Cadmon showed no signs of going back to work.

I'd been living in denial, allowing myself to believe there would be an eleventh-hour rescue. Lottery. Inheritance. A suitcase full of cash found in the backseat of a taxi. Hey, it could happen.

With no enthusiasm, I put my résumé together and began that mortifying ritual known as networking. The job-hunting books say to make a list of everyone you know, call them, and don't hang up until each person gives you three more leads. The problem was, out of ninety people on my list, only five called back. Well, a few phoned after midnight when they knew I'd be asleep. These were my so-called friends, my business associates, people I'd gone to bat for in the past. The five who called back were unemployed themselves, disappointed to learn I couldn't hire them at Myoki.

I looked into starting my own business and went to a franchise show at the Javits Center. For $50,000 to $200,000, I could own a Krispy Kreme store. A check-cashing company. A drug-sniffing dog firm. A bail-bonds business. Nothing called out to me.

As luck would have it, my closest friend, Faith, and I had lunch scheduled. We'd worked together many years ago at Myoki, umbilically united in battle as we struggled to survive the daily rantings of a tyrannical she-boss. Faith knew a lot about handling adversity. Her first husband, Rodney, switched teams three years into their marriage. He finally admitted what I'd always known – he was gay. The guy was sensitive. He had impeccable taste. He wore Lina Wertmüller glasses. He got regular fanny waxes. How could she not have suspected? Faith was devastated when it happened, but she handled herself with grace. They managed to stay friends and share custody of their golden retriever, Henry. I was trying to live up to her example.

Faith's story had a happy ending. In the ultimate stroke of good fortune, she found herself stuck in an elevator for two hours with a sixty-three-year-old multi-billionaire who was much kinder than his reputation would have you believe. They had a fairy-tale romance, the wedding to end all weddings, and then adopted two adorable girls from Pennsylvania.

Now she lived in a twenty-thousand-square-foot penthouse on Fifth Avenue with eight bedrooms and ten bathrooms, a pool, a gym, a meditation room, and a twenty-seat movie theater. She had help – a chief of staff with two assistants, a hairstylist, wardrobe stylist, masseuse, makeup artist, sushi chef, regular chef, trainer, weekday nannies and weekend nannies, all supported by maids and drivers aplenty. I won't bore you with the jewels Steven lavished on her, or the 32-carat diamond engagement ring. The Bentleys, Mercedeses, Lamborghinis, Hummers, Porsches, jets, and helicopters are hardly worth mentioning. Besides their castle in Scotland and private island in New Zealand, she and Steven owned homes in Southampton, Palm Springs, Palm Beach, and Paris. Since she was my best friend, I tried not to be jealous, but I must admit that at times, I wanted to slap her husband and say, 'Couldja just write me a check, for God's sake?'

We were there for each other anytime either of us had a problem. This time, Faith's senior assistant had arranged the lunch, so obviously she had something on her mind.

We met at my favorite restaurant, The Lever House, on a wet Tuesday afternoon. You were practically guaranteed to see someone famous there – Bill Clinton, Mike Nichols, Quentin Tarantino. Once we saw Bruce Springsteen! The roomful of jaded New Yorkers turned into flubbering Jell-O and applauded him when he got up to leave. It was kind of embarrassing.

'Whadja buy at Barneys?' Faith asked as soon as we were seated.

'Oh, just a trifle,' I said nonchalantly. See, my trick worked! I must admit it's tough to observe certain truths about yourself, like discovering you're so insecure you'd do *anything* to save face. Me, carry a Barneys bag so people would think I could still afford to shop there? Guilty.

'Have *you* lost weight?' Faith asked.

'I have. Thanks for noticing.'

'Aww, you're not able to eat with all that's happened,' she said.

'Yeah, well, it's called "the divorce diet." Plus I'm working out to exercise videos.'

'Could you use a treadmill?' Faith asked.

'Why, do you have a spare?'

'I just replaced my old one. You can have it.' Faith pulled out her BlackBerry and beamed a message to someone on her staff. Knowing her, the treadmill would be delivered that afternoon.

'Thanks. I figure I'm at a crossroad. If I go one way, I'll become a frumpy divorcée. If I go the other, I'll become a chic, desirable woman of a certain age.'

'Well, you look *great*,' Faith said. 'With that blond hair, I could almost mistake you for Renée Zellweger.'

Hmm. Did she mean the Renée Zellweger *with* the Bridget Jones weight or *without* it?

Faith changed the subject. 'So, how are the girls doing without Cad?'

'They're okay. They see him every other weekend. He calls a lot.'

'What about you? Do you miss him?'

'That's the weird thing. I don't. After he left, I realized we'd become more like business partners.'

'No sex?' Faith asked.

'Oh, sure, we did it. On the first Saturday of every month, in the same six positions, in the same order.'

Faith giggled. 'God, I hope that doesn't happen to us.'

'Just don't start calling each other "Mommy" and "Daddy" like we did.'

'Ooh, that's the kiss of death.'

'*I know!* Anyway, the girls and me, we're managing.'

'How about work? Anything new?' Faith asked.

I updated her on my career crisis.

'Ivy, do *not* feel bad about this. Did you see the front-page article in this week's *New York* magazine – "Failure: the New Success"? Failure's very hot right now. You're in.'

'Greeeaat,' I said.

'Look, give me your résumé. I'll pass it on to Steven. He's got so many companies. There's got to be a job for you somewhere.'

I would have preferred that she offer to ask her husband to support me, but barring that, this would help.

'Thanks. I'll do that,' I said. 'Say, what are you having?'

'Tuna carpaccio. It's my favorite.'

'I'll have vegetable soup.'

'That's it?'

'Yeah, when I go to restaurants now, I nurse a bowl of

low-fat soup. I'm practicing safe soup. But *you* should try the walnut-garlic paste on your bread. It's to die for.'

'Enough with the food. Back to business. Tell me, what do you *really* want to do?' Faith asked.

'I *really* want to feel what it's like to be dependent.'

'No, really.'

'Really,' I said. 'I should have listened to my mother and married a rich guy. Faith, you were *so* smart to marry Steven. I know you love him and all, but his wealth gives you such freedom. I swear, I'm gonna raise my daughters to marry well. They can always divorce well if it doesn't work out. If I ever remarry, it'll be to someone rich or with serious earning potential. I refuse to find myself in this position again.'

'Ivy, don't kid yourself. If you marry a guy with money, he'll just get a prenup. That's what Steven did.'

'No kidding. You have a prenup?'

'Of course. Steven promised to give me a million dollars for every year we're married. If we're married twenty years, I get a hundred million. And I agreed to have sex with him three times a week. I don't mind, though. He's not so handsome on the outside, but inside he's a sweetie. And all that power's a real turn-on.'

'Sex three times a week is spelled out in your prenup?'

'Absolutely. *And,* I agreed to stay under a hundred and ten pounds. See, Ivy, there's no easy answer for any of us.'

'Wait. I'm hung up on the sex-three-times-a-week thing. Does it define what you have to do? I mean, would a blowjob count or does there have to be penetration?'

'The contract spells everything out in pornographic detail. It's the bargain I struck to marry such a rich man.

But Ivy, forget about me. Let's talk about you. How will you support your family? You know, I read in a book that if you do what you love, the money will follow. So why don't you start a business?'

'I've thought of that, but I don't know what I'd do.'

'Steven says if you think of something people hate doing and make it easier for them, there's a business opportunity. That's why dog-walkers are in such demand. Not that I'm recommending you become one.'

We were interrupted by George, pronounced the French way, who took our orders. They were out of tuna carpaccio, so Faith chose poussin with foie gras, Brussels sprouts, and wild mushrooms instead.

'Don't worry about me, Faith. I'll figure this out. I'm sure of it.' *No, I'm not. I'm not sure of anything anymore.*

'At least you're optimistic,' Faith said.

'Speaking of doing something you hate,' I said, 'they're having the annual auction at the girls' school next week. Everyone's heard through the nanny grapevine that Cad and I broke up. I don't want to go alone. Would you be my date, pleeease?'

'Absolutely,' she promised. 'Now, I need *your* help.'

'Of course, anything.'

'I've been applying to kindergartens this year for Mae,' Faith said.

'Oooh, Faith, I'm sorry. *That* has to be about the worst experience a parent can have in New York. I remember how traumatic it was. Where are you applying?'

'All the impossible schools. Trinity. Harvard Day. Balmoral. Brearley. Chapin. Dalton. Spence. Nightingale. Hartley. St. Mary's. Horace Mann. Hewitt. I wanted

St. Andrew's but they wouldn't send an application. They'd given their quota to Caucasians and would only mail to minorities.'

'Faith, your husband's a billionaire. Doesn't that count as a minority?'

'I wish,' Faith said. 'It's gotten so much more competitive. Siblings and legacies get priority admission. Last year, Riverton had ten spots for kids who weren't sibs or legs, and more than six hundred children applied. And they gave five of those spaces to diversity kids.'

'I read that the year after Caroline Kennedy sent her youngest to All Souls, the school got fifteen hundred applicants for thirteen places,' I added, making matters worse.

'I know. And these days, schools want genius test scores and we had the worst luck. Mae took her ERB in November and her tester dropped dead of a stroke before she had a chance to record her results. When I took Mae for a retest, she refused to speak. She kept pursing her lips and pretending to zip them. I don't know what came over her. We're trying again next week.'

'I'm *so, so* sorry,' I said, truly sympathetic.

'Then there are the parent interviews,' Faith continued. 'Steven travels so much, I've had to do them myself. The schools don't like that. They think the father's not interested. When we went to Balmoral for Mae's visit, I laid out a perfectly lovely outfit. She insisted on wearing last year's Halloween costume instead. I could have died.'

'What was she for Halloween?'

'Barney the dinosaur. The other girls were in their party dresses and patent-leather Mary Janes and Mae was dressed as Barney.'

I started laughing. I couldn't help it.

'And there's more,' Faith added.

More?

'You know how they ask you those questions on the application and then give you about two lines to answer them? "What are your child's interests? What are your family's values?" Well, I squeezed my answers into the two lines. I found out later that I was supposed to write these moving essay answers. Like college! How was I to know that?'

'Oooh. I wish you'd asked me. I could've told you.'

'Anyway, what do you say about a kid whose main interest these days is excavating her boogers? Tell me? What do you say?'

9. If You Have to Ask

ow *would* one turn a booger obsession into a positive? 'Maybe you could have spun it to show a proclivity for science, a future doctor or biologist perhaps,' I suggested.

Faith gave me the fisheye. 'Ivy, I'm going out of my mind. How am I gonna get her into private school?' My friend was more upset than I'd ever seen her. I felt her pain. Getting Mae into kindergarten was out of her control. Everyone in New York knew a Weill, a Bloomberg, or at least one Hilton sister, so connections almost always cancelled each other out. Even having a wealthy father didn't guarantee a spot. Plenty of city kids came from money and had recognizable last names.

'Okay, let's think. Which schools are your favorites?'

'I guess St. Mary's or Balmoral. Ivy, can I taste your soup? Maybe I'll order it next time.'

'Of course.' I gave her a spoonful. 'Do you know anyone on the board of trustees at either of those schools? Ideally a current parent who's also a big donor?'

'I don't, but I'm sure Steven does. He knows everyone.'

'Well, do your homework. Find a few wealthy and

powerful friends who'll go to bat for you. Ask them to contact the headmaster and the head of development, *especially* the head of development. Tell them to talk about what a great addition your family would be, how philanthropic you are, and what an extraordinary child Mae is. And you know, she *is* extraordinary. She's just not performing when you need her to.'

'What do you expect? She's not a show dog,' Faith said.

'Faith, I'm on *your* side. Anyway, your friends should ask the schools to give Mae's application special attention, and they should promise that if she's admitted, Steven would serve as the chairman of the annual fund committee. Just tell Steven that he has to do this for you. He will.'

'Do you think it'll work?'

'Of course it will. You just haven't been rich long enough to naturally think this way. Trust me, helping each other's children get ahead is a time-honored tradition among the wealthy. Remember Tipper Bucket, who used to work in Consumer Debt Marketing?'

'I think so. Young black woman?'

'Yes. Well now she's assistant director of admissions at Harvard Day.'

Faith lowered her voice. 'Is it true Harvard Day's the feeder school to Harvard University?'

'No, that's what they want you to believe, but they're not even connected. Anyway, Tipper told me that schools can be bribed as long as it's done tastefully and everyone pretends it's a donation. She says it happens all the time.'

'Who knew? Okay, Ivy. It's a plan,' Faith said. 'God, what a nightmare. I feel worse about getting Mae into kindergarten than I did about getting shingles when Rodney turned gay on me.'

'Faith, don't say that. Remember the pain you were in?'

'Yes, but I had more control in that situation,' Faith said firmly. 'I'd take shingles over getting my kid into private school any day.'

∽

The Balmoral School auction was promoted as a community builder, but I didn't feel welcome. I'd budgeted $100 to spend. I know that was nothing compared to the indecent amounts other families would fork over, but I wanted to contribute in the piddly way that I could.

Faith and I walked around examining the smaller items for sale – paintings, autographed baseballs, theater tickets, that sort of thing. The organizers had written in suggested first bids, with most starting at $250. Finally, I found a pair of doggie sunglasses for Sir Elton from Mary Kate and Ashley's new pet accessories line. I penciled in my $100 offer and hoped there would be no bidding war.

Later, they were holding a live auction where terminally privileged parents would fight over one-of-a-kind items. This year there was a penthouse suite on the *Crystal Symphony* for a seven-day Italian cruise, a small part in a Martin Scorsese movie, one thousand copies of your child's book published by Doubleday, a dinner date at Rao's with George Clooney, and a chance to have Kevin Kline recite postprandial sonnets at the winning bidder's dinner party.

'What are postprandial sonnets?' Faith whispered.

'You obviously never went to private school, or you'd know what those were,' I told her.

'No. I attended the fine public schools of Paterson, New Jersey.'

'Right, I forgot you were from New Jersey. No wonder you don't know what postprandial sonnets are.'

'Do you know what they are?' Faith asked.

'Hell, no.'

Faith and I sat together at the dinner catered by the executive chef from La Tour d'Argent, who had flown in from Paris for the occasion. At first, no one at our table talked to us, and I pretended not to care. Then, Bitsy Frakas recognized Faith as Steven Lord's wife. I heard her whisper to Dolce de Nagy, 'Why didn't someone tell me she wasn't a nobody?' From that moment on, Bitsy, Dolce, and all the other wives got cozy with me in hopes of befriending Faith. Organizers made sure wine flowed freely to loosen parents up before going in for the big auction kill. The same group of twenty high rollers bid on everything, showing off for each other and the rest of the community. I know I was impressed.

When the date with George Clooney came up, Faith raised her paddle. 'It'll be your birthday present,' she whispered.

10. Park Avenue Penniless

'Are you *crazy*?' I said to Faith. 'I can't go out with George Clooney. He's the sexiest man alive.'

When the bidding got up to $10,000, I insisted she stop. 'I'd rather have the postprandial sonnets. Please get me those.'

'Not a chance. Kevin Kline's married. Besides, you've had a rough time, and I want to get you something special this year. You're going on a date with George Clooney if it's the last thing I do.'

The bidding was fierce. Dinner at Rao's was so famously impossible to come by that most people were vying for the meal, screw the date with George. An eleven-table Mafia-friendly restaurant open just for dinner, closed on weekends, Rao's has but one coveted seating a night. The only way to get a reservation is to know an insider who 'owns' a table, either a big shot like Tommy Mottola or a regular Joe from the neighborhood who just happened to grow up with Frankie Pellegrino, the owner. The President of the United States couldn't get seated at Rao's without the right connections. The place had become even hotter since Louis 'Lump-Lump' Barone whacked Albert Circelli in the dining room for insulting a guest who got up to sing 'Don't Rain on My Parade.' In the end, Faith's $35,000 bid – not including food – prevailed.

∽

On Monday, I interviewed at Citigroup. Vice President of Debit Card Marketing. They liked me. I could tell. But I was already bored with the work and I hadn't even taken the job. It was along the lines of what I'd done at Myoki, with more responsibility, a smaller staff, paying 30 percent less than before. Still, it would mean a regular paycheck and benefits. I had to consider it.

Meanwhile, next year's tuition bills arrived from the girls' school. Skyler's came to $25,950 and Kate's was $24,950 – a bargain because she was younger. I also held in my hand the annual fund solicitation I'd been sitting on. They would expect at least $5,000 per child if we were to have our names listed on the bottom ring of the giving tree. I couldn't bear the thought of contributing less and having our donation appear under the roots. Sadly, I realized I could no longer afford to keep the girls in their first-class, luxury school. The magnificent beaux arts mansion where they spent their days dressed in perfect little uniforms, lined up in two straight lines like Madeleine's class – it would all have to go.

Embarrassed, I called the head of admissions and told her we would probably need to withdraw next year. I explained that we loved the school but were experiencing an economic downturn. 'Is financial aid a possibility?' I inquired. 'No, what little we have is already committed. Just let me know by next week if you want your spaces,' she said. 'I have to replace the girls if they're not coming back.' She was cold and uncompassionate. Clearly, it didn't matter that Skyler and Kate had to leave. All that talk about how we were a community wasn't meant to include families who were down on their luck.

Drayton, that bottom-feeder, made a lowball offer for our apartment, contingent on my writing a glowing recommendation on behalf of the entire Bird family for his co-op board package. On principle, I should have refused. But I didn't have the stomach to put scruples before my overdrawn bank account. The market had softened. There was no bidding war, just one other bid. And after that deal fell through, Drayton's paltry proposition was our only possibility. With that, I would clear enough to give Cadmon half the profits and rent a small apartment in a semi-bad neighborhood.

I signed a lease on a place near Orchard and Delancey – the Lower East Side. The area had become trendy of late for its true grittiness and complete lack of hip, but so far the landlords hadn't caught on. Bargains could still be had. It was where my grandparents, like so many others, came when they immigrated to America. Then it was a neighborhood of pickle shops, pushcarts, tenements, and synagogues. In more recent years, there had been an influx of Latino and Chinese settlers. The elementary school in the neighborhood was terrible, but there was a charter program nearby that savvy parents clamored to get their kids into.

When I got to the registrar's office, she handed me a bunch of papers. 'The good news is we have open registration beginning tomorrow at noon.'

'That's great,' I said. 'I'll fill these out and bring them back.'

'Wait, you didn't hear the bad news.'

'The bad news?'

'Yes. Do you see the line that starts at our front door?'

'The one that goes clear to the Bowery? What's it for?'

'That's the line to register.'

'There's already a line to register?'

'Yup.' She lowered her voice. 'I suggest you get on line right now or you won't get your kids in.'

'You expect me to wait in that line for' – I looked at my watch – 'twenty-eight hours?'

'Only if you want to get your kids in.'

I thanked the woman and ran like a mugger to claim my space. Then I called Faith and asked her to pick up the girls and Sir Elton and keep them overnight.

'Ivy, you're not going to spend the night on the street, are you?' she asked. 'That's dangerous.'

'I most certainly am if it means getting the girls into this school. But would you do me a favor? Would you send over a pillow and blanket before midnight?'

'Ivy, girls like you don't stand in line all night for *anything*,' she said. 'Why don't I send one of our drivers to stand for you? You can take his place in the morning.'

I looked around at the moms and dads waiting in front of me. They were prepared with bags of food, blankets, pillows, pee bottles. Some were playing cards, others were reading; still others were talking on their cell phones. Parents were yelling at their kids to stay close by. The little ones were attracted to an albino man with a parrot on a leash. 'No,' I told Faith. 'I think I'd better do this myself.'

∾

As the sun was setting, a stretch limo pulled up to the curb. A uniformed maid stepped out of the backseat with a feather pillow, a blow-up mattress, and a down quilt. Then the chauffeur emerged, carrying a wicker picnic basket overflowing with fried chicken, potato salad, baked beans, rolls, brownies, and bottled water. There was wine for later, bagels with cream cheese for breakfast, and a Thermos with hot coffee-light, prepared just the way I liked it. Faith thoughtfully included a portable blow-up potty that zipped shut after every use. When the limo pulled away, the other parents circled like buzzards.

A plus-sized mama led the charge. 'What the hell're *you* doing taking up a space in this school? Don't you know how many poor people, with nowhere else to go, want their kids here?'

'Yeah, go back to private school, you rich bitch,' a nerdy guy who was emboldened by the crowd said. Others voiced similar sentiments, and not very politely, I might add.

I was completely out of my milieu, unfamiliar with the etiquette required to calm an agitated mob. In other words, I was fucked.

11. Nouveau Bitch

Surrounded by angry parents, I held up my hands to quiet them. That didn't work. So I closed my eyes and sang 'Close to You' like I meant it. Singing is a talent I have. Really, I have a captivating soprano voice. Everyone says that, not just me. Most people find 'Close to You' so painfully sappy that I thought it might shut the crowd up. It did.

> Why do birds suddenly appear
> Every time . . . you are near?
> Just like me, they long to be
> Close to you-oo-oo . . .

I took advantage of the mob's stunned silence to explain myself. 'Thank you,' I said. 'Please hear me out. I need to get my children into this school as much as you do. I'm not wealthy. I can't afford private. It just happens that my friend married a rich guy on the Upper East Side. She knew I'd be standing on line, so she sent things to make the wait easier. Do you think I'd be doing this if I didn't *have* to?'

The crowd mumbled. Then the nerd who called me a 'rich bitch' piped up. 'If your friend's got so much money, why don't you ask *her* to send your kids to private school?'

The other parents shouted, 'Yeah, yeah.'

'Even I have my pride,' I said. 'So would anyone like something to eat? I'm happy to share,' I added, trying to ease the tension.

No one took me up on my offer. *Fine, be that way*, I thought. Finally, Plus-Sized Mama broke the ice. 'So,' she said, 'you got a girl or a boy?'

'Two girls, six and almost eight. You?'

'My boy's five. My girl's eight. I'm takin' them out of the I've Got a Dream School.'

'What's wrong with the I've Got a Dream School?'

'No library. No PE. Parents don't care,' she said. 'School of the Basics is the third-best public school in the city. Their PTA's real active.'

'Maybe we can work on a committee together,' I suggested. 'I'm Ivy Ames.'

Plus-Sized Mama couldn't resist my natural charm. 'I'm Louise Fernandez,' she said, peering into my picnic basket. 'So, are those brownies homemade?' By midnight, we were exchanging recipes and singing 'Funky Cold Medina' to pass the time.

The line began moving at noon. By four, I'd registered the girls for their new school. I wondered which was better, waiting in line for thirty-two hours to sign your child up for public school or going through the string-pulling and scrutiny of applying to private school. Then I realized that the question was meaningless. This was how the world worked. Regular people stood in line and privileged folk took part in elaborate rituals designed to separate the wheat from the chaff. As Cad used to say, 'It is what it is.'

∞

On Friday, I joined Skyler's class for a field trip to the Martin Beck Theater on Broadway. I would miss being available to chaperone school outings like this when I went back to work.

Her class was performing in an assembly about the human body in April. Each child had been assigned an internal organ to play. They had to research the function and, in the character of their heart or liver or gallbladder, present a monologue on its role in the human body – a combination science/drama project. Harrison Ford's ex-next-door neighbor arranged the field trip. Her child, Harrison's goddaughter, was in Skyler's class. As a favor to the little girl, he had generously volunteered to teach the kids some basic acting techniques. I wanted to be there for Skyler, of course, but I also secretly fancied Harrison. I decided that if there was even the slightest chance he would throw Calista over for me, I had to introduce myself.

'I'm going to be a bile duct,' Skyler had told me a few days earlier. 'Will you help me research what a bile duct does?'

'A bile duct? Why in the world did they make you a bile duct? There are so many more interesting body parts.'

'I was supposed to be a colon,' Skyler explained. 'But when I wasn't looking, Bea talked to Mrs. Hatcher and said *she* wanted to be the colon, so Mrs. Hatcher took it away from me. All that was left was the stinky bile duct.'

How very like her father that Bea Bird was.

'Well, bile ducts aren't so bad. We'll make it interesting,' I promised.

My luck, Sassy also accompanied the class on the field trip. She kept her distance and pretended I wasn't there.

'Pee-puull, pee-puull, be your body part,' Harrison shouted. 'Electra, I want to see some beating from you. Hearts beat, you know. Skyler, open and close, open and close, let the bile in and out, in and out. Bea, dance like a spastic colon, let me see some movement. Elena, in and out, in and out, *feel* what it's like to be a pair of lungs. Michaela, you're not looking very brain-like, I want to see those synapses connecting,' Harrison said as he quickly snapped his fingers. While he directed, Mrs. Hatcher walked around and corrected the girls' positions. Harrison was so busy with the kids that he didn't pay attention to the mommies. That was a blow. I'd spent hours making myself gorgeous, while looking like I hadn't tried. That's not as easy as it sounds.

To our mutual chagrin, Sassy and I found ourselves seatmates on the bus going home.

'Aren't we lucky our girls are at Balmoral?' Sassy asked. 'Where else would they get acting lessons from one of America's top stars?'

'Yes, where else? You know, I think I'd like the school better if there was more diversity,' I added, attempting to set the stage for our impending departure to the Lower East Side. The Ames girls didn't leave because of financial problems. Heavens, no! Ivy wanted the girls at a school with *more diversity*.

'How can you say Balmoral doesn't have enough

diversity? Some parents have jets, others have yachts. Some girls are royal, others are common. Some families inherited their wealth, others are self-made.'

I was silent, wondering whether or not Sassy was serious. Given the earnest expression on her face, I guessed that she was.

'And of course,' Sassy stage-whispered, 'there's that adorable little black girl in their class, the one whose father plays for the Knicks. Not that her skin color matters, not that I even *notice* things like that. By the way, Skyler makes a wonderful bile duct.'

'Sassy, don't even go there. You know as well as I do that Skyler was supposed to be the colon.'

Sassy let out a nervous gravelly laugh. In addition to her perfect face and figure, Sassy had one of those sultry Kathleen Turner voices. 'Did you hear Drayton was promoted?'

'No, congratulations.'

'He'll be an EVP. He's playing in the majors now.'

'You must be proud.' *Gosh, I didn't think he was handsome enough to rise that high at Myoki*, I restrained myself from saying.

'How's Cad?' she asked.

'Fine, I suppose. I only talk to him when he picks up the girls.'

That wasn't *exactly* true. I'd received several late-night calls from Cad suggesting we try to patch things up. He swore he would never be unfaithful again. We'd had many good years together and Cadmon wanted to try to recapture that. I, on the other hand, knew there was nothing left to salvage, at least not for me. I'd never be able to move beyond his betrayal. Dad promised Mom he'd never cheat again, and then went on to break her heart and mine. 'I'm sorry,' I'd tell him. 'I don't want to be your wife anymore.' In fact, I was already interviewing lawyers.

'Are you in touch with Cad?' I asked Sassy.

'Oh, no. That was just a short-term fling. It was *purely* sexual. It never should have happened. Plus, frankly, his penis is rather small, don't you agree?' she said.

'Excuse me?'

'His penis. You know, he has one of those teeney-weenies. Just like two grapes and a gummy worm,' she giggled.

I glanced at Sassy. She returned my look expectantly. What? Was this supposed to be a girlfriend moment? Did she think we would bond over Cadmon's shortcomings? Yes, let's be best friends and make fun of *your* lover's — *my* soon-to-be-ex-husband's piddly little pleasure pickle. Won't that be fun? I don't know what happened. I'm usually such a controlled person. But at that moment, riding in that stuffy old school bus with no shock absorbers, I couldn't contain the rage I felt toward this ill-bred ninny. I could not – no, *I would not* let Cad's cockus erectus go unde-fended.

'No, Sassy. I don't think. CAD'S PENIS IS NOT SMALL. It's *AVERAGE*.'

'ALL RIGHT,' she said. 'Don't be so sensitive.'

Oh, dear. We were speaking rather loudly. Everyone on the bus was staring. Mrs. Hatcher was giving us a disapproving-teacher look. 'Sorry . . . so sorry everyone, forgive us, please,' I announced. 'Next time we'll use our inside voices.'

12. Closet Envy

eturning home from Skyler's field trip, I found there were two messages. Susan from Citigroup Human Resources called and so did Faith. I rang Susan back first and she made the offer I expected. It wasn't the dream job I'd hoped for, but there were no other options. I accepted it indifferently and we agreed I'd start in one week. I walked over to Faith's to tell her the news.

Her head of security escorted me upstairs.

'I'm in here,' Faith shouted. 'In the closet.' Faith was referring to her dressing suite. It was about half the size of my apartment. There was the marble bathroom, with its bidet, eucalyptus steam, aromatherapy pool, shower, Roman Jacuzzi, and cold pool. There was the wet-treatment room for wraps, scrubs, and hydrotherapy. The beauty salon was outfitted with anything a hairstylist or makeup artist would need to render Faith charity-ball ready. The massage and facial room was pure Zen. The dressing area itself was wall-to-wall mirrors, with a treadmill, elliptical machine, and bike in case Faith was too rushed to exercise in their downstairs gym. Faith's clothes, arranged by color and season, hung on motorized racks like they use at dry cleaners. She owned pieces by every la-di-da designer in the world. Four walls held floor-to-ceiling perfectly organized shoes by Manolo Blahnik, Jimmy Choo, Chanel, and other purveyors of strappy bejeweled footwear. Each pair was in its own box with a photo attached. In two other closets, hundreds of obscenely priced bags were lined up. Faith had come a long way from her days as an assistant manager at Myoki.

'Hi, Ivy. Over here.' Avi was blowing out Faith's hair while she talked to a geeky guy with a buzz cut. 'This is Vladimir Kahn, my closet director. Vladimir, this is my friend, Ivy Ames.' Faith had to speak loudly over the sound of the blow-dryer. 'Vladimir's creating a computer catalog of everything in my closet. Now I'll be able to go online and look through photos of my clothes organized by color, designer, degree of formality – whatever I want. When I pick an outfit and press "enter," it'll be delivered up front. Show her, Vladimir.'

Vladimir pulled up a photo of a Marc Jacobs flowery print dress. Below it, images of six pairs of matching shoes and six bags popped up. 'Which accessories, Mrs. Lord?' he asked.

'The Helmut Langs, definitely. And the Oscar de la Renta bag,' Faith answered.

Vladimir selected the three pieces, and the racks in Faith's closet started whirring and moving. Within seconds, the chosen items were assembled and waiting for her in the mirrored dressing area.

'Is that cool, or what?' Faith said.

'Cool. Except isn't that a Ralph Lauren dress?' I asked.

'Oh, my God. As if I would *ever* combine Ralph Lauren and Oscar de la Renta. Vladimir!'

'I'll fix it, don't worry.' Vladimir turned to me. 'We're still working out the bugs, but when we get this up and running, it'll cut Mrs. Lord's dressing time in half,' he bragged.

Avi put the finishing touches on Faith's hair. Christophe, Faith's stylist, came over to consult on tonight's makeup and outfit. He was holding a gorgeous cocktail dress. 'I'm seeing you in emerald-green Dior tonight, darling. With your Lucite stilettos and ruby red lips, you will be *taboo*, my love.'

'Whatever you say, Christophe. Now, everybody but Ivy, out. Out. I need to talk to her.' The room cleared before Faith finished the sentence. 'Ivy, I've got the *best* news. Your idea worked!'

'Which idea was that?'

'You know, getting Mae into private school. We got the wink-nod from two directors that if Steven chairs the annual fund and donates five hundred big ones next year, Mae's in. It's not official, but we were assured *personally* by both development heads that there's nothing to worry about. Not only that, they're falling all over each other to get us. We're being wined and dined like the King of Siam. That's why I'm getting all dressed up tonight. The head of St. Mary's is taking us to Masa!'

'And you only have to donate five hundred dollars. That's great,' I said.

'No, five hundred *thousand*. But it's worth it, don't you think?'

'Definitely, definitely worth it. You must be relieved, huh?'

'I am. I mean, I hate that she's getting in this way. But with her behavior at the school visits, my cheesy essays, and Steven not coming to the parent interviews, I don't see that we have a choice. Did I tell you she bit a girl at her Brearley visit? Drew blood.'

'That's terrible.'

Christophe poked his head in. 'Sorry to interrupt, gorgeous, but which jewels?'

'My emerald necklace from Cartier,' Faith answered.

Christophe looked like a broken man.

'What?' Faith asked.

Christophe's expression was grim. 'You will break my already fragile heart if you show up at Masa looking like you're trying too hard. You want to impress this head-master, yes, but in a way that says "I couldn't care less what *you* think, fatso." What does that call for, my little pupil? *Think. Think.*'

'Christian Tse!' Faith said.

'Eg-zaaaactly,' Christophe said as his head disappeared from view.

Faith stood up. 'Ivy, there's something I want to show you.' I followed her into the master suite. Faith dug through a stack of magazines in her nightstand and handed me last week's *New Yorker*. 'Did you read the article about that man who charges families forty thousand dollars to get their kids into college?'

'Uhm, I read it,' I said. 'He calls himself Dr. Margolis, right? He's a doctor of law. Like that has anything to do with college admissions. I can't believe anyone would pay so much.'

Faith and I retired to the sitting area. She pressed an

intercom button and ordered up a snack. 'I've been think-ing about our conversation last week. I would have given *anything* to have an expert like Dr. Margolis help Mae get into kindergarten. Why don't you start a company that does that? The advice you gave me was perfect. You could do the same for other people.'

'What would you have paid someone to help you?'

'Hell, we're paying half a mil to guarantee Mae a spot. If you'd been advising us all along, we could've done it on our own. I'm sure we'd have paid thirty or even forty thou-sand,' Faith said. 'Not to sound like one of those neurotic parents, but if you don't get your kid into the right kinder-garten these days, you can forget the Ivy Leagues.'

'Faith, most people aren't in your tax bracket. I don't think you could charge more than ten thousand for kinder-garten.'

'Well, think about it,' Faith said. 'If you decide to do it, I'll help you get clients. A bunch of Mae's friends are applying next year, and these parents would pay anything for an advantage.'

There was a knock at the door and a server brought in refreshments, which were more elegantly presented than high tea at the Plaza.

'Faith, your idea sounds tempting, but I just accepted an offer at Citigroup,' I said with no passion in my voice.

'Oh, well, that's *wonderful*,' Faith said. 'Congratulations, *really*.'

'You are *such* a liar,' I said, throwing my crustless cucumber sandwich at her. 'You and I both know what a drag this'll be. But I have to think of the girls. I have to be practical, right?'

'I guess. I mean, you *are* completely desperate,' Faith said.

'Yes, I am. Unless, of course, you and Steven want to adopt me.' Faith gave me a strange look.

'I'm just *kidding*,' I said. *Sort of.*

There was a hesitant knock at the door and Faith's closetkeeper stuck her head in. 'Your bath is ready, Mrs. Faith.'

'Thanks, Virginia.'

I followed my friend back to the dressing room, where her oversized Jacuzzi was steaming, filled with red and yellow rose petals. It smelled delicious. Near the bath was an exquisite basket of roses from Steven. He sent a magnificent bouquet to Faith, and smaller ones to Mae and Lia, every single week. *In a perfect world*, I thought, *every woman would be married to a man like Steven Lord.* Then I thought about mandatory sex three times a week. Would it be worth it? Glancing around Faith's dressing suite, I knew the answer.

13. Fired Becomes Her

I spent the next week lining up a part-time babysitter for the girls. I'd need someone to pick them up after school, help with homework, make dinner – all the fun mommy things I'd gotten to do for the last few months. Charles, an art student at Columbia, applied. I decided to give him a try. The girls only saw Cad every other weekend, so a little more testosterone in their lives would be healthy.

He spent the day with us on Friday, in training. *Here's the girls' school. Here's our nearest playground. Here's Sir Elton's dog run. Here's our favorite sushi place. Here's where you buy fish food for Beverly.* Handing over the baton was depressing, but necessary.

At 5:30 that evening, the phone rang.

'Hello, is your mommy home?'

'My mommy?'

'Your mommy, Ivy Ames.'

'This is Ivy.'

'Oh, Ivy, I'm sorry. You sounded just like a child.'

'No, it's me. I have a youthful voice.'

'It's Susan from Citigroup Human Resources. You aren't going to *believe* what I have to tell you!'

'What?' I asked. *You decided to increase my pay by 50 percent? You're putting me in charge of the whole department? You want to train me to be an investment banker? I couldn't imagine why Susan was calling.*

'They've eliminated your job,' she said.

'*What?* I haven't even started yet,' I complained.

'*I know.* I'm so embarrassed this happened, but I had no idea it was coming. There was a reorg announced yesterday and your box went away,' she explained.

'Do I get severance? I should, for all turmoil you've put me through.' *Feel guilty. Feel guilty. Feel guilty*, I telepathically divined.

'You can't be serious,' Susan said. 'Anyway, we'll keep your résumé on file, and I'll call you if anything else comes up.'

'You do that.'

What do you know? They fired me before I even started. What pricks! Unfortunately, I would have to do the same thing to young Charles.

∽

With no other prospects and little left from the Myoki severance, I decided to go into the private-school-admissions business. The more I thought about it, the better it sounded. I could do it. Innovation is often born of desperation. Well, I was desperate. I was beyond desperate. My only other option was to become a barista at Starbucks. That was out of the question. I have an MBA from Yale, for God's sake.

There was a slight problem with the admissions business. I had no experience. Does that *really* matter? I wondered.

No one knows what a kindergarten admissions adviser does. I could make it up. There were no licenses to get. No degrees required. No barriers to entry. I could become anything I pretended to be. People in New York re-create themselves all the time. Rudy Giuliani. Monica Lewinsky. Donald Trump. Why not me?

On Sunday, when the girls were with their dad, I wrote a plan. Approaching my future this way had worked in the past. Before I got married, I mapped out a strategy to acquire a handsome husband with good earning potential. Those were my requirements (I was young; what did I know?). In less than six months, I met Cadmon Ames III, and he fit the bill. I snared him by implementing Section B2 – joining a share house in the Hamptons. Cad and I met at a group dinner during my first weekend in Sag Harbor. The rest, as they say, was history. I *must* remember to dust off that plan.

On second thought, given recent events, maybe not.

I set two goals. First, become an expert on New York City private-school admissions. Second, find twenty clients willing to pay $10,000 each. To my surprise, I was excited about work. I couldn't remember the last time I'd felt that way.

PART 2

Educating Ivy

1. Kindergarten Wars

The path to enlightenment would be rocky. There were no books, no classes, no masters to bestow their wisdom on little Grasshopper. Theodora 'Tipper' Bucket, who used to report to me at Myoki and now worked at Harvard Day, offered to give me a tutorial on admissions. We met in a booth at the back of The Barkin' Dog diner in Queens, where I barely recognized her beneath the Yankee baseball cap and cheap aviator sunglasses.

'Tipper?' I asked doubtfully. 'Tipper Bucket?'

Tipper smiled. 'It's me. Only it's Bouquet now, like a bouquet of flowers.'

'Bouquet! How fancy.' From what I could see, Tipper's face was the same, quite beautiful in fact, but she'd gotten fat. I mean *really* fat. Her butt covered two thirds of the bench. It was a tragedy.

'How *are* you?' she said, holding her arms out for a hug. 'I'm so happy to see you.'

'Me, too,' I said, hugging back, feeling guilty that I'd secretly judged her for getting fat. Well, she wasn't fat as one normally thinks of fat. No, she was her same willowy self, but now there was a Volkswagen-sized mass attached to her butt. *Listen to me. What kind of shallow human being mentally mocks another for her imperfections?* Immediately, I vowed to fast next Yom Kippur for being so cruel in my heart to Tipper. 'What's with the disguise?' I joked.

Her eyes darted left and right. 'Now that you're going into this line of work, I can't be seen with you. There are others like you, but nobody knows who they are. Their names are discreetly passed around among prominent families, and I'm sure they make decent livings. But they have to stay underground or admissions directors like my boss, Cubby, will crush them like bugs.'

'Oh, my God,' I exclaimed. 'I had no idea. What do they have against us?'

'They say everyone should have an equal shot at getting their children into private school. They don't want advisers to learn their secrets and game the system.'

'But everyone knows it's not an equal playing field,' I said. 'People with money and connections have a huge advantage. If you're a normal white upper-middle-class lawyer or banker, you're screwed.'

'I know, I know,' Tipper conceded. 'But we have to *act* like everyone has a fair shot. Even when someone gives us a big donation to get their kid in, we pretend we don't make deals for admissions. But the child is always accepted – on his own merits, of course. We have a maniacal focus on ethics at Harvard Day – it's our number-one value, so it's critical that we maintain the pretense.'

The waitress appeared. Tipper jumped. 'Oh, my God, you scared me,' she said. We asked for coffee and a piece of chocolate cream pie with two forks.

'Frankly, I think you're nuts to become an admissions adviser. It's an ugly game. Think about it, Ivy. Who lives in Manhattan? The wealthiest, most accomplished human beings on the planet. They're sharks. And these are their children. They don't just *want* to get their kids into the most exclusive schools; they think they're *entitled* to it. Why would you choose to get involved with that?'

'You did.'

'Yes, but *you'll* be serving them. They have to suck up to me. If you start the business, I can *never* be seen with you again. Tonight I'll tell you everything I know, but after that, don't call me. If anyone asks, we *never* had this conversation.' Tipper spoke in a loaded and mysterious voice.

'Of course,' I said. 'I wouldn't dream of putting your job at risk.'

'Cubby is the most powerful woman in the private-school community. If she knew I'd breathed a word of inside information, I'd be blackballed from the industry.'

Tipper started out by telling me what I already knew – that there were five *official* elements to a child's application: test scores, parent essays, the child's visit, the parent interview, and the nursery-school report. A problem with any one of those could mean the difference between receiving a thin envelope or a thick one. Being the sibling of another student, or being a 'legacy' – the child of an alumnus – improved a kid's odds enormously. Who you knew and how adamantly they advocated for you helped. Donations carried weight, of course. Diversity was good, especially the visually obvious kind. Tipper was one of only two women of color on Harvard Day's staff, and her job included recruiting minority students for the school.

The chocolate pie arrived and we dug into it with fervor. I was still dieting, so I left the last piece. Tipper ate it shamelessly.

After a lesson on what goes on inside the admissions machine, Tipper ended by warning me *never* to let schools know if any of my little clients were in therapy or had learning disabilities – these were flagged for almost certain rejection. Also, many private schools get out of accepting kids with disabilities by not making their facilities wheelchair-accessible. Admissions directors were seeking perfect children, so that's what I should give them.

Tipper's eyes shot nervously around the room. She reached into her bag and removed some papers, then slipped them to me under cover of a menu. 'If anyone found out I gave these to you, I'd be dead.'

2. Kiddie Corrupt

onchalantly, I slipped the papers under my
yellow pad. 'What is this?' I said without moving
my lips.

Under her breath, Tipper replied, 'It's twenty of the best
parent essays Harvard Day ever received. They're priceless.
Every one of these kids got in. But you have to promise me
one thing.'

'Anything,' I answered.

'Read them, learn what you can, and burn them. If
these were found in your possession, I'd be ruined.' With
great effort, Tipper extricated her titanic tush from the
booth. She stood up to see if the coast was clear. Dropping
a ten-spot on the table, she said, 'Good luck, Ivy.
Remember, we *never* had this conversation. I only did this
because you were my mentor at Myoki. Now we're even.'

I was speechless. In the end, we left separately, just to
be safe.

∽

I had to get my hands on that test.

To get into kindergarten, four-year-olds took a test called

the WPPSI – the Wechsler Preschool and Primary Scale of Intelligence, to be precise. Since it was given by the Educational Records Bureau, folks around town just called it the ERB. For admission to the top-tier schools, kids needed world-class scores.

The ERB stayed the same from year to year, so I knew that if I could secure one, I could show my clients how to prepare their kids. Schools threatened that children caught having been coached would be eliminated from consideration, but it was common among rich families to visit out-of-town psychologists and pay thousands of dollars for their children to practice the test before taking the official one. I figured if I could see what was on it, I could teach parents and nannies how to get their children ready at home without ever exposing them to the actual questions.

The problem was, no psychologist would show me a copy, even when I offered to hire them as consultants. They were worried about losing their licenses. I tried the Internet, but no one was selling old WPPSIs, not even on eBay. The wall of silence that psychologists had built around these instruments was impenetrable. Damn them!

Desperate, I asked Faith for the name and address of the psychologist who first tested Mae, the one who died. Maybe I could get in touch with the family and offer to buy her copy.

I went to her building, hoping the doorman would tell me how to reach her next of kin. Unfortunately, Tanvir, the concierge, refused to divulge such sensitive information. As soon as I slipped him a C-note, however, he blabbed. It seems that her son, a Mr. Bendiner, would be visiting New York in the near future to clean out the apartment. Tanvir knew this because the place had been rented beginning next month. I gave Tanvir an extra ten-spot and my phone number and told him there'd be another C-note in it for him if he'd call me when Mr. Bendiner was in the apartment.

About a week later, the phone rang.

'Mrs. A, it's T.'

'T?'

'Yes, T, Tanvir from the building.'

'Oh, hi, T, how are you?'

'The robin has laid its egg,' he said cryptically.

'Excuse me?'

'The eagle has landed,' he said through clenched teeth.

'Ooooh, thanks, T.' We hadn't settled on a secret code, but I admired him for being so stealthy.

When I arrived at the late psychologist's building, Tanvir buzzed me up as soon as I paid him off. 'Hello,' I shouted. 'Is anyone home?' The door was ajar, and big black Hefty bags filled with clothes lined the hall.

A clean-cut guy wearing a Nebraska Cornhuskers cap stuck his head out of the bathroom and motioned me in. Tall and gangly with enormous ears, he greeted me with a boyish smile.

'Hi,' I said tentatively. 'You must be Dr. Bendiner's son.'

'Yes, I am, I'm Barry Bendiner,' he said. 'And you are . . . ?'

'I'm Ivy . . . My . . . Yoki. Ivy Myoki. Actually, I'm Jewish, married to a Japanese guy. He died. Long story,' I said, extending my hand. 'I just want to tell you how sorry I am for your loss. Your mother was a wonderful woman.'

'Yes, she was,' he said sadly, his eyes tearing up.

'I'm so sorry,' I said. 'Maybe I should go.'

'No, it's okay. It's nice to meet someone who cared about my mother. How did you know her?'

Think fast. Think fast. Come clean. Lie. Come clean. Lie. 'Well . . . I'm studying to be an educational psychologist, like she was,' I managed to reply. 'And I interned with her through . . . NYU. Your mom taught me everything I know about testing children. She was amazing with kids, but I'm sure you've heard that from other people.' I was ashamed of telling such blatant lies to this broken-hearted son, but not so ashamed that I didn't press on.

'I came by on the off chance that you might be selling some of her psychology books,' I said. 'It would mean a lot to me to have some of Dr. Bendiner's books in my own library, the one I'm just starting to build.' *Liar. Liar. God's gonna punish you.*

'Of course,' Barry said gently. 'All her work stuff is on the shelves in the den. Take a look.'

I walked into the room and immediately noticed a number of treatises on abnormal and educational psychology that I had no use for. On the bottom shelf – bingo – the entire WPPSI test was there for the taking. I'd hit the jackpot! *Go, I-vy. It's ma birfday.*

I gathered up the test materials. 'Barry, can I buy these from you?'

'You just take them, Ivy,' he urged. 'It would have meant a lot to my mother to have you own something she valued so much. I couldn't accept money from you.'

'Are you sure?' I asked, feeling like the complete and utter fraud I was.

'Absolutely.'

'Thank you, Barry. You'll never know how much this means to me,' I said, visualizing his mother pounding on the inside of her coffin in a desperate attempt to stop this travesty. I offered Barry a warm sympathy hug. I really did feel bad that he'd lost his mom.

3. I Have a Feeling We're Not on Park Avenue Anymore

Our moving day came on a rainy Tuesday at the end of April. Schlomo, Zev, and Moishe packed us up and hauled all the girls' stuff and my half of the household to our new home on the Lower East Side. Zev noticed the mezuzah on my door and couldn't resist asking, 'How can you move to *that* neighborhood, a nice girl like you, with two young daughters? They have gangs down there.'

What is it about Jews that we feel licensed to butt into one another's business?

'I'll be careful. Anyway, I'm happy about the move,' I told Zev, bubbling over with fake enthusiasm. 'I can easily cover the rent, and that's a huge load off my mind. My husband doesn't contribute a dime because he's unemployed. I'm getting a divorce. I have no income of my own. I can't possibly afford to stay on Park Avenue.'

Of course, I had just laid my whole life out before Zev with no hesitation, either. Why didn't I just add that my menstrual flow was especially heavy that day?

Our new apartment was a third-floor walk-up located above Kratt's Knishery, one of the oldest kosher delis in the city. On Sunday mornings, the line to get a table at Kratt's is worse than Space Mountain on Memorial Day. Customers stand three deep in front of the take-out counter waiting for bagels, lox, herring, nova, and sable. Michael Kratt, the fourth-generation owner of the building and restaurant, lived on the top two floors. The place was conveniently located between Hung-Goldstein Grocery and Lupe's Bueno Laundromat.

It didn't take long to set up the new apartment since the whole thing would have fit in my old living room. The tiny kitchen and living area were up front, and the two small bedrooms and a bathroom were in the rear. The bathroom and kitchen had recently been renovated. The wood floors were original and in reasonably good shape. The best part was that we had backyard rights. The fire escape outside my bedroom window led to a stairway that descended to the postage-stamp-sized property shared by the tenants.

On our first night in the new house, the doorbell rang. Yikes. That's when it hit me that we no longer had doormen. Anyone could show up – a murderer, a rapist, a Scientologist. I peeked through the hole and saw a large African American guy and a short, dark-haired white guy standing there. Without so much as a 'Who is it?' I opened the door. Not a smart thing to do in New York City.

'Hi,' the first guy said. 'I'm Archie Elliot. I live on the fourth floor. I think you know Michael, our landlord.'

'Hi,' Michael said. 'We wanted to welcome you to the neighborhood. Here's some stuffed cabbage and noodle pudding.' Michael handed me a covered dish.

'Gosh, that's so nice of you. This is just like the suburbs, I think. I've never actually lived in the suburbs. But, you know, I saw this happen on *Mr. Rogers' Neighborhood* a few years ago. Would you guys like to come in?' I asked.

'No, we can see you're busy,' Archie said, peering at the boxes behind me that the girls were using as tables for their sausage-and-pineapple pizza.

'These are my daughters, Skyler and Kate, and our dog, Sir Elton,' I added. The girls waved 'Hello.'

'Enjoy the food,' Archie said. 'Michael owns the deli downstairs. He's a great cook.'

'Really,' I said. 'And what about you, Archie, what do you do?'

'I'm an actor. A performance artist.'

'Have you heard of the Naked Carpenter?' Michael asked. 'That's Archie.'

'*Get out of town,*' I said. 'I live downstairs from the Naked Carpenter? I don't believe it.'

Archie blushed. Just a few weeks ago, Kate, Skyler, and I had watched him perform 'Handy Man' in Times Square. We threw money into his guitar case and he winked at us. There was a recent article about him in *Time Out.* You can find the Naked Carpenter almost every day in one of the hot tourist spots wearing only his Fruit of the Looms, a tool belt, hard hat, and work boots, strumming his guitar and singing. Visitors pay to pose with him. He's on postcards. He appears at corporate events. Apparently, he makes over $200,000 a year with his simple but profound concept. Lots of people think he's just another New York nutcase, but I think he's a genius. Anyone who manages to get paid that much, in cash, without having to deal with office politics, is wise beyond all measure.

'Have you met Philip, second floor?' Archie asked.

'Not yet.'

'He's a good guy,' Archie said. 'Quiet, but you'll like him. Anyway, welcome to the building. Let us know if we can help you out. I'm pretty handy. Really.'

I smiled, shocked, but grateful to have neighbors who would reach out to me. This would never happen on Park Avenue.

A week later, we met our elusive second-floor neighbor. The girls and I were jumping rope in the backyard after school, laughing and singing. For them it was playtime. For me, it was exercise. For Sir Elton, it was just one more thing to bark at.

> *Mother, mother, I am ill.*
> *Send for the doctor over the hill.*
> *Doctor, doctor, will I die?*
> *Yes you must and so must I.*
> *How many years will I live?*
> *1 . . . 2 . . . 3 . . . 41 . . . 42 . . .*

'Excuse me. *Hel-low.*' The man stuck his head out the window, interrupting my concentration. I messed up at forty-three. Only four more years to live. Gaaad!

'Yes,' I said, huffing and puffing. 'Hi. You must be Philip.'

'I am. I take it you're the new neighbors.'

'Yes, we are. I'm . . .' I tried to catch my breath.

'I'm writing up here. Could you keep it down? I work in the back and can't think with all that noise,' he said.

There was no need to get testy. We're all mature people here.

'Why don't you close your window, genius?' Skyler mumbled.

'*Skyler!*' I admonished. 'Don't worry, we'll be quieter,' I shouted.

He left and we resumed our fun. This time, Skyler jumped double dutch but we whispered our song.

> *Raspberry, strawberry, banana tart.*
> *Tell me the name of your sweetheart.*
> *Andy, Billy, Charlie, David . . .*

The man's head popped out the window again. 'Ex-CUSE me.'

We stopped. 'Are we still bothering you?'

'Yes.'

'But we whispered.'

'Your ropes are loud.'

'Fine,' I said. 'When will you be finished with your work?'

'In four or five hours.'

'Thanks for being so flexible,' I said.

'What are we gonna do, Mommy?' Skyler asked.

'Grab Sir Elton's leash. We're going to the park.' *Grrrrr*, I thought. *This never happened to Mr. Rogers.*

4. Kratt's Knishery

I wonder . . . would it be considered child abuse to gag my kids before sending them out to play? After three complaints from Mr. Hypersensitive, I was seriously considering it. Of course, I wouldn't tie the gags too tightly, just enough to muffle their screams. But first, I decided to bring the man food as a peace offering. Perhaps I could sweet-talk him into tolerating Kate and Skyler.

I wandered into Kratt's Knishery and was instantly hit with the smell of my grandmother Etta's kitchen. Ahhh – there's no mistaking the aroma of fresh beef brisket. The cases were filled with every artery-clogging Jewish delicacy that I adored – blintzes, chopped liver, gefilte fish, beef kishke, knishes, rugalach, kasha varnishkas. Living above the deli would be hell on my diet.

'Welcome. Can I get you anything?' Michael Kratt himself came over to help me. He was a good-looking guy in his early forties with thick black hair and deep dimples. I guarantee that every Jewish grandmother who ate here tried to set him up with her granddaughter or gay grandson.

'Hey, Michael. I'm looking for something really delicious that I can give to Philip, our neighbor. What do you suggest?'

'I'll tell you what. Sit down and I'll put together a tasting meal for you. Are you hungry?'

'Starved, thanks.'

I sat in a booth while Michael prepared a plate. Customers were popping in and out, and other employees took care of them. Michael handed me an overflowing plate and a cold Dr. Brown's cream soda.

'What is all this?' I asked.

'We have fresh beef brisket, potato latkes, chopped liver, knoblewurst on rye, kasha varnishkas, and some cinnamon Danish.'

'Nothing green?' I joked.

'Would you like some vegetarian chopped liver?' he asked seriously.

'I'll pass, thanks. It looks delicious.'

Michael went behind the counter to work while I sampled each dish. That old guy from *The Sopranos* was sitting at a back table having lox and bagels with a young hottie, either his granddaughter or his girlfriend. This was cool. Had I inadvertently moved above a celebrity haunt? Talk about dumb luck. Michael was oblivious to the star in our midst. He was too busy attending to an itsy-bitsy Jewish grandmother and her ancient humpbacked husband, who were buying cold cuts. The lady was lecturing Michael for not throwing in extra meat after the order was weighed like his late father used to do. 'Don't worry, Mrs. Goldofsky, I'm giving you an extra half-pound of whatever you like on the house,' Michael said.

'You mean free?' she asked.

'I mean free.'

'You're a good boy, Michael. Isn't he a good boy, Max?'

'He's a good boy,' Max agreed.

The food at Kratt's Knishery brought back memories of my childhood in Brooklyn – the happy part, that is. In the end, I bought a pound of chopped liver and a box of Ritz crackers for Philip. Michael didn't charge me for the tasting.

I brought the pâté home and transferred it to a Pyrex dish. Then I warmed it in the microwave so it would seem fresh from the chopping bowl. Satisfied that my neighbor would think it was homemade, I went downstairs, intent on bewitching him with my charm or chopped liver – whichever worked.

5. The Neighbor Downstairs

The moment he answered the door, I knew I'd brought the wrong dish. This guy was thin and lanky. He had that intentionally accidentally tousled look like those models in the Calvin Klein ads. Definitely a vegetarian and probably a runner. What was he? Twenty-three? Twenty-five? *Dammit*, I thought, *I should have worn makeup*.

I cleared my throat, bringing myself back to the moment. 'Hi, sorry to bother you. We didn't have a chance to meet last week when my children were annoying you. I'm Ivy Ames, and I'd like to offer you a nice bowl of chopped liver.'

He stared at me.

'It's homemade,' I added, sounding like June Cleaver trying to cajole the Beaver.

He stood there.

'If this is a bad time, um, I can come back.'

'No, it's okay,' he said quietly. 'Why don't you come in?'

I noticed that his apartment was exactly like mine except most of the interior walls were down and it was one big open room, like a loft.

'I'm Philip Goodman,' he said, taking the bowl of chopped liver out of my hands. We stood awkwardly in his living room for a few moments. 'Can I offer you some liver?' He smiled.

Whew. The guy's human.

We went into the kitchen, where he laid out a plate, some crackers, and two butter knives so we could sample the cuisine. 'I've never had chopped liver,' he said.

'I'm surprised. "Goodman" is a Jewish name and chopped liver is the mother of all Jewish dishes.'

'My father was Jewish and my mother was Greek Orthodox. We ate a lot of lamb.'

So he's not a vegetarian, I deduced. 'Well, for me, eating chopped liver is a spiritual experience.'

After spreading the liver on a cracker, he popped the whole thing in his mouth and began chewing. I watched him closely, looking for a sign of approval, gagging – *anything*.

'It's got an interesting flavor and texture,' he pronounced. I was gobbling up cracker after cracker even though I was stuffed from lunch at Kratt's.

Philip turned out to be civil, possibly even friendly. He was so low-key that it was hard to judge.

He told me he was a writer who did his best work afternoons and evenings. This did not bode well for my daughters' outdoor playtime. I asked him what he wrote. He'd published a book and written a screenplay, he said. These days, he was writing short stories until he settled on an idea for his next novel.

'I'm sure I've seen your book,' I declared. 'Reading is my hobby, and your name is so familiar. What have you written?'

He told me.

'Didn't *Resolution* win some big award? The Pulitzer Prize?' I asked.

'No, it got the National Book Award,' he said.

'Still, that's not chopped liver,' I said. Ha ha. I wondered if he was impressed with my extemporaneous ability to make jokes. It's my second-best talent after singing.

'No, you're right. I'm proud to have won it.'

'I read they're making *Resolution* into a movie. Is that true?'

'They are. That was the screenplay I wrote.'

As I talked to Philip, I realized who he was. Young, hip, attractive author whose celebrated debut novel made him a media darling. I'd read about him. I'd seen his picture in *Newsweek*, *People*, and the *New York Times*. A hardworking, intensely private writer who worked seven days a week and never partook of the city's hip party scene. What was a guy like that doing living under *me*? Suddenly, I wasn't quite sure what to say.

'What about you? What do you do?' he asked.

I talked about the new business I was starting. He said he couldn't believe parents would actually pay someone to get their kids into kindergarten.

'I hope you're wrong,' I said.

'Why should someone hire you?' he asked. 'What are your qualifications?'

That was a good question, and it reminded me that I needed to come up with a new spin on my biography. I wondered if I could make my position at Myoki – marketing credit cards to debt-burdened consumers – sound like a qualification for this job. What was this, if not helping parents market their children to private schools drowning in applications?

'With my marketing background, I can help parents package themselves and their kids so the schools will find them attractive,' I explained.

'That's sick,' Philip said. 'No offense.'

'Do you think?' *Hmm, I guess I'd better not use that line with clients.*

'So, how are we going to let your daughters play and me work at the same time?' he asked.

'I don't know,' I admitted. 'I don't want them to bother you, but they're noisy by nature. Do you have any ideas?'

He sighed. Not a pissy sigh. More like a thoughtful one. 'I prefer working in the back of the house because it's quieter there – at least it used to be. But it looks like I may have to move my operation to the front.'

I was floored. 'Thank you.' My chopped liver had done its work. 'I appreciate how decent you're being about this.' Uptown, there would have been complaints, fines from the board, a lawsuit. Then it hit me. South of Houston Street, neighbors brought food. The dress was casual. People made eye contact. This was the anti-uptown. We were most assuredly *not* on Park Avenue anymore.

6. Admission Impossible

I knew I couldn't advise parents on schools without having toured each one myself. I also wanted to meet the admissions directors so I could understand how to influence them. A small, clubby group of women who knew what big deals they were, each was capable of bringing the city's most powerful pooh-bahs to their knees.

Despite Tipper's warnings as to how schools felt about advisers like me, I decided to call a few, introduce myself, and see if they might offer a tour. Maybe Tipper was exaggerating. Besides, I couldn't think of a good ruse to get in the door.

'Are you mad? Families don't need to hire private admissions advisers to get four-year-olds into *kindergarten*. They're fine on their own. You'll be fanning the flames of hysteria that already make this experience so stressful. I have no interest in meeting you.' *Click*.

'I'm sorry, but we're committed to giving each family an equal chance to get into our school. We simply can't support someone whose only goal is to tip the scales in favor of people who pay them. What you're doing is unethical.

Shame on you.' *Click.* This, from the school where Faith and Steven would be paying $500,000 for Mae's spot.

The direct approach was a bust. I needed another way in. I considered borrowing a friend's child and applying to all the schools, using the kid as a Trojan horse. But that would be too expensive – application fees were $50 to $100 apiece and there were sixty-five schools. You do the math.

I turned to my friend Young Mi. She's one of the two women I fired when I left Myoki. Young Mi had plenty of time on her hands and I had an idea on how she, as a Chinese American, could help me get inside. She was happy to play along.

'Hi, I'm Young Mi Shin, a reporter with *New York* magazine. We're doing a cover story on the progress New York City private schools have made toward creating racial and cultural diversity. We know how committed you are to honoring differences at your school, and we wanted to profile your success in our article. We were wondering if it would be possible for us to meet you and to tour the school as well?'

Come on down! With the promise of a cover story, the directors couldn't have been more welcoming. Using my computer, I scanned the magazine's logo and created business cards and official-looking press tags for each of us. Young Mi, our reporter, asked the questions while I took photographs. Admissions directors gave us tours, showed us their curriculum, invited us to audit classes, and were surprisingly open about what took place behind the closed doors of their offices, providing insights that would have taken me years to learn. They were all so generous that I felt like a first-class heel having to write and tell them that our editor had killed the story.

7. Party Pooper

With the school year coming to an end, we decided to throw an early birthday picnic for Skyler in our new backyard. Last year, we'd given her the $18,000 Fifth Avenue Ultimate Sleepover Adventure party at FAO Schwarz. There had been a treasure hunt, movies, a shopping spree, toys coming to life, characters in costume, a dessert orgy – you name it.

This year's celebration would be more modest, but no less important because it would be one of the last times she'd see her private-school friends. It's only natural for kids to lose touch with classmates who move away. All the girls were coming, and Michael, bless his heart, offered to bake the cake and supply the food. Archie, the Naked Carpenter, volunteered to sing. 'Oh, that's way too kind of you,' I said. 'I couldn't let you guys go to so much trouble.' But let's get real here. I could and I did.

The phone started ringing the night before the party.

'Ivy, hi, it's Kathleen. Listen, I have such bad news. We decided to go to the Hamptons this weekend, so Lauren won't be able to make Skyler's party after all.'

'Ivy, it's Topsy. Günter didn't know about the party and

he bought Chloë matinee tickets for *The Lion King*. Anyway, he wants to take her because he spent so much for the seats. You understand.'

'Ivy, it's Barbara. Victor just upgraded his Gulfstream, and we decided to fly to the Cape this weekend. Rachel is so sorry to miss Skyler's party. Tell her "happy birthday" for us. Kiss, kiss.'

By Saturday morning, every girl in her class except Lourdes had cancelled. The whole thing struck me as odd. I called Celerie, Lourdes's mother. Celerie and I had been in the same dorm at Yale. She married a partner at Goldman Sachs after college, retired, and had children right away. Every time I saw her, I couldn't get over how she looked exactly the same as she had almost twenty years ago. What were the odds of that? If anyone would level with me, it was Celerie.

'Ivy, I wasn't going to say anything, but Sassy called all the parents and advised us that you're living next door to a crack den in the downtown projects. She said she couldn't let Bea go to Skyler's party for safety reasons. Meanwhile, Bea was so crushed about not going to Skyler's that Sassy decided to throw her own horseback-riding party at Claremont Stables, you know, the indoor ring? Lourdes is dying to go, but I didn't want to abandon you like that. Do you really live next door to a crack den?'

'No.' My heart dropped into my stomach. If I tried to talk, I would cry.

'Ivy, are you there? Are you there?'

'Mmmm.'

'Would it bother you terribly if I let Lourdes go to Bea's party? Lourdy will be such a pill if I make her go to a backyard picnic when she could have been riding at Claremont.'

'Mmmm, it's okay,' I said, hanging up quickly.

Michael knocked on the door and presented me with a magnificent two-tiered birthday cake topped with eight candles, plus one to grow on. Archie was carrying his guitar and the rest of the food.

'What's the matter?' Michael asked.

It must have been obvious something was wrong. I told them what had happened. 'What kind of mother could be so cruel to a child?' Archie wanted to know. Michael just shook his head; he couldn't believe it. *Welcome to my world*, I thought.

Skyler walked in and started clapping when she saw her cake. 'It's so beautiful, thank you,' she said, hugging Michael. Turning to me, she begged, 'Mommy, can I get dressed now, pleeeease?' We had gotten her a new Paul Frank outfit for her party, and she was dying to put it on.

'Skyler, honey,' I said. 'Look outside, it's gonna rain for sure. I just called all the girls and cancelled the party. We'll reschedule it for a sunny day, what do you say?'

'Aaaaaaw. I want my party. Can't we do it inside?' Her lower lip was trembling.

'Skyler,' Michael said, taking her hands, 'how about we have *our own* indoor party today, and after, we can go out on the town together? Then you'll have two parties. This one, and the one you'll reschedule with your friends for a sunny day.'

'Yeah, honey, I promise we'll do it again. And maybe next time you can invite some of the new girls you meet in the neighborhood,' I said.

Skyler nodded glumly. We called Kate to join us and made the most of a sucky situation. Later, Michael took us to the American Girl Place off Fifth Avenue where Kate and Skyler took part in the Doll Hair Salon Spectacular. Then we joined eighty or ninety ethnically and historically diverse dolls, all strapped in their booster seats, for tea at the Cafe. The girls loved it, but it gave me the willies. I felt like I was in a *Bride of Chucky* movie taking place at It's a Small World. And that's just weird. Michael seemed to enjoy the meal. His kindness elevated him to a whole new level in my eyes, I can tell you that.

8. Agony on the Upper East Side

I was just about ready to open my doors for business. But first, I needed to get the inside scoop on what *really* took place during admissions. I suspected that the schools were giving me the official story and that it was the parents who would dish the dirt. I was right. With the exception of one mom, who burst into tears and hung up on me after proclaiming the season she applied for her son 'worse than the year I had fungal disease,' mothers and fathers all over Manhattan eagerly spilled their guts.

They described the admissions experience as a harrowing ride on an emotional roller coaster. Parents were forced to apply to ten or twelve schools just to get one or two acceptances. Their hearts ached watching their four-year-olds subjected to such intense scrutiny and outright rejection. Thousands, perhaps millions of dollars were spent annually for psychotherapists by anxious Manhattanites whose egos took a severe beating during the experience.

'Why do you think they wanted to know if I'd had a difficult birth?' one mother asked. 'Whether or not we had a summer house was none of their business,' a father complained. 'When they asked about my father, I wasn't sure if they wanted to know his pedigree or if they cared what kind of man he was,' another man said.

Nursery-school directors, who often had more than thirty children applying to kindergartens, were forced to become brokers. They had to juggle the placement of *every* child, often playing favorites and selling out one family in favor of another. 'The Michaelsons wouldn't take a place if you offered them one, but the Sandlers would. And just between you and me, the Sandlers are one of my "A" families. The Michaelsons are "B" at best. Can I interest you in Canyon Sandler?'

Before they'd make an offer, most admissions directors wanted parents to put in writing that *their* school was the family's first choice and promise to enroll if offered a place. In the end, after making the monumental effort of applying to ten schools, parents felt compelled to put all their eggs in one basket. Four-year-old best friends who were applying to the same schools were forbidden to play together by their competitive parents. It was just too tense.

Applying to private school was the single most dreaded activity of New York City parents. If Faith was right, this could be a gold mine. *Yippee! I* do *have a future*, I thought.

9. Try, Try Again

I sat at the kitchen table behind a pile of bills. Electric. Telephone. Water. American Express. Visa. Medical insurance. I couldn't get over how quickly my severance had run out. *Let's see, if I pay the minimum on each bill, that should keep me afloat until I have income.* Then I realized I couldn't afford the minimum.

I stooped to calling Cad. 'I need you to send me some money.'

'How much?'

'Ten thousand would help.'

'Ten thousand! *Are you crazy?*'

'Cad, you haven't given me anything for the girls since we broke up. A thousand a month for each child sounds reasonable.'

'Ivy, you know I'm not working . . . Ivy? Ivy, are you there?'

'I'm here.'

'If I was working, I'd give it to you. I just don't have it.'

'You could sell your Porsche. I sold *my* car.'

'No one would buy it. Someone ruined the paint job . . . Ivy? Ivy?'

'Look, Cad, I know you have money and I need you to send me some. Liquidate your IRA or 401(k). I don't care. Just send something for the kids.'

'I can't do that. The tax consequences . . .'

'Cad, screw the tax consequences. Your children have to eat. *Jeez*.' I banged down the phone.

I dialed Faith's number, intending to ask for a short-term loan. Then I hung up. Better save that for when I'm desperate.

Aha! I'll get cash on my Visa card and pay American Express, insurance, and the phone bill. Then I'll call Con Ed to work out a payment plan for electric. I don't think the government lets single mothers with children lose their electricity.

There was no getting around it. I needed clients and I needed them yesterday.

Faith promised to start telling her rich friends about me. Still, I had to let other people know about my service. How would people learn about me? There wasn't even a section in the Yellow Pages for kindergarten admissions advisers. Prostitutes had their own section, but my specialty didn't. Go figure.

I decided to advertise. Radical. Never seen it done before. But I couldn't think of any other way to get the word out.

With wealthy clients as the target, I looked for publications that appealed to the rich. After researching the options, I tested a few headlines in small ads placed in the *New York Observer*, *5th Avenue*, and *Big Apple Parent*:

Getting your child into a top NYC kindergarten is overwhelming.
Let Ivy Ames advise you behind the scenes. 212-555-3427.

**The right kindergarten could be your child's ticket
to the Ivy Leagues.**
Let Ivy Ames help make it happen! 212-555-3427.

**You'll need to earn over $750,000 to pay for your
child's private school.**
Shouldn't you hire Ivy Ames to get it right? 212-555-3427.

The ads ran. I waited.

I waited some more. And more.

Two weeks after my ads hit, the business phone finally
rang. Whew. I was starting to worry.

'Hello, Ivy Ames speaking.'

'Is Sam there?'

'Sam?'

'Sam Harrison.'

'I think you have the wrong number.'

Damn.

Maybe I needed bigger ads. I made flyers and posted
them on trees in playgrounds and on bus stops near nursery schools. I scheduled a workshop for September called
Surviving Private Kindergarten Admissions. With luck, the
attendees would become clients. I posted ads for my workshop in children's stores, day-care centers, Mommy & Me
locations, and the like.

The phone rang again.

'Hello, Ivy Ames speaking.'

'Hi, I saw your ad and I wanted to see about getting
help. My daughter's applying to kindergarten next year.'

Yesssss! This one's gonna bite. I could taste it.

'Certainly, let me tell you how I work. First, I'll meet

with you and your child. Do you have a daughter or a son?'

'I already told you, I have a daughter, Lizzie.'

'Oh, right. I have two daughters myself. Anyhow, we'll meet, and based on our conversation I'll recommend schools you can apply to, and I'll help you complete your applications, including essays, and I'll get your daughter ready for her ERB, and I'll prepare you and your daughter for interviews, and I'll help you leverage your connections, work with your nursery-school director, write thank-you notes and first-choice letters, and I'll advise you through the wait-list process.' I spoke like one of those telemarketers who don't take a breath between sentences so the customer won't hang up.

'Can you help me get financial aid?'

'Excuse me?'

'Financial aid. With private school so expensive, the only way we can afford it is with assistance.'

'I'm sure I can help you with that as well,' I declared. 'Anyhow, if you're interested, I accept MasterCard, Visa, American Express, and personal checks.'

'This is a service you have to pay for?'

'Yes, my fee is $10,000.'

'ARE! YOU! OUT! OF! YOUR! FUCKING! MIND?!' *Click.*

I took that as a 'not interested.'

Three other people called, each more sticker-shocked than the last when I quoted my fee. This was beginning to get me down.

One more call.

'Hello, Ivy Ames speaking.'

'Ms. Ames, this is Dr. Klein. I'm a gastroenterologist with offices on Madison Avenue. I saw your ad on a tree in the park near my apartment.'

Oooh, a doctor! 'Do you have a child, Dr. Klein?' I asked, deepening my voice to make it sound more professional.

'No, just a dog. But I do have a large gastroenterology practice that specializes in treating Manhattan parents who are going through the private-school admissions process. September is my Christmas season, Ms. Ames. That's when I see a spike in gastrointestinal problems suffered by overanxious parents. Anyway, I was wondering if you'd be interested in trying a little cross-promotion with me. You've probably seen my ads on buses and subway trains all over Manhattan. Well, I was thinking that you and I might partner on a campaign that leverages the symbiosis between school admissions and GI problems. How does this sound to you: *"If the thought of applying to kindergarten makes you sick, call Ivy Ames for admissions advice and Dr. Klein for relief from gastrointestinal symptoms."* Then I'd list both our phone numbers. What do you think?' he asked.

I *was* desperate. But the idea of linking private-school admissions with a guy who tells you to bend over and drop your pants struck me as off-putting. Don't ask me why.

'Dr. Klein, I know who you are. I've seen your pictures on the subway a thousand times. Thanks for thinking of me – but my gut tells me to pass.'

◦◦

Three weeks had gone by since my ads were placed and not one sale. I turned to Faith, who theorized that perhaps wealthy people wouldn't respond to an ad for this kind of service. Maybe it was too gauche. She promised to hold a luncheon in my honor and invite all her girlfriends who were applying their children to kindergarten. 'It'll be like shooting fish in a barrel,' she said.

The euphoria I'd felt while putting the business together was gone. What made me believe I could start a company? The idea was absurd. Why would anyone pay $10,000 to get her kid into school? I couldn't pull this off. What an idiot I'd been to spend so much time on this crazy scheme. I was a single mother with two children to support.

What had I been thinking?

10. Radical Humiliation

On the Friday of the fourth week that my ads were running, I lay on the couch consuming baked potato chips, Diet Coke, and low-fat ice cream, smoking a cigarette and watching reruns of *The Golden Girls*, which, I'll have you know, can be seen on at least one cable channel twenty-four hours a day. For her sake, I hope Bea Arthur gets residuals. What a talent she is, even with that man voice of hers. I contemplated the hair on my legs by the light of the TV. If I stared long enough, maybe I could actually see it grow like corn in a field. This was boring. Let's see. Who starred in *Dynasty*? Jane Wyman, Lorenzo Lamas, Abby Dalton, William Moses. He was cute. Didn't he marry that actress Tracy Nelson? I started to imagine what I'd be doing if I'd never been born when something familiar caught my eye. It was *me* on television, looking as ugly as a catfish, trying out for *Radical Reinvention*. I sat up.

'. . . no, I *beg* you to choose me for a radical makeover because I just got fired, my pet died, and I caught my husband taking a bath with another woman . . . and they were naked. Now, I'm gonna have to start dating again *and look at me.* Who would want . . . *this?* Plus, my mother died, I'm about to lose my home, I had to fire my nanny, my maid, and my kids' tutors. I have to color my *own* hair and do my *own* nails. My psychic says I'm gonna get hit by a bus. And have you ever seen a frown line this deep? I need . . . no, I'm *desperate* for Botox.'

Simon Starkey, the show's host, came on. 'Tune in Thursday night for a special edition of *Radical Reinvention* – "Auditions – Uncensored, Uncut, Ugly!" You'll see tapes of show hopefuls who were *so lame,* even *we* couldn't help them. You won't want to miss our must-see "Reject Show" this Thursday night at eight. If you want to feel better about yourself, *be there.'*

OH! MY! GOD! How could they do this? I didn't know whether to be more upset about not being picked as a contestant or about being publicly portrayed as an even bigger loser than I really was. It was one thing for me to audition for the show in the privacy of Skyler's bedroom, to exaggerate my patheticness so they'd choose me, but quite another thing for them to air the tape just to humiliate me on national TV. This was irresponsible journalism. This was an outrage. Heads were gonna roll.

I called the network and asked to be connected to the *Radical Reinvention* show. After going through four people, alternatively howling and wailing my case at them, I was finally transferred to Ms. Ball in Legal.

I exploded when she picked up. 'Ms. Ball, I want my audition tape taken off your promo this instant or I will call my lawyers and sue your ass until I own your moronic show. You have no right, *NO RIGHT AT ALL,* to portray me like that on national television without my permission.'

'But Ms. Ames, didn't you read the fine print in your application? You gave us unlimited rights to use your tape for content, promotion, publicity, marketing, and advertising of our program. I'm afraid there's nothing you can do about it.'

What? Nothing I can do? I agreed to all that? Gaaah. Think. Appeal to her humanity.

'Ms. Ball, making fun of my misfortune is cruel. What kind of organization are you part of? This'll backfire. You'll see. People will hate your network and all its affiliates for being so callous toward people like me who are down and out.'

'Ms. Ames, humiliation sells. It's the cornerstone of reality TV. Audiences love watching people degrade themselves. We've made billions of dollars on that one idea.'

This was not working. *Think. Think. Think. Appeal to her bottom line.*

'Ms. Ball, after all my misfortune, and *now this*, well, I can't take it anymore. I may have to kill myself. And you know what? My suicide note's gonna say that it was seeing that audition tape on TV that pushed me over the edge. Then my family will sue you and I don't care what I signed, they'll win.'

'Oh, my God, would you *really* do that? A suicide would blow our ratings sky-high. You can't buy that kind of publicity,' she said.

'It sounds to me like there's nothing you wouldn't do for ratings, Ms. Ball.'

'Pretty much.'

Is there no way out of this? Think.

'Well, Ms. Ball, even though you've so brutally exploited

me, I'd be willing to drop the whole matter if you'd give me the radical makeover I asked for.'

'Let me be brutally honest with you, Ms. Ames. *No*.'

'But why not?'

'Nothing personal, but you're a train wreck. Even *we* can't fix you. If it'll make you feel better, we've made you the featured star of our "Reject Show." Everyone will see you on national TV. You'll get your fifteen minutes.'

'I don't want my fifteen minutes,' I whined. 'I want plastic surgery so I can be pretty and someone'll marry me. I want a new life. Is that too much to ask?'

'Sorry, hon, no can do. Goodbye. Good luck.' *Click*.

I hung up and dissolved into tears. How could this have happened? Had I gone too far with the Jaclyn Smith kelly-green pants suit? Or was it the vegetable oil I'd sprayed in my hair? What difference did it make? My last hope for rescue had been dashed. I couldn't find a job. My business was a failure. I'd disgraced myself on national TV. I picked up the phone and ordered a large loaded pizza from Ray's.

11. Manhattan Madness

Chewing cold pizza, I reflected on my troubles. Why was life such a struggle for me? Why couldn't I have it easy like Sassy and Faith? Sassy was so beautiful. Faith was so rich. *It's not fair. You're making it too hard for me, God. If you could cut me one break, just one, I'd never ask for anything ever again. I promise.*

The telephone rang. It was Faith. At least *she* loved me. I started to tell her about my crummy luck with *Radical Reinvention*, but she cut me off. 'Turn on the news,' she insisted. 'You won't believe what's going on.'

I turned on Channel 4. Chuck Scarborough was covering a breaking story. They were showing live pictures of Harvard Day. The children had been evacuated. I caught sight of my friend and informant, Tipper, on camera looking distressed. She was talking to the police. Her butt looked even *more* enormous on TV. It was so sad.

'There is a frightening hostage drama going on at the Harvard Day School,' Chuck said earnestly. 'Apparently the children are safe. They have all been evacuated and are walking to St. Martin's School on East Eighty-fourth. Let me repeat this for parents just joining us. The Harvard

Day students *are safe*, and parents should meet them at St. Martin's.

'Meanwhile,' Chuck continued, 'a hostage situation is unfolding inside this exclusive Upper East Side private school.' He motioned to a gorgeous redhead standing to his right. 'This is Lara Long from the posh Harvard Day School. Lara, I understand you were present when this drama began. Can you bring us up-to-date?' He stuck his microphone in her face.

'Well, Chuck,' Lara said excitedly, 'I work for Cubby Sedgwick in the admissions office. She was meeting with a father who applied his son to our school this year. The boy didn't get in, and the man was appealing the decision. Anyway, Cubby must have given him bad news because there was yelling. I started toward the door and that's when I overheard him say that she'd never take another child if she didn't take his son. I ran out of the office and called the police. Then I pulled the fire alarm and the children filed out of school at an orderly pace as they would in any fire drill.'

'So it was your quick thinking that saved the lives of hundreds of Harvard Day children?'

'Yes, Chuck, I guess it was,' Lara answered, beaming.

'Now, Lara, what grade was this child applying for?'

'He was applying for kindergarten, Chuck.'

'Kindergarten?' Chuck mugged directly into the camera, making an exaggerated incredulous expression.

'Yes, Chuck, but you have to understand that anyone who matters knows that *our* kindergarten only accepts the crème de la crème, so it's not surprising that parents become distraught when their children don't get in.

Cubby'll reconsider a decision, especially for a child who made the wait-list.'

Chuck turned to his left and introduced Emily Cone, a disheveled mother, along with her two children, six-year-old Esme and baby Engelbert. 'Mrs. Cone, are you shocked by what you're witnessing today – Harvard Day's director of admissions taken hostage by an apparently desperate father?'

'Chuck,' she said breathlessly, 'I'm just surprised it doesn't happen more often. What private schools do to parents applying for places is unconscionable. We applied a few years ago and I'm still reeling over the experience. This father must have flipped out. I hope this serves as a wake-up call to private schools that parents can only take so much.'

'Emily, I have to interrupt you,' Chuck said. 'There appears to be some kind of activity taking place inside the school. The SWAT team is moving in. Let me repeat: the SWAT team is moving in. For parents who are just tuning in, your children *are* safe. They *have* been evacuated. They can be picked up at St. Martin's School.'

They kept the camera focused on the school, but all the action was happening inside. Finally, they switched back to Sue Simmons at the anchor desk, who promised to update us on any developments as this story unfolded.

'My God,' I exclaimed to Faith, who was still on the other end of the line watching TV along with me. 'I'm shocked. This is terrible. I hope Cubby's okay. She was really nice to me when I met her.'

Faith said she was sorry, but she had to run. She wanted to be in the limo when Mae was picked up from her playdate. You had to hand it to her. She could have delegated the task to her driver and nanny, as so many privileged mothers do, but she was determined to be there herself.

I turned back to the TV, where pandemonium was breaking out behind Chuck. I could see Tipper with a group of people in the background. They were hugging each other.

Soberly, Chuck announced that the hostage drama had ended in a terrible tragedy. The man had shot and killed Cubby Sedgwick, then turned the gun on himself. His wife told police about her husband's rage and disbelief over their son's rejection from Harvard Day. He had promised his wife that he would change Cubby's mind if it killed him. Sadly, it had.

12. The Best Publicity Money Can't Buy

My phone rang at 7:00 P.M. It was a reporter from the *New York Times*. They were covering the Cubby story and wanted to interview me for an accompanying piece on how difficult it was to get a child into prestigious private kindergartens in New York City.

'How did you find me?' I asked in disbelief. 'I'm just curious,' I added. This was huge!

'I was doing a Nexus search and your ads came up. I thought you might know the anguish parents experience when they apply to private schools.'

'Oh, I do,' I assured the reporter. 'I've had to talk parents off ledges over this.' I'm no dummy. I knew this was one of those life-defining moments. With every ounce of authority I could muster, I bared my soul, telling the reporter everything she wanted to hear about the heartbreak of kindergarten admissions in New York City – the extraordinary lengths to which mothers and fathers would go for a coveted spot at a top school. Having just interviewed so many parents, I recalled some of the wildest stories I'd heard, telling them as though they were my own. May God forgive me.

'Do you have my name? It's I-V-Y, A-M-E-S.' Just make sure you get that right.

The moment I hung up, the phone rang again. And again. The *Wall Street Journal*. The *Daily News*. The Associated Press. *People*. *Time*. *Forbes*. *Larry King Live*. *Farmer's Digest*. *Farmer's Digest?* The story had captured the nation's fancy, with America in disbelief over the apparently misguided values of Manhattan's most elite citizens. The press was wetting their pants over this. Since I was the only kindergarten-admissions adviser they could actually find, the media wanted my comment. Remind me never to trust experts on TV.

I was dying to call Faith to tell her about my good fortune, but the phone wouldn't stop ringing.

Barbara Walters's assistant called. They wanted to discuss the rarefied world of private-school admissions on *The View*. Would I be willing to appear on camera? *Would I!* At 11:00 P.M., I had Katie Couric on one line and Diane Sawyer on the other, both asking for interviews the next morning. I hated to disappoint Diane, but I went with Katie because I've always believed that the two of us could be friends if only we met under ordinary circumstances, like having our daughters in the same class. I can't explain it, but I had a hunch that she just might invite me for coffee after the interview.

Talking to the media, I marveled at what a gifted actress I was. All my research had paid off. Even *I* believed I knew what I was talking about and that I'd spent fifteen years in the field.

The phone stopped ringing around midnight. I turned on the answering machine so I could get some sleep before my 5:00 A.M. *Today* show pickup. Maybe they'd send a stretch. How cool would that be! I called my best friend's chief of staff, who in turn patched in my best friend, waking her from a sound sleep. 'Faith, I'm sorry to call so late, but I need your help.' I explained what had been going on, and she promised to send one of her nannies over by 5:00 A.M. to get the girls up and ready for camp. She also promised to stop by herself to pick up my messages, clear the answering machine, and tape my appearances on TV.

Faith, who lived the most exciting life of anyone I knew, was thrilled by my good fortune.

That night, I prayed. '*God, I'm really sorry about Cubby's murder, may she rest in peace. You know I never would have wished it on her and I feel terrible about it. But for reasons not apparent, her tragedy is bringing me lots of opportunities. Please God let this senseless killing be the break I need to burst on the scene like this year's "It" girl. Let every family with a toddler that can afford an apartment in the 10021, 10028, and 10128 ZIP codes reach out to me. Then, Lord, help me find the perfect school for every child you put in my path. God in Heaven above, please do these things in the name of Cubby Sedgwick, so that her death won't have been in vain. Amen.*'

13. Surprising Developments

I was exhausted after doing *The View*. I had to walk that thin line of entertaining the audience with wacky admissions stories without alienating viewers who might become clients. It was a challenge.

At Myoki, executives got two weeks of media training before they were allowed to talk to the press. I'd never been high enough on the food chain to get trained. Still, I held my own, I thought. I had Star and Meredith in stitches.

Faith was waiting for me when I got home. She gave me a hug before getting down to business.

'Okay, here's a list of press calls you need to return,' she said as she handed me two handwritten pages of publications that ranged from the *Washington Post* to the *Irish Echo* and shows that included *60 Minutes* and *Jerry Springer*. 'Even better, here's the phone log of parents who want to hire you. The first page lists people who live on Park Avenue, Fifth Avenue, and Central Park West. I've been quoting them twenty thousand for your services.'

'Are you out of your mind?' I cried. 'No one's gonna pay that much. That's ludicrous.'

'Ludicrous? Do you see the four names I crossed off on

the first page? Those are the only people who squawked about the price. The people on the second page don't have the gold-plated addresses, so I only quoted them ten grand. The two people with stars by their names called from the hospital. Their wives had just given birth. They want to hire you now, but I think you should keep them in mind for the future. The woman whose name is underlined in red is pregnant with her first; she wants you on a monthly retainer for the next four years. You can decide about her. I think you should start by calling the twenty-thousand-dollar prospects and only go to the second page if you have to.'

I was speechless. Stupefied. Incredulous. My mind was boggled.

'Oh ye of little faith,' Faith sang. 'I *knew* you could do it. I *knew* this was a brilliant idea. Thank you, thank you,' she said, taking bows to an imaginary audience.

Over the next several hours, I returned calls. Faith would pick up the girls so I could strike while the iron was hot.

I sat down at my kitchen table and began dialing. The parents were relieved to hear from me. By the third conversation, I had my patter down, describing what I'd do to improve their child's chances, always stating that there were no guarantees with this process, but also assuring them that my past clients had done *extremely* well, *wink wink*. I thought a few of these people were going to reach through the telephone lines and kiss me. Others were standoffish, but I could hear them relax as soon as they concluded that help had arrived.

From what I gathered, parents were freaked out about the Cubby incident and all those news stories on how tough it was to get into private school. The hostage-taking father turned out to be a popular Park Avenue gynecologist whose child was at the Secret Garden Nursery. 'There but for the grace of God go I,' they must have been thinking.

My close was particularly artful. After describing the service, I added that in the interest of quality I would only take ten clients a year. I said I had eight confirmed and would surely have ten by the end of the day. If they wanted to join my exclusive roster, they should messenger a check by 8:00 tomorrow morning. I gave them Faith's swanky address. They might not be so enthusiastic if they knew where I really lived.

By 7:00 that evening, Faith had received five checks for $20,000 each, one cigar box filled with old bills totaling twenty grand, plus a beautiful Prada bag containing $20,000 in crisp hundreds. These parents were taking no chances.

It shocked me that people would pay so much. Not that I was complaining. I decided to limit my practice to seven families. If I could do an outstanding job with seven, they would tell their friends and I would be established. Plus, with so few clients, I could spend more time with my own daughters. If anyone else called, I'd suggest my September workshop. At $300 a head, that would be a profitable evening. I was thrilled. I just wished Mom were alive to enjoy my success. She would have reveled in it.

∽

Faith sent Kate and Skyler home that night in one of her town cars with a box containing juicy pot roast, salmon cakes, mashed potatoes, macaroni salad, and chocolate cake.

Normally, her chefs cook low-fat, but I'd been through such a stressful experience that Faith insisted comfort food was required.

I sent the girls to invite Michael, Archie, and Philip to join us. I was wired and in the mood to celebrate. Faith had packed enough food for a small wedding, so why not share?

Archie wasn't home, so Skyler taped a note to his door inviting him to stop by. Michael was leaving for a blind date, but he said he'd stop by if it ended early. Philip accepted our invitation.

Shortly after, the doorbell rang and Philip appeared with a cold bottle of Chardonnay. My stomach did a double flip when I saw him standing there. Even though he was in jeans and a T-shirt, he'd taken the time to comb his hair and shave. Cleaned up, he looked like a young Ashton Kutcher. How could I have missed that before? *Stop it, Ivy. You're at least ten years older than he is. You have upperarm jiggle, stretch marks and a C-section scar.* Still, dare I dream? *Moi?* Demi Moore.

'What can I do to help?' he asked.

'Not a thing,' I told him. 'The girls are setting the table and dinner'll be ready in a few minutes.'

'I read that article in the *Times* today,' he said. 'You were quoted quite a bit.'

'I haven't seen it,' I answered self-consciously. That wasn't true. I had a dozen copies of the paper stashed in my closet. But I didn't want Philip to think I cared about superficial things like reading about myself in the most highly regarded newspaper in the United States.

As I put the reheated food on the table, I told him

about the amazing events that had transpired in the last twenty-four hours (leaving out the part about *Radical Reinvention*). The way I'd lost faith in my business. How I'd become the beneficiary of Cubby's tragic death. The way I'd blathered authoritatively to the press. The families who were crazy enough to pay $20,000 to get their kids into school. That was the only part of the story that got a rise out of Philip.

'How do you feel after all that drama?' Philip asked.

'Well, Dr. Phil, I feel confused, guilty, excited, and afraid, all wrapped together, I suppose.'

He smiled. 'Ivy, you didn't cause Cubby's death. You're just capitalizing on the fallout. Under the circumstances, I think God will forgive you.'

How does he know I'm worried about that?

'Now that you've taken these clients, do your best to help them get what they want. For some reason, the universe gave you a gift just when you needed it. Accept it. Be grateful,' Philip said.

What a wise and knowing young man he is, I thought. I couldn't believe how I'd misjudged him when we first met. We joined the girls at the table and dug into Faith's yummy meal. Philip opened the wine and poured us each a glass. Skyler talked about her first day at Central Park Zoo camp, and Kate sang a song about the *Titanic* sinking that she'd learned at the Jewish Community Center.

Sir Elton wouldn't stop begging for food, which was kind of embarrassing. Ever since we'd moved downtown, it was like he'd never been trained. His former pet psychologist would have had a field day with this.

Philip listened to Kate and Skyler's stories about their

day, and talked to them like they were people, not little children. My daughters were starry-eyed.

As I put the girls to bed, Philip did the dishes. He did dishes!

We still had wine left over from dinner, so I poured myself another glass. Philip switched to beer. 'Thanks for helping clean up,' I said.

'My pleasure, I'm glad you invited me,' he answered as we settled in to talk.

'Would you like to see my debut on national television?' Faith had left the tape of my appearances on the *Today* show and *The View*. I was dying to see how I looked.

'Sure,' he said.

I put the cassette into the machine, and we watched. *Oh, my, I sound so authoritative. I'm good. But, ooooh, are those jowls? What are jowls exactly? I think I have them. And my voice, gaaah. So Minnie Mouse. I must consider doing cartoon voice-overs if this new business doesn't work out.* When the tape ended, I rewound it and hit the PLAY button. I was trying to act like it was no big deal and only worth watching twice.

'Mommmm!' Kate yelled from her room. 'Waaa-ter.'

'I'll be right back,' I told Philip.

A few minutes later, I walked into the living room and froze. My appearance on *The View* had ended and the tape was still playing. Philip was watching.

'. . . no I *beg* you to choose me for a radical makeover because I just got fired, my pet died, and I caught my husband taking a bath with another woman . . . and they were naked. Now, I'm gonna have to start dating again *and look at me*. Who would want . . . *this*? Plus, my mother died, I'm about to lose my home, I had to fire my nanny, my maid, and my kids' tutors. I have to color my *own* hair and do my *own* nails. My psychic says I'm gonna get hit by a bus. And have you ever seen a frown line this deep? I need . . . no, I'm *desperate* for Botox.'

14. Getting to Know You, Getting to Know All About You

I snatched the remote and turned off the television. Philip looked at me and said, 'Did you see that commercial?'

'What commercial?'

'That lady looked like you. Rewind the tape. I'll show you.'

'You think I look like *that*?' I asked, feigning hurt.

'No, no, you're *much* prettier. She just reminded me of you. Maybe it was her voice. It had the same, um, lilting quality as yours.'

'Maybe,' I said. I brought Philip a cold beer and poured some more wine for me. My heart was hammering madly. My face was flushed. My ears were ringing. I felt dizzy. I'd broken out in a cold sweat. To center myself, I silently repeated my mantra: *Barneys, Barneys, Barneys, Barneys* . . .

'So, are you from New York?' Philip asked, oblivious to the state of my nerves.

I took a deep, cleansing breath. 'I'm from Brooklyn originally. We moved to Manhattan when I was eleven.'

'Was your family moving up in the world?'

'Not exactly.' I told Philip how we'd left Brooklyn after Dad had one too many affairs.

'That must have been hard. Did you see your father much after you moved?'

'No, I never talked to him again. My mother was so angry about his infidelity that I would have felt like a traitor if I'd tried to find him. A few years after we came to Manhattan, we heard he'd moved to California and married again. Then, about five years ago, Mom told me he'd died. I don't know how she knew.'

'Sounds like you had a tough time.'

'When I was young, yes, but a lot of good things happened later. I earned a scholarship to Yale,' I began.

'I went to Yale, too.'

'No kidding. When were you there?' I asked.

'Late nineties. You?'

'A few years before that.'

'Anyway, sorry to interrupt,' Philip said.

'You're not interrupting. I was just saying that things were difficult when I was young, but they got much better. I went to an Ivy League school. I had a good marriage for a long time to a man who gave me my daughters. I had a lucrative career. And because of the struggles my mother and I went through, we were close. We talked constantly. She was interested in every boring detail of my life. She died last August.'

'I'm sorry.'

'Yeah, me, too. Do you want another beer?' I asked.

'I'll get it.'

Nice butt, I thought as he walked to the kitchen. *Ivy, stop it! Admiring a man's ass at your age, that's just wrong. Pull yourself together.* As I watched Philip pop the bottle cap off his beer, Sir Elton jumped into his seat. I pushed him down. He knew he wasn't allowed on the furniture. 'How'd you end up here, Philip? On the Lower East Side.'

'I moved a few years ago after *my* mother died. I'd been living with her on the Upper West Side. She had an apartment at the Dakota and I didn't want to stay there alone. I'd already taken this place as my writing studio, so I moved in. I was working all the time anyway. It was therapeutic. I slept here, on the floor. Finally, I called one-eight-hundred-M-A-T-T-R-E-S and they sent a bed. It was supposed to be temporary, but I got comfortable. I sold the Dakota apartment last year. It made sense financially.'

'Can I ask you how your mother died?'

'Sure. It's still hard to believe. My mother was a writer, like me. She'd just finished a book about plastic surgery and her publisher was sending her on tour. A doctor she'd interviewed offered to do work on her at a discount. She was having a facelift and she died during the procedure.'

'Oh, my God,' I said. 'Such a tragedy. I've always heard that could happen, but I never really believed it.'

'Believe it,' Philip said, shaking his head. 'The irony was, she had a beautiful face for a woman her age. But she wanted to look younger. Like so many people, she bought into society's shallow pursuit of beauty. I think plastic surgery is obscene.'

'Yeah, me too,' I said.

'Anyway, let's not talk about that. How'd you end up on top of Kratt's Knishery?' Philip asked.

'It's a boring story. My husband and I broke up. After we sold our apartment on Park, this was all I could afford on my own.'

'How are your kids handling the breakup?'

'Okay, I guess. They see Cadmon twice a month. With that, they get more of his attention than they did when we were together.' I was about to tell him more when the doorbell rang. *Probably Archie or Michael,* I thought.

I opened the door, and there was Cadmon, speak of the devil. *Fuck, fuck, fuck.*

15. Scrambled Eggs to Go

'What are *you* doing here?' I whispered.

'Hey, I saw you on national TV telling the world I cheated on you. *How could you do that to me?*'

'*Shhhh.* Not so loud. Anyway, you did cheat on me.' I hadn't focused on the fact that my little promo would embarrass Cadmon. At least there was a silver lining.

'And you looked like a migrant farmworker on St. Patrick's Day. How could you let yourself be seen like that?'

'It's called *acting.* They paid me to look like a hag for dramatic effect.' *Hmmm. Good excuse. Remember to use it again.* 'Cadmon, I'm busy right now and I'm tired. Would you leave?'

'Do you have company?' he asked, pushing the door open and peering inside.

By then Philip was standing up and saying goodbye. I introduced him to Cadmon. 'Philip, you don't have to go. Cadmon's not staying.'

'No, that's okay. I have an early morning tomorrow. Nice to meet you,' he said to Cad as he left.

'So who's the jailbait? I hope I didn't interrupt anything between you,' Cadmon said insincerely.

'Cad, please, why are you here?'

'Can I interest you in a nightcap?' he asked, picking up the wine I'd been drinking and flashing his Ultra-Brite smile, the one that melted my heart in Sag Harbor.

I stared at him with my arms folded.

He got down on his knees and began begging, not for real, just for effect. 'Ivy, why are you being so stubborn? I'm sorry, for the hundredth time. I made the biggest mistake of my life. I was down on myself for being unemployed. You were always working. I reached out to Sassy. That was stupid. I know. Please, can't you forgive me?'

'Cadmon, I forgive you. I'm past it now, really.'

'And I forgive *you* for broadcasting my failure as a husband on national TV. So, let's try again. I miss you.' Unexpectedly, he pulled me toward him and started to kiss me. His breath smelled like stale beer and his face felt like sandpaper.

'Cad, no,' I said, pushing him away. 'Look, stop. Listen to me. I was so . . . hurt when you cheated on me. I just . . . I can't go through that again.'

'I told you that was the last time it would ever happen, and I meant it. Please, I miss you. I'm helpless without you. I don't know how to do laundry. I can't make my bed. I can't even scramble an egg.'

I smiled. What Cad needed was a maid. 'Cad, since you left, I've had time to think. And I don't want the marriage we had anymore. I want to be with a man who prefers *me* to golf. Someone who helps with the kids without my having to ask. A guy who counts his blessings every single day because I'm in his life. If I can't have that, I'd rather be alone.'

Cadmon stood silent for a few moments. I could *see* his thoughts flowing as he processed the conversation. 'I can change. Just give me a chance. Tell me what you want me to do and I'll do it.' He looked so earnest standing there.

I laughed. 'No, Cad, you'll never change.'

He seemed offended. Then he smiled. 'You're right. I won't, will I? I'm a selfish pig and that's what I'll always be.'

I didn't argue. 'Tell you what, I'll teach you how to make scrambled eggs. But after that, you're on your own.'

Cad let out a sigh and walked into my tiny kitchen. He pulled a saucepan out of the cabinet. 'Okay, what now?'

'First, you need the right tools,' I explained. I got the frying pan, added some butter, broke two eggs and scrambled them while they cooked, just the way Cad liked them. 'This isn't so hard, is it?'

We sat silently at the table while Cad ate. He stood up to leave. 'Are you sure about this?' he asked.

'Positive.'

Cad said goodbye and left. As always, I washed his dirty dishes.

16. Cubby's Legacy

I called Tipper the next morning to offer my condolences over her boss's death. Of course I didn't say anything about how big her butt looked on television.

'Tipper, are you okay? Is there anything I can do?' I asked.

'I'm okay, I guess,' she answered. 'Actually I'm numb. Cubby was such a role model for me. I can't believe she's gone.'

'I know. The whole thing's such a shock.' After losing my mother, I understood that nothing I'd say would help.

'They're burying her this afternoon,' she said, her voice breaking up. 'I don't know how I'm gonna get through this.'

'Make sure you don't wear mascara,' I advised.

'The thing is, Mr. Van Dyke, the headmaster, appointed me admissions director in Cubby's place. He said I was her protégée and the only one who would know how to carry on in her tradition. I feel so guilty that it took her death to make my dream come true.'

Join the club, I thought.

'Tipper, you didn't cause Cubby's death. You're just accepting the unexpected benefits that came out of it. I'm sure God will forgive you. The universe is giving you a gift, and it's your responsibility to accept it gratefully,' I said, repeating Philip's advice. Hey, it worked for me.

'You're right, Ivy. I need to pull myself together so I can carry on Cubby's legacy.'

'That's right. Now go out there and make Cubby proud.'

'Thanks, Ivy. I appreciate your call. Let me know if there's anything more I can do to help you.'

We hung up. I felt bad for Tipper. She admired Cubby and was ill equipped to handle the mixed blessings brought on by her death. I, on the other hand, was holding up well.

17. Tots with Résumés

O ver the next week, I scheduled meetings with my new clients. My first appointment was always after 10:00 A.M., which gave me ample time to work out. I'd become semi-obsessed with exercise. Happily, this new business would be perfect for balancing my own needs, motherhood, and career.

It was already June, and we had work to do before my clients left for the Hamptons, the Italian Riviera, or wherever the heck they'd be summering. I planned to assess the children as soon as possible to get a preview of how they'd test. Then I'd show the parents and nannies what to do with each child over the summer to improve their scores. If there was time, I'd work on their essays. I was excited about getting started, but anxious, too.

Dear God, please help me do a brilliant job with my clients, especially since I don't know what I'm doing. Also, Lord, I want to clarify something that's been bothering me. I'm not complaining, but when I prayed the other day and asked you to cut me a break, I didn't mean that someone should die. So from now on I'd appreciate it if no one else has to lay down his or her life to further

*my career. I think I can do it on my own from now on.
Amen.*

❧

The clients turned out to be a surprise. Before meeting them, I thought they would all be rich, neurotic, and demanding. Well, a few were. Others were quite wonderful, people I could imagine becoming friends with. On Monday morning, I donned an old Armani suit, dusted off my Coach briefcase, grabbed the Barneys shopping bag, and met my first client, Wendy Weiner.

Just as my former analyst used to do, I set up a file for each family in which I would keep detailed notes after every visit. I even made a crib sheet of all the clients and their kids. I was having trouble remembering who belonged to whom. I'm told this is what happens to peri-menopausal women. The indignity!

Monday, A.M. – *Wendy Weiner* – 6/14/04
Wendy Weiner (pronounced 'weener') is a divorced mother with the whiniest voice I've ever heard emitted by a human being. Not that I'm criticizing. Wendy has one child, Winnie. Any woman who would name her child Winnie Weiner is automatically suspect in my book. Winnie and Wendy live on Central Park West, near 98th. They have a nicely appointed junior four, with the dining room neatly screened off and transformed into Winnie's bedroom. The windows are old, the floors scuffy parquet, and the walls mint green, thick with forty years of paint. The place needs to be gutted and redone, but my guess is Wendy can't afford it. Especially after hiring me.

This will be Wendy's second try for Winnie. Last year, she applied to thirty-five schools and got into none. Wendy became so obsessed with finding the perfect educational environment that she gave up her law practice and made school-hunting a full-time job. She is enraged that Winnie wasn't accepted anywhere and blames it on her nursery-school director. Says she's anti-Semitic. (Note: Winnie went to the same school as Skyler and Kate. Her director is as Jewish as bagels and lox.)

Winnie is a sweet-natured, exotic-looking child. Tiny with coffee-colored skin, green-brown eyes and waist-length hair; I was immediately drawn to her. She showed off her room, told me which books were her favorites, introduced me to her fish (shades of Kate) and entertained me with a puppet show. Winnie's ERB scores last year were solid. I'm sure she presented well. The problem had to be the mother. After meeting Winnie, I am determined to help her because Wendy can't do it alone.

Monday, P.M. – *Johnny and Lilith Radmore-Stein* – 6/14/04

The Radmore-Steins used to be the Radmore-Ratfin-klesteins, but they changed the name so their son Ransom wouldn't get teased. They live in a massive co-op at 820 Fifth Avenue, some say the best building in New York City (it's rumored that you have to be worth a billion to get past the board). Their apartment is *Architectural Digest*-perfect. No surprise – it was featured on the cover of last April's issue. When the maid, or housekeeper, or butlerette, or whatever she was, led me through room after magnificent room toward the library where I met the couple, I kicked myself for oohing and aahing like I'd never been in such an opulent apartment (and other than Faith's, I hadn't).

As chairman of one of the largest newspaper conglomerates in the country, Lilith is a well-groomed woman with a horsey face and a gummy smile. Except for the fact that she is never without Mrs. Butterworth, her teacup Yorkshire terrier, Lilith is all business. She reminds me of Anna Wintour, but that's probably because she never took off her sunglasses. We discussed the process we would follow, talked about schools that interested her (easy – it has to be Stratmore Prep), strategized about the contacts she has on Stratmore's board who could help, scheduled a meeting to assess Ransom, and did our brainstorming for their essays right then and there. I got some entertaining stories out of Johnny, her polo-player husband, who is laid-back in the way that beneficiaries of large fortunes often are. Lilith had little to add. I suspect that she doesn't spend much time with her son and that Johnny doesn't spend much time with her.

Ransom is *un enfant terrible*. Marvys, his weekday-afternoon nanny, brought me to his very own three-bedroom apartment (located next door to his parents'), where he lives under caregiver supervision at all times. Marvys explained that this way the main apartment is always clean and Ransom is in spitting distance of his parents. The enormous living room, with its million-dollar views of Central Park, is reminiscent of Pee-Wee's Playhouse. I expected to detest the little prince, but instead I felt sorry for him. Wearing one of those $500 imported Bon Point short outfits with leather suspenders, Ransom greeted me with two water balloons, thrown like hand grenades from his tree-house on a fake but real-looking oak. Amused by his own hilarity, he laughed so hard that I worried he might give himself a hernia. 'W-watch Watch this, watch this,' he said as he stuck his hand in the opposite armpit, flapped his arm, and made real-sounding fart noises. 'Wanna hear me d-d-do the alphabet?' he asked. 'Sure, why not?' I said. Ransom swallowed a quart of air and proceeded to burp the A-B-C song. 'His parents must be very proud,' I remarked to Marvys. Here he is, ladies and gentlemen – rich boy who has everything but his folks' attention. The most exclusive private schools are filled with dozens of Ransoms, so I know he will be welcomed along with his parents' money.

Tuesday, A.M. – *Ollie Pou* – 6/15/04
Ollie is Jamaican, the single mother of a boy named Irving. She is a maid by profession. Working for the Radmore-Steins, Ollie was delivering a tray to Lilith's bedroom when she overheard her boss telling Johnny that she had hired Ivy Ames to make sure Ransom got into the best school. Ollie wants Irving to go to the best school, too.

We met at a coffee shop on Second and 73rd. Ollie made me promise not to tell Lilith that she'd hired me. 'Mrs. Ames, she's as mean as she is cruel. If she knew I'd called you, she'd make me pay.' When I suggested that she might be exaggerating, Ollie told me stories that made my toenails curl. She claims that Ransom is as heartless as his mother. He once played a trick on Irving by hiding his pet snake in Irving's Power Rangers lunch box. When Irving opened the box to eat, he discovered the dead gopher snake in the thermos compartment. Ransom threw such a hissy-fit that Lilith made Ollie replace the reptile out of her wages. 'Snakes are expensive, Mrs. Ames. It had was to take me three weeks to pay that off.' *It had* was *to take me? That's gonna be a hard sell on the Upper East Side.*

I assured Ollie that our relationship was confidential, but suggested that she couldn't possibly afford me. 'I had was to use my life savings, Mrs. Ames. If you can help my boy go to a good school now, he'll get a scholarship to college, and that will change his whole life.'

Irving colored on his activity placemat as we spoke. He is a serious boy with light brown skin and curly black hair who wore a blue polyester suit and a clip-on tie to our meeting. Irving wants to be a doctor someday and can name all the bones in the human body. The kid fancies himself an explorer and knows the continents and oceans. He asked me if I wanted to hear them. I said of course. By gum, the kid knows more geography than I do. I'm certain Irving won't be hard to place, and I can probably help Ollie get financial aid. I agreed to take Ollie on one condition – she has to let me give back her $20,000. As desperate as I am for cash, I can't take her life savings.

Tuesday, P.M. – Omar Kutcher – 6/15/04

Omar Kutcher, a single father, is New Jersey–born, mob-connected, and ill-bred. He's short and stocky with unusually long arms, like Cro-Magnon man's. His back is so furry that hair emerges from his collar and goes up his neck to his head with nary a pause. I can see that he thinks of himself as Cary Grant, debonair and irresistible. Power must do that to people. By paying someone off or threatening someone's life (there can be no other explanation), he was approved by the toughest co-op board on Park Avenue. With his wife, may she rest in peace, as decorator, he spent a fortune gussying up his apartment, but the effect is gaudy and tasteless – a veritable Graceland in the sky. He still has a wing to do, but he said that after his wife died in an unfortunate accident, he doesn't have the heart to finish the job. Omar personally took me on le grand tour, crowing with self-adulation when he revealed his bookcase with the secret door that leads to the panic room. The pride he takes in his home is sweet, almost poignant, to observe. It almost made me forget that the *Post* calls him 'Kutcher the Butcher.'

Both Maria, four, and Omar Jr., two, have Asian eyes. I assume they got these from their mother. Nothing will do for Maria but Sacred Heart or Marymount – two of the city's best all-girl Catholic schools. Omar is also willing to consider The Balmoral School, as that's where Gwyneth went, and Chapin, as that's where J. Lo went. (Neither is true, but we'll just let that slide.)

Maria is pint-sized and spoiled. Anytime her father says no to her (which isn't often), she turns her back, crosses her arms, screws up her face, and wails like a car alarm (just as her mommy used to do before her untimely death, Omar explained). Omar adores the kid. 'Ain't she a pistol?' he said over and over again. I think I can leverage her diversity, and maybe dangle a large donation (cash!) in front of some development directors. Hopefully she'll deliver strong ERB scores and her nursery-school report will be stellar. Omar's reputation as a mob boss, however, which would have been an asset in Staten Island, might be a deal breaker among the Manhattan elite, whose own ethics are of course beyond reproach. As long as Omar doesn't strong-arm a school into taking Maria (in which case my work will be done), I'm going to earn my $20,000 on this one.

Wednesday, A.M. – Willow Bliss and Tiny Herrera – 6/16/04

Willow and Tiny are lesbians. Tiny is a two-hundred-pound pink-haired film and television producer who reminds me of Giggles, a troll doll I used to have. Willow is a stunning African ex-model who gave up her career to stay home and care for their wheelchair-bound adopted son. Both of Jack Henry's parents were killed in the fiery car crash that robbed him of his ability to walk. Willow first saw Jack Henry on 'Wednesday's Child,' a program that features tough-to-place children. No one wanted this toddler, who was black and disabled. Willow called Tiny on the set and told her she had found the child who was meant to be theirs. By Friday, the boy was home.

I have to hand it to these women. They make sure Jack Henry has the best medical care and provide him with excellent therapists, nutritionists, and psychologists. Willow is his constant companion, offering stimulation and love. By the time he was four and a half, Jack Henry had the vocabulary of a seven-year-old and was already reading Captain Underpants and the Attack of the Talking Toilet, a second-grade-level book. He's fascinated by history, plays the flute, and draws beautifully. The boy speaks three languages – English, Spanish, and an African dialect called Twi – and can put together a 150-piece jigsaw puzzle with help. He loves to take rides with his two moms on their custom-made bicycle-built-for-three.

Tiny and Willow want Jack Henry to have the best education money can buy at a school that will welcome their unusual family and accept their son's special needs. I told them that Jack Henry's intelligence, verbal skills, and easygoing disposition, along with the gay-black-disabled combination (the Triple Crown of diversity) would make him a top draft pick among applicants. I predict Jack Henry will have his pick of schools.

Wednesday, P.M. – *Stu and Patsy Needleman* – 6/16/04

Stu will be a problem. A slight man with curly orange hair and delicate white skin, Stu must have told me six times that he works for Steven Lord, one of the world's richest men. From what he says, Stu is Steven's most trusted protégé, a tycoon-in-waiting. I didn't let on that my best friend was married to Steven and that their daughter barely got into private school herself.

Stu thinks he *is* Steven. He expects me to be available 24/7 and to wear a beeper. He says he's going to hire another educational consultant to give him a second opinion on everything I advise. And if he doesn't have at least three top-tier schools from which to choose, he will enlist all of Steven Lord's resources to ruin me. (My first threat!) Patsy, his mousy blond wife, wears the permanent expression of someone who's just bitten into a lemon. She says nothing during Stu's diatribes. How she stays married to this loser, I will never understand.

After explaining how many hundreds of thousands of dollars he's invested to stimulate his daughter's brain, Stu presented Veronica's curriculum vitae: Madison Play

Group, The Brick Church School, swimming lessons at the 92nd Street Y, French at Le Jardin a l'Ouest, music at Diller Quaille, Suzuki method for violin, manners at the Eloise Institute of the Plaza, elocution at Toastmasters for Tots, cooking at the French Kids Culinary Institute, computer at Future World, chess at the Dalton School Chess Academy, singing, dancing, and acting at Babes on Broadway – nothing as pedestrian as Gymboree for this would-be prodigy.

In her defense, Veronica's training shows. She was the only child who shook my hand when we were introduced, saying, 'It's very nice to meet you, Mrs. Ames.' (Note: teach all the other children to do that.) Veronica has thick red hair and big green eyes that are sandwiched between a fuzzy unibrow and a generous nose that will someday have to be fixed. She borders on fat, which is a problem. According to Tipper, at the kindergarten level, private schools accept cute kids almost exclusively. Many become geeks later, but all start out as swans. I feel bad for Veronica. What she needs is relief from her overbearing father and a good eyebrow-waxing.

Friday, A.M. – *Greg and Dee Dee Epstein-McCall* – 6/18/04

Dee Dee met Greg when both were students at Northwestern. They eloped to Las Vegas because Dee Dee's family didn't want her to marry a gentile and Greg's family didn't want him to marry a Jew. It was easier that way. Dee Dee's family sat shiva for her after she married Greg, and they haven't spoken since. Greg's mother, distraught over her only son's 'mixed-race' marriage, had a breakdown and was hospitalized for three months in a Connecticut sanitarium (although 'officially,' she was wintering at Canyon Ranch). Still, Greg's family is kind to Dee Dee and always includes the couple in family events. When Moses was born, Dee Dee and Greg decided to raise him as a Jew and Greg says that this disappointed his parents.

Greg works for his father, Buck McCall, who owns the largest shipping conglomerate in the world. In spite of everything, Buck adores Moses. When Moses demonstrated a talent for dunking a ball into his Fisher-Price basketball hoop, Grampa Buck bought his grandson an NBA team (held in trust, of course). Greg assures me that he can obtain reference letters for Moses from any dignitary or billionaire through Buck's connections.

Dee Dee is a stay-at-home mom who cares for Moses and volunteers for B'nai B'rith. She was concerned that I would think they were neurotic New Yorkers for hiring me. I assured her she was not neurotic and that my clients are all nice, normal people who just want help through a difficult process. She asked if anyone would find out they'd hired me. I said our relationship was strictly confidential and no one would know about it. I promised to stay in the background, and explained that my job was to make *them* look good.

Dee Dee wants Moses to go to one of the Jewish day schools, and Greg agrees. From what I observed, he always goes along with Dee Dee. Still, I suggested they consider some secular schools with large Jewish communities because only three of the day schools are worth going to. At four and a half, Moses already speaks English and

Hebrew. I instructed them to tell the tester that Moses is bilingual when he takes his ERB. Private schools don't expect bilingual kids to do as well on their verbal sections, and they'll be impressed that he speaks two languages. Greg thanked me profusely for the tip. He says I'm a godsend (his *exact* word). He promised to recommend me to all their friends after Moses gets placed. I *love* this family.

IVY'S CLIENT CRIB SHEET

Wendy Weiner	whiny voice
Winnie Weiner	rejected by 35 schools (blame mom)
Lilith and Johnny Radmore-Stein	Lil – CEO with teacup Yorkie, Johnny – a polo player
Ransom Radmore-Stein	stutters, burps alphabet, arm-farts
Ollie Pou	Lilith's maid
Irving Pou	future doctor, dead snake
Omar Kutcher	a mobster
Maria Kutcher	a pistol
Willow Bliss and Tiny Herrera	lesbian couple, Willow – model, Tiny – pink hair
Jack Henry Bliss-Herrera	high intelligence, disabled

Stu and Patsy Needleman	Stu – works for Steven Lord, Patsy – lemon face
Veronica Needleman	unibrow but great résumé
Greg and Dee Dee Epstein-McCall	Greg – has billionaire dad (Buck) Dee Dee – wants Jewish school
Moses Epstein-McCall	loves basketball, owns team

18. Makeover in Manhattan

ot long after I started working with my clients, Faith insisted that I take a break and come for a massage. As the two of us lay on our respective tables being rubbed, pounded, and hot-stoned, we updated each other on our lives. I confessed my infatuation with Philip while lamenting the fact that even though I was working out, I wasn't morphing into the pinup girl I once was. Truth be told, I never was a pinup girl. But there was a time when I was rather fetching.

Of course, Faith sprang into immediate action. She insisted on assembling her dream team to fix me. Emergency sessions were scheduled with Ken Gomez, fitness guru; Avi Portal, hairstylist to the stars; and Raquel Morley, makeup artist with her own show on public-access cable. As an early Christmas present (and I mean *really* early – it was only June), Faith signed me up for six months of the Metro diet. Every day, right at my front door, they would deliver three gourmet meals and two snacks totaling 1,200 calories. If I ate nothing else, exercised religiously, and drank eight glasses of water a day, the pounds would have no choice but to melt away. It wasn't *Radical Reinvention*, but Faith guaranteed that if I followed the program, I would be transformed. Everyone should have a best friend like Faith Lord.

When Ken 'Six Pack' Gomez showed up at my door, I must admit I was intimidated. His arms and chest were large and defined, his muscles hard and sculpted. Never have I felt like such a marshmallow.

'So what do you think?' I asked, after showing Ken my treadmill and weights.

'Let's see what you normally do,' he said.

Walking briskly on the treadmill at 3.4 miles per hour, I could tell that Ken was impressed. 'Pretty good, eh?' I asked, huffing and puffing like a gym rat.

'You're not even breaking a sweat,' he said. 'Let's see you jog.' He increased the speed to 4.5 miles per hour, and I was forced against my better judgment to run. After five minutes, I was soaked, winded, and pooped. I had to stop. It was embarrassing.

'Don't worry. You need to work your way into it, that's all,' he said.

What a kind man that Ken Gomez is, I thought. Ken designed a program in which I'd alternate walking and running on both flat and inclined settings. In six weeks this would come easy, he assured me. I would see him again at that point so he could make the workout tougher.

I showed him how I lifted my three-pound weights. Apparently my form was completely wrong and three pounds was too easy for me. Oh, well. Ken pulled seven- and ten-pound dumbbells out of his gym bag and demonstrated the right technique and movements to add definition to my body. He watched me do sit-ups, which he said were perfect (thank you, *Abs of Steel*). I promised to follow his program, and he invited me to stop by his gym anytime for more instruction. Apparently, Faith had Ken on retainer.

Later, Avi and Raquel stopped by to do my hair and makeup.

'Who did your *color*?' Avi asked. It was more of an accusation than a question.

'I did.'

'You must promise me you'll *never* bleach your own hair again,' he said firmly. 'The damage will take me hours to repair.'

'Scout's honor,' I said. Of course I knew you shouldn't color your own hair. But at the time, I couldn't afford a professional and I *really* wanted to be blond for self-esteem purposes.

Over the next five hours, my locks were painted with toxic chemicals, wrapped in foil, baked under a lamp, cut, blown, slathered with product, and ironed. As my hair baked, Raquel gave me a makeup lesson. She insisted I could transform myself as radically with makeup as I could with plastic surgery. That felt like a stretch, but I must admit that she made me look pretty darn hot if you ignored all the foil in my hair.

After the dream team worked their magic, I may not have been hot yet – but I was definitely getting warmer. Anytime I thought about cheating on my diet or skipping a workout, I imagined myself standing naked in front of Philip with my old body. Need I say more?

19. It's Not About the Brains

elping parents find schools for their children was more rewarding than any job I'd ever had. For the first time, I was contributing to society (though some may argue that it was high society).

Soon, I was evaluating kids. I created my own version of the ERB test that told me exactly what each child needed to work on over the summer. I, in turn, instructed their parents and caregivers on just what to do. We'd reassess in the fall.

Ransom's parents, the Radmore-Steins, asked if I would tutor their son until they left for Cannes in August. Lilith was too preoccupied with her newspapers to give Ransom personal attention, and Johnny just plain didn't care. I told them that tutoring wasn't included in my fee. 'No problem,' they said. I seriously did not want to tutor the boy, so I quoted them $300 an hour and they immediately said yes. I could have asked for twice that.

Stu Needleman explained that he was far too busy to work with Veronica. (Patsy, of course, was a complete pinhead – not qualified to teach their daughter anything.) He insisted that I personally prep Veronica by having her memorize the answers to the questions on the test.

'Stu, that's not a smart thing to do. She may say something to the tester about having been tutored. If she does, you're screwed.'

'I'm willing to take that chance,' Stu answered. 'This is one of the few instances where I have control, so I plan to use it.'

'Stu, your four-year-old daughter would be cheating to get into school. Are you sure you want to put her in that position?'

'Ivy, I didn't need to pay you twenty grand for *that* piece of advice. My competition is going to look for every advantage, and so will I. If you don't want to help us, I'll find someone who will,' he said, his face turning purpler and purpler. Could he burst?

'Let me bring up one last concern, Stu,' I plowed on nervously. 'What if you teach her the test and she aces it and – God forbid – gets into a school that's too hard for her and she fails? Do you want *that* on your conscience?'

Stu looked like he wanted to strangle me with those elfin hands of his. 'Veronica is smart. She has Needleman genes. She'll be a superstar like her father,' he answered slowly and loudly as if he were talking to a dim-witted adult, signaling that he'd had quite enough of my lip.

'Fine, Stu, I'll teach your daughter the answers to the test, but I'm doing this under protest. My rate is three hundred an hour. And I charge an extra fifty dollars an hour if you want me to tutor her to take the test without acting like she's been tutored.'

'*Are you on drugs?* I won't pay you a penny over seventy-five. And you'd better get this done in five sessions.'

We hondled, finally settling on $150 an hour and ten sessions – and I insisted on taking Veronica for a 'day of beauty' as a reward for her hard work. Of course, I really wanted to get my hands on the ugly duckling to see if I could make her more visually appealing.

20. Rarefied Heirs

By the end of June, I had brainstormed with my clients to elicit as much information about their lives as I could. The fruit of our sessions would become the basis for application essays, answering questions like:

- Briefly describe your child (e.g., personality, temperament, distinctive qualities, strengths, talents, enthusiasms).
- What values are important to you? How do you communicate these values to your child?
- Write a letter to your child, to be given to him thirteen years from now on graduation. Explain why you chose (school name) for him/her above all other schools.

I took reams of notes and then asked each family to write a few paragraphs profiling their child and family. This way, I could pick up on each parent's 'voice' in the final, edited draft. Everyone except the Radmore-Steins were game. They didn't want anything to do with essay-writing and said my voice would do just fine.

Stu Needleman, anxious to light a fire under me, turned his piece in first. The facts were there, but poetic it wasn't. These were his first two paragraphs and it deteriorated from there.

> *Veronica is a hippy girl with lots of energy. At four, she ran her first 5k and won of course. Now she's training for the iron-kiddie competition, where she'll swim, trike, and run against the top toddlers in the world.*
>
> *Veronica has empathy. She is worried about where her cat will sleep when it is dead. She felt bad when her maid burned her hand ironing Veronica's undies. She also enjoys finging and dancing.*

Since his family was the only one that turned its assignment in by deadline, I complimented Stu on the wittiness of his prose and remarked on how little doctoring I'd have to do to it. But between you and me, how did this man ever graduate from college?

ꙮ

I knocked on Philip's door. We hadn't seen each other since our evening was so rudely interrupted by Cadmon. I'd been busy with clients, and Philip seemed to have dropped off the face of the earth.

This time, I brought a plate of chocolate-chip cookies. Even though they were made from packaged Toll House cookie dough, they were technically homemade because I baked them myself. For some reason, I felt compelled to bring food to Philip. I suppose it gave me license to show up uninvited.

He smiled when he saw me standing there. Freshly baked cookies were so superior to liver. I don't know what I'd been thinking before. What man gets excited about a woman bearing liver? Philip invited me in, and I noticed appreciatively that his writing desk and computer were now located in the front of his apartment. He seemed engrossed.

'I thought you'd like a break,' I said. 'I brought chocolate-chip cookies.'

'Thanks,' Philip said appreciatively. 'Can I pour you some milk?'

'Absolutely.'

We scarfed down the cookies and caught up with each other. I told him about my clients and asked what he was working on. He mentioned that he was starting a new novel.

'That's wonderful,' I said. 'What's it about?'

'Sorry, I never talk about a book until I've completed the first draft. It's bad luck.'

'Of course,' I said. 'Actually, I was going to ask you to help me write these application essays that I have to do. And I pay the big bucks.'

'Oh, *that's* why you brought the cookies. You're trying to butter me up,' he teased.

'No, not at all. I just thought you might like to earn some extra money. Plus, the truth is, I need help. Writing isn't my strength.' I showed Philip Stu's first attempt, and he agreed that it sucked. There was no reason to believe that any of my other clients would do better.

'I'll give it a try,' Philip said. 'What would your clients say if they knew a published author wrote their essays?'

'Well, this particular father would think he deserved nothing less. But the rest of the parents would be thrilled, I'm sure. I'll give you credit, don't worry.'

'*No, don't,*' Philip implored. 'I'd rather people not know that I'm writing essays for private-school applications.'

'You only need to write six. There's one client, Ollie – I'll write hers myself.'

Philip wanted to charge $50 for each essay. He was giving me a special 'neighbor' discount. I insisted semi-adamantly that he take $100 per question, but he refused. What more could I do? I gave him the detailed notes from our brainstorming sessions along with Stu's sorry first attempt. I also handed over the golden essays Tipper had given me to use as examples. Two days later, I found an envelope under my door with the revised Needleman piece. I won't bore you with the whole thing, but feast your eyes on how Philip improved Stu's first few paragraphs.

> *Veronica possesses a fervent passion for life. There is a maturity about her that is balanced by a bewitching charm and a delightful sense of humor. She is athletic and enjoys running, swimming, and biking in competitive toddler events.*
>
> *Veronica has a unique sensibility. That, along with her loving nature, reveals a heart not always present in a child so young. When her precious cat, Princess, fell out the window, it wasn't enough to tell her that the kitty had gone to heaven. Veronica was concerned about 'Who will*

brush her? Who's going to hold her when there's thunder?' After our housekeeper burned her hand ironing, Veronica begged us to let her press the remaining clothes herself. She was devastated when we drove past a farmer harvesting corn in the Hamptons. She asked that we stop the car so she could throw herself in front of his combine to save the corn from being killed. We are not surprised that our daughter is so big hearted – consideration of all living things is at the core of the Needleman family values.

Veronica takes many different classes, from language to music to public speaking, but her favorite activities are singing and dancing. Recently, a renowned talent scout tried to sign her, but we felt she was too young to star on Broadway. Veronica loves choreographing her own shows and helping her seamstress sew sparkly costumes for all her performances. Veronica Needleman has accomplished more in her four and a half years on earth than many adults achieve in a lifetime.

Whoa. What a difference a little editing by a professional makes. After the essays were delivered, my clients couldn't get over how I'd gotten their prose to sing. They complimented me on my flair for the written word and patted themselves on the back for hiring such a talented adviser. At Philip's insistence, I didn't reveal that their ghostwriter had her own ghostwriter.

PART 3

Ivy on
Her Own

1. Was It Something I Said?

riday evening, I squeezed the girls into Cad's scratched-up Porsche for their weekend with him. *He really ought to get that thing fixed,* I thought.

I ran into Michael as I was returning home. He was locking up the Knishery. 'Good Shabbas,' I said.

'Oh, are you religious?' he asked.

'No, but I figured you must be, owning a kosher deli and all.'

Michael smiled. 'I'm reformed. Want to grab some dinner? I see you're on your own.'

'Sure. Barrio Chino for tapas?' I suggested.

'I just ate there last week. Steak?'

That was fine by me. We grabbed a cab to Washington Square and walked over to the Knickerbocker. A neighborhood joint that's been around forever, the place is a Greenwich Village institution. It's always packed, especially on weekends, when there's jazz.

Michael ordered steak with a side of creamed spinach. I chose the liver and onions. Since this wasn't a date, breath wasn't an issue.

Michael excused himself and went over to say hello to a table of actors. I assumed they were actors because one guy was wearing makeup, but heck, this being the Village, you never know.

'Sorry. They're deli customers. They've been coming for years.'

'Actors?'

'No. The guy in the studded vest owns a tattoo-and-piercing shop on St. Mark's Place. The man in drag is a psychiatrist. I don't know the woman sitting to his right, but the guy whose back is toward us is Bruce Wagner.'

'The writer?'

'You know him?'

'I've read his books. I guess you know a lot of interesting people from the Knishery.'

'I do. Everybody eventually makes the pilgrimage to Kratt's. The mayor. Hillary Clinton. Oprah Winfrey. Mrs. Goldofsky.'

'*Mrs. Goldofsky comes to the Knishery?* Just kidding. Oprah comes?'

'Couple of Sundays ago.'

'How could I have missed that? Did she stand in line?'

'You bet. You know how tolerant my Sunday crowd is of cutters.'

'Oh yeah. Last Sunday, I tried to sneak in just to snag a few bagels and they almost lynched me. I had to go to Hung-Goldstein's.'

'Traitor.'

'Have you ever thought of opening a second location?'

'I did. You know the Hotel New York–New York in Vegas? A few years ago the owners wanted me to open a Knishery there. It just seemed like too much trouble, flying back and forth, managing two restaurants.'

'You could have licensed the name and concept and let them run it.'

'I could have, but then I wouldn't control the quality. Plus, I can't stand the idea of creating a Disneyland version of my restaurant. Kratt's is the real deal. It looks the same today as it did sixty years ago.'

I smiled. 'You know, I've been coming to the Knickerbocker for almost twenty years. It hasn't changed, either. My soon-to-be-ex-husband used to take me here when we were first dating.'

'Really? I took my ex-wife here, too. Hope we don't run into either of them tonight.'

'God forbid. When we first started coming, we'd see Harry Connick, Jr. singing and playing piano. He made a hundred bucks a week then – at least that's what he told us. Cad and I used to talk to him and he always said how famous he was going to be. Of course, we didn't believe him.'

'Shows what *you* know.'

Michael and I talked easily, enjoying each other's company along with our steak and liver. Mine was so rich, I knew I'd have to sleep sitting up that night.

We listened to Tessa Souter, a rising star in the New York City jazz scene. She was accompanied by Victor Lewis on drums, Kenny Barron on piano, and Russell Malone on guitar. When Tessa finished her set, Michael went over to the bar and said something to the owner. Next thing I knew, he was playing the piano and singing 'It Had to Be You' with Victor and Russell backing him up. I didn't know whether to be impressed or mortified. Nobody but me paid attention to the change in entertainment, so I decided to relax and enjoy his talent, which was almost as impressive as my own singing.

'Where did you learn to play piano like that?' I asked when he sat down again.

'My mother made me take lessons when I was a kid. I was miserable about it until I got older and realized that girls were attracted to musicians. I wanted to become a professional, but my father died and I had to take over the business until it could be sold. Then I got married and needed a reliable source of income, so I stayed with the deli. You know how real life gets in the way of your dreams sometimes.'

'Yeah, I hate when that happens. Do you think you'll ever get married again?'

'I do. I'm a romantic guy. If it weren't for the wife I chose, I would have loved being married. What about you?'

'Maybe. But this time I'm marrying a guy with money – or at least serious earning potential.' *I can definitely see myself as part of a fabulous Manhattan power couple,* I thought.

'So that eliminates me.'

'I'm afraid so,' I said sympathetically. 'I hope you're not too crushed.'

'I was just joking. But you weren't, were you?'

'Oops. Sorry, not really, no. The thing is, I married for love the first time and look where it got me. Now I'm a single mom with two kids to support. No safety net. I have to be practical.'

'Ah, I see. Check please.' Michael motioned to the waitress. I think I'd offended him.

'Michael, I'm just being honest with you. It's not like you wanted to marry me.'

'That's true. I would not want to marry you.'

'I feel terrible. I'm sorry. It's been such a nice evening. Please, let's just forget what I'd said. I'm a good person. Really.'

'I'm sure you are. But the thing is, I'm not comfortable spending time with someone who doesn't think *I'm* good enough. You can understand that, can't you?'

'I think you're great. You're just not the person I would marry. That's different.'

'Is it?'

'Yes. Do you want to marry a Jewish girl?'

'That would be nice.'

'It's the same thing. I want to marry a mover and shaker. You know, like the president of a major corporation or a famous actor or writer. Someone who's fabulously successful.'

'Some people think *I'm* fabulously successful. My mother always did. Personally, I'm crazy about myself.'

I laughed nervously. 'Michael, you're a wonderful man. But I know myself. The lifestyle I aspire to is expensive. If I marry again, it's got to be to a man who can support my girls and give me that big New York life. Please don't take it personally. Can't we just be good friends?'

'Mmm, I don't think so, Ivy. But don't take it personally.'

∞

Man, did I blow it with Michael. I adore the guy. He's just not husband material for me. Is it a crime to want to marry a man with ambition? Does that make me a monster?

I did learn one good lesson. I will never again talk about this with anyone except Faith.

I sent Michael a bouquet of flowers along with a heart-felt note of apology. But from that night on, our relationship changed. Michael was polite, of course. He's too well-mannered a guy not to be. But the warm and friendly Michael I had come to know was gone. And I had no idea how to win him back.

2. Identity Crisis

The top twelve private schools in the city were known as the Baby Ivys. It was every status-conscious New Yorker's dream that their child attend one of these schools, since they were a pipeline to the Ivy League colleges. Even more important, having your kid at a Baby Ivy was vital for avoiding humiliation when asked the inevitable question: 'So where does your child go to school?' The names of the Baby Ivys could be spoken with pride. The names of second- and third-tier schools were typically muffled by a cough or change of subject. Everyone understood that if your child didn't attend a first-tier school, you must be a second- or third-tier family.

Before my clients left for vacation, we put together the lists of schools where each would apply. I encouraged everyone to stretch for the Baby Ivys, but I insisted that they also select two safety schools. The exercise was straightforward for everyone except Willow and Tiny, who needed a gay-friendly community with full wheelchair access (which eliminated many of the best schools in the city). Wendy Weiner also struggled with her list. She was persona non grata at the thirty-five schools that had rejected Winnie last year. Before advising

Wendy, I called Eleanor Dubinsky, her former nursery-school director, to find out why Wendy had failed so miserably.

'It was two things,' Eleanor explained. 'First, she applied to thirty-five schools, and when interviewers asked her where else she was applying, which they *always* ask, she actually *named* the other thirty-four schools. They thought she was completely over the top, which of course she was.

'Plus,' Eleanor whispered, 'how do I say this delicately? That *voice*. Who wants to sign up for thirteen years of that excruciating sound?' Personally, I suspected that Eleanor had queered the deal for the Weiners, not wanting to be responsible for passing Wendy on to institutions where she had continuing relationships.

Based on this intelligence, I urged Wendy to move Winnie to a no-name local nursery school so Eleanor Dubinsky couldn't sabotage Winnie again. I told Wendy to apply using her ex-husband's name and to let him handle the parent interviews. We could bleach Winnie's hair, apply her under the name of Winona whatever-her-dad's-last-name-is, and start with a clean slate.

It was then that Wendy mentioned there was no ex-husband in the picture. Winnie was the product of artificial insemination with an anonymous donor.

'Fine,' I told her. 'We'll get an actor to pretend to be Winnie's father.' See, there's no stumping me.

Wendy vehemently objected, not to the subterfuge itself, but to being excluded from taking an active part in it. She reluctantly agreed to the plan after I assured her there wasn't a chance in hell that any private school would knowingly accept her daughter after last year's debacle. Winnie's only hope was to ditch her mother.

3. Southampton Holiday

The summer after I lost my husband, my job, and my home turned out to be the happiest I could remember. Since I'd turned sixteen and was legally employable, I'd been one of those overly responsible girls who never took a break from work for fear of having to justify any unexplainable résumé gaps. Every professional and personal choice I'd made took into account how I would position that decision to some nameless, faceless interviewer considering me for my next job.

The only responsibilities I had over the summer were tutoring Ransom and Veronica and editing Philip's essays so my clients would be ready to submit their applications in September. Compared to life at Myoki Bank, this didn't even qualify as work.

Philip became a visible presence in our lives, but not a romantic lead. *Grrrrr.* I had this mad crush on him, but he wasn't biting. Still, I was delighted that we were beginning to see each other regularly. Whenever he completed an essay, he would hand-deliver it, joining me for a meal or quiet drink. I looked forward to his visits, and I dressed up and put on makeup every day in case he showed up.

By the time he gave me the sixth essay, I was bemoaning his obvious lack of interest. I decided that he must think of me as just a friend or, worse, a mother figure.

For the last two weeks of August, Faith invited the girls and me to Southampton, where she and Steven had a house on Gin Lane. It was one of those twenty-million-dollar estates that you drool over in the *Sotheby's Fine Home and Estate Catalog*. Faith (with the help of the best decorators money can buy) had transformed it into a warm and cozy home filled with impressionist paintings, beautiful rugs, colorful fabrics, and elegant clutter. It was child-friendly while remaining a feast for the eyes. Every morning, Faith and I would run on the beach. Later, we'd all swim in the frigid Atlantic Ocean, then dive into her heated pool, and finally take a Jacuzzi. The children spent their days jumping on the trampoline, riding the miniature horses, bowling in the private alley, scaling the climbing wall in Faith's gymnastics pavilion, or giving Sir Elton a bath. At night, Faith's chef would barbecue for picnics we'd hold on the beach. Then we'd all bundle up in the outdoor beds to watch the latest movies on their screen under the stars.

Faith encouraged me to invite Philip to join us for a few days over the long weekend. Actually, she relentlessly insisted until I had no choice but to ask him. Amazingly, he said yes. He said yes!

With Philip coming, I asked Faith to recommend someone to give me a bikini wax *just in case*. She suggested the top pubic stylist on the East Coast, Francesca Gregorio. I'd heard of her, of course, but couldn't spare $250 to clean up my nether region. 'No problem,' Faith said. 'She's making a house call on Tuesday. She'll do us both. My treat. What do you need?'

'Just a shaping. If I feel kinky, I might go Brazilian.'

'Ivy, Ivy, Ivy.' Faith shook her head sadly. 'That's *so* yesterday. Francesca's an artist. She can do anything. You can have a full-frontal defoliation. Or better yet, think about a pubic picture. She's bringing her colorist. I'm getting a strawberry this time, but she's done a heart, a cherry, and a bull's-eye before.'

'She colors and shapes your pubic hair into a strawberry? No offense, Faith, but that's just weird.'

'It's adorable. Bikini topiary's the rage. They did a whole thing about it on the E! Entertainment channel.'

'Guess I missed it. I'll settle for a cleanup and shaping. If I happen to get lucky with Philip, I'd rather not have a bull's-eye between my legs. It seems so calculated.'

∽

On the Friday evening Philip arrived, we left the girls with Faith's weekend nanny and had dinner at Savannah, a charming restaurant near the train station. It was one of those warm, perfect evenings, and we were seated in the back garden. Steven asked how Philip and I met, and to my embarrassment, he outed me for showing up at his door bearing chopped liver.

'Are you crazy, Ivy?' Faith said. 'Nobody likes liver. How could you not know that?' She turned to Philip. 'Admit it, you thought she was strange, didn't you?'

'No, I thought she was kind of cute,' he answered, giving me a smile.

He thought I was cute! He likes me. He really likes me. I felt like Sally Field. *Play it cool*, I cautioned myself.

'But did you *enjoy* the chopped liver?' Faith pressed.

'No, not really. I think it's a taste you have to grow up with,' he answered. 'Sorry, Ivy,' he said, looking at me for forgiveness.

'Don't you guys read *Gourmet*? It's a known fact that chopped liver is one of the six sexy foods. That plus oysters, figs, caviar, chiles, and chocolate. Hel-loow, it's an aphrodisiac,' I said.

'Maybe for Jewish people, but trust me, not for anyone else,' Faith said.

'You don't know what you're missing.' I said. 'Have you ever tasted warm chopped liver right after it's been chopped? Mmmmm. Just thinking about it makes me hot.'

'I don't think any food is sexier than food fed to you by a lover,' Philip said.

Faith and I stared at him. After picking my chin up off the floor, I croaked, 'That, too.'

After dinner, Steven invited Philip to join him outside for a cigar. Faith and I waited for dessert.

'Philip doesn't strike me as a smoker,' I remarked to Faith after they left.

'You're probably right. But show me the man who can say no to a big Cuban cigar. It's a guy thing. Now you won't be able to kiss him tonight,' she teased.

'Since I haven't kissed him yet anyway, I don't think cigar breath will be a problem.'

'He's cute,' Faith said seriously. 'What I wouldn't give for one night with a stud like that.'

'Faith, Philip is *not* a stud. He's a prodigy, an intellectual giant, a publishing wonder boy. I'll grant you, he has a nice ass, but that's purely secondary. And anyway, why would you be interested in Philip? You're with one of the most accomplished men in the world.'

'I know, and I love him to death. But he's at least thirty years older than Philip.'

'And he looks great for a guy in his late sixties.'

'Yeah, I know. When I first met Steven, the idea of sleeping with a man older than my dad was just gross. But then he dazzled me with his wealth and power and charm. Now I *adore* him. But with Steven, it's what's *inside* that's sexy. Every once in a while, I can't help it. I fantasize about being with a younger guy. Is that terrible?'

'It's perfectly normal,' I assured Faith. *Like I know about these things.* 'Did you agree to threesomes in your prenup? Why not invite a gorgeous man to join you?'

'I can't. The agreement defines "threesomes" as one man and two women. Steven has these lesbian fantasies.'

'Eeeuw.' I covered my ears. 'Too much information, too much information, la la la la la.'

As we giggled, I noticed a pint-sized visitor approaching our table. It was Veronica, my little student, who was having dinner with her endearing parents, Stu and Patsy Needleman.

'Hey, little pumpkin,' I said to her. 'Meet my friend Faith.'

'Hi, I'm Veronica, it's very nice to meet you,' she said politely while shaking Faith's hand. *I must, must, must remember to teach all my clients' children to do that as soon as I get back.*

To my chagrin, Stu came over. He was sporting a second-degree sunburn that hurt to look at. Patsy followed her usual two steps behind. I introduced them to Faith.

Stu ignored her, while long-suffering Patsy was silent, looking down at her feet.

'I tried to call you yesterday and you weren't available,' he accused.

'I'm sorry, Stu, but I've been here for the last few days.'

'Ms. Ames, I should be able to reach you anytime I have a question.' He pronounced 'Ms.' like 'Mizzzzzz.' 'Steven Lord would have my ass in a sling if I left my job for even a day without letting important clients know how to reach me. That was *completely* unprofessional,' he chided.

'Okay, Stu, from now on you'll always know how to find me,' I said as I jotted my cell-phone number on a cocktail napkin. Oops, transposed two numbers. Gosh, I hate when I do that.

'It was urgent that I talk to you,' he continued. 'I want a written and oral briefing on the questions Patsy and I can expect to be asked at each of our interviews.'

Like this couldn't wait until winter, when they would actually go to the interviews? Poor Patsy and Veronica were cowed by his bullying, even though it wasn't aimed at them. Faith just sat there with her mouth open. I knew what she was thinking.

'Again, my apologies, Stu. From now on, you'll be able to reach me anytime you want.'

'You disappoint me and you *know* what I'll do,' he said, waving his stubby little pointer finger at me. 'I'll use every last resource of Steven Lord to bring you down, missy.'

Did he just call me 'missy'? 'Oh, Stu, let me introduce you to my friends, Steven Lord and Philip Goodman,' I said, gesturing to our dates, who were now standing behind the Needleman family.

'What's this about using every last resource I have against Ivy?' Steven's antennae were up. He didn't become one of the world's richest men by being a boob.

'Oh, he's just joking, Steven,' I said. No point humiliating the asshole. He's still a client. 'You know Stu, don't you? Your junior lieutenant.'

'No, I don't believe we've met,' Steven said. 'What division do you work in?'

Stu's face was bright red. 'Oil and Gas, sir.'

'Well, it's nice to meet you, Stuey,' Steven said, slapping Stu's back. 'Any friend of Ivy's is a friend of mine.'

Steven turned to sit down. 'Oh, Mr. Lord, sir,' Stu began, 'do you think – would it be possible – would you do me the honor – could I have my picture taken with you?'

'Sure, do you have a camera?'

'Patsy, the camera,' Stu barked. The 'chop-chop' at the end of the sentence was implied. Patsy instantly retrieved it from her purse. Steven put his arm around Stu and both smiled while Patsy snapped away.

'Thank you, sir,' he said practically prostrating himself at Steven's feet. 'You don't know how much this means to me.'

'My pleasure,' Steven said.

As Steven and Philip sat down, dessert was served. This was Stu and Patsy's cue to skedaddle, which they quickly did, but not before I gave Veronica a big hug and promised her that day of beauty in September.

As they walked away, Stu reviewed the pictures on their digital camera. 'Jesus fucking *Christ*, Patsy,' he said, 'you cut Steven Lord's head off in every shot! Can't you do *anything* right?'

Faith started to open her mouth, but I interrupted. 'Don't even start, Faith. I know Stu's a jerk, but his daughter's a sweetheart. I'm determined to get her into a wonderful school so she'll have something good in her life to make up for that overbearing father of hers.'

'But how can you put up with him treating you like that?' she said.

'Not to brag or anything, but I spent fourteen years at Myoki Bank, *remember*? Graceful acceptance of humiliation was part of my daily Zen practice there.'

'Ivy, you have the patience of a saint,' Steven said. 'To Ivy,' he toasted, and everyone joined in.

4. Sex on the Beach

A fter dinner, Philip and I went to the Driver's Seat for a nightcap. One of the oldest anti-chic restaurants in town, the place had a wood-paneled bar in the front room, a dining room in the back, and an outside patio that appealed to the few would-be Beautiful People who frequented the joint. We sat in front, where the bronzed bartender hobnobbed with the patrons, mostly locals.

Philip downed a few beers to my one glass of wine. I pressed him about his book, which he seemed reticent to discuss. 'Soon,' he promised.

'Is it something I'll enjoy reading?'

'I hope so,' he answered. 'You'll be in it.'

'Wow,' I said. 'I'm going to be in your book? I don't know what to say. No one's ever put me in a book before.'

'Let's just say you're inspiring me to write this story, and without you I never would have attempted it.' He took my hand in his, reached over, and kissed me. It was a small, tender kiss on the lips, but I don't think I've ever received a nicer one. Part of me wanted to savor the moment – make it last like a five-course meal at

Chanterelle. The other part wanted to throw Philip down in a booth and have my way with him. Tear off his shirt. Run my fingers through his chest hairs. Squeeze his perfect round orbs (whatever those are), explore every crevice of his body with my teasing, flickering tongue. Pleasure him as no woman ever –

'Do you want to take a walk?' Philip asked.

'Sure.'

As Philip took my hand, butterflies fluttered in my stomach. I'd forgotten the feeling of new love. We strolled up Jobs Lane to Main Street, looking into windows filled with knickknacks so superfluous you'd only buy them if you were a millionaire on vacation. We eventually wandered into Bookhampton, one of the few stores open late. It was my idea to see if Philip's book was in stock. It was! I wanted to buy one, but Philip said he'd give me a copy for free. Later, we hoofed it back to Faith and Steven's. They'd taken the car, but we didn't mind the walk. It was a warm night and the moon was almost full. Some unidentifiable creatures (mosquitoes perhaps?) were chirping. It smelled like it might rain.

'Such a beautiful night, don't you think?' I said as we meandered along in the darkness.

'Beautiful,' Philip said. He stopped walking, looked at me for a moment, then drew me toward him and kissed me so deeply and with such intensity that I understood for the first time the phenomenon known as 'melting in his arms.' Philip Goodman, man of few words, had communicated his feelings perfectly.

We walked the rest of the way to Faith and Steven's without talking.

When we arrived at the gate, Philip got all serious. 'Can I ask you a question?'

'Sure,' I said.

'If you'd been out drinking one night and the next morning you woke up on the beach, completely naked with no memory of how you got there, would you tell anyone?'

I thought for a moment. 'No, definitely not.'

'So would you like to go to the beach with me?' he asked.

I laughed. 'Did you just make that up?'

'Nah, it's an old joke. I'm surprised you fell for it.'

'I'm extremely gullible.'

'So do you want to go to the beach with me?' he asked.

'Are you joking?'

'No, I'm asking.'

'Okay.'

He grabbed two beers from the outdoor refrigerator and we walked down the wooden path to the ocean. The sky was freckled with stars.

'Come on, let's sit,' he said.

We sat near the water, on the packed sand.

My teeth were chattering lightly even though it was warm and there was no breeze. I wondered if we were going to have sex on the beach. I'd never done anything that daring before, and to tell you the truth, it seemed like it would be uncomfortable. But I didn't say anything.

'See that ship over there?' Philip said.

'It's a cruise ship,' I pointed out.

'Have you ever gone on a cruise?' he asked.

'Yeah, you?'

We looked at each other and smiled. This was awkward. Philip reached over and brought my face to his and kissed me gently on the lips. 'Mmmm,' I said. Philip's tongue met mine and we kissed slowly. Then we lay back in the sand and made out more urgently, our bodies pressed together like Burt Lancaster and Deborah Kerr in *From Here to Eternity*.

'I never knew it could be like this. Nobody's ever kissed me the way you do,' I said.

'Nobody?'

'No, nobody,' I said laughing and kissing him again. All of a sudden, the water rolled up and soaked us both. 'Shit, that's *freezing!*' I said, jumping up.

We ran to higher ground. 'Let's get out of these wet clothes,' Philip said.

'Really?'

'Really,' he said.

'Okay.' I started to take off my pants and noticed that Philip was already naked. 'How did you get undressed so fast?' I asked him.

'I can't wait,' he said. 'Do you know how long I've been thinking about this?'

'Is that so?' I said, pleased. I threw my clothes behind us so the surf couldn't reach them. I silently blessed Faith for giving me the dream-team makeover, but still wondered how my body looked to Philip. If only we were in bed, where I could artfully drape the sheets over my trouble spots. Could he see my cesarean scar? I stretched my upper torso, pushed my chest forward and threw back my shoulders to look trimmer. One can only hope that moonlight and ocean spray act as soft filters.

Peeking at Philip's body, I noticed there wasn't an ounce of fat on the guy. His enormous erection was at full attention in anticipation of my affections. I would have been completely mesmerized by his naked loins were it not for all that scratchy sand sticking to my body. What if he got some on his penis? That could hurt.

We started kissing again. Soon, we were embracing and I forgot about the sand. I felt myself getting wetter as he pressed his muscular body against mine. I prayed silently that he preferred my soft womanly flesh to those bony young models he was probably more familiar with. He kissed me gently on the lips, then eased his face down to lick my neck, suck my breasts, and . . . was the bikini-wax a success? *OH. MY. GOD. Not only is he gorgeous, he's also generous in bed or sand or wherever.* I moaned.

We were startled by a jeep driving down the beach. Philip's head popped up. He put his finger to his mouth. We were quiet as sandcrabs and didn't move. Still, the jeep parked about ten feet away.

A man with a flashlight got out and started toward us. 'Shit,' I said to Philip.

'Shhh,' he said, sitting up. 'Let me do the talking.'

The man stood in front of us and flashed his light right at my boobs. I swear he did it on purpose. 'I don't s'pose you two know it's against the law to be nekkid on this beach.'

'No sir,' Philip said. 'We didn't realize. We'll get dressed.'

'I'm afraid I'm gonna have to arrest you,' he said.

5. Shocking News

I could not possibly get arrested for being nekkid on the beach. Faith would never let me live that down. '*What!* Please, your honor, no. Don't arrest us. We'll put our clothes on; we'll leave. No one has to know about this,' I pleaded. The horror!

'Sorry – it's the law.'

'Officer, wait,' Philip said. 'We're staying right there at Steven Lord's house. Let's go talk to him. I'm sure he can help straighten this out.'

'Ah, houseguests of Steven Lord. Uh-*huh*.' The cop thought for a moment, then went over to his jeep and called for backup.

I got up to fetch my clothes. 'Freeze!' the officer ordered, pointing his flashlight at me. 'Hands up.'

I stood, naked, with my arms in air, while the cop leered at my body in the spotlight. It was creepy and flattering at the same time.

'Uhm, sir, can she sit down?' Philip asked.

'*Huh?* Oh. Yes,' the officer said.

I dropped to the sand like a rock. A few minutes later, sirens were blaring and flashing red lights brightened the sky in front of Faith's house. A group of teenage boys who had been partying up the beach came over to see what was going on. They stood behind the cop, staring and giggling like we were some kind of freak show. The pimpliest of the kids pulled out a camera phone and snapped a picture of us. I felt like the village slut. Yeah, I know, I was sitting on the beach buck naked next to a man in his birthday suit, but still!

'What's the matter, never seen a woman without her clothes on before?' I hissed at Pimple Boy.

'Never one as old as my mom,' he answered, cracking up his friends.

This was so humiliating. Lights were turning on at Faith's house. A few minutes later, Steven and Faith, in their matching bathrobes, were descending the wooden stairs to the beach with two cops. I hoped that we hadn't interrupted any contractual sex.

'Are these your guests, Mr. Lord?'

'Yes, they're with us,' he said. Faith was trying to suppress her laughter behind Steven. I wanted to kill her.

'Well, if that's the case, we'll let 'em go this time.' The cop turned to us and warned, 'Next time, take it inside.' He looked at the teenagers. 'Okay kids, show's over. Do your parents know you're out at this hour?' Nya-na, nya-na. Now it was their turn to get in trouble. When the cop turned his back, I shot them the bird, proving that I could be just as immature as they could.

∽

Saturday was as magnificent a day as a vacationer could hope for in Southampton. Eighty-eight degrees at noon, a gentle breeze, clouds so wispy they didn't even count. Steven took Philip to Sag Harbor on his jet helicopter to see the new golf course he was building. Coptering ten miles was overkill, but I guess that's what happens when you have too much money.

I was teaching the girls how to build a proper sand castle. Mae and Lia were filling their buckets with wet sand, while Skyler and Kate handled construction. We made an enormous hill with four towers on top, surrounded by thick retaining walls.

'Let's build a moat,' Skyler suggested.

'Good idea, every castle has a moat,' I agreed.

I showed them how to dig a deep canal that circled the hill and then swirled out toward the water like a snail. Each time the waves came in, our canal filled up. It was extremely cool. The kids wanted to make the moat deeper, so I left them to it and went to join Faith. Sir Elton was sleeping under the beach umbrella.

'Okay, I want to know every detail,' Faith said, putting down the newspaper. 'Is he a good kisser? How's his body? I couldn't tell because he was sitting. Did you go all the way or did the cop bust you before you had a chance?'

'Faith, don't ask me that. I'm not the kind of person who kisses and tells.'

'Come on, it's *me*. I told you what's in my prenup. And that's highly confidential.'

'Okay, okay, he's a great kisser, there's no fat on his body, and no, we didn't have a chance to do it. That stupid policeman ruined everything. Maybe tonight, we'll see. Can I have the "Arts" section when you're done?'

'I'm done. Here,' Faith said. We both ignored the front

page and the 'Metro' section, preferring to stay uninformed and oblivious while on vacation.

My cell phone rang. I fished it out of all the junk in my beach bag, almost missing the call. It was Bonnie, my old assistant.

'Ivy,' she asked hesitatingly, 'have you heard the news?'

It's never a good sign when someone starts a conversation like that. 'What news?' I asked.

'The Myoki tragedy, did you hear?'

My stomach lurched. I jerked to attention, terrified to hear what she had to say, knowing she was about to put a damper on my vacation.

'Three people died,' Bonnie said.

'*What*? What happened? Oh, my God, who died?'

'An executive vice president, a vice president, and a secretary.'

'How did it happen? Oh, my God.'

'What? *What*?' Faith was asking. I held up my hand to shush her.

'We were having a team-building meeting in the Everglades. I was there helping Drayton. He made me his assistant after you left. Anyway, the executives had just finished swimming with alligators. Remember last year's off-site, when you swam with dolphins? Well, this time, Drayton wanted to do something more in keeping with reality.'

'I can't believe Myoki would let its executives do something like that. They *rode* alligators?' I asked.

'No, not exactly. We swam in a swamp where alligators were known to live. The goal was to feel the fear and do it anyway. We had this keynote speaker who talked about leaders who carry on in spite of great risk. The swim was our chance to look danger in the face and defy it. But the gator swim wasn't the problem. It went fine. Afterward we celebrated with a barbecue on the boat. While we were eating, the consultants set up a hot-coal fire walk on the aft deck. They say if you can walk across burning coals in your bare feet, you can do anything. Supposedly, they'd had fire walks on this boat before, but this time, something went wrong. The coals ignited the wood on the deck and the ship went up like it was doused with gasoline. It happened so fast. No one was wearing life jackets.'

'What did you do?'

'I jumped. Everyone did. But our leftover ribs fell in the water and attracted the gators. They were swimming all around us. First they went for the food, then us. A rescue boat came, but not fast enough to save everyone.'

'Bonnie, I can't imagine.' I was out of breath just listening to this story. 'What about Drayton and Konrad? Did they make it?'

'Drayton's dead. Olive Armstrong, too. She's the one who took your place after they fired you.'

'*What?*' I interrupted indignantly. 'They replaced me? Those bums. I was fired to save money. That's what they said.'

'Yeah, well, you know Myoki. No one ever tells the truth. Anyway, do you want to hear the rest of the story or not?'

'Yes, of course. Sorry.'

'Konrad's secretary, you know, the songwriter – he's gone. Ivy, here's the worst part. I was right next to Drayton when an alligator burst out of the water. Drayton grabbed me. I thought he was trying to save me. Instead, he pulled me in front of him like a shield. Can you believe it? Somehow, and I don't know how, I managed to dive under him and the gator latched on to Drayton. Then it started spinning him. That's what alligators do. They spin and drown their victims. Then they tear them apart piece by piece before they eat them. Did you know that?'

'No, I didn't. I mean, it's never come up before. What about Konrad?'

'He's alive, if that's what you mean. But he lost half his face, including his nose. He'll never be the same.'

'Oh, my God, that perfect face.' I couldn't imagine what Konrad would do without it.

'I know. I'll bet he loses his job after this,' Bonnie said. 'At his level, the aesthetic standards are so high. He won't be able to compete with the heavy hitters. If they can't use him on the cover of the Annual Report anymore, what's the point?'

'You're probably right. What about you? Do you still have a job?'

'I don't know,' Bonnie said. 'We just got back last night. If I'm not too traumatized, I'll go in on Tuesday or Wednesday to find out. You know Myoki, they'll use any excuse to reorganize.'

'Bonnie, if there's *anything* I can do, just ask.'

I hung up, and told Faith everything. Reaching for the 'Metro' section, we spotted the headline: THREE EXECUTIVES EATEN ALIVE IN OFF-SITE GONE AWRY.

'Faith, do you realize I might have died if Drayton hadn't gotten me fired? The woman who took my place was *eaten*.' Like someone who just missed getting on a plane that crashed, I didn't know quite what to make of my good fortune. Truth was, I felt like whooping, wailing, and testifying – 'Hallelujah, I'm alive, I'm alive, Thank you, Lord Jeezus, I'm ALIVE!' But that would have been in bad taste. Secretly, and I knew it would be unthinkable to say this, I felt that Drayton and Konrad deserved it. There. I thought it. They were mean to me, so God punished them, right? They were greedy sleaze-buckets who finally got theirs. Talk about being up to your ass in alligators, ha ha ha. I was so witty and clever when it came to puns. *Oh, dear God, I can't believe what I'm thinking. What kind of monster am I?*

Dear Lord in Heaven, forgive me. I take it all back. I'm sure Olive Armstrong was a fine person even though she took my job. And songwriter-secretary, his dreams of a future in musical theater – dashed for all eternity. Please God, bless these people. I am so sorry for them and their families. I mean that with all my heart. And I regret any wicked or inappropriately humorous thoughts I may have had. I was in shock. Thank you God for your understanding and forgiveness regarding this matter.

I had a hard time enjoying the rest of the weekend knowing that Drayton, Olive, and songwriter-secretary had met such gruesome deaths. And Konrad, the Face. Like a surgeon who lost the use of his hands, what would he do now? I kept imagining what it must be like to be bitten, chewed, and spit out by an alligator. Would death be instantaneous or would you actually feel your bones snapping and your flesh ripping? It was too hideous to contemplate. But the possibility that there might be senior-level openings at Myoki was oddly intriguing.

On Saturday night, I slipped into Philip's room after everyone had gone to bed.

'I can't sleep,' I whispered.

Philip lifted the covers and motioned for me to join him. I climbed under the sheets, which were warm from the heat of his body, and snuggled close. He kissed me softly. His touch was so tender. He made me feel cared for in a way that I could barely remember. Tears started to flow. I couldn't help it.

'What's wrong?' he whispered, caressing my hair.

'I don't know. I feel so bad about what happened to the people I used to work with. What if I'd been there? My girls wouldn't have a mother. I can't put it out of my mind.'

'Shhhh. You're safe.' He kissed me more deeply this time. Then, his face moved down and he bit my neck. 'Do you like it when I do this?' he asked as he began to unbutton my nightgown. If he thought he could distract me from thinking about the Myoki tragedy, he was right.

'Mmmm, I like it.'

'How about this?' he whispered, sucking my nipples.

'Yes, please don't stop.'

Philip slipped my nightgown off and reached inside my panties. He rubbed me slowly and gently before removing them. As he moved down and began kissing me between the legs, I was so thankful I hadn't gone for the bikini topiary. He looked up. 'How's this?' All I could do was clutch the bed and moan with pleasure. Reaching down, I beckoned him back. I couldn't wait any longer. As soon as he was on top of me, I felt for his erection. I wanted him inside me and I wanted him now. In seconds he was moving in and out with such urgency that the shabby chic headboard banged against the wall and the bedsprings squeaked with each thrust. *Bang. Squeak. Bang. Squeak.* I tried not to moan or scream too loud so as not to wake the others in the house. I needn't have bothered. Faith told me later that she and Steven had put pillows over their heads to muffle the noise. I hope that doesn't mean I'll never be invited back.

When we had finally satisfied our lust, I snuggled into the crook of Philip's shoulder and fell into a deep sleep.

Late that night, I was awakened by a terrible dream. Drayton pushed me off a boat into an alligator-infested swamp. He and Konrad and all the other senior people from Myoki were laughing at me as I struggled to escape the clutches of an enormous bull alligator with two rows of razor-sharp teeth. Just as the beast snapped off my leg with its deadly jaws, I woke up terrified. *Breathe. Breathe. Breathe,* I said to myself. Then I noticed someone sitting calmly in the reading chair across from the bed. My stomach flipped. It was Drayton.

6. Andy's Open House

You probably think I'm crazy. Drayton was dead. But I swear on my daughters' lives it was him. Ridiculous. I checked to see if I was awake. Could this be a very realistic dream? No, I was definitely awake. I must be hallucinating. I looked at Philip, who was sleeping soundly by my side, then back at Drayton. He smiled at me. *Yeow. O dear God, I hope Drayton hadn't been watching us have sex earlier. Nah. Get your mind out of the gutter.* I reached over and shook Philip.

'Philip, wake up. I had a nightmare. Will you hold me, please?'

Philip smiled and wrapped his arms protectively around me. I looked up and Drayton was gone. After a half hour, when I felt certain Drayton's ghost wouldn't return, I said goodnight to Philip and snuck quietly back into my room. Between Philip and Drayton, I'd had enough excitement for one night. I needed to sleep.

∽

It rained Sunday morning, then cleared up in a heartbeat, as though God flipped the weather switch. As saddened as I was about the Myoki tragedy, I pulled myself together to go to brunch at the old Andy Warhol estate in Montauk. The Lords got invited to all the best parties.

The real estate firm of Allan M. Schneider hosted the event. The Warhol property, which could be had for a mere fifty million dollars, boasted a seven-bedroom main house, two guesthouses, a staff house, a caretaker house, stables, and a pool. It was on 122 acres of undeveloped land with 600 feet of oceanfront – unheard of in the overdeveloped Hamptons. Liza Minnelli, Elizabeth Taylor, Jackie Kennedy Onassis, and Mick Jagger were just a few of the famous houseguests who had visited in years past. Virtually anyone who could write a personal check for fifty mil was invited – industrialists, media moguls, movie stars, rappers, pop singers, heirs and heiresses. We were told to get there early, as parking would be a problem. The property could only accommodate seven jet helicopters.

We said our goodbyes to the girls, who were engrossed in a papier-mâché project with Victoria, their weekend nanny and former Spence kindergarten teacher. Faith stole all her nannies from the best private schools.

'Look, Mommy, I'm making a bird,' Skyler said.

'And I'm making a SpongeBob,' Kate said, showing me her square creation.

Mae was making an erect penis. Then she explained that it was a fish. I guess we know what was on my mind. Lia was meticulously constructing a blob.

'You guys are doing a wonderful job, aren't they, Faith?' I said.

'I pronounce them gifted,' she agreed.

Brunch was catered by Loaves and Fishes, home of the $70-per-pound lobster salad. The place was buzzing with the top 1 percent of the top 1 percent of the wealthiest humans on the planet, along with a few hangers-on such as myself. There was a respectable showing of business honchos like Henry Kravis and Ron Perelman with their gorgeous second or third wives. Ira Rennert was a no-show. He owned a hundred-thousand-square-foot, hundred-million-dollar compound in Sagaponak with twenty-nine bedrooms, thirty-five bathrooms, and parking for more than a hundred. Compared to Ira's, Andy's was just a starter escape.

The grounds were swarming with celebs. Inside, my heart was atwitter. Outside, I maintained a Buddha-like composure, blasé and underwhelmed. That's what New Yorkers do around famous people. Christy Brinkley. Jerry Seinfeld. Yeah. Cool. Whatev. Billy Joel. Paul Simon. Do I know you? P. Diddy. Alec Baldwin. Yawn. Matthew Broderick, Sarah Jessica. Check please. Philip and I people-watched, since neither of us knew anyone in person, only by reputation. Frankly, I was a little miffed that not one star made an effort to get to know us. With no one to talk to, we decided to explore the property on our own. Personally, I preferred Faith's estate, which was thirty million dollars cheaper, but hey, that's just me.

We scoped out the master suite in the caretaker's house. 'Check out this closet,' Philip said.

I peeked in. It was just an ordinary man's walk-in about half filled with clothes. Nothing special. 'You haven't seen a closet until you've seen Faith's,' I told him.

'No really, come inside,' he said.

'What?'

Philip pulled me toward him and kissed me roughly. He shut the door and began to undress me.

'Why, you bad boy,' I said as we got naked. I couldn't believe how exciting my life was becoming. Cad and I never indulged in the pleasures of the flesh beyond the safety of our marital bed. But look at me now! Steamy hot sex in Andy Warhol's estate's caretaker's closet. I reached down and held Philip's engorged penis in my hand, then knelt to take it in my mouth. That's when we heard voices in the bedroom. Instinctively, we dove behind the curtain of hanging clothes. A man with a southern accent was giving a tour. I prayed, *Please don't open the door. Please don't open the door.* He opened the door.

'Here's the closet. It's like any other closet you might see anywhere. Except this closet has two naked people in the corner hiding behind the clothes.' Everyone laughed. He shut the door and the tour moved on. With all the security at this party, it was a miracle that yet again we had escaped arrest.

When the coast was clear, I quickly got dressed. 'I've never been caught naked in my life and now look at me, twice in one weekend. What are the odds?' I growled.

'They're pretty high when you fuck in public places,' Philip said.

'Well, call me a prude, but from now on, let's only have sex in private. If Faith and Steven found out we'd been caught again, they'd *never* invite me back. An open invitation to the Hamptons is something you don't screw around with, Philip,' I barked.

'Okay, calm down. Why don't we go eat?' Philip said.

'Good idea,' I agreed. 'Let's get out of here.'

We joined the line for the buffet, which was next to the pool. Children were splashing and screaming. The adults were eating at tables dressed by Versace to promote their new couture houseware line. A reggae band was play-ing Bob Marley songs, making for a Caribbean party–like atmosphere. It was more like a poolside buffet at the Jamaican Ritz Carlton than an open house.

'Try the lobster salad,' I told Philip. 'I hear it's amazing.'

'Hey, I know you.'

I looked up. Pimple Boy was filling his plate with greasy foods he had no business eating.

'You're the two we saw on the beach the other night. *Mom, Dad, there they are!* The people I told you about. The naked grown-ups.' *Thank you, Pimple Boy, for broad-casting that little factoid to the entire brunch line. Perhaps you'd like to borrow the band's microphone and tell everyone around the pool.*

'You must be mixing us up with someone else,' Philip said quietly.

'No, it was you,' Pimple Boy accused. He pulled out his cell phone, punched a few buttons, and as quick as you can say 'Clem Kadiddlehopper,' there we were, naked on the beach. It was the first time I'd ever seen a nude picture of myself. Who-o-oah! Thanks to my workouts, I looked pretty darn good. I wondered if there was any way I could get a print. 'See!' The kid held the photo up for everyone's viewing pleasure. 'See! See! See! Told ya!' he said.

Philip reached over and snatched the phone out of his hand. Then he hurled it into the swimming pool, thereby destroying the only good naked picture of me that would probably ever be taken.

'Hey, whadja do *that* for?' Pimple Boy whined. '*Mo-om!*'

'That was an expensive phone,' his mother huffed. 'I hope you're planning to pay for it.'

'Hey, you show naked pictures of strangers standing next to you in line, you deserve what you get,' Philip said.

∾

The week after Labor Day was complicated. I was ecstatic over my budding relationship with Philip. At the same time, my heart was aching over the alligator tragedy. It took way too long to fall asleep, and when I did, my dreams were violent and disturbing. I always awakened with a vague feeling that something dreadful had happened. Then I'd remember. I couldn't stop thinking about getting fired. If not for that, I would have been on that sinking ship during Myoki's ridiculous off-site.

Having been given a second chance at life, I resolved to get it right this time. Never again would I stay in a stale relationship, have fake friendly conversations with people I hated, or work at a job I detested. I vowed to ignore everyone else's expectations, listen to my heart, and do whatever interested *me* from now on. I would no longer bother with shallow concerns like how fat I looked, how deep my frown line had become, or how pathetic it was to buy knock-off designer purses. *So what. Who cares? Not me. I'm deeper than that now.* Regretting the time I'd wasted on plastic values, I pledged to focus on what mattered – being an accomplished mother, working out for my heart and not my figure, eating fresh vegetables and not frozen, living every moment mindfully, and dedicating myself to important causes like peace and world hunger.

I swore that from then on, my life's litmus test would be 'What would Mother Teresa do?' A few weeks later, I changed that to 'What would Ivana Trump do?' It sounds strange, but it made sense. Ivana's a beautiful, tough woman who is first and foremost a good mother. She came from nothing and married a billionaire. Later, she confronted his lover, just like I did Cad's. Then she had head-to-toe plastic surgery and became even more beautiful. Mother Teresa may be a saint, but Ivana's a god.

7. Extreme Makeover

On Friday, I took Veronica for her day of beauty at the Kiddie Cuts Salon and Spa to reward her for learning the answers to the admissions test, which I had taught her against my better judgment. Patsy joined us and was more relaxed and talkative than I'd ever seen her. After lightly perming Veronica's hair, one of their most renowned stylists gave her a chin-length bob that flattered her face. Later that day, celebrity eyebrow sculptor Pablo DiSorrento spent an unprecedented two hours on her unibrow, charging us double. With that and a simple mustache waxing, you could finally see her little face, which was surprisingly angelic. Even with her chubbiness, Veronica was ready to compete for a spot at any private school. After buying a slimming black linen interview suit with matching patent leather shoes and lacy party socks at Saks, Veronica announced that the perfect end to the day would be a stop at McDonald's for a Big Mac and Serendipity for a frrrozen hot chocolate.

'Patsy, does Veronica eat at McDonald's very often?' I asked as we nursed our frrrozen hot chocolates.

'Well, she gets at least one meal there a day, sometimes

two,' Patsy answered. 'Either McDonald's or Wendy's. We alternate.'

'How about dessert? Does she go to Serendipity every day?'

'I know what you're getting at, Ivy. Veronica's a bit heavy, right?'

'Yeah, she is. I don't think it's healthy for her to be at this weight.'

'It doesn't help that she dips her food in Coke,' Patsy lamented.

'What?'

'She dips everything in Coke before she eats it – eggs, cherries, crackers, McDonald's french fries, whatever.'

'Could you substitute Diet Coke?' I suggested.

'I'll try. You don't think the artificial sugar's bad for her?'

'It's not good. What about vegetable juice? Could you substitute that for Coke?'

'No, don't think so. Veronica prides herself on the fact that nothing green has ever passed her lips.'

'Hmmm. Does she exercise much?'

'She competes in those iron-kiddie races, but she never trains for them. Other than dance, all the classes she takes are pretty cerebral.'

Cerebral? Pinheads don't use words like 'cerebral.' What was Stu talking about? Patsy was plenty smart.

'Oops,' Veronica said, as she spilled her drink all over the table. A waitress instantly appeared, cleaning up the mess. 'Don't worry,' she whispered to Veronica, 'I'll get you another.'

'Patsy, I think you need to get Veronica on some kind of low-key diet-and-exercise program. In kindergarten, children probably won't make fun of her, but as she gets older, they will. I was chubby, and my classmates gave me a hard time about it. God forbid Veronica gets teased at school.'

'You're right. I've always felt guilty that she's so big. I'm a terrible cook, so I take the easy way out, which is fast food. I'm such a bad mother, so incompetent,' she lamented. I figured that was Stu talking.

'No, you're not. Look, I'll help you put a program together for Veronica. I'll stop by on Monday and we'll come up with some meal plans, find a few quick recipes, and make a shopping list. We can check out the *Big Apple Parent* for some athletic programs Veronica can join.' I would never have imagined that this new career of mine would involve days of beauty, clothes shopping, nutrition, exercise, and psychological counseling. I marveled at my dedication and wondered if the *Wall Street Journal* might like to do a profile on me. *Mental note: get a publicity still and media kit as soon as possible.*

Surviving Private Kindergarten Admissions was coming up next week. I figured I'd have twenty-five to thirty parents. In fact, thirty people enrolled and I turned another thirty away. If it went well, I'd definitely schedule another one. The weekend would be spent preparing for the class. Speaking in public always made me a nervous wreck.

8. Ivy the Brave

My luck, New York City braced itself for a hurricane on the day of my workshop. Earlier in the week, we'd been watching the weather reports, not taking seriously the possibility that Hurricane Hannah would venture this far north. The last time the city had been hit with such a storm was September 27, 1990, when Hurricane Bob struck. I remember because that was the day I got married. People tried to tell me it was the best possible luck to have a hurricane on your wedding day, but I knew better. The electricity had gone out just after Oscar Beauman, stylist to the socialites, washed my hair. Without power and light, there could be no blow-dry on the most important hair day of my life. Half the guests didn't show. The rabbi married us by candlelight, which actually turned out okay. There was no band, no dancing, no dinner, and a melted cake. To this day, I wonder if our wedding debacle was God's way of telling us he objected to the union.

Even though Hurricane Hannah was headed our way, weather reports indicated that the storm would blow out of the city well in advance of my workshop. It didn't. By the time I decided to cancel, most of New York had lost power, cell phones weren't working, and it was impossible to reach anyone. We were told to stay indoors and tape big X's on our windows with masking tape. That seemed dumb. Would masking tape really protect a window in 100-mile-per-hour winds? But Archie came over and did it for me, just in case. That's just one of the benefits of living downstairs from the Naked Carpenter.

'Do you think anyone'll come to my workshop?' I asked Philip.

'No, of course not.'

'You're probably right, but I want to put up a sign saying it's cancelled.'

'Are you crazy?' Philip asked. 'They're predicting gale-force winds. All kinds of debris'll be blowing around. It's too dangerous.'

'I have to put a sign up. I'm sure no one'll show, but if they do, I want them to think I'm professional.' I remembered Stu's rude accusation in Southampton two weeks ago.

'All right,' Philip said. 'I'll go with you. I can't believe anyone in his right mind would be outside tonight, but if it's important to you, let's do it.'

Archie came down to watch the girls, but Skyler was having none of it.

'Mommy, don't go. There's a hurricane. You're supposed to stay inside.'

'Honey, I'm just going to put a sign up to let my clients know there's no workshop. I'll be back soon.'

'What about me and Kate? What about Sir Elton?' she whined.

'Archie'll keep you safe. I'll be back as fast as I can.'

'I *hate* your stupid clients,' Skyler said.

I walked over to my daughter and gave her a hug. 'Skyler, I wouldn't leave if I didn't have to. We need my clients to pay the bills. They're depending on me to take care of them.'

'So are me and Kate,' she said sadly.

'Oh Lord, maybe I shouldn't leave,' I muttered.

Skyler sighed. 'Don't worry about me. I'll survive. God forbid I should hurt your career.'

Where did she learn that? I wondered. *Oh yes, from me.*

Archie called to Skyler to come to the other room. He and Kate were dancing to the music of his battery-powered radio. She ran off.

I agonized over leaving the children, but I felt had no choice. The moment Philip and I stepped outside, my umbrella turned inside out, broke apart, and flew away. I struggled to breathe in the torrential rain and raging wind.

'This is nuts,' Philip yelled. 'Let's go back.'

'No, I need to get a sign up. You go back, I'll be okay,' I screamed. My backpack was soaked, as was everything inside it, including the paper I'd brought for the sign. But I was determined. Philip didn't leave my side. His willingness to risk life and limb was a testament to his deep and abiding commitment to me, I decided.

'The subway's closed,' he shouted when we finally reached the train. A deck chair from someone's balcony blew by and almost clobbered me.

'Holy shit,' I shouted. This was beginning to feel like an exceptionally stupid idea on my part. We continued to push our way uptown, hugging the sides of buildings for stability. A police van drove alongside us and stopped.

'What are you doing outside?' the cop yelled. 'It's dangerous, take cover.'

'I'm trying to get to my mother on Eighty-seventh and Lex, officer,' I screamed. 'She's old and afraid to be alone.'

The cop motioned for us to get in the van and said he'd drive us. Thank the Lord. I was soaked and exhausted by then. I'm not sure I would've made it to 87th Street on foot.

When Philip and I arrived at the church where the workshop was to be held, we were astonished. Sitting patiently on those ass-numbing folding chairs that can be found in every church basement across America were thirty wet and disheveled parents, ready to master the intricacies of private-school admissions.

I introduced myself to the group and announced that class was cancelled. 'Come back next week, same time, same place, and we'll do it then.'

'Wait,' one father said. 'We went through hell to get here in this storm. Look at us. We're drenched. We're exhausted. But we're here. Please don't cancel. We *need* the information you were gonna give us. If we don't get our Trinity and Horace Mann applications in, we'll be shut out. I have to insist that you do the workshop tonight like you promised. You took our money. Now give us the class.' The other parents nodded their heads yes emphatically. I wondered if they were about to turn into an angry mob.

'Are you people out of your minds? We're in the middle of a hurricane. You abandoned your children, risked your lives. For what? For a class about getting kids into private schools! Get some perspective, man,' Philip said. God, he was sexy when he took charge.

The dad leading the group seemed unsure of what to do next. A small woman who resembled a wet Siamese cat tried to negotiate a compromise. 'Prease,' she said. 'We're here. It's too dangerous to go outside now. Why don't you teach as much of the workshop as you can? Someone can watch the weather and when the eye of the storm passes over and it's safe to go out, you can stop. That way, we can get started on our apprications. We can reconvene next week to finish – what do you say?' She curled her lower lip down, tilted her head, and made the universal sad-puppy-dog *mmm-mmm-mmm* whimper. I looked around at the other parents, who sported similar needy expressions and also made pathetic sound effects.

Ooooh, this was dramatic. It was up to me to save the day. I glanced at Philip, who rolled his eyes skyward. How could he possibly understand how important this was to these parents? How abandoned they'd feel if I let them down? 'Okay,' I said courageously. 'I'll *do* it.' I'd never experienced such a natural high. For the first time, I was helping people in need, and it felt good. I made a note to myself to think about becoming a volunteer firewoman as soon as I lost more weight and got into fighting shape. As the deadly winds blew outside, I bravely lectured on, telling these devoted mothers and fathers how to write killer application essays. Philip watched the weather and reported back to the class when the eye of the storm passed over. All the parents except two hustled home before the next surge of wind and rain began, buoyed by my pledge to return next week and guide them through the rest of the admissions process.

A pasty old gazillionaire approached me after everyone had left. How did I know he was loaded? One need only look at his trophy wife, who was decked out in vintage Chanel and Manolo Blahniks and carrying one of those wait-listed black Hermès crocodile bags. I saw one on eBay recently for $27,000, not that I was looking. You'd definitely have to be rich to wear designer in a hurricane.

'Before we go, would you mind taking a look at our son's ERB scores?' the man asked.

Philip appeared anxious to leave, but I agreed to take a quick peek. They both seemed nervous. The moment I saw the boy's results, I understood why. In every category of the test, the kid had scored below 50 percent.

'We're raising a moron, aren't we,' the man said sadly.

'No, don't be ridiculous. Fifty percent is average. Lots of kids don't test well. That doesn't mean they won't be successful in life,' I explained. 'Don't you dare look at your son any differently because of this. I'm sure he's a terrific child.'

'But is he terrific enough to get into Harvard Day or Horace Mann?' the woman asked. 'Would they take him with these scores?'

'It's unlikely, I'm afraid.'

Tears dripped down the woman's cheeks and she began beating her husband's chest. 'Why? Why did this happen, Sidney? What's *wrong* with Ethan? Is this our fault? Call somebody. Pay someone off. How are you going to fix this, Sidney? How, how?' Sidney just stood there, numb. It was all very theatrical.

'I'm sorry,' I said, handing him my card. 'If you'll call me, I'll give you more advice, maybe suggest some alternative schools to apply to. But for now, I think we'd better get out of here before the weather changes.'

'Can we give you a ride?' Sidney offered.

'That would be great,' I said. 'Would you drop us at Philip's house downtown?' I had an image to protect, so I couldn't reveal that I lived there too.

Thanks to Sidney and his Chanel wife, we were chauffeured home in a Bentley. I took that as a sign of good fortune ahead. Not for Ethan, who was doomed to disappoint his parents, but for us.

9. The Plot Thickens

By October, Lilith Radmore-Stein was a woman obsessed. She was convinced that influence would be the key to Ransom's acceptance at Stratmore Prep, the only school she really wanted.

Lilith hired Intelligent Choice, a jury consulting company, to investigate and analyze each trustee on Stratmore Prep's board. They would recommend whom she should attempt to sway and how best to prevail upon them. We met at Lilith's antique marble table with the Louis XVI chairs in her office conference room. Johnny was absent, supposedly playing polo in Argentina. As we assembled, Lilith lavished her attention on Mrs. Butterworth, her Yorkie. As the little yapper dog licked her face, Lilith kissed back. 'She's such a sweet puppy, aren't you, Baby Butterworth, aren't you? You're Mommy's little girl, aren't you? Yes you are, yes you *are*. Yessssssss!' It was nice to see that Lilith had a nurturing side.

Once everyone was seated, Lilith asked, 'Ivy, how many spaces will Stratmore Prep have for white non-siblings, non-legacies this year?'

'Gosh, Lilith. I don't know. Schools never release that information ahead of time.'

'Ivy, Lilith Radmore-Stein does not understand the meaning of the words "I don't know." *I want answers,*' she said evenly. 'Call whomever you need to – the mayor's office, the Parents' League, the school itself. Are you up to the job for which I hired you? If so, then get me the fuckin' answer to my goddamn question. Have I made myself clear?' For a Fortune 100 CEO, Lilith had a real potty mouth.

'Yes, you're being clear. I'll get you the answer right away,' I said calmly. *Shit, I guess I'm supposed to know inside stuff like that,* I thought. *I'll e-mail Tipper tonight. Maybe she'll call Stratmore Prep and get me the answer. I hate looking dumb in front of clients.*

Lilith introduced Mort Small-Podd, the president of Intelligent Choice. Mort dove into his PowerPoint presentation, analyzing each Stratmore Prep director while highlighting any professional or personal hot buttons in intimate detail. The consultant suggested the most valuable favor Lilith might bestow on each board member, with the help of *her* powerful connections, to ensure their full endorsement of Ransom Radmore-Stein's acceptance:

Board Member	Favor
James Fritz	make his mistress disappear
Eric Redd	arrange a job with Dreamworks for his son
Biff Hyatt	find bone-marrow donor match for his mother
Buzz Wendell	gain FDA approval of his company's over-the-counter botulinum toxin type-A home injection kit

Murray Miller	Secure the Town of East Hampton's approval for his proposed backyard heliport
Arthur Quinn	Eliminate his rival, George Maisel, from consideration for the chairmanship of American National Foods
Frederick Thomas	Secure hair-replacement therapy for him that isn't obvious
Skippy White	Stop hostile takeover of his company, White Star
Cornie Nielson	Get attorney general to drop indictment on charges of tax evasion

Mr. Small-Podd followed up with a series of diagrams blueprinting what Lilith needed to do to put herself in a position to bestow each of these favors. For example, to get the attorney general to drop the tax-evasion indictment against Cornie Nielson, she might threaten to run a story in one of her newspapers exposing the affair the attorney general recently broke off with his son's sixteen-year-old girlfriend. Mr. Small-Podd emphasized that Lilith needed only one board member in her pocket, as the others would rubber-stamp his recommendation and the director of admissions would comply.

'What do you think, Ivy?' Lilith asked, scratching Mrs. Butterworth's head.

I think I'm in waaaaaaay over my head. That's what I think. I want to speak to my attorney.

'You knoooow,' I said slowly . . .

Think. Think. Think. I think this could be against the law.

'I believe Ransom will test off the charts on the ERB,' I began. 'He's acing all the practice tests I'm giving him, and his improvement on symbols and pattern blocks is nothing short of miraculous. You and Johnny will interview beautifully, of course, as will Ransom. It seems to me that you could rely on the old-fashioned but effective promise of a large donation and call it a day.'

'Given that approach, Ivy, what chance does Ransom have of being admitted – one hundred percent?'

'The only person in New York City who ever had a hundred-percent chance of getting her children into private school was Caroline Kennedy.' It went without saying that Lilith was no Caroline Kennedy. 'I'd estimate his chances at eighty to eighty-five percent with the traditional approach that I suggest. But those are the same odds that any major player has under the best of circumstances.'

Lilith smiled, showing as much gum as teeth. I wondered if a cosmetic dentist could fix that problem. 'Oh, but you see, I want better,' she said calmly.

'Lilith, influencing Stratmore's trustees in the way that's being recommended here is risky,' I said. 'It's one thing for board members to accept donations on behalf of the school, but these are all personal favors you're talking about. Some people might call them bribes.'

Lilith looked at me like I'd just fallen off a watermelon truck.

Lilith turned to Mort. 'Mr. Small-Podd, if I follow your approach, what is the percentage chance that Ransom will get in?'

'One hundred percent, Lilith. I guarantee that if you

follow my advice, Ransom will be wearing the Stratmore Prep blue blazer next year,' he said.

'Fine.' Lilith smiled. 'Ivy,' she continued, 'you advise us on Ransom's tests, the essays, and interviews. I will rely on Mr. Small-Podd to guide us through the influencing phase of this project.' With that, she stood up and left, leaving me and Mort Small-Podd alone in her *très* elegant conference room.

Oh, so we're a team, are we? Just like Johnnie Cochran and Robert Shapiro.

'Ivy, it's going to be wonderful working with you,' Mr. Small-Podd gushed. 'I hope you'll consider bringing me in to consult with *all* your other clients.'

'Let's see how this case goes, Mort. I'll *absolutely* consider it.' *Over my dead body,* I thought to myself.

10. Cabby with a Heart of Gold

fter the meeting with Lilith, I grabbed a cab and made a mad dash to the public library. I needed to research whether or not I could go to jail for what Lilith was about to do. In the old days, I would have consulted a lawyer. Today, that was a luxury I couldn't afford.

'Forty-second and Fifth, please.' As we headed downtown, I realized that I'd left my Barneys shopping bag in Lilith's conference room. Damn. 'Sir, I forgot something at the building I just came from. Do you mind circling back and waiting for me while I run in to get it? You can leave your meter running.'

'No problem,' the cabby said. He was a large Indian man with a kind face.

When I got back into the taxi, the driver said, 'You should always make lists so you don't forget. That's what I do. I can't remember anything. See, here's my list.' He held it up for me to see:

- ABC
- IRS

- Milk
- Plane ticket
- Call Sanjeev

'Do you have to go to ABC Carpet?' I asked, sticking my nose where it didn't belong, as usual.

'No, I have to call ABC News. They are making a documentary of my life.'

Get out of town! A documentary of a cabby's life. Will wonders never cease? 'What's so special about your life that they're making a documentary?'

'Well, miss, I've been driving a cab in Manhattan for twenty years. All that time, I saved my tips, scrimped on dinners, movies, and clothing for my family. Working fifteen-hour days I saved enough to open a school for girls in the Indian village where I grew up, Doobher Kishanpur. In my village, many girls were illiterate. Not anymore. Now they have their own school. It's named after my mother, Ram Kali, who never learned to read or write. In New York City, I am a hardworking but poor immigrant. In Doobher Kishanpur, I am a philanthropist,' he said proudly. 'And ABC News is going to make a documentary about this.'

'Wow. That's incredible. That must have cost you a fortune, opening a school.'

'Money buys much more in India than in New York. I send twenty-five hundred dollars a year to the school. That pays for five teachers, the school building, books, uniforms, supplies. Right now, we have one hundred and eighty little girls, but we're expanding to open a high school for five hundred.'

'How do you decide who gets to go there? Do the girls

apply?' I wondered if there were any similarities between the application process for girls' schools in India and those in New York City.

'If a parent brings a girl to our school, we will take her. If she wants to learn, we will teach her. Our school is simple. The students sit on the floor and write on small chalkboards.'

'That's really incredible, Mr. . . .'

'Sharma, Om Dutta Sharma. We have a foundation now, and others contribute. When I'm ready to retire, I'm going to sell my taxi medallion and give the money to the school. In America, it's all about getting for yourself. But it's more important to give to others, don't you agree?'

'Yes, I do. I'd like to give you some money,' I said. 'I don't have a lot on me today, but here's forty dollars.'

'That is very generous of you. That will pay a teacher's salary for a month,' Mr. Sharma said appreciatively. 'God bless you. Oh, and be sure to watch the *Today* show next week. They are doing a segment on me also.'

When Mr. Sharma dropped me at the library, I asked for his card so I could send more money for his school. As I live and breathe, I never would have expected to meet such a saintly man driving a New York City cab. *He must be a highly evolved soul,* I thought. *Way higher than me.*

৩৩

I was in the library, surrounded by legal texts that I could make neither heads nor tails of, when my cell phone rang.

'Hello,' I said.

'Is this Ivy Ames, school-admissions adviser?' the voice on the other end asked.

'Why, yes it is, how can I help you?'

'Ms. Ames, there's a gentleman who wants to speak with you. He's waiting outside the library in a Rolls-Royce.'

'Who is this?' I demanded as the speaker hung up.

11. A Tempting Offer

Who knew I was going to be at the library? Was someone following me? Could this have to do with Omar Kutcher? I *knew* I shouldn't have taken on a mobster client. Was I tied to the family forever? Would he kill me if I tried to leave? *Naaaah. You are being so overly dramatic,* I told myself. At this point, curiosity got the best of me, so I gathered up my papers and Barneys bag and went outside.

There was the car. A beautiful Rolls-Royce Silver Cloud. The windows were blacked out, so I couldn't see inside. An elegantly uniformed chauffeur, who obviously doubled as a bodyguard, opened the back door for me. I hesitated. I wasn't keen on walking through the valley of the shadow of death just yet.

A handsome, well-dressed gentleman stuck his head out and told me to get into the car. 'I won't bite you,' he said. *Well, if you won't bite me, then by all means I'll jump right in.*

'Who are you?' I demanded, not moving a muscle.

'I'm Buck McCall,' the man answered. 'Moses McCall's grandfather.'

'Oh, why didn't you say so?' I said as I got in.

The driver returned to the car and electronically locked all the doors. He made no attempt to turn on the motor, so I assumed we'd be meeting in the locked Rolls. This was rather exciting, I must say.

'Ms. Ames,' he began. 'You're helping my son and his wife get Moses into school, are you not?'

I had promised Dee Dee that our relationship would be confidential. I wasn't quite sure how to answer that.

'What makes you think I'm helping them?'

'Greg told me. He also showed me the essay your boyfriend wrote about Moses. Nice,' Buck said.

How could he know Philip wrote that? Is my house bugged? Does Buck McCall employ Mort Small-Podd?

'Ms. Ames,' Buck continued. 'I know that my son and daughter-in-law want Moses in a Jewish school. If he goes to a Jewish school, my wife, who is already heartsick over their marriage, will lose her will to live. It's hard enough on us that they're raising him to be a Jew, but sending him to one of those schools where he'll wear a yarmulke, speak Hebrew, and grow those girly ringlets . . . well, I can't let that happen.'

'But Dee Dee is determined, and Greg wants whatever Dee Dee wants.'

'My son is a pussy, Ms. Ames. But I'm not.'

Uh, yeah. That was coming through loud and clear. 'Why don't you try talking to Greg, Mr. McCall? I'm sure he respects you. Tell him how you feel.'

'No, Greg doesn't listen to me or his mother. Whatever the wife wants, Greg wants. It means nothing to him that it's *our* blood running through the child's veins. We've tried, but we can't get our son to think like we do. So now

I'm asking for your help. I would like to hire you to convince my son and daughter-in-law not to send Moses to a Jewish program and to make sure that he gets into and goes to a top secular school.'

I sat there, stunned. My lower jaw hung open. *Oh, my God. He wants me to be a double agent.* I looked around the car. *I'm on* Candid Camera, *right?*

'I'm prepared to pay you well. I know you're a struggling single mother in the midst of a divorce. I have in my hand a check for one million dollars. The moment Greg enrolls Moses in a secular school, it will be deposited into your checking account. With a million dollars, you could send your daughters back to The Balmoral School, hire a tutor for Kate, pay for summer camp, move to a better neighborhood.'

Okay, now I'm creeped out. What else do you know about me? My bra size? The last movie I rented at Blockbuster? I'm sure I don't need to give you my checking-account number, because you know that, too. I may have cocked my head at this point. I remember that no words were exchanged.

'As a show of good faith, Ms. Ames, I've arranged for your daughters to resume their dance lessons at the Alvin Ailey School. Here's a letter confirming their enrollment. This is just a taste of the good things you'll be able to give your children if you help me with my modest request. This is my cell-phone number.' He handed me a card. 'If you need anything to make this happen, anything at all, call me. My resources are at your disposal.'

Without warning, the bodyguard-chauffeur opened the car door, causing me to jump in fright. That was my cue to exit stage right.

12. A Difference of Opinion

A million dollars just for steering Moses Epstein-McCall away from a Jewish school. *Could this be the miracle rescue I was praying for?* But it would be unethical. *Nobody would get hurt.* I'd be betraying people who trusted me. *I could retire.* Honor. *Bribery.* Integrity. *Betrayal.* This was the conversation between my conscience and me as we rode the bus home from the library. Mom was on one shoulder advising me to do the right thing; Dad was on the other telling me to take the cash. I wondered what Ivana Trump would do.

Once home, I ran a hot bath, adding bubbles and calming essential oils. With the lights out and two candles burning, I lay still in the tub, meditating, hoping the answer would reveal itself. It didn't. The water got cold. My fingers got wrinkly. I became bored and I dried off. Then I turned on Dr. Phil and made a deal with the universe. If the theme of today's show was ethics and morals, I would *not* take the million dollars. If it was about anything else, I would. Ha! Ha! The show was about women who had no self-respect. A sign from God that I should take the bribe, perhaps?

Later that evening, Philip interrupted my angst with a bottle of my favorite champagne, Veuve Clicquot.

'What's this?' I asked.

'It's my birthday,' he said with a smile.

'Oh, my God! Happy birthday, Philip. I wish I'd known. I'd have gotten you a card,' I said, as he popped the cork.

'Oooh, a card, you must really care for me.'

'I do. I'd have bought you an expensive present, too.' *Lie.* I couldn't afford it. But it's what I would have liked to do for him.

'Well, since you didn't get me anything, I have an idea.'

'What?'

'Do something special just for me,' he said, kissing me tenderly on the lips.

'Mmmm, that can be arranged,' I said.

We made out like teenagers for a few minutes, but when Philip started to unbutton my skirt, I stopped him. The girls were sleeping in the back. 'Let's have our champagne,' I said, trying to distract him. 'Tell me what you did for your birthday.'

Philip poured us each a glass. 'Cheers,' he said as we clinked our glasses and tasted the champagne. 'Well, I finished the first draft of my manuscript.'

'Congratulations. Does this mean you're ready to talk about the book?'

He hesitated, then spoke. 'It's still pretty rough. But I'll tell you a little. Okay,' he began, 'I'm writing a novel based on the life of Ariana Nabokov von Geltenburg Chopra Gross, a grande dame of high society who was a German spy during World War Two, and the mistress of Winston Churchill *and* Adolf Hitler.'

'Both men at the same time?'

'Yes. Her story has love, sex, murder, passion, ambition, betrayal, wealth – you can't make this stuff up.'

'Wow,' I said. 'But what about *me*?' I asked. 'Which character am I?' Not that I'm egocentric or anything, but he did say I'd be in the book.

'You're the main character.'

'Okay, now I'm really confused.'

'Let me explain,' Philip said. 'This book is *loosely* based on a real person, yes, but it'll be fictionalized. As I wrote, I pictured Ariana as you. Imagining you as my heroine inspired me to write what I hope will be a bestseller. I got the biggest advance of my career, and two studios are interested in the movie rights.'

'Shut-uuup!' I said. 'Would you do me a favor?'

'Anything.'

'Marry me. I *really* need to be rescued right now.' I told him about Lilith's crackpot scheme and Buck McCall's little bombshell.

Philip was silent for a moment. Then he spoke. 'Ivy, I'm a simple guy. I don't think I could be married to someone who leads such a complicated life.'

'It didn't used to be like this.' I sighed. 'What do you think I should do?'

'I don't know. What's more important to you? Self-respect or money? Hey, you just gave me an idea for my next book – an exposé of you and your crazy clients. We'll call it *Telling Tales Out of School*.'

'Ha!' I said, throwing a pillow at him. 'How about *Telling Tales Out of Prison*, because that's where I'll be when you write the book.'

'I'll visit you every month, I promise.' Philip laughed.

'I'm serious, Philip. I don't know what to do. That offer Buck McCall made is tempting. And truthfully, I think the secular schools *are* better than the Jewish ones. I'd be doing Greg and Dee Dee a favor if I swayed them the way Buck wants me to. No one would get hurt.'

'You're not actually thinking of taking it, are you?'

'Of course I'm *thinking* about it. I don't get million-dollar offers every day!'

'Ivy,' Philip said, 'look at yourself. Since you started this business, you've lied to those admissions directors, that dead psychologist's son, the press. You capitalized on Cubby's murder. Now, you're talking about buying off a trustee so some rich woman's sniveling brat can get into a chichi school. And you're considering selling out one of your favorite clients for a million dollars. What's next?'

'Oh, like you've never lied before,' I said.

'No, not the way *you're* doing it,' Philip said. 'It's becoming second nature to you, and it's not attractive.'

'Philip, this is business. It isn't real life. In the corporate world where I come from, *everyone* plays fast and loose with ethics. You're just not used to it because you're a writer. With school admissions, having a great kid isn't enough. You need *more*. Nobody follows the rules – not the schools, not the parents. If I don't get down in the mud with everyone else, I won't win . . . for my clients. I won't win for *them*.'

'Ivy, listen to yourself. Is this the kind of role model you want to be for your daughters?'

'Don't bring the girls into this. I'm considering this *because* I'm responsible for them. Their whole lives would change if I do this one favor for Buck McCall.'

'You mean if you take his bribe. Ivy, if being in this business means you have to become a fraud and a cheat to get what you want, then find something else to do. Lying doesn't suit you. And it doesn't suit me, either.'

'Philip, how can I make you understand? If I play it straight, I fail. These clients gave me their money. They're depending on me to get their kids into the best schools. I've come too far to back off. Please don't ask me to give it up. That's a sacrifice I can't make right now.'

'So I guess you'd rather give *me* up instead?' Philip asked.

'Of course I don't want to give you up, Philip. I want you *and* I want my business.' My voice barely broke a whisper.

Philip looked at me for a minute, then rose. He walked over to the window and stared outside. What was he thinking? A fire truck with its siren blaring raced by. Philip stood motionless for what felt like an eternity. 'I can't be with a person who's willing to live like that, Ivy, I'm sorry,' he said quietly. Then he walked out the door.

13. No Amount of Money . . .

*L*ilith called for an ERB dress rehearsal so she could see the results of my tutoring. As a former businessperson, I understood that it was *only* results that mattered. Unfortunately, I'd be depending on a four-year-old to demonstrate the quality of my work.

We met in the conference room on Lilith's converted Boeing 727. It had four bathrooms, each with 24-carat-gold fixtures, a steam shower, and a bidet. There were two bedrooms, a playroom, an office, and a conference room. She and the family were jetting to California to visit her West Coast presses, so the six hours over would give Ransom ample opportunity to demonstrate his mastery of shapes, analogies, mental math, vocabulary, and comprehension. On arrival at some private airport in L.A., I'd be whisked to LAX to catch the red-eye back to New York. I couldn't imagine a more perfect day.

Before we got started, I gave Lilith the news that Tipper had uncovered on my behalf. Stratmore Prep had thirty places. This year, fifteen would go to siblings, seven to minorities, and eight to Caucasians. They expected four hundred applications for those eight spots. It would be easier to get into Harvard University than Stratmore Prep this year.

'I love a fight,' Lilith said. 'Don't I, Mrs. Butterworth? Does Mommy love a good fight? Yes she does, yes she does, Mommy *loves* a good fight,' she said, kissing her pup's face while Mrs. Butterworth licked her back enthusiastically.

'Well, top ERB scores are the first step on the road to victory,' I said. 'Ransom, let's show Mommy how smart you are.'

Laying out a four-piece frameless puzzle of a telephone, I asked him to put it together and tell me what it would make.

Ransom moved the pieces around slowly until he had made the telephone perfectly except for its cord and plug.

'Can you find where the plug goes, Ransom?'

'The p-p-plug goes in the trash, 'cuz if there's no plug, Mommy can't talk on the phone.'

'Let's try something besides puzzles,' I suggested quickly. 'Ransom, can you tell me how a magazine is like a newspaper?'

'Parents read 'em at breakfast when they don't wanna t-t-talk to each other,' he answered, sliding down in his chair.

Lilith listened with a stony expression on her face.

'How is a plane like a train?'

'They take mommies away from their little b-b-boys,' he ventured, now completely under the table.

I turned to Lilith and praised Ransom the best I could. 'It's impressive that he understands I'm looking for common categories here. Lots of children his age don't get that.'

'Ransom, I need you to get back into your seat,' I said.

He didn't move.

'Ransom, I can't hear your answers when you're under the table, you silly-willy,' I said in my cajoling sing-songy voice.

He didn't move.

'Ransom, if you don't get in your seat right now, I'll have to *tickle you*. I me-ean it.'

Ransom didn't move, so I climbed under the table and assumed tickle position with my fingers. That's all it took. Ransom scrambled up into his chair, giggling. That kid loves to torture me.

'Let's try vocabulary,' I suggested. 'Ransom, I'm going to show you a picture. You tell me everything you see.' I held up a picture of a woman reading to her son. She was so engrossed in her tale that she didn't notice that a pot was boiling over on the stove behind her.

'The mommy's reading the sock market instead of the book the boy wanted. When she's not looking, he's gonna pour hot w-w-water on her head and watch her d-d-die,' he said.

'His verbal skills are far above age level,' I explained to Lilith. 'Most kids only say the words "mother" or "child" or "book" when they see this picture, but Ransom is elaborating beautifully.'

'Ivy, I've seen enough. Marvys, take Ransom to watch a movie.' Lilith waved them out dismissively.

No, Ransom, please don't go, I thought. *Your mommy scares me.* But he and Marvys left as ordered.

'Ivy, what have you done to my son?'

'Excuse me?'

'His answers . . . they were so . . . so wrong.'

And your point, mother who gave birth to and hired the people who raise this child you ignore?

'Sometimes, Ransom gives me answers like the ones you just heard. But usually his responses are less' – *what's the right word for it?* – 'emotionally charged.'

Lilith shot me a searing look. 'Ivy,' she said, 'I trusted you with my angel. And today you brought me, I don't know, who *is* this child I just saw? What did you do with my son? This is not my baby. My baby is smarter than this . . . this dunce who missed *every* answer.'

Oh, I get it, you're disturbed about his mistakes, not the possibility that he might follow through on his latent desire to murder you. But I held my tongue. She was a client, after all. I decided to ask the question that had been on my mind. 'Lilith, is Ransom in speech therapy?'

'Heavens, no.'

'Haven't you noticed his stutter?'

'Of course I have. What kind of mother do you think I am? But I would never put him in speech therapy. They'd write about it in his nursery-school report. Then Stratmore Prep would reject him.'

'I think the schools are going to notice that he stutters when he goes for interviews.'

'You know, Ivy, I don't remember asking you about his speech. I remember asking you why he got so many questions wrong.'

'Yes. Right. Well, *of course* Ransom knows more than you saw today. He was showing off. That's common with children who don't spend much time with their parents. I assure you, Ransom will perform in the top five percent when he's tested. He is one of the smartest children I've ever worked with,' I lied.

'You'd better be right.' Lilith smiled as menacingly as a person with extreme gums can. 'If Ransom doesn't score high enough for Stratmore Prep, I'll make it my business to get *your* children kicked out of whatever fancy program they're in so you can see what it's like having *your* babies in a second-rate school.'

Okay, now she's threatening the kids. Thaaaat's it. *Not gonna take it.* 'Lilith,' I said evenly, 'if you're trying to scare me, you'll have to do better than that. My children are already in a second-rate school and I like it just fine. Help me here, Lilith. How is it *possible* that you don't see your son is crying out for attention? Why'd you bother to give birth to Ransom if you can't pencil him in for ten minutes a day? You give that mutt more love than you give your son, for God's sake.'

Oops. Lilith's face turned bright red. Her eyes bulged and I swear I saw blood vessels popping.

'MRS. BUTTERWORTH. IS. NOT. A. MUTT. I should fire you for saying that. But I won't, because it's too late to replace you. You make sure that Ransom aces his ERB. That's why I hired you.' With that, she turned and marched out, leaving me alone in her flying conference room wondering why anyone would need four bidets on her private jet. Sadly, the mystery would remain unsolved because next thing I knew, the plane was descending for an unscheduled stop in Minneapolis. There, I was unceremoniously ditched, sent home in a commercial jet that didn't have even one bidet.

14. I See Dead People

As fall progressed, my clients' children took their admissions tests. The top nursery schools brought in the best testers so kids could be evaluated in a familiar, comfortable environment on a day when they were healthy and in a good mood. The rest of the city's children had to go to the sterile ERB offices to be seen by whichever psychologist was available on whatever day they could get an appointment. There, little ones were known to become hysterical when asked to go with testers because they thought they'd be getting a shot. Except for Irving, all my kids went to nurseries that gave the ERB on-site.

Faith called to see how I was holding up after Philip dumped me.

'I'm hangin' in. It's tough. I miss him.'

'I'm sure. Have you seen him at all?'

'No, we're avoiding each other. And Michael barely speaks to me, either. Remind me *never* to get involved with anyone who lives in my building.'

'Well, I have something to cheer you up. Are you busy this afternoon, say about one?'

'No, why?'

'One of Steven's entertainment pals, Les Moonves, gave me two tickets to go to a taping of John Edward's *Crossing Over* show.'

'The guy who talks to dead people?'

'No, the guy who reunites people in the physical world with those who have crossed over.'

'Yeah, I've seen the show. And you think listening to people talk to their dead relatives will cheer me up why?'

'Hey, just being with me will make you feel better.'

'You're right about that,' I conceded. 'But you don't really believe he's talking to spirits, do you?'

'I'm not sure,' Faith said. 'But if it's real, maybe you'll get a message from your mom. And if it's bogus, we'll still have fun.'

'All right, I'm in,' I said. 'It'll be an adventure.'

Later that day, Faith and I were sitting front-row center (the VIP seats, of course) at a West Side sound stage watching John Edward commune with the other side. First, he did a private reading with a soap-opera star I'd never heard of. Her mother, aunt, and the unborn child she miscarried all came through. She appeared to believe everything they were saying, but she's a professional, so it could have been a performance.

Next, John came out to the gallery to do readings. That's what he calls the studio. My stomach turned somersaults when he looked into the audience. *C'mon Mom. C'mon. C'mon. If you're out there, make yourself known.* But he skipped right over me and went for a gay couple in the back who'd lost their adopted teenage son to AIDS. It was so sad. The entire audience was sobbing and honking as they blew their noses.

After the commercial break, he pointed to the area where Faith and I were sitting. 'I think I'm over here,' he said.

'I see a male figure to the side who recently passed. That would have to be a husband, brother, or friend. He passed on the eighth of the month or in the eighth month, but eight is a significant number to him. Does this make sense to anyone?' John asked.

We looked at each other and shrugged.

'I'm definitely over here,' he said, indicating with his hands the area around where we were seated.

'He's telling me that he paid a visit to this person after he passed and the person saw him. He wants this person to know that it *was* him; they weren't hallucinating,' John added. My eyes widened, but I didn't raise my hand. Surely it can't be . . .

'He's making me feel like I need to bring up *Sesame Street*. He's showing me Big Bird from *Sesame Street*. Is "Big Bird" or "Bird" significant to anyone?'

My stomach did a triple flip off the high dive. Slowly I raised my hand.

'Does this make sense to you?' John asked.

'Yes, it does,' I said.

'I'm definitely with you,' John stated.

Even in death, Drayton Bird was torturing me. *What is it with him*, I wondered. We detested each other in life. *If Faith arranged this as a joke, I'm gonna kill her.*

'This man passed from a drowning. But he's making me feel like there was more to it. I'm seeing blood. Does this make sense?'

'Yes,' I said. To my surprise, tears began to pour down my face. Faith shoved a Kleenex into my hand.

'He says you think his passing was painful, but it wasn't.

It happened quickly,' John said. 'He's telling me that the two of you didn't get along in life and he wants to acknowledge that it was his fault.'

'Yes,' I said, nodding my head, still weeping.

'Oh, really, I see, wow, whoa.' John was looking at someone right over me who wasn't actually there. Apparently, they were having a psychic conversation.

'I'm not sure if I understand this, but let me repeat what he said,' John remarked, looking at me again. 'He's saying he betrayed you in life, but you should thank him, because his betrayal *saved your life?* Does that make sense?'

'Yes,' I said, putting my head in my hands and bawling like an inconsolable child. Isn't it just my luck to appear on TV having a big fat cry?

'He says that the two of you had a major, and I mean a MAJOR karmic connection. According to him, you died to save him in a past life, and his mission, or purpose if you will, in *this* lifetime was to return the favor. Now that divine balance has been achieved, he can move on.'

I looked up at John. 'Do you mean to tell me that that double-crossing, sanctimonious, lying, insincere, hypocritical traitor was really my cosmic *friend?* He picked a *fine* way of showing it.'

Oh, dear God. Did I just say that out loud?

John and the audience were laughing. 'Did I ask you for an opinion?' John said. 'But thank you for sharing.'

I had this horrible vision of Sassy and her children flipping through the channels and stopping on this show just as I said those terrible things about Drayton.

John switched gears. 'He says there's someone with a "B" connected to him. "Bee Bee," "Beatrice . . ."'

'Bea, that's his daughter.'

'Who's the "S" name?' John asked.

'That would be Sassy, his wife.'

'He wants you to let Sassy know he's okay. He says it's important that you tell her about his visit today. He's asking if you'll keep an eye on her and help her because she doesn't have your strength.'

'Okay,' I said, nodding.

'He's laughing about the last time you saw him. He says he overheard you reveal a secret that he wasn't supposed to know. He's razzing you from the other side,' John teased with a smile.

'Oh, my God,' I said. '*He knew?*'

'Do you care to enlighten the rest of us?' John asked.

'No, not on national TV,' I said. Everyone laughed.

'He's saying that he's not the person you wanted to hear from today and he hopes you won't hate him for grabbing the spotlight and stealing time that was meant for someone else,' John added. 'He's saying that by telling you *this*, you'll have confirmation it's really him because that's the kind of man he was in life.'

Yes, he often took what didn't belong to him, the jerk, I thought but didn't say. Then I apologized profusely in my mind to him for thinking such a mean thing. He was, after all, dead.

15. What About Me-ee?

My business phone rang. It was that mini-mogul, Stu Needleman. Ever since he learned I was Steven Lord's friend, he'd become nice to me in that phony you're-friends-with-someone-important kind of way. Now, he only threatened to ruin me about half as often as he used to. Stu calls at least three times a day to obsess over some aspect of his school search, sometimes more. I just tune him out, say uh-huh a lot, and ponder universal questions like electrolysis vs. waxing, Japanese hair-straightening vs. orange-juice cans, that sort of thing.

'Ivy, I've just heard something very disturbing,' he said ominously.

'What did you hear, Stu?'

'I can't believe it's true,' he added, clearly saddened by the news. I thought he might cry.

'What? Tell me,' I asked again. I couldn't imagine what this was about.

'I heard that *you*, my private-school-admissions adviser, send your own children to *public school*. Is it *true*?' he demanded.

'Mommy, Mommy, Kate won't get out of the bathroom and I need to use it,' Skyler said, interrupting my conversation.

'Not now,' I said firmly to Skyler.

'Oh, they aren't there now?' Stu said.

'No, they are,' I said to Stu.

'But Mommy, it's an emergency. I got my period,' Skyler insisted.

I held my hand up to shush her.

'How can you advise me on private schools when *you've* chosen public? And *why* in God's name would you send your children to public school?'

Did Skyler just say she got her period? 'Stu, I made a different decision for my own daughters. That doesn't mean I'm not qualified to help you.'

'*But why?*' he asked, in a state of profound disbelief that anyone he knew other than his maid or garbageman would willingly send her children to public school.

Because my husband had an affair and we broke up. Because I lost my job and had to eliminate every luxury in my life except rent and food. Because by starting a business to help parents get their children into private schools, I no longer make enough money to afford it for my own kids. There, are you satisfied?

What I really said was, 'I chose public because it was the right decision for my children and my family. Just like I'm going to help you find the right place for Veronica.'

'Mooo-ooom!' Skyler yelled. 'I need you no-o-ow.'

'I hope you're not going to suggest public school to me, Ivy,' he said, 'because if you did, I would fire you on the spot, you know that?'

'Stu, how many times have you fired me already? Three? Four? This was the right choice for *me*. I know it's not the right choice for you.'

'Fine,' he said. 'As long as we've got that straight.' As usual he hung up without saying goodbye.

I sat for a moment, eyes closed, massaging my neck, listening to Skyler pound on the bathroom door where Kate had locked herself in. 'Kate, let me in right now, you monkey turd,' Skyler screamed.

'I know you are, but what am I?' the little voice behind the door answered.

'I mean it, you twerp,' Skyler yelled.

'I know you are, but what am I?' the voice replied.

A suspicious silence followed. I opened my eyes and peeked around the corner. Skyler was outside the bathroom door holding *Harry Potter and the Order of the Phoenix* over her head in clobber position. 'Oh, Ka-ate, come ou-out. I have a sur-PRISE for you.'

'*ARE YOU CRAZY!*' I leapt from my chair like my ass was on fire and grabbed the makeshift weapon. '*What were you thinking? Don't ever do that again. Have I made myself clear?*' Skyler nodded her head and stormed into the living room. People say that fighting between siblings is normal, but sometimes I wonder. Hitting, biting, scratching, kicking, and screaming seem normal. Whacking your sister on the head with an 870-page hardcover book seems excessive. Or is it just me?

I followed Skyler into the living room. She was sitting on the couch next to Sir Elton, flipping angrily through *Teen People*. 'Did you really get your period?'

'Like you care, Mom.'

'Well, did you?'

'No, but I wanted to talk to you and I knew *that* wasn't enough to get your attention.'

'Skyler, how many times do I have to tell you not to interrupt me when I'm on the phone with a client?'

'Mommy, you care more about your clients than you do about us. You only pay attention to them.'

I pushed Sir Elton off the couch and sat down next to her. 'You've got that wrong, sweetheart. Come here,' I said, pulling Skyler into my lap. 'I care more about you and Kate than anyone else in the world. It's just that I have to work for my clients when they need me. Don't ever think I don't care about you, baby. Tell me what you wanted to talk about.'

'Puberty.'

'Puberty? What about it?'

'Mommy, I don't want to grow hair in places I can't even mention.'

'Yeah, I know, it's a pain, but it happens to everyone,' I said.

'Do you think I'll grow a mustache?'

'I doubt it. Tell you what, this weekend we'll go to the bookstore and get you a book about puberty. We'll read it together and talk about what to expect.'

'*Eeeuw.* I can't read a book like that with you. You're my *mother*. I'll read it myself and ask you questions if I have any, which I probably won't.'

'That sounds like a plan,' I said, hugging my girl.

16. Don't Spit on the Nice Lady

A s I walked by the girls' bedroom, I wondered about Skyler's accusations. *How could she think I cared more about my clients than about my own children? Maybe I should carve out an hour a day of alone time with each child. That would help. But do I have a full hour to give to each girl? I'll just have to cut back on my workouts. Wait, no. Those are for the family. I have to look good to attract a new stepfather for the girls. Okay, thirty minutes. Yes, that's realistic. From this day forward, Kate and Skyler will each get a half hour alone with me every night. No excuses.* Then the phone rang. Omar, my favorite mobster, was calling to report a situation. I immediately erased Kate and Skyler from my mind. *Sorry, girls, I'll iron out the details tomorrow.*

Omar and Maria had just interviewed at Hartley, one of the few schools that completed the entire admissions process in one visit. First, Maria and Omar toured with the director, who, I knew, would have been secretly judging the way father and daughter interacted while they meandered through the building.

As they entered one of the kindergarten classrooms for

a look, Maria was immediately attracted to a cage with a rabbit inside. She went over to it, put her fingers in and pulled out a half-eaten piece of spoiled lettuce that the critter had been salivating, peeing, and pooping on for days. Turning to her father, she held up the lettuce and asked if she could eat it. Omar said no, of course, at which Maria folded her arms, turned her back, screwed up her face, and . . . he knew what was coming next. 'Fine,' he said, 'eat the damn thing. But if you get salmonella, don't come running to me.' Satisfied, Maria munched on the disease-ridden greens. The mortified director witnessed the entire episode.

Continuing their tour, the director asked Maria what she wanted to be when she grew up. 'An assassin,' Maria answered. This was something she had probably picked up watching the Power Puff Girls, but coming from Omar Kutcher's daughter, it wasn't deemed remotely cute.

Finally, while the director interviewed Omar in her glass-enclosed office, a teacher assessed Maria in the mini-classroom located right outside the door.

Omar thought they might have blown the interview. While the director grilled him, he could see through her glass walls that something was going awry between Maria and the teacher.

'Maria kept shaking her head. At one point, she turned the box of crayons over on the floor and refused to help the teacher clean it up. How am I supposed to concentrate on *my* interview with that going on outside? Then it got worse. Maria stood up and turned her back on the teacher and started screaming, you know the way she does? She's such a pistol, that kid. That's when the teacher pulled me out of *my* interview. Maria was hysterical. She started yelling at me, saying "I know why you're doing this. It's because you hate me, isn't it? Isn't it?" Miss Ice Queen said our interview was over. It lasted five minutes,' he explained. 'Did we blow it?'

'Yes, you blew it,' I confirmed. 'We can write *that* school off.'

'I feel like killing that frigid bitch,' he said. He was not kidding.

'I don't think that'll be necessary, Omar. This wasn't one of the best schools, anyway. Even if they'd taken Maria, we would have turned them down.' Truthfully, if Maria was going to blow an interview, this was the one to blow. Hartley was a third-tier school, everyone's safety choice. People automatically assume that any boy or girl who goes there is a loser.

Omar sounded distressed. 'Ivy, I'm a powerful man. I don't know if you know that.' Uh, yeah, I'm aware.

'Everyone respects me. *Everyone*. Anyone who doesn't pays the price. But my daughter, my own flesh and blood, I don't know how to reach her. She hates me.'

Gee, could the fact that you bumped off her mother have something to do with that?

'Omar,' I said. 'There's nothing harder than being a parent. You have to keep trying with Maria. Be patient. Be loving. I'm sure she's just acting out because she lost her mother. Maybe she could use some play therapy.' I held my breath, hoping I hadn't gone too far, not wanting a repeat of the Lilith incident.

'Can you recommend someone?'

Oh, my God. He's taking my advice, I mentally squealed.

'Not offhand, but I'll do some research and find you the right person.'

He sounded relieved.

'Omar,' I said, reaching for my notebook that listed the trustees for each school, 'I think we're going to have to tap into some of that power of yours. Let me read you a list of board members for the schools you're applying to. Tell me if you know any of them. Maybe we can find one or two who'd pull strings for Maria.'

'Okay,' he said. We reviewed the list together and identified two trustees at different schools who, as he put it, 'would take a bullet for me.'

'Great,' I said. Now I can add colluding with the mob to my list of wrongdoings. I wonder what the penalties are for extortion in this state?

'Can you get in touch with these men next week?'

'Done,' he said. 'It's like that Bob Dylan song says.'

'Which song?'

'"You Gotta Know Somebody."'

'Right, it's like that. Anyway, don't stop going to interviews, and try to get Maria excited about her visits. What's her favorite thing to do with you?'

'That would be going to The Little Shop of Plaster.'

'You take Maria to The Little Shop of Plaster? That's so sweet,' I said, imagining this universally feared mob boss painting little plaster kittens with his daughter. 'Why don't you promise that if she does her best at each interview, you'll take her there after every visit?'

'You mean bribe her?'

'Yeah, I can't believe you didn't think of it yourself, Omar.' *Oops. Faux pas.*

He laughed.

Completely out of left field, Omar got mushy on me. 'Ivy, you're a beautiful girl. You're single. I'm single. Let me take you to dinner tonight.'

Oh yeah, let's go out on a date, fall in love, and get married. Then I can be Maria's new stepmother and you can kill me when you're tired of me. I think not.

'Omar,' I teased. 'You are *so* naughty. I can't date you. You're my client. I make it a rule never to date clients. I need to stay objective.'

There was an unnaturally long silence on the other end of the phone. Finally, he spoke. 'Then how about we go out *after* Maria gets into one of these schools?' He didn't sound happy. Omar 'the Butcher' Kutcher is not used to hearing the word 'no' from anyone but his little pistol.

'Absolutely. There'd be nothing standing in our way then,' I purred suggestively. *Shit. Now I'll need to join the witness protection program.*

17. The Bitch in Burberry

On Sunday, Sassy and her brood were coming for a barbecue, weather permitting. I reached out to her, as I'd promised Drayton I would on national TV. It was a good thing because Sassy was deeply depressed. She had just put her new (my old) apartment on the market. Apparently, Drayton had left her without insurance, and she could no longer afford the place. At first she declined my invitation, but she finally agreed after I promised to tell her more about my experience with John Edward.

Without asking permission, Skyler and Kate knocked on our neighbors' doors and invited Philip, Archie, and Michael. They all said yes. *Damn. I haven't seen Philip since our argument. And Michael acts like I don't exist. What prompted them to accept?*

At least the weather cooperated. We had one of those Indian-summer evenings, warm enough to eat outdoors if we wore sweaters. Sassy arrived wearing Burberry plaid jeans that made even her perfect ass look fat.

I wasn't sure how she would respond to our downscale apartment and plebeian neighbors. I took her on a tour of the place, which she pronounced 'cozy.' Then she asked how much it cost. The kids played in the yard while the grown-ups settled in at the picnic table. Sir Elton wouldn't stop humping Sassy's leg, which was inappropriate and he knew it. I banished the pug to my bedroom for the evening. Sassy acted cool but polite when I introduced her to Michael, Archie, and Philip. When she found out that Archie was the Naked Carpenter, she downgraded her demeanor to frosty.

'And what do you do?' she asked Michael.

'I own Kratt's Knishery downstairs.'

'What a darling little place! Are you able to make a living on that alone?' she said, batting her eyelashes all innocent-like.

'Sassy, I don't think that's any of – ' I started.

'The Knishery and a few other investments. Stocks, bonds, real estate,' Michael interrupted.

'Oh, I'm impressed. Who would imagine that a small business owner in *this* neighborhood would be such an astute investor?'

Come on, Sass, would you play nice? I thought.

'Michael is a man of many surprises, Sassy,' I said. 'So, Philip, how's your new book coming?' I asked, changing the subject.

'Oh, are you a writer?' Sassy said, perking up as soon as she realized that there might be someone closer to her caliber at the table.

'He won the Pulitzer Prize for fiction,' Archie bragged.

'*Really,*' Sassy said, deeply impressed.

'No, no, it was the National Book Award,' Philip explained. 'Archie, could you pass the mustard?'

'I haven't heard of that one,' Sassy said. 'Is it a big deal?'

'Huge,' I said.

'And, they're making it into a movie starring Nicole Kidman and Denzel Washington,' Archie added.

Even *I* didn't know that. Barely broken up and we've already lost touch. Tragic.

'Did you get to meet Denzel and Nicole?' Sassy asked.

'Yes, I did.'

'Aaaaaannnnd?' she pressed.

'They were cool,' Philip said quietly, as he slathered mustard all over his hot-dog bun.

'Well, what's your new book about, Philip?' Sassy asked.

Before he spoke, Philip took a bite of his hot dog and then washed it down with beer. 'It's about an unusual woman during the forties named Ariana Nabokov von Geltenburg Chopra Gross,' he started.

'She was a spy during World War Two, and both Winston Churchill and Adolf Hitler's lover,' I added enthusiastically.

'Yes. I just worked on a scene today where Eva Braun walks in on Adolf and Ariana making love in the Führer's suite at the Berlin Ritz. You should have seen the fur fly,' he laughed.

'Sounds like a fun read,' I said. God, I missed Philip. I wondered if he still thought of me when he wrote about Ariana. I noticed that everyone had finished eating, so I gathered up the leftovers and threw away the dirty paper plates and plasticware.

Michael brought out a succulent cinnamon-peach pie. He had baked the top crust in the shape of a peace sign, and he whispered to me that he was calling a truce between us. I gave him a hug and thanked him for giving me another chance.

'I have news,' Sassy trilled. 'I'm starting a home design business.' She looked at us expectantly. *What? Are we supposed to applaud?*

'That's wonderful, Sassy. I'm sure you'll be very successful,' I finally said.

'My apartment's for sale, and everyone who sees it remarks on how beautifully decorated it is, so I decided to hang out my shingle,' she said.

The other guests congratulated her.

'Are you getting any action on the apartment?' I asked.

'There've been lots of lookers. But I'm hoping my case'll be resolved so I can take it off the market.'

'Are you suing Myoki over the accident?'

'Yes, but that'll take years. I plan to come to a quicker settlement with United over Drayton's ashes.'

'What happened to his ashes?' I asked.

'I flew to Maui to spread them on the beach and United lost the suitcase I packed them in.'

'You packed your husband's ashes?' Michael asked.

'Well, I couldn't very well carry them on board with all the security these days. Anyway, they traced them to Guam and then they disappeared. They're still looking. If they don't find them soon, United'll have to compensate me for my emotional distress.'

'You must feel terrible about it,' Philip said.

'Not really,' Sassy said, chewing a mouthful of pie, 'but don't tell United. I was just gonna scatter them in the wind. They're worth a lot more to me lost than found.'

'Speaking of ashes,' Michael interrupted, 'Antonio Banderas ate in our restaurant last week.'

'What does that have to do with ashes?' I asked.

258 The Ivy Chronicles

'Nothing. I just don't like to talk about death,' Michael answered.

'I love Antonio,' Sassy said. 'Who was he with?'

'Melanie Griffith.'

'What did he order?' Sassy asked, apparently fascinated with all things celebrity. Until then, I hadn't realized just how truly shallow she was.

'He had knockwurst on rye, matzo ball soup, and rugelach for dessert.'

'Did Melanie eat dessert?' Sassy pressed.

'Yeah, she did. I'm surprised. She was looking a little zaftig,' Michael answered.

'What does that mean? Sassy asked.

'Chubby,' Michael said.

'Thanks. I don't speak Hebrew. You know, I read in the *Observer* that Antonio and Melanie just bought an apartment on Fifth. If they come in again, here's my card, Michael. Would you give it to Melanie? Maybe tell her about me?' Like Melanie Griffith would hire Sassy Bird, amateur decorator, complete stranger, to do her magnificent new apartment. Right.

'If they come in again, I promise to give it to her,' Michael said. You had to hand it to Michael. He's a mensch.

When the barbecue was over, I declared the evening a success and felt smug about being so kind to Sassy, even though I'd been intermittently snide in my mind. Maybe in time we'd become friends and I'd be less judgmental.

As Sassy and her children were leaving, she gave me a heartfelt hug.

'Thank you for having me,' she said. 'This was the first time I've felt happy since . . . you know . . .'

I took her hand in mine and squeezed it meaningfully. 'I know,' I replied. 'I'm glad you had fun, and we'll do it again very soon.'

'And thanks for introducing me to Philip. He's so sexy. I invited him to dinner next Friday and he's coming,' she said, sounding kind of breathless.

WHAT! *Why you despicable decorator-slut. You destroyed my marriage. You stole my apartment. You ruined my daughter's party. Now you want the love of my life, too?*

I looked up at Heaven, closed my eyes, and prayed for a moment. *Drayton, I'm sorry, but I can't help your wife anymore. You have to release me from my obligation because I can't do it, buddy. I can't. I won't. I'm sorry. You're on your own, pal.*

'Don't you think he's a little young for you, Sassy?' I asked.

'Heavens, no. I'm at my sexual peak. He's at his. It's perfect.'

I swallowed. 'I'm pretty sure he's gay.'

'Well, we'll just find out next weekend, won't we?' she giggled.

'Yeah, I guess we will,' I giggled back. 'You be sure to let me know.'

I closed the door behind her, sat down, and wept.

PART 4

In Search of Class

1. A Cautionary Tale

Stu was on the phone and he was seething. This was not unusual.

'Veronica's ERB scores came today,' he began.

'Is there a problem? Didn't she do well?'

'Her numbers were fine,' he said. 'She scored ninety-eight percent and above on all the sections.'

'That's wonderful, Stu. Congratulations,' I said. *So why are we so grumpy today?*

'The writeup on the second page *could* present a bit of a problem,' he chided.

'What did it say?'

'Let me just read you what the tester wrote under "Contributing Factors."' Stu began: 'Her ease with test was evident from the outset. She displayed an almost psychic comprehension of directions, correctly beginning each task before she was even told what to do. Throughout the session, Veronica made comments such as "I've done this before." "My tutor showed me how to play that game." "You skipped a question." "I'm not sure. Can I call Ivy?" Veronica is either a gifted clairvoyant or was coached for this test. Her scores are not reflective of her genuine capabilities.'

Listening to him read, I felt sick. I *knew* it had been a bad idea to teach Veronica the answers, but no, Stu *had* to do it. I didn't want to say 'I told you so,' but *I TOLD HIM SO.* The fact that the tester *openly* accused the family of cheating was devastating. Usually, psychologists resort to disguised language understood only by admissions directors. For example, 'Susie gave up easily when confronted with difficult tasks,' really meant 'Susie is a loser who will never amount to anything.' 'A delightful child' not paired with other gushing superlatives really meant 'There's nothing special about this kid.' ERB reports were filled with cryptic hints, allusions, and hidden messages decipherable only by admissions directors privy to the code. In Veronica's case, they hadn't even made a pretense of disguising their opinion. Not good.

'Ivy, this is unacceptable,' Stu said.

'Stu, you knew it was a risk to teach her the answers to the test.'

'I never should have let you talk me into that. It was cheating and I was always uncomfortable with that,' he said.

'Excuse me?'

'I'm furious with you for insisting on teaching her the test. You've probably ruined her chances at every school. Now we'll have to move to *Scarsdale,*' he hissed.

'Stu, it was *you* who insisted I teach her the answers, remember? I told you I was doing it under protest.'

'No,' he argued. 'I told you I was *letting* you do it under protest. So far, your service has been pathetic, Ivy. I'd have been better off on my own.'

'I'm sorry you feel that way, Stu. I know you're disappointed about the test. But I do think I provided real insight when you put your list of schools together. And I know you'll agree that my work on your essays made a difference,' I reminded him.

'What are you talking about? I wrote my own essays.'

'Stu, I spent hours editing your first draft.' Kind of true. *It was really a famous author who put in hours of his time rewriting your so-called essays, but still.*

'Ivy, your revisions were a disgrace. I threw them out and used what I wrote myself.'

Does this man have a death wish? I wondered, remembering his inarticulate, mistake-filled essays.

Stu laughed bitterly. 'I should fire you right now, Ivy. But I won't. You'd better deliver what you promised. If you don't, I will hunt you down and make your life a living hell. I don't care if you *are* Steven Lord's friend, this is my daughter we're talking about. If you ruin *her* life, I'll ruin yours.' And with that, he slammed down the phone.

2. Black Like Me

Winnie Weiner's interviews were coming up. Since Wendy had burned her bridges with thirty-five schools last year, we had to keep her in the closet and find someone to pretend to be Winnie's father. I considered asking Cadmon, who had been quite the charmer when we interviewed for Skyler and Kate. Then I thought, *naaaah*. He hadn't been calling lately, so why go there?

During our barbecue, it had occurred to me that Archie might be game. He was a performance artist. This would be a good opportunity for him to work with his clothes on.

'So, what do you think?' I asked him after explaining the job.

'This is what you do for a living?'

'Not usually. But Wendy screwed herself last year and she can't show her face again,' I explained. 'We're desperate.'

'And this little girl is black?' Archie asked.

'No, she's white.' Whoa! That gave me an idea. *Her chances would improve if she were a minority candidate,* I mused. *We could take her over to Golden Glow and put her in the spray-tanning booth.* 'On second thought, we may be able to present her as African American.'

'Oh, really? How would you do that?'

'Don't worry about the details. Leave them to me.'

'What happens when she starts going to school next year? How long do I have to play her father?'

'Good question. Maybe you can show up with her alone in the beginning. Then you can start bringing Wendy with you, as your new girlfriend. We'll ease you out of the picture slowly. How does that sound?'

'Okay,' Archie said. 'Why not? This should be interesting. Will you give me a script?'

'How good are you at improvisation?'

'There are those who say I'm gifted. But you'll need to help me understand my background and motivation.'

'You got it. And I'll brief you on each school and what you can expect them to ask. I promise there won't be any surprises. Oh, and Archie, one more thing.'

'What?'

'Don't say anything about being the Naked Carpenter. That won't sell at Balmoral.'

'Of course. I know that. When can I meet my daughter?'

'Stop by later. Her mom's bringing her over so we can change her appearance. We don't want anyone recognizing her from last year.'

That afternoon, Wendy and I cut Winnie's long hair and dyed it Clairol Deep Chocolate #43.

'What do you think, Winnie?' I asked her.

'I like it. I look different.'

'You look pretty. Did your mommy explain to you why

we're making you look different? How it will help you get into a wonderful new school?'

'Yes. It's for my own good. And I have to keep it a secret.'

'Are you good at keeping secrets?'

'Yes. Like the secret about Mommy having her face-lifting operation. I didn't tell *aaaanybody*.'

'Good girl,' I said. *Shit. We're dead*.

Later, Wendy and I took Winnie for a double-dark misting at Golden Glow and bought her an African-inspired outfit to wear on her interviews. She would easily pass for Archie's daughter. I was particularly thrilled by the prospect of presenting her as a diversity candidate. That would quadruple her chances!

You may find this hard to believe given my track record, but I was worried about how this charade might affect Winnie. Were we permanently warping her psyche? How much therapy would she someday need in order to get over this? But what choice did we have? No private school would take her if they knew whose daughter she was. I was deeply conflicted about our little scheme, but I decided to go ahead with it. I couldn't think of an honest way to ensure that Winnie got the education she deserved.

'I have two questions,' Wendy asked in that squeaky dolphin voice of hers.

'What do you need to know?' I said.

'When she gets in somewhere, how long do I have to keep her black like this?'

'Well, I'd say you start the year as dark as she is now. Then each month, lighten her hair and skin just a shade. By the end of the term, she can be herself again and

I doubt if anyone will notice the change. It'll be a gradual transition,' I explained.

'And what should I tell her school now? About why she looks so different?'

'Tell them that she has a part in an Off-Broadway show,' I suggested. 'They'll buy that.'

And that's how Winnie Weiner, nice Jewish girl from the Upper West Side, adored student of Rodeph Shalom Sunday School, became WaShaunté Washington.

3. Mad About George

According to to Sassy, she and Philip were an item. I couldn't believe it. How could he not see that she was a phony and a liar?

I'd never told Philip about the part Sassy had played in the breakup of my marriage or how her husband had so deftly screwed me out of my job. If I mentioned it now, it would look like a smear campaign.

Sassy had taken to calling me every time she and Philip went out. I was her new best friend. When she told me that *she* was his inspiration for the main character of his new novel, I almost puked. Was that just a pickup line he used?

I missed Philip. Then again, maybe I just missed having a man. Luckily, the date with George Clooney that Faith had bought me at auction was coming up. He lived in Los Angeles and couldn't schedule it until he was going to be in New York. The timing couldn't have been better. I craved the attention of a hunky guy. It didn't matter if he was an auction prize. I could pretend.

In preparation for my date, I was given full access to Faith's closet with Avi Portal on hair, Raquel Morley on makeup, and Christophe directing. It was obvious that Christophe didn't relish the assignment. While my hair was being ironed, he paced back and forth talking to himself. 'Purple Alberta Ferretti. No. Too froufrou. Blue Missoni with tummy cut-out. No. Impossible with that tummy. Gold Roberto Cavalli blingbling wear. No, too predictable. Karl Lagerfeld turquoise tulle. No. Too prom queen. *I have it!* Dolce and Gabbana leather miniskirt. Miu Miu see-through black tee. That's so crazy it *just* might work. *It just might work.*'

In the end, it did work. 'What kind of footwear does this ensemble call for?' Christophe asked.

'Manolos?' I ventured.

Christophe looked like he'd just witnessed his dog being run over.

'No?' I said.

'My dear, dear Ivy. You are about to go out with the sexiest man on the planet. Do you know what I would give to be in your shoes? I would give anything. *AN-NEEEE-THING!* Your job is to bring this man to his knees until he begs for mercy, slay him, end his misery, and then send him to his glory. That calls for . . . *WHAT?*'

'Jimmy Choos?'

'YES! You will wear red lace-up Jimmy Choo fuck-me boots. Nothing else will do.'

'Red?'

'If you learn *nothing* from me, learn this,' he said dramatically. 'When in doubt, *always* wear red.'

Avi gave me a feng shui haircut and blow-dry, which was something he'd just learned from a California Zen stylist at the International Hair and Makeup show. The look was balanced, sexy, and infused with positive Ch'i. He placed a Bagua Map over my head, then added extra-bright highlights in the love and marriage area. My past experience with feng shui hadn't been so good, but I figured why not try again? Frankly, I'd have my hair's astrology chart done if there was a chance it would make George Clooney love me.

In the end, I looked pretty darn hot; at least that's what everyone in Faith's closet said. I know, I could practically have given birth to the girls George usually takes out. Still, I wanted him to think I was pretty.

By 7:00 P.M. on Friday, I was made-up and coiffed, wearing my drop-dead designer outfit, awaiting the arrival of George's stretch. Every five minutes, I was in the bathroom with stomach cramps.

At 7:36 P.M., an obnoxious motor sound filled the room. *Oh great. The Hell's Angels must be having another rally outside the house.* The girls and I peeked out the window, and lo and behold, there was George Clooney getting off a beautiful red-and-chrome Harley-Davidson right in front of our building. He took his helmet off and looked around, trying to figure out where I lived. Within five seconds, my entire block of neighbors had congregated around him. It was as if a truck had driven up and down the street, megaphone blaring, announcing his arrival. Even Philip walked outside to see what the commotion was about.

The whole scene would have been thrilling if not for the crisis. Three independent events had converged to create the perfect fashion emergency: (1) George Clooney was approaching my door; (2) Our transportation would be a motorcycle; and (3) I was wearing a miniskirt and white underwear. If I rode the bike, my panties would show. Even worse, I'd have helmet hair for the entire evening. *Damn*. I ran into my bedroom and quickly put on an ancient black lycra girdle so no one would see a big white spot between my legs as we rode. I grabbed one of Kate's scrunchies to pull my hair back, panicked that all my primping would be for naught. This would have to do. Disaster averted.

The doorbell rang, and Kate ran to the door to answer it. I hung back, not wanting George to think I was anxious or anything.

'Are you Ivy, my date?' he asked Kate.

'No,' she giggled, 'that's my mommy.' He smiled that gorgeous George grinned smile and Kate melted. 'Would *you* be my new daddy?' she asked.

George grinned and ruffled her hair. 'Aren't *you* the cute one.'

'No, really, *would you?*' she insisted.

I walked into the room, mortified. *Oh, fuck it. He's got to be used to girls throwing themselves at him by now.*

'Hello,' he said, shaking my hand. 'I'm George Clooney.' Like I didn't know that with every fiber of my being.

'Hi,' I answered. 'I'm Ivy Ames, the lucky girl who won you at auction.' *Act normal. Act normal. Act normal.*

He smiled again. *Oh, I can't stand it! What a hunka hunka man.* I wanted to jump up and down and scream like a teenager at a sixties Beatles concert, but I restrained myself. He offered me his arm ever so gallantly and said, 'Shall we?'

I had purchased a disposable camera to record this moment, but it seemed like such a dorky thing to do that

I left it sitting on the table. There would be no tangible evidence of our evening together. I'd have to commit every second to my fallible memory.

'Wait,' I said, changing my mind. 'Can I get a picture? It's not every day that we meet someone like you.' *Hot diggity, this could be the centerpiece of my annual holiday letter!*

'Of course,' he said.

We shot the whole roll. George alone. George alone with each of us. George with all three of us. George with the two girls. George alone with me and Sir Elton. George with Sir Elton. George with the family and Sir Elton. George with June, a college girl who was babysitting. He was a sport.

After we said goodbye to the girls, we walked outside. There must have been fifty neighbors, including Philip, standing there. That alone was worth the $35,000 that Faith had spent on this.

The crowd applauded. I was deeply embarrassed but pretended not to care.

We got on the motorcycle and he gave me a helmet. Goodbye hairdo. 'Make sure you put your arms around my chest and hold on real tight,' he said. *Like I need you to tell me that?* As I hugged his chest and plastered my body against his back, I fantasized that we were in bed together, spooning. On a scale of one to ten, how pathetic does that make me? Don't answer that.

We drove to Rao's uptown, on 114th Street. A model intercepted us at the door and acted like she and George were old friends, air-kissing him on both cheeks. *Hel-loow? My name is Ivy. Get your paws off my date or I'll take you down*. George politely extricated himself from her clutches and introduced me.

'Oh, hi,' the floozy said. 'I thought you might be his aunt or something.'

'No, I'm his girl,' I said sweetly, moving to position myself between him and the tart. It didn't matter. George went off to schmooze the owner, who was standing at the bar. Turning my back on the trollop, I silently wished her a loveless marriage to a short, bald, fat guy who would bring her nothing but misery. I joined George, who introduced me to the owner, who was called Frankie No on account of all the people he's turned away, including Madonna. The bartender, Nicky the Vest, offered me a drink. Frankie walked us to our table.

Dinner was spectacular. Frankie No serenaded the diners with an old Sinatra tune. Then a guest sang Puccini. We were treated the way Rao's treats everyone – like royalty. George turned out to be a real card. At one point, he had me laughing so hard I blew wine out my nose.

After dinner, we choppered down to Balthazar for a drink.

The place was packed, but they kicked out a table of mere mortals and gave us their seats. People he knew from the entertainment biz dropped by the table. Fans stopped over to tell him how much they enjoyed his work. Women brazenly gave him their phone numbers right in front of me. I tried to be gracious, but I wasn't having fun.

He must have sensed that because he suggested we leave after one drink. 'Where can we go that's quieter?' he asked.

'My house,' I offered.

When we arrived home, I excused myself to go to the bathroom and take off my girdle, *just in case*. We each got a beer out of the fridge and went outside to sit at the picnic table. It was a cool evening, so he put his arm around my shoulder to keep me warm. 'Oh, do that to me one mo-oh time, I can ne-vah get enough of a man like you-oo,' I sang softly. Corny, I know, but effective. He reached over and kissed me like he used to kiss Nurse Hathaway on ER. *Yes, if you insist, I will go to bed with you.*

'I'd better go,' he said. 'If I stay, we may do something we'll both regret.' *No, it's okay, George. I won't regret it. I promise.*

I stood up and told him what a wonderful evening I'd had. We walked around the side of the house and he got back on his Harley. Before he put his helmet on, he took my face in those large, manly hands of his, the same hands that captained the *Andrea Gale* in *The Perfect Storm*, and he kissed me again gently, deeply, easily. *Ooooh, when it comes to love I want a slo-ow hand.* Don't worry, this time I didn't sing.

4. The Curse of the Kid Parent

P hilip called out to me as I was leaving to take Skyler to her dance lesson the next day. I swear he'd been lying in wait.

'Hi,' he said.

'Hi back.'

'I see you're dating a movie star now.'

'No, we're just friends.'

'That was a friendly kiss he gave you in the backyard last night.'

Yes! He'd been watching. He'd seen my once-in-a-lifetime moment with George Clooney. *There IS a God.*

'Well, who knows where any friendship is destined to go?' I said cryptically. *Yes, I might become George Clooney's lover and wife. See what a prize you broke up with, Philip? You fool.*

Philip looked at me strangely. He was jealous.

'Well, bye. We've got to go,' I said. 'Skyler, hold my hand while we cross the street.'

'Is that so we'll die together if a car hits us, Mommy?'

'Very funny.'

Skyler and I walked to the corner and waited for the

bus that would take us to the Alvin Ailey studio. After an eternity, it arrived and we boarded with a motley crowd of neighbors. As we took our seats, Skyler said, 'Mom, why don't we buy a car again?'

'We can't afford it, honey.'

'I wish I'd gotten the money parent,' she mumbled.

'What?'

'You know. Daddy made the money and you took care of the kids. You're the kid parent and Daddy's the money parent. If we'd gotten Daddy, we wouldn't be poor,' Skyler said.

'Excuse me?' I said. 'I'll have you know that Daddy's made no money for the last year. I've been the kid parent *and* the money parent. And before that, I always pulled my weight financially.' *Stop it, Ivy. You do not need to defend yourself to an eight-year-old. That's Penelope Leach 101.*

'Mommy, it's okay,' Skyler said, patting my knee. 'Everyone knows the man makes the money.'

'Honey, that's not true.'

An old lady got on the bus, but there was no seat for her. 'Here, take mine,' I offered, getting up. For the rest of the ride, I stood next to Skyler.

She looked up at me. 'I'm tired of being poor, aren't you?'

'We're not poor. Why would you say that?'

'Mommy, look at the facts. We don't have a car. We don't have a driver. We don't have a jet. We don't have a pool at our country house.'

'Honey, we don't have a country house.'

'And that's just sad.'

'Most people don't have those things, Skyler.'

'Everyone *I* know does.'

'Your new friends don't.'

'Yeah, but I made those friends after we got poor. Can't we go back to being rich, Mommy?'

'Skyler, it's a good thing I put you in public school. I hope it wasn't too late.'

'Chloë and Mardet won't be my friends anymore because I go to public school. What's wrong with public school?'

'*Nothing*. Your old friends are being snobs.'

'That's another thing, Mommy. None of my old friends'll come over anymore because we live next door to a crack house.'

'We do *not* live next door to a crack house.'

'Mommy, *pleeeease* can't we go back to the way things used to be? Why'd you have to start that dumb business?'

'Skyler, I lost my job and I started the business to support you.'

'Then get your old job back so we can be rich again. Maybe Daddy would come home.'

'Skyler, sweetheart, they wouldn't give me my old job back even if I asked. And Daddy and I aren't getting back together. I'm sorry.'

'I wish you'd never been born.' Skyler crossed her arms and looked out the window, tears welling in her eyes.

'Skyler, if I hadn't been born, then you wouldn't have been born,' I said as I pressed the button signaling the bus to stop.

'No. Daddy made me once and he could make me again with another woman,' she said just loud enough for everyone on the bus to hear. The old lady who took my seat smiled. She tapped me on the leg and asked, 'Teenager?'

'No, she's eight.'

'Better you than me,' she said, shaking her head.

5. Not Our Kind...

Ollie Pou, my maid with big dreams, was a joy to work with. She never threatened me. She never belittled me. She never fired me. She was always kind, always respectful. In fact, she reminded me a lot of Mom – determined to give her child a better life than she'd had.

Ollie met with me before every interview so I could prep her for the visit. She took copious notes and reported back after each session. She was my prize pupil, the one client I could count on to stay with the plan. Things were progressing perfectly. I'd compose a thank-you letter for her after each school visit. Then she'd handwrite it. Ollie had beautiful penmanship, and having such elegant personal notes in her file would be a plus.

Ollie's only obvious mistake took place during her first interview. We met to debrief immediately after her visit and I saw that she was wearing a royal blue suit with rhinestone buttons, a matching hat with ostrich-feather trim, dyed silk pumps, and a purse that coordinated perfectly with the outfit. It would have been fine for a wedding or church, but it was all wrong for a private-school interview. If she wore it, someone was sure to laugh behind her back.

'Where did you get that suit?' I asked.

'Do you like it?'

'Yes, it's gorgeous. Although, I don't think it's quite right for interviewing.'

'It's my dress suit. I wore it to my niece's wedding last summer.'

'It's too fancy to wear when you meet with the directors. Let me lend you something more conservative.' Ollie wore a size smaller than I did, but she shopped my closet and picked out a black Christian Dior suit that Faith had handed down to me. The lady had taste.

Irving's test scores were over the top. Even better, his behavioral write-up could not have contained one more gushing adjective. I would be meeting with his nursery-school teacher next week to show her how to write a school report that would sell any child. Irving was the first student she'd ever had who was applying to private school.

Willow Bliss, Tiny Herrera, and Jack Henry Bliss-Herrera were my other favorite family. They lived in a comfortable apartment at 1040 Park Avenue, one of the most exclusive co-ops in town. It was filled with gorgeous artifacts from around the world, like the ancient praying Buddha they'd hand-carried back from China. I always felt at ease, surrounded by the bright oranges, reds, and pinks of their apartment. Willow would prepare elaborate dinners from scratch. Not even the vegetables were frozen.

On this particular night, Jack Henry treated us to a concert, singing 'Nobody Knows the Trouble I've Seen' and both Oscar Mayer wiener songs, three interesting choices. Willow explained that D.W. sang the first song in an episode of *Arthur*, so I shouldn't read too much into the selection. For his second tune, he just loved the words: 'Oh I wish I were an Oscar Mayer weee-ner . . .' For the third song, he was just showing off that he could spell such a big word: b-o-l-o-g-n-a.

'Why do you want to be an Oscar Mayer wiener?' I asked Jack Henry.

'Then everyone'll be in love with me,' he explained.

'We already are,' Willow said, giving him a kiss.

Tiny told us about a new animated TV series she was developing for Nickelodeon – *Marvin and the Magic Wheelchair*. It's about a boy named Marvin who flies all over in his amazing wheelchair, performing heroic acts. Tiny felt the show would go a long way in helping children become more accepting toward disabled kids.

We had applied Jack Henry to some of the top-tier schools on the Upper East Side, since that's where they lived. I also convinced his moms to try a few schools in Greenwich Village. Uptown, Jack Henry would always be the gay-black-disabled triple-header. Downtown, the lesbian thing wouldn't be a blip on the radar screen.

After visiting a few Upper East Side private schools, Tiny was starting to agree. She was also concerned that being one of the only black children in his grade might prove overwhelming for him. I suggested that we meet with an older boy of color who was currently attending a Baby Ivy to find out what the experience was like. I just had to dig up a kid like that.

'The courses they offer at the private schools are amazing,' Tiny said. 'Take a look at this.' She showed me Harvard

Day's high-school curriculum: The History of New York City from Eight Perspectives, The Tragic and Comic Modes, Theory of Computation, Theory and Ear Training for Jazz Musicians, Astrophysics. 'I'm sure you won't find classes like this at any public school.'

'You're right. Jack Henry could take fabulous courses if he went to private school,' I said.

'But would it be worth going through school as an outsider?' Tiny asked. 'I mean, with his disability and having me and Willow as parents, he'll always be different. I wonder if being one of the few black kids in his class would make it even harder for him.'

'I don't have the answer to that, Tiny. You know, I was different from the kids I went to school with. I was fat and poor. My classmates tormented me because of it. But I have to believe we live in more enlightened times,' I said.

'Me, too, Ivy. I was always different. And not to the extreme Jack Henry is. That's what worries me.'

Tiny and Willow were about to interview at Stratmore Prep, the most conservative school in the city. 'You know,' I began delicately, 'Stratmore Prep is not going to be as welcoming to lesbians as other schools. Maybe at *this* school, and only this school, just one of you should interview. You can say you're a single mother. I think Jack Henry's chances would be better.'

Tiny and Willow looked at each other. 'You mean hide the fact that we're lesbians?' Willow asked.

'Well, yes,' I said.

'But if Jack Henry got in, it would be under false pretenses,' Willow said.

And your point?

'Ivy, we won't do that. We want Jack Henry in a school that knows who we are, knows who he is, and says yes to us based on that. Living our lives honestly is what we're about,' Tiny explained.

Wow. That was something. Principled clients. They were proud of who they were and willing to sacrifice to maintain their values. I admired Tiny and Willow, even though I thought they were being chumps in this instance. 'That's fine,' I said. 'Just know that your chances won't be as good at this school. If you're willing to accept that, so am I.'

'We are,' Willow said. 'We want to find the best school for our son, but not at the expense of our integrity.'

Yeow. These girls had guts. I worshiped them.

'Do you know if your nursery school has sent out Jack Henry's school report yet?' I asked, changing the subject.

Tiny and Willow exchanged worried glances. 'Oh, didn't we tell you about that?' Tiny asked.

'No, is there something to tell?'

'Well,' Tiny explained. 'About a month ago, Jack Henry began having a "behavior problem." ' Tiny made quotation marks with her fingers when she said 'behavior problem.' I don't know why people do that. It's so goofy.

'Every day, during art, he would draw or paint pictures of the car crash where his parents died and he was paralyzed. We didn't even know he remembered the accident. He's never spoken of it. The images were violent and disturbing. He made two or three a day. Finally, the director called and asked us to tell him not to make car-wreck pictures anymore. On his psychiatrist's advice, we told them no. She felt the art was helping him work through the tragedy and it could set him back emotionally if we made him stop. The director said if he didn't change his behavior, she'd put it in his school report. We told her to go ahead. We weren't going to step in. This went on for a few weeks. Finally, Jack Henry's teacher took him aside, against our wishes, and told him he had to stop making those pictures or she wouldn't let him paint anymore.'

'Did he stop?' I asked.

'Oh yes,' Tiny explained. 'He listens. But now, he draws pictures of the *Hindenburg – catching* on fire, exploding, breaking in half, passengers falling to their deaths, that sort of thing. We watched a History Channel documentary on it. I guess it made an impression.' She handed me a stack of drawings Jack Henry had done on that theme. Whew. These were powerful images of havoc, destruction, and incineration. 'God knows what they said in the school report,' Tiny said.

෪

Patsy let me take Veronica out on three occasions. Without telling her parents, I applied my favorite little pork bun to the only three schools in town that didn't require the ERB. They weren't top-tier schools. They were small, progressive, nurturing programs that might be perfect for Veronica.

Pretending to be her single mother, I regaled the schools with stories about Veronica's many interests and talents. She genuinely is an exceptional child, and I tried to help them see that. Veronica enjoyed her visits, which were low-key playgroups with teachers observing from the sidelines. Except for the fact that she spilled her juice at snack every single time, she performed beautifully. Two of the three schools seemed interested.

My concern, of course, was that no Baby Ivy would take her after that damning ERB report. Maybe I'd be able to offer Stu a private-school alternative that would be a better fit for his daughter. How I would convince him of this, I had no idea.

6. A Hoi Polloi Holiday

The admissions process came to a screeching halt until after New Year's, so I could enjoy the holidays with my daughters. Kate and Skyler's school was holding a fair to raise money for their library. As in, the school didn't have one.

The charter program I'd slept on the street for was called School of the Basics. The principal, Jennifer Rachelson, was a no-nonsense educator who advocated an old-fashioned, traditional approach. The children wore uniforms. The focus was on reading, writing, and arithmetic. The girls were separated from the boys for math and science.

I was happily shocked by how much help School of the Basics provided for Kate's learning disability. In kindergarten, she had been diagnosed with dyslexia. Our private school regretted to inform us that they didn't have the resources to help. She either had to keep up on her own or find a new school. They strongly recommended that we get extra support three to four days a week. It didn't occur to them that the additional $15,000 a year for special-education tutors might be more than we could manage. Of course, when she was first diagnosed, we hired help without thinking. Today, it would be out of the question.

The public school, on the other hand, provided a free learning specialist and kept Kate after school for special review sessions with her teachers. For the first time since kindergarten, she didn't feel like the dumbest kid in class.

Skyler faced a different problem. Her private-school friends looked down on her now that she was in public school. That was driven home when, as a community service project, her old class came to School of the Basics to tutor the 'disadvantaged' public-school kids in Skyler's grade. It hurt to see my daughter belittled by girls whose opinions mattered so much to her. At the same time, I was secretly relieved to see her traveling in different, more humble circles.

Of course, I had to become more involved in the public school. There were committees to raise money for all the extras that were standard in every private school – a library, an after-school program, classes in music, art, and phys. ed. Would my daughters graduate appreciating the difference between Manet and Monet? Pucci and Gucci? Would they be on a first-name basis with the children of the power elite? Not likely. On the other hand, both were happy and learning. Both were getting a more realistic view of how the rest of the world lived. I'm not going to lie to you. If money were no object, I never would have taken them out of the sheltered world of private school. But under the circumstances, we were doing just fine.

At noon on Sunday, the girls and I walked out of our building and headed for the fair. The line to get into Kratt's was twice as long as usual. *Good for Michael*, I thought, *the Knishery is hopping.* I vowed to have a heart-to-heart with him about expanding. The place was a gold mine.

Faith and Steven's limo drove by just as we reached Hester Street. They were joining us. We caught a ride with them for the last few blocks. Archie came with Wendy and Winnie. It warmed my heart to see how seriously he was taking this gig. With background music provided by a parent salsa band, the fair had face-painting, balloon animals, sand art, a bake sale, and an arts-and-crafts zone where children could make their own holiday presents – no grown-ups allowed. That's where Kate, Skyler, Mae, Lia, and Winnie spent their time.

'How's Winnie handling her new image?' I asked Wendy.

She frowned. 'Not so great. Her friends didn't recognize her at first. So the teacher explained that Winnie looked different because she was in an Off-Broadway play. Then Winnie told everyone that she changed her skin and hair to help her get into a better school. You should have heard me backpedal with the teacher. I just can't get her to lie.'

'You've got to impress upon her how important it is to keep the secret. If schools find out she's not really black, no one will take her.'

'I know. I'm trying,' Wendy said. 'I hate to say it, but I think this was a mistake.'

'It might have been, but it's too late now to find another father. You have to stay the course. I *know* you can do it.'

'Of *course* I can,' she said. 'I'm a Weiner, and a Weiner never quits.'

I put my arm around her. 'That's the spirit. C'mon, let's go to the potluck.'

After dinner, a silent auction was held. It featured smaller-ticket items than those offered at the girls' old school. Principal-for-a-day. Dinner for four at Kratt's Knishery, arranged by me. Hip-hop lessons by Gabriel Fernández, husband of Plus-Sized Mama, who was now my good friend and co-chair of the book-fair committee – that sort of thing. There were no dates with George Clooney or penthouse suites on the *Crystal Symphony*. We stayed for both the potluck and the auction. Skyler was thrilled when she found out she would be principal-for-a-day, a gift from me. I bought break-dancing lessons for Faith and Steven, which they thought would be a hoot.

When the fair was over, Principal Rachelson made a big announcement. To her delight, the auction had raised $104,900! Forty-nine hundred dollars from school parents, and $100,000 from one of the world's richest men, who happened to be in the courtyard at that very moment trying to learn how to spin on his head.

7. Oprah's Favorite Things

Wednesday after the fair, I went to Kratt's after dropping the girls at school. I'd been avoiding the place ever since Michael and I had that fight. But since he reached out to me with that peace-sign-shaped piecrust, it was time to return the gesture by stopping in to eat. Plus, I thought I might casually bring up the idea of expanding. I knew he was against it the last time we talked, but the place got busier every week. It would be a service to the people of New York City.

I sat at a window booth waiting for Michael to notice me. He didn't. That could only mean he wasn't there. Peeking in the back, I spied him having a heated discussion with two women who were up to their elbows in flour. I hustled back to my table, waiting for him to emerge.

'What was going on back there?' I asked when Michael finally came out. It wasn't like him to be so stressed.

He sat down and put his head in his hands. 'You know *The Oprah Winfrey Show*?'

'Of course.'

'Well, she does a program near the holidays called "Oprah's Favorite Things," where she picks items she particularly likes – clothes, electronics, food, that sort of thing – and she does a show about them. A few weeks ago, we got a call that Oprah chose our cinnamon-cheese coffee cake as one of her favorite things. She tasted it last fall when she ate here. They asked us to send two hundred tins of coffee cake for everyone in her audience, so we did.'

'That's great, isn't it?'

'Well, sure. The show aired a week ago Tuesday. Did you see the line on Sunday? It went all the way to Broome Street.'

'I did! I saw it on my way to the kids' fair.'

'The problem is, we've gotten more than twenty thousand orders for cakes, and we have to fill them in the next two weeks. I don't see how we can do that.'

'Can't you hire more workers?'

'I have. See the two women in the back? All they do is bake coffee cake. I have a second shift that comes in after dinner. My cousin's wrapping and boxing as fast as he can. I hate to say it, but I think we're going to disappoint a lot of people.'

'How many orders are you filling a day?'

'About five hundred, and the requests keep coming.'

'You'll never get it done at that rate.'

'I know. That's what I've been saying.'

'I'll help,' I volunteered.

Michael smiled, flashing those dimples. 'Would you prefer to box or bake?'

I thought for a moment. 'No, we need to think bigger. You know how, in the olden days, neighbors used to help their neighbors by having barn-raising parties?'

'Yeah, I remember seeing that on *Little House on the Prairie*.'

'You watched that show?'

'Every day after school. I was in love with Mary, the blond sister. But don't tell anyone.'

'You mean the *blind* sister.'

'That, too.'

I laughed. 'Okay, here's my idea. Let's organize a party to fill the orders. We'll invite our neighbors to help.'

'Ivy, my naïve tenant, I hate to burst your bubble, but this is New York City in the twenty-first century. People aren't as neighborly as they were in the days of *Little House on the Prairie*. But thanks for the suggestion.'

'Hey, don't be so cynical. It's a good idea. If I could get you a bunch of volunteers, would you feed them?'

'Sure, I guess.'

'Then don't worry. You cook. Leave the volunteers to me.'

That afternoon, I made flyers for KRATT'S COFFEE CAKE-BAKING PARTY, to take place Saturday night after sunset, from 7:00 P.M. until 7:00 A.M. I posted the invites all over the neighborhood – at the girls' school, the boys' club on Canal, and the Henry Street Settlement House. We advertised entertainment by the Naked Carpenter and free food for anyone willing to work.

After Friday's lunch at School of the Basics, Principal Rachelson lent us the school's industrial ovens. No way could Michael's equipment handle 20,000 coffee cakes. With Plus-Sized Mama in charge, our PTA book committee held a bake-a-thon in the school's kitchen for twenty hours straight. As each batch of cakes cooled, two of Faith's drivers loaded and delivered them to the Knishery for packing and mailing.

By 10:00 P.M. Saturday, only a handful of volunteers had shown. Faith was there, supervising cake packing. Ollie Pou boxed and labeled the packages. Tiny and Willow processed charges for orders. Wendy Weiner served food to hungry volunteers, not that we had many. The Goldofskys were there, of course. They never seemed to leave. Even the kids pitched in. When the Naked Carpenter finished each set, the children sang old standards like 'The Wheels on the Bus,' 'Head and Shoulders, Knees and Toes,' and that perennial favorite, 'If You're Happy and You Know It, Clap Your Hands.' I was moved that so many clients and friends had answered my call for help. But what about the neighbors?

'I don't get it. It's after 10:00. Where is everyone? I put signs up all over,' I said.

'Ivy, this *is* New York. I think you're expecting too much. We'll get through most of the work with the volunteers we have,' Michael said. 'You've done an amazing job.'

'But I wanted to get it *all* done for you,' I said. I thought for a minute. 'Stay here. I'm going recruiting.'

'Ivy, don't. It's Saturday night. There's a full moon.'

'What's that got to do with it?'

'The city's extra-dangerous when the moon is full. More crime. More accidents. More rats crawling out of the sewers.'

'Eeeuw. Why'd you have to tell me that?' I said.

'The point is, you shouldn't be out alone at this hour.'

'You're right. So come with me,' I said.

A less-than-enthusiastic Michael put his cousin in charge of the Knishery. We left in search of volunteers.

'Let's go to Cosette's. There's always a crowd outside,' I suggested.

'No, I can't,' Michael said. 'They'll be furious if I steal their customers.'

'They're not customers. They're sad, rejected people who will never be let in.'

'Doesn't matter. They need the crowd to look hot. It's their shtick,' Michael said. 'Plus, have you seen the size of their bouncers? I'd rather not die tonight.'

'Fine. Okay. Let's think. What about this?' I said. 'There's a homeless shelter at St. Dominico's on Hester Street. The food's lousy. There's no TV. No music. I'll bet we can find volunteers there.'

'How do you know the food's lousy?'

'I'm guessing.'

'That might work,' Michael said. 'Let's go.'

The church was open, but there was no sign of the shelter. A janitor who was wiping Pledge on the pews told us where to go.

Father Christopher stood at the basement door welcoming people who were seeking shelter. We introduced ourselves and told him about our plight. 'Would you be willing to make an announcement about our cake-baking event?' He agreed, but only after extracting a promise from Michael to donate all the food Kratt's couldn't sell to his shelter. He said their food was lousy (*see, I was right!*). He'd eaten at the Knishery and knew the cuisine was superb. Father Christopher offered to pick it up every night. Michael was happy to oblige. Usually he tossed his less-than-fresh food. It was a win-win, as they used to say at Myoki.

Twenty minutes later, we led a motley crew of nineteen volunteers back to Kratt's. Those who came were happy for something to do. The promise of good food and music was a powerful draw. We divided them up into packers, bakers, and box labelers. By midnight, the place was humming.

'Ivy, I don't know what to say,' Michael said. 'I thought I'd seen it all.'

'See, Michael, sometimes people surprise you. I *knew* we'd find volunteers.' I noticed a few more neighbors had arrived, so I asked them why they'd come.

'Food, definitely,' a bleached blonde with five visible face piercings declared.

'The entertainment. I just love that Naked Carpenter,' said a nurse who had just finished her shift. 'Is he married?'

'I wanted to help,' a red-cheeked Irishman said.

'What did I tell you, Michael? People giving to other people. Neighbors helping neighbors.'

'Plus, I was hoping to meet girls,' the guy added.

Mr. and Mrs. Goldofsky were packing cakes into tins under Faith's supervision. Mrs. G. took this as an opportunity to make introductions. 'Michael Kratt, this is my granddaughter, Miriam Goldofsky. Michael, Miriam is a docta. Miriam, Michael is *the* Kratt from Kratt's Knishery.' She lowered her voice so that we all paid close attention. 'He owns buildings all over the Lower East Side. You could do woise.' Michael and Miriam smiled at each other and went outside to talk.

By Sunday morning, we had baked and boxed enough coffee cake to fill all the orders and then some. Michael was ecstatic and exhausted at the same time. While the rest of us said goodnight, he opened the Knishery to a gaggle of hungry New Yorkers clamoring for their Sunday brunch. I went to sleep, with visions of coffee cakes dancing in my head.

8. A Mysterious Benefactor

'Let's go look at the tree at Rockefeller Center,' I suggested to the girls on the Saturday before Christmas. Even though we celebrated Chanukah, New York was amazing this time of year and we never missed the big tree or holiday windows.

'Yeah!' Skyler and Kate screamed. They were suckers for decorations, too. We bundled up in our winter coats, scarves, and hats and hoofed it to Fifth Avenue and 49th Street just for the exercise. The girls whined about the long walk, but I distracted them by pointing out cool holiday decorations along the way. When we arrived at Rockefeller Center, the sidewalks were jam-packed with visitors who all had the same idea we did. It was too crowded to get near the tree, so we stood across the street and gazed at the top of it, which was the only part we could see.

'Come on, let's get in line and look at Saks' windows,' I suggested. After half an hour in the dense crowd, we reached the first display. The mob carried us past the windows like swimmers caught in the undertow. Kate and Skyler were so jostled, they couldn't have seen much beyond the backs of the taller people in front of them.

'Wasn't that fun, Mommy?' Kate said after we blew past the last window.

'It sure was,' I said. Did she *really* think that was fun? Frankly, I was overwhelmed by the crowd, my feet hurt, I needed to pee and was starved. Otherwise, I was enjoying myself immensely. Then I had a brilliant idea. 'Come on, girls, let's go to Tavern on the Green.' We headed west through Central Park. As a native New Yorker, I knew that the best Christmas decorations were at Tavern on the Green's patio, where trees were strung with lights of every color and shrubs had been pruned to resemble everything from King Kong to delicate swans. You could grab a hot dog, sit for free at an outdoor table, and marvel at the gorgeous setting. Plus, I could probably talk my way into their bathroom, even though we weren't eating there.

Ahhhh! I thought as I rested my weary bones in a chair and gazed at the symphony of multicolored twinkling lights. The girls ran around exploring the topiary and flirting with the maître d' at the front door.

A hostess approached me. 'Excuse me, are you Ms. Ames?'

'Yes?' I said, certain that they were about to kick us out for freeloading on their beautiful patio.

'Your table is ready.'

'Oh, but we aren't eating here. We were just resting our feet, if that's okay.'

'It's fine, but you see, a gentleman came by and reserved a table for three in your name. He's taken care of the bill.'

'You're kidding! Who was it? What did he look like?'

The hostess laughed. 'Now, I can't tell you that. He wants to remain anonymous.'

This was rather exciting. A mysterious stranger was treating the girls and me to dinner. Will wonders never cease? Could I have a secret admirer who saw me sitting here and thought I was pretty? I fooled with my hair and smiled at no one in particular. If I'd known we were eating at Tavern on the Green, I would have dressed better. *Oh, well, let's just enjoy the unexpected treat,* I thought to myself.

We were escorted to our table, where a bottle of Veuve Clicquot was already chilling on ice. Three gifts were waiting for us. *What in the world* . . . Kate and Skyler couldn't contain their enthusiasm. 'Can we open our presents?' they both asked.

'Sure,' I said, looking around to see if someone I knew was watching us. I didn't see a soul. This was beginning to feel creepy. How could someone know we were going to be at Tavern on the Green when *I* hadn't even planned to be here? The girls tore into their packages and practically wee-wee'd with glee when they realized they'd each been given the Fendi book bag that Skyler had been salivating over all year. Not one of the fakes you buy on Canal Street, I might add. The *real thing.* 'Swee-eet,' Skyler said.

My box contained a Prada periwinkle python-print bag. Inside, there were ten crisp $100 bills along with a note:

Dear Ms. Ames,

I know how tight things can get over the holidays. Hope this helps you make your daughters' holiday wishes come true. More

show of appreciation to come, of course, when
Moses is admitted to the right school. Don't let
me down.

Sincerely,
Buck McCall

*I don't have a secret admirer. I have Buck McCall. Damn
him for doing this.* The money and gifts made me feel
cheap, like a hooker. And it made me feel ashamed because
I knew I would keep them.

9. An Unexpected Gift

On Christmas night, it was me all by myself. Cadmon had the girls for the holiday week. Faith and Steven had taken their kids on a photographic safari to Africa. Archie was visiting his parents. Philip would most certainly be with Sassy. According to her, they were practically married.

As it turned out, Buck McCall wasn't the only client who remembered me at the holidays. That was nice. Tiny and Willow sent a yummy bottle of wine accompanied by a card that Jack Henry made. Omar gave me a flat-panel plasma-screen TV that was probably stolen. Stu sent a gift certificate for dinner at La Côte Basque, a nice gesture that would have been nicer had the place still been in business. Ollie mailed me a $50 gift card from Macy's that I knew she couldn't afford. The Radmore-Steins sent a clock with Lilith's ghastly portrait covering most of the face. It gave me a chuckle whenever it was 9:15 or 3:45. That's when the hands of the clock formed a big black mustache right under Mrs. Radmore-Stein's nose, so artfully photographed by Annie Leibowitz.

I went to Blockbuster, but it was closed. Returning

home, I noticed that Philip's lights were on. There were people in his apartment. Sassy's Land Rover was parked in front. I guess she was slumming. *As soon as she snares Philip, he'll be living on Park Avenue in my old apartment,* I thought sadly. With his help, maybe she could afford the place.

Trudging up the stairs, I let myself in. Faint sounds of Christmas music and laughter could be heard from below. I made brownies. I was lonely, and eating a pan of them would ease the pain. Uncorking the wine Tiny and Willow had sent, I settled in for the evening to drink, think, and sing the blues. Sitting on the sofa, I dug into the brownies with a spoon. Why bother cutting them when I'd be the only one eating? *This is ridiculous,* I thought. *I refuse to feel sorry for myself tonight.*

I went down to Kratt's for dinner. It was quiet, and Michael was cleaning up behind the counter.

'You don't look so good,' he said when he saw me.

'Thanks.'

'No, I mean, you look kind of sad.'

'I am. The girls are with Cad and I miss them. I thought I'd come down for dinner.'

'I'm sorry, but we're about to close.'

'Oh. Oh, well.'

'Why don't you come upstairs and let me make you something to eat?'

'Really?' I said.

'Really.'

'That would be so nice,' I said. I meant it.

We walked upstairs to his apartment. It was the first time I'd been there. When I tell you it was beautiful, I mean it was *très* exquisite. He had two stories. The whole bottom floor was one big open living room, kitchen, and dining area. There was this hypnotic sheet of water that flowed like glass down a black granite wall in the entry. The floors were light oak. The beautifully designed furniture was simple and inviting at the same time. There was no clutter. Michael's bedroom and library were upstairs, he said. And there was a roof deck with a Japanese garden that he promised to show me when the weather was warmer. The feng shui felt perfect, and I wondered if Master Li had helped him place his furniture.

'I love your place,' I said. 'It's so harmonious.'

'Thanks.'

'It's not what I expected,' I added.

'You mean it's not what you'd expect a deli owner to live in?'

'Michael, will you *ever* get over our evening at the Knickerbocker? Everything I said that night came out wrong. And how many times did I say I was sorry? Like fifty, not to mention the flowers.'

'Okay, okay. I won't bring it up again.'

'The reason your apartment isn't what I expected is because it's in such an ordinary-looking building,' I explained.

'That's the thing about New York,' Michael said. 'All over the city, there are buildings you couldn't imagine living in because of how they look on the outside. Then someone invites you inside and they turn out to be show-places. You have to look past the façade, you know?'

'You're so right.'

Michael walked into the kitchen and opened the fridge. 'How do you feel about pasta with a lobster marinara sauce?'

'You eat shellfish?'

'Shhh. Let's keep that between us. It's classified information.'

'Now I know two secrets about you. You're a kosher-deli owner who eats shellfish and you used to be in love with that slutty shiksa from *Little House on the Prairie*. What else are you hiding?'

'If I told you all my secrets, I'd have to kill you,' he said, smiling. 'How about some wine?' He opened the door to a small, cool room that contained hundreds of bottles from all over the world. I selected my favorite, Conundrum.

Michael prepared the meal while I watched, sipping my drink. As he worked, I put on a Harry Connick, Jr. CD. The food was as delicious as any I'd ever eaten. And being with Michael was relaxing. 'You are one surprise after another, do you know that?' I said.

'I am? How?'

'You can cook, play the piano. Your apartment is beautiful. You collect wine. You're charming. And yet you're a deli-man. You're just not what a deli-man is supposed to be.'

'Excuse me? You made *me* promise not to bring that up, and now you did. You obviously don't know deli-men, Ivy. What do you think they're supposed to be like?'

'Well, they're supposed to be simple, family-oriented, overweight, living in apartments that haven't been updated since 1955. And they smell like lox.'

'So I've disappointed you.'

'No, not at all. In fact, I propose a toast. To Michael, the Renaissance Deli-Man.'

'I'll drink to that,' he said. We touched our glasses and took a sip. 'And to Ivy, my coffee cake angel.'

'It was a pleasure to help,' I said.

'Would you like to dance?' he asked.

'Okay. I'm not the greatest dancer.'

'Don't worry, just follow my lead.'

We danced to the music of Bobby Caldwell. Michael was surprisingly easy to follow. I didn't step on his toes once. I fit snugly next to his body, too. Truth be told, I melted like butter into his arms and when Bobby started singing 'Old Devil Moon' I had this irresistible urge to kiss him. Was it the wine?

'You are beautiful, you know,' he said.

'No, I am not beautiful. I'm anything but beautiful.'

'Is that what you think?'

'That's what I think.'

'Well, at least you're pretty. Would you concede that?'

I laughed. 'Thank you.' I needed to be careful. This was the kind of conversation that could lead to romance. And I wasn't attracted to Michael that way.

Too late. Michael brought his face to mine and kissed me, parting my lips with his tongue, moving it slowly around in my mouth. Then he began to bite my neck lightly. 'Oh, God,' I moaned. A warmth was spreading from the top of my chest to the depths of my crotch.

The next thing I knew, we were lying on the rug in front of the fireplace. I don't remember how we got there. Michael was looking into my eyes and touching my face. He gently kissed my eyes, my mouth, my neck. He unbuttoned my shirt one button at a time, revealing more and more as he slowly moved down my chest. Then he helped me take the shirt off. I removed the rest of my clothes while he watched. 'I knew you would have a beautiful body,' he said. I looked around the room. Was he talking to *me*?

'Do you have protection?' I asked.

'I do,' he said. 'I'll be right back.' He ran upstairs, leaving me naked on the rug. But the room was warm and I was buzzed from the wine. I didn't even notice time passing. Michael was back, standing in front of me and taking his clothes off. This time I watched, curious to see what his body looked like. I was not disappointed.

Michael lay next to me and began stroking my body. 'Your skin is so soft. And you smell like lemons,' he whispered. He lifted his face and brushed his lips to mine. I kissed him back, then moved down his body, nuzzling my face into his chest, exploring every inch with my hands and eyes. Mmm, he had just the right amount of hair, enough for me to run my fingers through, but not one of those thick rugs like Omar Kutcher's. *Gaah! Do not think about work. Be here now. Center yourself*. I did. Soon, I was attending to his hard-on with my tongue. It was the first time I ever enjoyed giving a blowjob. I never liked them with Cad. *Stop! Do not think about Cad. Pleasure him slowly. Relax. Be at one with the penis. Will you look at that?* Michael had a little brown discoloration on his right ball. Didn't Michael Jackson have some kind of mark on his private parts? *Stop! Do not bring Michael Jackson into this. Concentrate on the blowjob. The blowjob is all there is. There is nothing else. Wait, yes, there is.* I turned my attention to the rubber lying next to us. Opening it, I placed it over his erection and rolled it down as erotically as I could.

Michael sat up and helped me lie down. He reached between my legs and slipped his fingers inside. *I can't remember ever being this wet. Not with Cad. Not with Philip. Hel-loow. Don't think about other men. Re-laaaaaax. Mmmm, that's good.* Michael moved on top of me and we began to fuck, first slowly, then harder and harder. We varied positions I don't know how many times, a nice change from the six ways Cad and I always did it. The experience was almost spiritual, like eating chopped liver. *For God's sake, Ivy, forget Cad. Forget chopped liver. Focus on Michael being inside you. Be conscious of his weight. Fuck mindfully. Fuck reverently. Have your-self a mer-ry little orgasm. Stop singing. Let go. Let go. Let go.* I came. Then Michael shuddered and collapsed on top of me. *Oh, for Heaven's sake, he's crushing me. Would it be rude to push him off so soon? Wait one minute. One Mississippi, two Mississippi, three Mississippi* . . . I moved my head to the right, locating an airhole for my nose. Finally, he rolled over and lay next to me.

Michael looked at me and smiled. 'Merry Christmas,' he said.

'Mmm, happy Chanukah,' I replied.

10. On Second Thought

ig mistake. I never should have done it with Michael. I knew it the minute I woke up on December 26th. He was my good friend, and this was bound to change everything. If we had a relationship and then broke up, that would be one more neighbor I'd have to avoid. Plus, as much as I wished this weren't true, it bothered me that he just owned a deli. If he wanted to expand and open a chain of Knisheries, that would be one thing. But he was perfectly content with his one location on Delancey and Orchard streets. Michael was amazing in hundreds of ways. But he wasn't the powerhouse I needed.

Maybe I could keep having sex with him until a more appropriate candidate showed up. *No, that would be sick and wrong.*

I went down to the Knishery to say what needed to be said, praying that Michael wouldn't take it too hard.

As I sat in my favorite booth, Michael caught my eye from behind the counter. He smiled, poured me a cup of coffee, and brought over some cinnamon rolls. Before he sat down, he kissed my cheek.

'How are you this morning?' he asked.

'I'm fine. That was wonderful last night,' I began.

'It was, you animal,' he teased. Then we both started talking at once. 'You first,' he said.

'No, you,' I insisted.

'Okay.' Michael came to my side of the booth and took my hands in his. *He's gonna say he loves me. Be gentle. He's a good guy. Do not break his heart.*

'Ivy, last night was amazing. I don't think I've ever been with a woman who lost herself so completely during sex. You made me feel like there was nothing in the world except the two of us. It was unforgettable, really. But I don't think we should take it further.'

'*What!*' I couldn't believe my ears. Michael was dumping *me?* 'Is it because I have children?' I asked. It had to be something like that. It couldn't be me personally.

'No, I love your kids. I want children of my own. The problem is, at the end of the day, I know I could never marry you. So I don't think we should even start a relationship.'

'You've *got* to be kidding.'

'No. I realized it some time ago. That's why I wanted to make up with you. Last night, I got carried away. The wine. The food. You.'

'But what's wrong with me? I'd be perfect for you.'

'No, no, you wouldn't. You're a wonderful person, but our values are too different.'

'I've got good values. What's wrong with my values?'

'Nothing is *wrong* with them. They're just different from mine. You care more about material things than I do. You want to live a big New York life. I know you don't have that right now, but if you were given the chance to get it back, you'd take it in an instant. I'd never choose that. I'm comfortable living on the Lower East Side, managing my deli, hanging out in my apartment, working in my garden. I love seeing the Goldofskys every Sunday. I enjoy cooking and baking. I'm happy with my simple life. The two of us don't want the same things, Ivy. So, let's just agree to be friends, okay?' He smiled at me. *Lord have mercy on my soul. Those dimples.*

'I can't believe what you're saying,' I said. The lump in my throat made it hard to speak.

'I'm sorry, Ivy. Trust me. This is best for both of us.'

'But the sex was so good,' I whispered.

'I know,' he agreed.

'Do you think we could just have sex sometimes?' I asked. 'It could be meaningless.'

Michael laughed and kissed my hands. 'Ivy, it pains me to say this, but no. It would be too awkward. We live in the same building. We see each other all the time. Let's just be friends, please?'

I nodded. Tears were streaming down my face. Don't ask me why. This is exactly what I'd wanted.

11. Happy New Year!

I spent New Year's Eve with my furry date, Sir Elton. And another pan of brownies and a spoon. The phone rang. I answered it right away in case it was the girls.

'Ivy, it's Stu.'

Oh, what good news. Exactly the guy I didn't want to talk to on a lonely New Year's Eve.

'Stu, it's a holiday. I was taking the night off,' I said. What nerve to call me tonight of all nights! Does it not occur to this megalomaniacal Neanderthal that I *might* have important plans?

'Well, since you picked up, you can answer my question.'

'Fine, what's your question?' I asked, trying not to sound too impatient.

'Once Veronica is in kindergarten, what should we be doing to build up her résumé so she'll get into a top college like Harvard or Yale?'

'You called me on New Year's Eve for that?'

'Yes, I need to know. I'm writing Patsy and Veronica's life plans tonight, along with my own. It's something I do every year at this time. I want to get this into our long-term goals. Do you think I should get her started in a hospice? Maybe we should train her for speed skating so she can be in the Olympics. Or do you think competing in triathlons would be enough? We need to find her a hook for college, and the sooner we start, the better.'

'Stu, Veronica's four. Why don't you wait to see what interests *her*?'

'She'll be interested in whatever I decide.'

Okay. I give up. 'I think you should go for speed skating. Having an Olympic gold medal will set her apart from the average student-council presidents and theater geeks,' I said. Plus, it might be good for her weight problem, which of course I did not say.

'It's just too bad we didn't have any international accomplishments like that to write about in her kindergarten essays,' he lamented.

'Yeah, too bad, Stu. But most kids under four don't achieve worldwide celebrity, so it's not like she's behind the eight-ball or anything. Will that be it?' I asked sweetly.

'Did Patsy tell you I was promoted?'

'No, she forgot to mention it. Congratulations.'

'It was in my life plan last year. And it happened. That's the beauty of these things. State your intention and let nature take its course. Next year, Steven Lord is going to *personally* draft me to fill a plum position in his organization,' Stu predicted. 'That's my number-one goal. Just watch and wait. I'll make it happen.'

'I'm sure you will. Now, is that it?' I asked politely.

'Yes, but I may call you back later if I have more questions.'

'You do that, Stu,' I said, as I hung up and unplugged the phone.

12. Behind Closed Doors

After the holidays, there was a flurry of interviews to complete. By some cosmic coincidence, all my clients were interviewing at Harvard Day on January 12. Well, maybe it was because I'd submitted all their applications on the same day. As usual, everyone called me afterward with a full report:

'So you won't be needing financial aid?' Tipper asked Archie.

'No, that won't be necessary. I can afford the tuition,' Archie explained.

'That's wonderful,' Tipper said. 'Archie, can I ask you a personal question?'

'Of course,' Archie answered.

'How did WaShaunté lose her mother?'

Archie began to speak and then put his head in his hands and sobbed. 'I'm sorry, but it's still such a raw wound.'

Tipper handed him a Kleenex.

'She was on her way to Kenya to volunteer with the World Hunger Organization. It was always important to Hola to be part of the solution, not the problem. Anyway, she was on a small plane with six other volunteers that went down in a remote section of the African jungle. They only had one candy bar and a box of apple juice between them. After ten days of waiting and hoping to be rescued, there was no sign of help. On the eleventh day, they knew that someone would have to die and be eaten so the rest of the group could live. They were preparing to draw straws when Hola, selfless as always, volunteered to be the one. A fellow passenger handed her a pistol and she made the ultimate sacrifice. Just as they finished eating her torso, a rescue party arrived and everyone but my beloved Hola was saved. Do you want to know what the real irony was?'

'What?'

'Hola is an African name that means "savior."'

Tipper shuddered. 'That gave me the chills. You know, I saw a movie on the Lifetime Channel that was just like that about two weeks ago.'

'Did you now?' Archie said. 'Did you happen to notice the message they flashed at the beginning of the show, "inspired by actual events"?'

'Noooo,' Tipper gasped, her hands covering her mouth.

'Yesssss,' Archie confirmed, nodding his head up and down.

༅

Against my advice, Lilith brought Ransom's weekday-afternoon nanny to their interview. She wanted her there in case they were asked questions about Ransom that neither she nor Johnny could answer. Ignoring all my instructions, Lilith wore her dark glasses during the interview. She carried Mrs. Butterworth in her $14,000 Birkin bag, which had been specially modified with airholes.

Further ignoring my counsel, Johnny opted for an Armani running suit instead of a conservative Brooks Brothers look. I don't know why they even hired me.

'What do you and Ransom like to do together as a family?' Tipper asked.

'Can I answer that, dear?' Lilith asked Johnny.

'Of course, darling,' Johnny answered.

'Often I have to work weekends, and Ransom always begs to join me. I'm chairman of American Standard Papers, as you know, the largest newspaper and publishing conglomerate in the world. I usually have speeches to prepare, and Ransom likes to watch me work. If I'm holding a Saturday conference call, Ransom will make silly faces to see if he can get me to laugh while I'm talking on the phone. It's really very cute,' she said, recalling her son's antics.

'Oh, I thought you didn't like that, dear?' Johnny asked.

'Oh, no, I do, darling. I think it's adorable,' Lilith corrected him, giving him the hairy eyeball.

'It says in your nursery-school report that your secretary always attended Ransom's parent-teacher conferences. If Ransom attended Harvard Day, we'd have to insist that at least one parent be present. Would that be a problem?' Tipper asked.

'No, not at *all*,' Lilith said. 'Those conferences seemed like such a waste of time in nursery school. I mean, what was there to say? He excels at Play-Doh? He's good on the jungle gym? Give me a break. But now that he's going to *real* school, of course we plan to be there.'

'Is Ransom good on the jungle gym?' Tipper inquired.

'You know, I'm not sure.' Lilith looked at Johnny, who

appeared stumped, too. Marvys jumped in with the answer. 'He's a little gymnast. Can't keep him off the monkey bars when we go to the park.'

Johnny tried to change the subject. 'Oh, honey, let's let Marvys tell Tipper that hysterical story she told us,' he begged.

'Honey, I can tell that story as well as Marvys. You see, Tipper – I can call you Tipper, can't I? I was taking the corporate jet to one of my printing plants in Cincinnati. Anyway, remember that U.S. Airways plane that crashed on takeoff last week? Ransom must have heard about it on the news because he ran to Marvys in tears, just crying his little eyes out, saying, "Marvys, a plane just crashed. I'm afraid Mommy was on the plane that crashed." We all got *such* a chuckle out of that, *as if I'd ever fly commercial.*'

ᦞ

'Mr. Butcher, I mean Kutcher, I'm sorry, can you tell me how Mafia, I mean Maria handles frustration?' Tipper asked, flummoxed.

'Tipper, I can't lie to you,' Omar said, using his Marlon-Brando-as-the-Godfather voice to spook her. 'Ever since her mother died, may she rest in peace, Maria's had a hard time when things don't go her way. Sometimes she screams, other times she refuses to speak to me. Once she got so mad that she dropped a whole set of china off the balcony. I tell ya. Sheeee's a pistol.'

'My gosh, that's terrible,' Tipper said. 'How would a child even get an idea like that?'

'Her mother, may she rest in peace, used to do all

those things when she was frustrated,' Omar explained. 'Anyway, by the time she comes here, none of that will be a problem. She just started play therapy with a top child psychiatrist.'

Tipper made notes in the file. 'That's wonderful, Mr. Kutcher. Do you have any questions for *me*, sir?'

'Yes, I do. I've been wondering – do many of your graduates go to college?'

'Yes, just about every one.'

'Ah, excellent, excellent,' Omar stated. 'Tipper,' he continued, 'I notice that you're not wearing a wedding ring.'

'Oh, I'm not married, Mr. Kutcher.'

'Tipper, you're single, I'm single. Let me take you to dinner tonight,' he said romantically. 'I'd love to take you to David Burke & Donatella. They make the best lobster in New York City.'

Tipper hesitated. It had been years since a man had hit on her. For one brief and shining moment, she basked in the glory of the proposition. Then she remembered who was asking. 'Oh, Mr. Kutcher, that's nice of you. But we're not allowed to date parents of applicants. It would be a conflict of interest,' she said politely.

'Of course,' Omar said. 'Is there no way I can *twist your arm*?'

'No, Mr. Kutcher, you . . . you . . . just can't.'

'Then how about we go out *after* Maria gets into Harvard Day?' he asked.

'That sounds . . . delightful.' Tipper swallowed hard while trying to act natural. 'I'd love to go out for mobster, I mean lobster, with you.'

❧

'So, you two are sisters?' Tipper asked Willow and Tiny.

'Oh, no, didn't you read our essay? We're lesbian partners,' Tiny explained.

'Right,' Tipper said. 'I remember your essay. I was *so* moved by it. 'If Jack Henry were to come here, you'd definitely want to meet Max Kanter and Howard Honiblum. They're our gay family,' Tipper explained.

'Are those the only gay parents in the school?' Willow asked.

'Right now, yes, but don't let that discourage you,' Tipper said. 'We're super gay-friendly at Harvard Day, and we want more families of that persuasion.'

'That's good to hear,' Tiny said. 'Jack Henry is different enough with his disability. We don't want kids teasing him because he has two mothers.'

'Speaking of his disability, do you expect he'll be in a wheelchair for his whole life, or is this something he'll grow out of soon?' Tipper asked, smiling.

'Chances are, he'll always need a wheelchair,' Tiny explained.

'Will you be providing some kind of companion to assist him throughout the day?'

'We weren't planning to. He's self-sufficient,' Tiny said.

'Well, isn't that wonderful.' Tipper noted it in the file.

'I see here that he's black, too,' Tipper said. 'We're always on the lookout for minority candidates who have the right stuff. Besides working admissions, I head up the diversity council,' Tipper bragged. 'Will you be applying for a scholarship?'

'No,' Tiny said. 'We can handle the tuition.'

'I notice in his school report that Jack Henry draws pictures of . . . fiery car crashes. Does he still do that?'

'No, he gave it up,' Tiny answered.

'Excellent,' Tipper said.

'Now, he's doing a series based on the *Hindenburg*,' Tiny added.

'Oh my, how grown-up. Do you have any questions for me?' Tipper asked.

'Yes, I do,' Willow said. 'How many children of color would be in his grade?'

'Well, that depends on how many qualified applicants we receive. But our goal is to have at least one child of color in each of our four kindergarten classes. Of course, that could be *any* color – black, Indian, Chinese, Hispanic. Sometimes I wonder if we should split them up like that. Maybe it would be better to put all the minorities together in one class, so they wouldn't feel alone. I don't know, what do you think?'

'I would think a child would feel pretty isolated being the only minority in his class,' Willow said. 'Let me ask you this. How many other disabled children attend Harvard Day?'

'Well, actually, I'm not sure. Do you mean children in wheelchairs?' Willow and Tiny nodded.

'Do you mean now or historically?' Tipper asked.

'I guess both,' Willow said.

'That would be . . . none. We've never had one. Anything else?' Tipper asked, smiling.

Willow and Tiny shook their heads.

'I'm intrigued by your hair,' Tipper added. 'It's so pink.'

'Do any of your other parents have hair this color?' Tiny asked.

'No, our parents tend to be more conservative,' Tipper said. 'But don't worry, we're very open-minded and accepting of people's differences.'

'Super,' Willow said.

∽

'So, Mr. Needleman, it says in Veronica's ERB report that the tester believes she was coached. Do you have a response to that?' Tipper asked.

'We enrolled her in a general enrichment class after nursery school. When she said she had done the games before, we believe she was referring to activities from that program,' Stu explained.

'The tester specifically mentioned in the report that Veronica asked to call Ivy for help. That wouldn't be Ivy Ames, school-admissions adviser?' Tipper asked.

'Never heard of her,' Stu said.

'May I say something?' Patsy asked. Stu shot her a dirty look.

'Of course,' Tipper said.

'We made a big mistake, Tipper. We did have her coached. Ivy told us not to do it, but we were so stressed-out about the process that we did it anyway. We were wrong. Please don't hold it against our daughter. She's a wonderful little girl and I'd hate to see her penalized because of our stupidity,' Patsy said.

'Honey,' Stu said to Patsy, 'we coached Veronica on *Ivy's* advice. She *insisted* we do it, *remember?*'

'Stu, you are so full of shit.' Patsy looked at Tipper. 'It was Stu's idea and it was a bad one. Please forgive us, Tipper.'

'Patsy, calm yourself,' Stu said to his wife. 'Tipper, Patsy's been under a lot of pressure lately and it's caused her to become confused. She's under a doctor's care now and is heavily medicated. Pay no attention to what she says,' Stu said calmly.

Patsy stood up. 'Stu, the only pressure I've been under lately is the pressure of living with you. You're a bully, a liar, a boor, and a cur. I want you out of the house by the end of the day today,' she screamed at him. Politely, she turned to Tipper and smiled. 'Now, if you'll excuse me.' And Patsy walked out of her Harvard Day interview.

'Will there be anything else?' Tipper asked Stu.

'Did I mention I work for Steven Lord?'

೦ಾ

'So, Ollie, I see you'll be applying for financial aid,' Tipper mentioned.

'Yes, well, I can't afford tuition, so a scholarship would be good,' Ollie said.

'And you work for the Radmore-Stein family?'

'Yes.'

'You know, Ollie, if Irving comes here, he'll be playing with children who come from the world's best families. All first-tier homes. Would you be comfortable with that?' Tipper asked in a politely condescending way. God forbid Ollie should find herself lost and confused in first-tierdom.

'Of course. Irving gets along with everyone. He's a good boy.'

'Does Irving ever play with the Radmore-Steins' son?'

'They used to play, but not again,' Ollie explained. 'Once that boy wanted to check the air-conditioning vent above his room. He make Irving go first and Irving got stuck. The fire department had was to come get him out. Of course, I had was to pay to fix all the damage the firemen made to the wall,' Ollie told Tipper.

'You *had to pay* to fix the damage,' Tipper said.

'Right. I had was to pay three weeks salary. One next time, the boy and Irving played hide-and-seek with his three little Ratfinklestein cousins from Niagara Falls. Irving hid in the clothes dryer, but Ransom and his cousins went off to play something else. He had to wait an hour for them before he give up. He had was so upset when he seen they'd gone to the park and left him. After that, I stopped bringing Irving to the boy's apartment. I didn't think they was right for each other.'

'*Were*. You mean you didn't think they *were* right for each other,' Tipper said.

'Right, they wasn't right for each other at all.'

'I think you made a wise decision,' Tipper said, going back to the Radmore-Stein file and making a few notes.

'Ollie, your son's scores on his ERB test are *very* impressive.'

'Well, he's bright. I know something good gonna become of that boy. I'm proud of him.'

'You should be. He tested beautifully, and his school report is one of the best I've ever seen. Your essay was heartwarming, too.'

'Does that mean you'll take him?' Ollie asked.

'Well, he's just the kind of student we love having here, Ollie.'

'Greg McCall?' Tipper asked.

'Tipper Bucket?' Greg asked back.

'No, Tipper "Bouquet." It's "Bouquet" now. I went back to my ancestral pronunciation. I can't believe it's really *you*,' Tipper squealed, practically tinkling in her Lane Bryant granny panties. 'When I saw the name, I wondered. But last I heard, you were living in Chicago.'

'We moved back after college. Do I get a hug?' Greg said.

As they embraced, Dee Dee looked on, confused. 'How do you two know each other?' she asked.

'We worked together at Camp Flaming Arrow in the Catskills,' Greg explained. 'We were the counselor leaders for the Kickapoo tribe. Whenever they held ceremonies on their sacred grounds, Tipper and I would hide in the bushes and make sure they didn't burn down the woods. That was a great summer. Wasn't it?'

'It was. I just can't believe Moses is your son,' Tipper said. 'I saw his application and read your essay, but I didn't put two and two together. He sounds like a wonderful boy.'

'Thanks, we think so,' Greg answered.

'And Dee Dee, it's nice to meet you. Is this the Dee Dee from school you used to talk about all the time?' Tipper asked.

'The very one,' Greg said proudly. Dee Dee was beaming.

'Dee Dee, you were his favorite topic. Greg was always "Dee Dee this" and "Dee Dee that." I feel like I know you.'

'I'm so happy to see you again, Tipper. I can't believe I ran into you,' Greg said.

'I can't, either. We *must* get together for drinks and dinner one night. Greg and Dee Dee, you are *exactly* the kind of family we love accepting at Harvard Day. I hope you'll give us serious consideration,' Tipper said, recalling just how rich and philanthropic Greg's father was.

13. Nose-Pickers of Park Avenue

As their parents met with Tipper, the children were introduced to Mrs. Olson and Mr. Taymore, the teachers who would be interviewing them in small groups. Unlike most schools, Harvard Day reported back to parents, letting them know how their children had fared. Based on their feedback, I was able to put together what transpired. . . .

'Okay, kids,' Mr. Taymore said, 'go tell your parents you'll be leaving them for a little while to play and have fun, but let them know that they'll be all right and you'll pick them up later.'

The children did as they were told and then, following Mrs. Olson's instructions, they formed a choo-choo train and chugged upstairs. Veronica Needleman was the engine and Maria Kutcher the caboose. They chugged into a sun-drenched classroom, filled to the brim with kindergarten staples like easels, blocks, crayons, books, computers – an environment hard to resist for all but the most jaded child. Of course, many children who passed through these doors were, indeed, jaded.

'Okay, boys and girls, let's form a circle.' The kids

followed the teacher's instructions and plopped their bottoms on the carpet below.

'My name is Mr. Taymore, and I'm a teacher here at Harvard Day. This is Mrs. Olson, our psychologist. I coach the chess team at school. The thing I can do that I'm most proud of is run a mile in five minutes. Something I find interesting and want to learn more about is ancient Egypt. Now we'll go around the circle and let each of you tell us about yourself.'

Three hands shot up like lightning. 'Me! Me! Me!' The anxious children waved their hands desperately.

'Let's go in order,' Mr. Taymore said. 'Veronica, you first.'

'My daddy yelled at my mommy today before we came here,' Veronica announced. 'My mommy has shit for brains!'

'I'm sorry about that, Veronica, but what I'd like you to do now is tell us about *yourself*, what you're proud of, what interests you,' Mr. Taymore said.

'Oh, okay, I'm Veronica. I'm four and three-quarters years old. I like to sleep and eat. But, what I'm most proud of is . . . um . . . I can pee standing up like my daddy.'

The children giggled and Mrs. Olson cleared her throat in warning.

'Mr. Taymore, I wanna learn about ancient Egypt, too. Were you alive then?' Veronica asked.

'No, that was before my time, Veronica.' Mr. Taymore pointed to Jack Henry.

'My name is Jack Henry. I'm gonna be famous when I grow up because I have a gap between my two front teeth. That's rare. See,' he said, smiling like a jack-o'-lantern. The children oohed and ahhed.

'When I grow up, I'm gonna be a millionaire,' Jack Henry added proudly.

'What are you going to do to become one?' Mrs. Olson asked.

'Save.'

'I see,' Mr. Taymore said, and he called on the next child.

'My name is WaShaunté. I'm gonna be famous, too. I'm going to be just like Dr. Martin Luther King Junior.'

'Hmmm,' Mr. Taymore said. 'Do you want to be like Dr. King because he's black like you? And because he was a hero?'

'No, that's not it. If I was like Dr. King, my birthday would be a holiday and we could all take the day off,' Winnie-WaShaunté explained. 'Anyway, I'm just pretending to be black so I can get into a new school. My skin is *really* pink. My hair is *really* yellow. My mommy changed my colors.' Winnie-WaShaunté put her finger to her lips and whispered, 'but don't tell anyone. *It's a see-cret.*'

Mr. Taymore and Mrs. Olson were confused. Wasn't this the child who didn't have a mommy? They exchanged looks that said We'll talk about this later.

'Do you want to know what I'm proud of?' Winnie-WaShaunté said. 'I'm proud I can read minds. I'm psycho.'

'WaShaunté, you're psychic, not psycho,' Mr. Taymore said.

'Robin is Batman's psychic,' Winnie-WaShaunté said.

'No, he's Batman's sidekick, not psychic,' Mr. Taymore explained patiently.

'That's what I said – psychic, a superhero's assistant,' Winnie-WaShaunté said.

'Ooh, ooh, ooh,' Jack Henry raised his hand, waving it wildly. 'Did you see the *Batman and Robin Chanukah Special* this year? It was *awesome*.'

'Ooookay . . . let's move on . . . Ransom, what about you?' Ransom was so busy mining his nose that he didn't hear his name called. Mr. Taymore cleared his throat. 'Raaaansom.'

'Sorry,' he said, partaking of one final morsel. 'My n-n-name is Ransom Radmore-Stein.'

'Radmore-Heinie. Did you say Radmore-Heinie?' Maria asked, giggling.

'You want a knuckle sandwich, Chickbutt?' Ransom threatened.

'Children, don't be rude. Ransom, continue,' Mrs. Olson said.

'I'm proud I learned how to c-c-congregate verbs. Do you want to hear me do it?'

'By all means,' Mr. Taymore said.

'I f-f-fuck today. I fucked yesterday. I will fuck tomorrow,' he said, beaming with pride.

Mrs. Olson gasped audibly. Mr. Taymore ignored Ransom.

Veronica raised her hand. 'Yes, Veronica,' Mr. Taymore said.

'What does "fuck" mean?' Veronica inquired.

'Oh, I know, I know,' Maria said, waving her hand furiously. '*Call on me. Me! Me! Me! Me!*'

'Let's not discuss it,' Mr. Taymore said. 'That's not a nice word.'

Maria leaned over to Veronica and whispered, 'It's means "sexing," you know, when the man puts his penis in the woman's bagina to make a baby.'

'*Oooh, gross,*' Veronica said. 'My daddy would *never* do that.'

'Girls, that's enough. Maria, please introduce yourself,' Mrs. Olson said.

'My name is Maria Kutcher and my daddy is a butcher. Did you know there's no Santa Claus?'

'*What!*' Jack Henry said. 'That's not true.'

'Oh, yes, it is,' Maria said, nodding her head. 'My daddy told me and he's a wiseguy. And there's no Easter Bunny, either.'

'Hhhhhhhh,' Jack Henry gasped, clapping his hands to his mouth.

'And there's no t-t-tooth fairy,' Ransom added.

'So I guess there's no God,' Jack Henry said, looking to the teachers for verification.

'Good reasoning ability, Jack Henry,' Mrs. Olson said, making notes in her file.

With that, Mrs. Olson took three of the children and Mr. Taymore took two. They went to separate tables, where they drew pictures of their families, counted little bears, added, subtracted, and demonstrated their ability to write and recognize letters. Maria didn't know her hexagons from her parallelograms. Ransom didn't know his numbers. Otherwise, the children managed well. A snack of rice cake, fruit, and apple juice was served. Maria wouldn't eat her peach because of the 'bone' inside. Veronica spilled her juice.

'Okay, children, everyone line up and we'll go pick up your parents,' Mrs. Olson said.

'Who farted?' Maria accused.

'Don't look at me. I'm innocent,' Jack Henry said.

'He who smelt it d-d-dealt it,' Ransom said in Maria's face.

'He who denied it supplied it,' she said right back at him.

'Veronica, start walking toward the door,' Mr. Taymore said, ignoring the flatulence fracas.

'*Pssst.*' Maria tapped Veronica on the shoulder. 'What's your favorite holiday?'

'Saturday.'

'*Pssst.*' Maria tapped her again. 'You wanna have a play-date with me?' Maria asked as they choo-chooed back to their parents.

'Sure,' Veronica said, digging her Rugrats Filofax out of her Cinderella backpack as they marched downstairs. 'What's good for you?'

'I'll call Daddy and ask,' Maria said, whipping her cell phone out of her SpongeBob purse. 'He's holding my Power Puff Palm 'cuz it didn't fit in my bag.'

⁓

That afternoon, an intimate group of two boys were set for their interview. Mr. Taymore introduced himself again and invited the candidates to do the same.

'Hi, I'm Moses Epstein-McCall. I like to watch sports on TV and play T-ball. I can speak Hebrew. Did you know that every Jewish prayer starts out "I broke my toe in Illinois"?'

'I think you mean *Barukh atah Adonai*,' Mr. Taymore said.

'That's what I said. "I broke my toe in Illinois." Oh, and my most proud thing is I can turn my penis inside out. Wanna see?' Moses began to unzip his fly.

'No,' Mrs. Olson insisted, frantically waving her hands. 'Everyone will keep his penis confined to his pants, please.'

'I own a basketball team,' Moses added.

'Cool,' Irving said.

'Now, Moses, you don't own a basketball team,' Mr. Taymore said.

'Do so.'

Mr. Taymore and Mrs. Olson looked at each other with raised eyebrows. 'Where did you get that knot on your head, Moses?' Mr. Taymore asked.

Moses touched his lump. 'Oh, I bumped my head on my bump bed. Did I tell you my uncle died last year? Yeah, I'm gonna dig him up soon.'

Trying to suppress a smile, Mr. Taymore called on Irving.

'My name is Irving Pou. If you dig up your uncle, he's gonna be a skeleton. If you want, I'll come wich you and tell you the names of his bones. I'm gonna be a doctor someday.'

'You can come,' Moses said. 'It'd be good to have a doctor there.'

'I have a pet mouse that lives in my mom's closet,' Irving said.

'Neat!' Moses said.

'Don't you have a problem with mouse droppings?' Mrs. Olson asked.

'Oh, no. I trained him to poop on Post-it notes.'

As with the earlier group, Mrs. Olson and Mr. Taymore observed Moses and Irving in the classroom. Counting. Drawing. Block-building. Both boys demonstrated an extraordinary flair for scissors. Irving forgot the words to 'The Farmer in the Dell.' Moses ate most of his Play-Doh, a transgression that would, of course, be overlooked in light of his family's donor potential.

14. Let's Go to Luckenbach, Texas

Stu held me responsible for the breakup of his marriage to Patsy.

'This is all *your* fault, Ivy! If you hadn't put ideas into Patsy's head, none of this would have happened!' Stu screamed so loudly that I had to hold the phone away from my ear.

'Stu, don't you think you might have had *something* to do with it?'

'*No, Ivy, I don't!* Patsy and I were *happy* before you came along. We *never* argued. Patsy agreed with me on *everything*. The day we hired *you* is the day our lives fell apart.'

'And you think *I'm* responsible?'

'I don't think it. *I know it!*'

'Okay, Stu, how can I make this up to you?'

'You can get me my wife back, that's number one. You can get Veronica into a top-tier school, that's number two. And, after that, *I never want to see your sorry face again!*' He slammed down the phone.

After Stu's ass-reaming, I walked outside, sat on the bench in front of Kratt's, and wept. Thirty-nine years old, and all I wanted was my mommy.

I wasn't good at getting yelled at. At Myoki, yelling was for suckers. Only rubes revealed their hand so aggressively. At Myoki, we smiled at our enemies while scheming behind their backs, devising cunning ways to even the score. My expert ability to fight back through passive-aggressive means had been honed under the tutelage of such gifted maestros as Drayton Bird and Konrad Kavaler. That's how I survived fourteen years there. When someone screamed at me as Stu had, I regressed and became five-year-old Ivy Schechter, whose mommy and daddy used to scream and fight when Daddy came home smelling of perfume; at least that's how my former shrink explained it.

So Stu's tirade drove me to tears, and I went outside to cry myself out. Sitting on the bench with my head in my hands, sobbing, I heard someone say, 'Are you all right?' I looked up, and there stood Philip with two D'Agostino bags in his hands.

'Do I *look* all right?' I asked. 'I'm upset because my client yelled at me.'

'Did you do something wrong?'

'I don't know.' I told Philip about Stu's accusations as objectively as I could.

'This guy sounds like a real jerk. If I were his wife, I'd leave him, too.'

'Thanks.'

Philip sat next to me, putting down his bags. 'What about the rest of your clients? Are you doing better with them?' He seemed genuinely interested.

'For the most part, yes. But all the tricky-dicky stuff this job requires is driving me insane. I thought I'd given that up when I left Myoki, but it seems I can't get away from it. I'm too resourceful for my own good. And now I've instigated so many crazy plots, there's no going back,' I complained.

'It can't be *that* bad.'

I updated him on my latest shenanigans. How we'd disguised Winnie so she'd look black. How we'd hired Archie to pretend to be Winnie's father. How Omar was strong-arming trustees to get Maria in. How we'd helped Veronica cheat on her ERBs.

Philip asked me lots of questions about how we managed to change Winnie's color, how she was handling the charade psychologically, who Omar was extorting, how Veronica had cheated on her test – and, more to the point, what she had said to get herself caught. I was pleased that he was taking such an interest in my life. Maybe there was hope for us.

I went on to remind Philip of how Lilith Radmore-Stein was planning to bribe a Stratmore Prep trustee and how Moses McCall's grandfather was still offering me $1,000,000 to betray his son. The only clients who weren't mixed up in smoke and mirrors were Ollie, Tiny, and Willow. Philip couldn't believe all the extras Buck had given me in anticipation of the big payoff.

'I don't know what to say,' Philip remarked. 'Wow!'

'Wow, indeed,' I answered. 'And there's something else I should tell you.'

'What?'

'I'm considering accepting Buck McCall's offer. I'm thinking of taking the money, getting out of this business, and moving to Luckenbach, Texas.'

'Luckenbach, why?'

'I don't know. It's in a Waylon Jennings song. You know, *"I'm goin' to Luckenbach, Texas, with Waylon and Willie and the boys."* It sounds so easy. I could buy a house outright, put the girls in public school, get a used Ford, and become a cashier at the local Piggly Wiggly.'

'So *Green Acres* is the life for you?' Philip joked.

'It may be,' I said seriously. I felt my chin wobbling. 'Philip, I've done some really bad things. You're lucky to be rid of me.'

'I miss you,' he said quietly.

'I miss you, too,' I whispered. 'But, hey, it sounds like there's a wedding in the cards for you and Sassy. I'm happy for you, I guess.'

He laughed. 'Where did you get *that* idea?'

'From Sassy, where else?'

'It's not true,' he said. 'I've had dinner with her a few times, but that's all.'

'Isn't she inspiring you to write your new book?'

'Who told you *that*?'

'Sassy, who else? She told me you said she was the inspiration for the lead character in your new novel,' I said.

He laughed. 'I talked with her about the relationship *you and I* had. I told her *you* had inspired me to write the main character in my book. She must have said that so you'd think badly of me. I guess she wants to keep us apart.'

'God, she's so dishonest,' I said. 'You broke up with *me* for that. Why do you stay with her?'

'She's not my girlfriend, Ivy. I haven't even slept with her.'

'Oh, my God! She told me what a wonderful lover you were, how you definitely weren't gay,' I exclaimed.

'Gay?'

'Not important,' I muttered. 'Listen,' I said to Philip, 'I can understand why you might not want to build a life with someone as unprincipled as me, but can we at least be friends again?'

'Oh, Ivy,' he said, 'I want that, too.'

It wouldn't have broken my heart if Philip had argued the point, insisting that my principles weren't *so* bad and maybe there *was* a future for us. I wouldn't have objected if he'd swept me into his arms, carried me upstairs, and made love to me like he had last summer. But he didn't. He only wanted to be my friend. Just like Michael. Always the friend, never the girlfriend.

15. An Important Introduction

The phone was ringing when I went inside. It was Sassy. I wished she'd stop calling me. Still, I asked her how she was. Always having fake-friendly conversations with people I can't stand, that's me.

'I'm not well, Ivy, not well at all. United found Drayton's ashes, so there goes my pain-and-suffering award. And someone made an offer on the apartment. I'll have to take it.'

'I'm so sorry.'

'Thanks. One good thing happened, though. I got my first paid decorating job. I'll be doing the bedroom of one of Bea's friends. The girl's mom felt sorry for me because of Drayton. It's a pity commission, but I'll take it. I can't believe I have to support myself. I could kill Drayton for putting me in this position.'

'I know how devastated you are about having to work,' I said. Life can be so cruel.

'Yes, I am. But that's not why I called. I need to ask a favor. Philip's taking me out Saturday night to cheer me up and Irma can't babysit. Can I leave the children at your house, since you live so close to Philip and I'm sure you don't have a date? I could pick them up in the morning.

Things are *really* heating up between us. I'm hoping he'll propose. We have so much in common, you know. He's attractive. I'm attractive. He's a famous writer. I have *many* famous friends. And the sex with Philip, well, it's amazing. *Amaaaazing.* I wonder how much time I should let pass before I marry again?' She blabbered on like a schizophrenic Chatty Cathy doll.

'Gee, Sassy, I'm glad to hear you two are so much in love. I wish I could help you Saturday, but darn it, I have plans.'

'Won't you change them?' she said, making pathetic whimpering sounds. 'It would mean a lot to Philip and me. Especially after my awful news about the ashes. And you promised Drayton's spirit you'd help me, remeeeember?'

Did you ever? 'I'm sure about Saturday night,' I said. 'But I can help you with something else. Something more important. I have a client, a nice gentleman, very rich, who lost his wife recently. Anyway, she was right in the middle of redecorating their apartment when she passed. Do you want me to recommend you to him, to finish the job?'

'Oh, that would be wonderful. Would you do that? Would you call him today?' she asked. *Could this woman be any pushier?*

'Sure,' I said. 'It'd be my pleasure. If he calls, his name is Omar, just so you'll know who it is.'

I invited Omar to have dinner with me at Kratt's. Michael must have thought it strange, my consorting with a notorious mobster, but he didn't say anything. I ordered the beef-brisket-and-potato-pancake special and encouraged

Omar to do the same. He updated me on the last of his interviews and assured me that his trustee friends were working behind the scenes. It looked like Maryvale and St. Andrew's were in the bag.

'Plus, I think that director at Harvard Day *really* liked me. She wants to fuck me. I'm sure she'll offer Maria a space,' he boasted.

Tipper? Not possible.

'But here's the best part, Ivy. I'm already seeing changes in Maria. She got angry last night when I told her it was time for bed. She folded her arms, turned her back, screwed up her face, but didn't scream! Can you believe it? She didn't scream! What a pistol my girl is! We're making progress, and it's all because of that fancy psychiatrist you recommended. I'm forever in your debt, Ivy,' he said kindly. 'If you ever need anything, anything at all, just ask.' That *was* good news. It's always nice to have a mob boss owe you one.

'I'm happy for you, Omar. And guess what? I have another recommendation. Remember when you told me you needed to finish your apartment? Well, I have a friend who's a talented decorator. I think you'll like her work. She's also a beautiful single woman who lost her husband not too long ago. I think she's lonely, and you might be able to fill a certain void in her life.'

'Say no more, Ivy. Give the broad my number. Va-va-voom!'

Omar had such a way with words.

16. The Kids' Limo

On Saturday, Faith picked us up in her chauffeur-driven kid stretch, the one stocked with juice boxes, rice cakes, a DVD library of children's shows, a twenty-four-inch plasma-screen TV, first-aid supplies, changes of clothes, and Pull-Ups. This was a must-have for every billionairess mom juggling the demands of children and obscene fortune. Of course, her personal chauffeur drove the less conspicuous Mercedes Maybach whenever Faith was *sans* children. We were on our way to the Museum of Natural History, always fun and educational, but more important, an expedition guaranteed to wear out the girls. As is often the case with children, the reality didn't live up to the fantasy. The day started out as a real whine-fest.

'I want to see "Shrek Three-ee,"' Lia said.

'They haven't made it yet. We're going to the museum,' Faith said.

'I haaaaate the museum,' Lia wailed. 'It's the most boring place eeeee-ver.'

'Lia, would ya put on your anti-whining cloak?' Mae said.

'I wanna eeeeeat,' Kate said. 'Let's go to Popeye's for chicken.'

'Yeah, yeah,' said Mae. 'I love Popeye's.'

'Nooooo,' Skyler said. 'I only eat chicken nuggets, not *reeeeeal* chicken.'

'Guess what, everybody? My mommy's gonna have a baby,' Mae announced.

'What!' I turned to Faith. 'Why didn't you tell me?'

'Busted.' Faith smiled guiltily. 'Sorry, Ivy, we didn't want to say anything until I was three months along. I wanted to be sure before telling you.'

'Congratulations,' I said, hugging her. 'That's so exciting.'

'Do you know if it's gonna be a boy or a girl?' Kate asked.

'No, we don't know yet,' Faith said.

'Do you know if it's gonna be black or white?' Kate asked.

'We're pretty sure it'll be white,' Faith said, smiling.

'Mommy, Mae's tweating me like a skunk,' Lia tattled.

'Say it, don't spray it,' Mae said to her sister.

'See what I mean, Mommy?' Lia snitched.

'She kicked me first for no apparent reason,' Mae said.

'No, Mommy, Mae diswespected me. She called me a pubic hair. That's the weason,' Lia insisted.

'You bwabbewmouth,' Mae said to Lia, making fun of her speech impediment.

'What's a pubic hair?' Kate asked Lia.

Lia shrugged. She had no idea. But it sounded bad.

'Mae, leave your sister alone or we'll turn this car around right now and take you home.' She turned to me.

'I think having another one of these will be delightful, don't you?'

I laughed. 'You should have asked. I would have given you one of mine.'

'By the way,' Faith said, 'my closetkeeper, Virginia, just quit. Keep your ears open for someone, would you? We have the agency working on it, but so far we haven't liked anyone they sent over.'

'You got it,' I said.

'Lia, did you just wet your pants?' Faith said, noticing a big wet stain on Lia's crotch.

'No, I went swimming,' she said with her head hanging down.

'Come here, let me change you.' Faith reached below the seat of her well-stocked limo for some dry clothes.

'I do it,' Lia said.

'Fine.' Faith handed her some dry panties and a skirt. 'Just remember, the tag goes in the back.'

'We're almost there,' I announced as we turned onto Central Park West. 'Everyone get your shoes on.'

'Mommy, Mommy,' Kate shouted, 'what if you could go back in time and stop either my birth or Skyler's. Which one would you stop?'

'Neither, I love you both.'

'No, but if you don't stop one of us from being born, everyone in the world including you would die.'

'Oh, well, when you put it that way, I guess I'd stop *your* birth,' I said.

'I *knew* I was the favorite,' Skyler said. '*Yessssss!*'

'Do you *really* wish I was never born?' Kate asked.

'Of course not, but don't ask me silly questions like

that. I could never choose between the two people I love most in the universe.'

'Mommy.' Lia was pulling at Faith's sleeves. 'Mae just called me the F-curse.'

'You'd better not have,' Faith said to Mae, 'or I'll have to wash your mouth out with soap.'

'What if I just *think* the F-curse? Is that okay?' Mae asked.

'No,' Faith said.

The car pulled up to the museum steps and the kids noticed the hot-dog stand in front. 'Let's have hot dogs!' Mae said. 'Yeah, yeah,' the others agreed. Finally. Consensus.

'Mommy, I wish Daddy would quit his job and become the hot-dog man,' Mae said.

'Me, too,' Lia agreed.

Faith looked at me wistfully. 'Sometimes, I wish that's all he were, too. Life would be simpler.'

'Are you out of your fucking *mind*?' I whispered, tugging on Faith's arm.

'You're right. I don't know what I was thinking,' Faith said, shaking her head.

17. Snooty with a Chance of Attitude

Dinner at my house is a less-than-casual affair. Kate, Skyler, and I sit at our tiny table. Sir Elton annoys us, begging for scraps. There's no silver bell that I ring to signal the chef in the kitchen to bring on the next course. There's no chef. There's no separate kitchen. There's no next course. It's broiled steak or some Crock-Pot dish that cooks itself while I work. *The Rugrats* is on. Conversation between us is minimal because we are lost in the world of Tommy, Chucky, and Angelica.

'Which Rugrat do you think is the smartest, Kate?' Skyler asks.

'Tommy,' Kate answers.

'But which Rugrat do you think *looks* the smartest?' Skyler asks.

'Chucky,' Kate answers.

'Has anyone heard the new Madonna album?' I ask, looking for common ground with my daughters.

'Ma-DON-na!' Skyler says. 'She's *so* over with.'

'Madonna's old. She's gonna die soon,' Kate adds, feeding Sir Elton her steak.

'Kate, don't give the dog people-food. And eat your steak. It's good for you.'

'Did you see the animated steak on *The Simpsons* last night?' Kate asks Skyler.

'Yeah, I saw it. But you know what's even more delicious than animated steak? *Animated ribs!*'

'With animated barbecue sauce!!!' Kate adds.

I'm sorry to say that this is the kind of spellbinding repartee that goes on at our dinner table. But by 7:00 P.M., I don't have the energy to top off a day of work, cleaning, errands, school, dog-walking, baths, homework, and refereeing with meaningful conversation. I'm spent. My plan to pass half an hour of daily quality time with each of my daughters was a bust. My new plan to schedule meaningful conversation for weekends when I'm fresh seems to be working. For now, I've come to accept and embrace my less-than-perfect reality. So the three of us sit, chewing, each in her own private stupor, six eyes converged on Nickelodeon.

The phone rang. It was Sassy, calling to thank me for introducing her to Omar. Apparently, he had given her a huge commission to complete his renovation and they were getting along famously, *FAMOUSLY!* Bully for them. I hung up as quickly as I could, not wanting to miss the part where Angelica got her own talk show.

The knocking at our door took me by surprise. *Now what?* The universe was conspiring against my seeing the climax of *Rugrats*. It was Archie, Winnie's fake father. I invited him to sit in the kitchen with us where I could keep one eye on him and the other on the show.

'I'm concerned about WaShaunté's interviews,' Archie

began. 'We went to St. Andrew's today and had a bad experience.'

'What happened?'

'You know how the kids are supposed to come to that visit prepared to talk about something important to them?'

'Yes.'

'Well, WaShaunté brought her security puppy, the one she's been sleeping with since she was a baby, you know, Red Puppy?'

'No, I don't know Red Puppy specifically, but that sounds like a good item to bring.'

'Well, *it wasn't*,' Archie explained, miffed. 'As someone who calls herself a professional, I think you should have advised me better on this one.'

'Excuse me?' I said. 'Archie, you aren't even the actual father. You just play one in real life.'

'There were six kids at the interview, and they all went in with the teacher. I stayed back talking with the rest of the parents as usual, and the conversation got around to what each child was going to share. One mother told us that her son was studying anatomy and had brought in an earthworm he was going to dissect for the group.' Archie sniffed.

Good grief. What kind of four-year-old boy has the fine motor skills necessary to dissect an earthworm? 'Skyler, would you please turn down the volume?'

'I can't hear the TV with you two talking so loud,' she said.

'Turn it down *now*.' She did.

'Another mother told me her daughter was a student of modern dance and was going to perform Alvin Ailey's

Aspects of a Vibe, a twenty-minute jazz piece. Then a Jamaican babysitter mentioned that the little boy she takes care of, a white boy I might add, had taught himself Mandarin Chinese and would be reading a traditional Mandarin story to the group in the *ancient* form of the language. Of the two kids left, one was going to tell an African folktale. Another was reciting postprandial sonnets. We sent WaShaunté into a situation where she was *way* over her head, and *somebody* should have known better,' he accused.

'Postprandial sonnets?' I asked. 'What are those?'

'I have no idea. But I guarantee they're more complex than *Mother Goose.*'

I sighed. 'I'm sorry, Archie, I should have known this. You're right. It's just that at most schools, children only have to draw shapes or pictures, count, write letters, stuff like that. St. Andrew's takes gifted kids, but I didn't realize they would expect so much raw talent from four- and five-year-olds.'

'Well, in the future, I'd appreciate it if you'd do your homework before casting us to the wolves like that. Apparently, the other children made WaShaunté feel like a baby for bringing in her special puppy. This was no ordinary show-and-tell.'

'I'm sorry, Archie. It won't happen again.'

'See that it doesn't,' Archie barked.

You could have scraped me off the floor. Archie was morphing into Stu Needleman. On the one hand, it was good to see that he was taking his role as WaShaunté's (I mean Winnie's) father so seriously. On the other hand, he didn't have to be so snippy about it.

PART 5

The Importance of Being Accepted

1. Not to Be Rich and White in New York City

Tiny, Willow, and I knocked on Isaiah Jenkins's door. I'd hidden behind a parked car and watched the boy leaving Stratmore Prep. He looked about sixteen. Boldly, I quasi-stalked him home to 128th Street and rang the bell. Introducing myself, I explained to his mother, Deirdre, that I had some friends who had adopted a black child and wanted to know what it was like to be one of the few children of color in an exclusive private school. Deirdre told me how happy Isaiah was at Stratmore and what a difference it had made in his life, and she graciously made a date to introduce her son to my friends.

Entering Deirdre's small but cozy living room a few days later, we smelled and then noticed a plate of boiled mini-hot-dogs laid out in our honor. Isaiah and the four of us devoured the weenies before we got down to business.

'Isaiah,' Tiny said, 'Willow and I have a little boy who's applying to private school. He's black, like you. We're trying to decide whether private school's right for him. Can you tell us about your experience at Stratmore Prep? Have you been happy there?'

'I like my school okay. I've made friends, and the teachers are nice. I've learned a lot, I guess.'

'You love it there,' Deirdre said. 'Show a little enthusiasm.'

'The thing is, Mom,' Isaiah started, 'I'm not sure they should send their son.'

Deirdre's mouth dropped open.

Isaiah turned to Tiny and Willow. 'I've been going to Stratmore Prep since kindergarten,' he explained. 'When I hang out in my own neighborhood, people think I'm different. No one talks to me, no one plays ball with me, no one invites me over. They call me "Boozhie," you know, bourgeois. I don't fit in here. I don't have it.'

'What don't you have?' Deirdre asked.

'You know, *it*, my identity, my groove, my black soul. I've tried to fit in, but how can I? I talk like I'm white, I walk like I'm white, I dress like I'm white. Have you ever heard me say "whaddup dawg" or "yo" or "thang"? I sound ridiculous.'

'I can teach you to be black, Isaiah. You don't need to go to school in the neighborhood to learn *that*,' Deirdre said.

'You can't teach me. You're yuppie black. You've made it so I don't belong with my own people, Mom. And I don't belong at Stratmore Prep, either. I go to school with kids who don't look like me, don't live the way we live. Their parents won't let them come to my house. I think you should have let me live the life I was born to.'

'Isaiah, I sent you to Stratmore Prep because I thought

it would open doors that staying in Harlem never could. When I grew up, I was never exposed to the privileged world you operate in every day. I wanted you to be part of that. I was trying to do my best for you, that's all.'

'I know you were, Mom. I'm only saying that it's made me an outsider at home *and* at school. I don't think it was worth it,' Isaiah said. He turned to Tiny and Willow. 'Maybe this won't matter for *your* son. He's being raised in the white world already. He may not care about identifying with his own people.'

Tiny, Willow, and I listened, fascinated. This was particularly interesting to me because lately Skyler had begun talking with a Puerto Rican accent. I'd been telling her to stop, not realizing that perhaps she was trying to fit in with her new friends.

'Isaiah,' Deirdre said, 'why didn't you tell me this before?'

'You never asked.'

When Tiny, Willow, and I left Isaiah's house, we were all lost in our own thoughts, none of us sure if the advantages of a private-school education would outweigh the part of Jack Henry's soul that the experience might extinguish.

2. A Crisis of Conscience

On Sunday morning, I met with Greg and Dee Dee at Kratt's to discuss their first-choice letter. After standing in line for forty-five minutes, we finally got a table, ordered coffee, bagels, lox, sable, and cream cheese.

'I like the Shalom Day School. What about you Greg?'

'I like Shalom Day, but I also like Harvard Day. I know it's not technically a Jewish school, but don't they have a large contingent of Jews in the parent body?' Greg asked.

'Huge. They have a huge contingent of Jews,' I replied.

'It's got a much finer reputation than Shalom Day, Dee Dee,' he explained.

'Much finer,' I agreed.

'Yes, but Moses won't speak Hebrew at Harvard Day. He won't learn Jewish traditions,' she argued.

'That's true, Dee Dee,' Greg said. 'But a lot of the kids go to Hebrew school across the street at Temple Hillel. And the kids from Harvard Day get into the best Ivy League schools,' he added.

'The best of the best,' I agreed.

'Are you two ganging up on me?' Dee Dee asked.

'No, not at all,' Greg answered. 'If you want Shalom Day, we'll try for it. But let's at least make Harvard Day our second choice, okay?'

'Okay, deal,' she said. 'Ivy, go ahead and send our first-choice letter to Shalom Day. Harvard Day'll be our second choice.'

'Done,' I said.

The two of them left to go shopping on Orchard Street, leaving me alone with my coffee and thoughts. *What to do?* I wanted that million dollars so badly I could almost spend it. I needed it. I deserved it after all I'd been through. I looked over at Michael, who was working hard to serve the hungry crowd. What would he think of me if I took Buck's bribe? Could I ever tell him? Could I live with myself if I betrayed my clients? Dad would have done it in a heartbeat. Philip, Tiny, and Willow wouldn't have. But they were stronger than I was. My conscience unequivocally said, *'Don't do it,'* but my practical self, the one with two kids to support, screamed, *'Do it! Do it! Do it!'*

Maybe I should move away, forget this year ever happened. I could make this the last lie. The lie that ends the lying. At this point, I had no dignity left anyway. I'd been so corrupt that there was nowhere to go but up. This could be my final wayward act, and then I'd reform. That sounded like a fair solution, so I pulled out a yellow pad and composed this letter to Shalom Day:

Dear Rabbi Jacobson,

    Dee Dee and I would like to thank you for considering Moses Epstein-McCall for admission to your kindergarten class next year. We want nothing more than to send our son to a school steeped in Hebrew tradition such as Shalom Day. You are our first choice. If you offer Moses a place, we will accept.

As you could probably tell at our interview, Dee Dee is absolutely committed to Shalom Day. I want you to know that I am willing to do anything to ensure Moses's acceptance. I'm sure, like most New Yorkers, you have heard of the McCall family (McCall Hall, McCall Performing Arts Center, McCall School of Medicine at NYU, McCall Stadium). If you take Moses, we would be happy to discuss an immediate seven-figure donation to Shalom Day, the only condition being that you rename your school McCall Day.

Although we will be major donors to the school, we won't abuse our position by asking for special treatment too often. We do have one request, however. It is imperative to Moses's ongoing treatment that his psychopharmacologist be allowed to observe him in the classroom bimonthly. We would appreciate it if his teacher would welcome the doctor and spend time with him following each visit, providing an update on any unusual or disruptive behaviors Moses may have exhibited at school.

Again, many thanks for considering our son for admission next year. We look forward to being active members of the McCall Day community next fall.

Sincerely,
Greg McCall

3. Who Yo Daddy?

A rchie stopped by again. I was worried about him. He was taking his role as Winnie's father *waaaay* too seriously.

'Ivy, we visited The Balmoral School yesterday, and I have to insist we withdraw the application,' he said.

'Why? It's an excellent school. My own girls went there.'

'I'm sure the education is wonderful. The mansion is amazing, and I liked the ballet studio and the roving masseuse, but that's not the point,' he explained.

'What *is* the point, Archie?'

'This very sophisticated junior, Antoinette, gave the tour. She had just gotten back from the Bahamas, where one of her classmates had a Sweet Sixteen party. Her parents flew the whole class, in a private jet, to Eleuthera for the weekend. From what she said, *that's normal*. Ivy, WaShaunté comes from humble roots. She would never fit into a world where the children around her don't understand what it means to be hungry.'

'Archie, remember, WaShaunté's name is Winnie. She isn't really black. She's a white Jewish girl from the Upper West Side. She'll manage.'

'Even if that's true . . .'

'Which it is; you know that, don't you, Archie?'

'Yes, of course I do. Ivy, I don't know if you've been to Balmoral lately, but the older girls are all anorexic. They carry Prada backpacks and wear uniforms designed by Steven Tyler. When I asked Antoinette what she was learning at school, she recited the rankings of the buildings on Fifth Avenue by status. That's just wrong,' he said. 'If WaShaunté goes to that school, what kind of person will she grow up to be?'

'Archie,' I said. 'Her mother put Balmoral on her list. It's what she wants. There's nothing I can do. Once Winnie gets in somewhere, she'll be out of your life and mine forever. Have you told Wendy about your concerns?'

'We talk after every interview. I've been straight with her about my feelings. We're having dinner on Friday. I'll tell her then.'

'Just don't forget that this is an acting job, it's not real life.'

'Yes, but it's WaShaunté's real life.'

4. Undue Influence

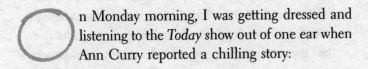

On Monday morning, I was getting dressed and listening to the *Today* show out of one ear when Ann Curry reported a chilling story:

The Justice Department is looking into reports of corruption involving the Food and Drug Administration, American Standard Paper, and Phizz Pharmaceuticals. Independent sources alleged that Lilith Radmore-Stein, the chairman of American Standard Paper, bribed Lyndon Pratt, the former chairman of the FDA, by arranging for her company's publishing subsidiary to purchase his novel *Approval Hell*, a roman à clef about the inner workings of the FDA. In exchange, just before leaving office, Chairman Pratt overrode the FDA ban and approved Phizz Pharmaceutical's new over-the-counter botulinum toxin type-A home injection kit, a wrinkle-reduction therapy for the do-it-yourself crowd that works like Botox.

Expected to be marketed as 'Baby Face,' the product had been opposed for some time because of the high occurrence of patient error when the toxin was self-administered during trials. In two out of ten cases, subjects injected the product into the wrong muscles and nerves, causing complications such as droopy eyes, frozen grimaces, and other expressions most commonly associated with stroke victims.

Approval of Baby Face will mean hundreds of millions of dollars in profits for Phizz Pharmaceuticals. Sources close to the Justice Department confirm that Mrs. Radmore-Stein arranged for then-Chairman Pratt's intervention in Baby Face's cause in an attempt to induce Phizz's CEO, Buzz Wendell, to influence the approval of her son's kindergarten application to the exclusive Stratmore Prep School, where Mr. Wendell is on the board of trustees. Spokespersons for former Chairman Pratt, Mrs. Radmore-Stein, Mr. Wendell, and Stratmore Prep all expressed shock and denied the allegations.

No! This can't be. How did this come out? The only people who knew were Lilith, Mort Small-Podd, me, and then Chairman Pratt and Buzz Wendell, I suppose. If I do jail time over this, I will be so pissed off.

The telephone rang. It was that reporter from the *New York Times*, the one I'd hoodwinked last spring. She was doing another story on the cutthroat world of New York City private-school admissions in association with the Baby Face scandal. Could she ask me a few questions? 'No comment,' I said, and hung up on her.

The phone began ringing off the hook. The *Wall Street Journal*. The *Daily News*. The Associated Press. *People*.

Time. Newsweek. Forbes. Quilting News. Quilting News? 'No comment.' 'No comment.' 'No comment.' What could I say? I was there when Lilith planned the crime. *Does that make me an accessory to a felony?* I wondered.

Am I going up the river?

5. Ivy in a Pickle

I dropped the girls at school and immediately went to the Knishery looking for Michael. He was a businessman. He'd know what to do. Unfortunately, I was told, he'd taken a few days off to go snowboarding in Canada. *Snowboarding? Michael? Screw it, I'll find Philip.* Luckily, he was home.

'I'm in big trouble,' I said.

'What's the problem?'

I told him about the report I'd heard on the *Today* show and all the press that had called.

'The thing is, I *knew* Lilith Radmore-Stein was planning to influence a board member at Stratmore Prep. But I had no idea she would bribe the chairman of the FDA. Do you think they'll arrest me? Am I an accomplice?'

'I don't even know if what you did is a crime.'

'What should I do?' I asked. 'I can't afford a lawyer. I can't go to prison. I'm responsible for two little girls. And don't say I should have thought of this in the first place, because I know that.'

'Ivy, I'm no lawyer, but it seems to me that you should call the Justice Department. Tell them you're a witness and you want to come forward with information,' he suggested. 'Then, if you accidentally did something illegal, they'll cut you a break. They want to nail high-profile crooks, not nobodies like you. If you help them develop their case, I can't believe they'd charge you with anything.'

'That's a good idea. I'll throw myself at their mercy. But before I drop the dime on Lilith, I'll deal.'

Philip looked at me strangely.

'You know, if I sing before I bargain, I won't have any leverage. Don't you watch *Law and Order*?'

'No, not really,' said Philip.

Philip called directory assistance and got the number for the New York City branch of the U.S. Justice Department. He went through six people before finding an investigator assigned to this case. When he'd explained the situation, they invited me in for an 'informal chat.'

6. To Tell the Truth, Part 1

hilip and I headed downtown to headquarters, which was really the Federal Building on lower Broadway. He insisted on accompanying me for moral support. When we arrived, Mr. Baker was waiting. He looked nothing like the detectives on television. If I'd seen him on the street, I would have tagged him as a thirty-year-old investment banker. I introduced Philip and asked if he could stay. Mr. Baker said that would be okay. Then he asked if he could tape my statement.

That's when I made my move.

'Mr. Baker, I know what happened here. I was a witness to a meeting where Mrs. Radmore-Stein concocted this preposterous plan. I was there and I told her it was a bad idea, but she obviously went ahead with it. I wasn't involved when she put the plan into motion. But I knew what she intended to do. Anyway, I'm willing to tell you everything I witnessed, but I'm worried that I'll say something incriminating and you'll want to prosecute me. I have two little girls, Mr. Baker. I can't go to jail. If you want *this* canary to sing, you have to agree not to bring charges. And I want it in writing. Frankly, Mr. Baker, if you don't deal, I'll lawyer up right now.'

'You've obviously watched a lot of television, Ms. Ames,' he said. 'I'll be right back.' He left the room.

'Do you think that's a yes?' I whispered to Philip.

'I don't know, Ivy. This is my first time in the pokey,' he whispered back, smiling.

'Look.' I pointed to a mirror on the wall. 'I'll bet that's a two-way mirror. Do you think they're watching us? *Don't look.* Act natural.'

'It probably is a two-way mirror,' Philip whispered.

Mr. Baker came back with a piece of paper entitled 'Cooperation Agreement.' It said I wouldn't be prosecuted for any crime if I told them everything I knew about Case Number 5708982 and agreed to testify should that be required. It was a standard form that he tore off a pad. *They must make deals like this all the time*, I thought.

Mr. Baker signed the paper, as did I, and he handed me the yellow carbon copy. He turned on his tape recorder. With that, I spilled the beans on Lilith. I described the meeting in her conference room and fingered Mort Small-Podd, whom they didn't know about yet. He asked me lots of questions about school admissions to get a better understanding of why parents would take such risks to get their children into private school. Motive. Obviously, he was trying to establish motive. I suggested to Mr. Baker that the smoking gun just might be the fact that more than four hundred boys would be competing for eight Caucasian spaces at Stratmore Prep. Four hundred well-mannered little gentlemen versus alphabet-burping, armpit-farting Ransom Radmore-Stein. I rest my case.

After hours of being grilled with no relief, I asked Mr. Baker if we could take a break and eat. He agreed and was nice enough to give us complimentary lunch tickets to use in the Federal Building's basement cafeteria.

As we were looking for a place to sit, I spotted a friendly face. 'Ollie,' I called out, waving. She waved back and invited us to join her. I introduced her to Philip and asked what she was doing there. Did it have something to do with Lilith?

Ollie explained that she was being interviewed just like we were. 'Are you a witness?' I asked her. 'Did you see anything?'

Ollie said that something terrible had happened. About a week ago, Stratmore Prep had phoned for Mrs. Radmore-Stein. Thinking it was about Ransom's application, Lilith had taken the call immediately. After a few moments, Ollie heard her boss screaming, 'I'll have your fuckin' ass, Ollie!!' She went to Lilith's study to find out what she had done now.

It seems that Stratmore Prep just wanted to verify Ollie's salary. They were discussing Irving's financial-aid package in committee, and fact-checking was part of the process. In making the call, Stratmore Prep inadvertently revealed to Lilith that Ollie had applied Irving to their kindergarten this year.

Ollie said Mrs. Radmore-Stein was seething. Did Ollie not understand that Irving was competing with Ransom? Lilith demanded. If Irving got in and Ransom didn't, Irving would have stolen what was rightfully Ransom's. And even worse, if they *both* got in, Lilith would have to attend school events with . . . with . . . with *the domestic help*. Did Ollie think they would both become class parents and carpool together? She told Ollie she was fired and that she would never give her references.

Before Ollie left the room, she had the audacity to ask

Lilith for her wages. Although her weekly salary was $400, Lilith deducted $100 for taxes and Social Security and $200 for room and board in Lilith's one-room basement maid's quarters. The balance was just $100. On hearing the words 'Can I have my $100 for the week,' Lilith lost it and began throwing her plaques and awards at Ollie to drive her out of the house.

'I had was to run for my life. I thought she was gonna knock my teeth down my throat.'

Ollie had known this day was coming. Not necessarily over this, but at some point Lilith would banish her from the kingdom just as she regularly expelled other staff members who displeased her.

Ollie was no dummy. She'd always known that she needed some dirt on Lilith so that when Lilith screwed her, she'd have a way to fight back. For that reason, Ollie always kept her eyes and ears open. Recently, while cleaning Lilith's bathroom, she'd overheard Lilith tell Johnny that the chairman of the FDA had agreed to approve Mr. Wendell's new injection kit if she would publish the chairman's book. She went on to say that Mr. Wendell had promised to get Ransom into Stratmore Prep if his injection kit was approved.

Ollie knew there was something fishy about that arrangement. She believed it might be something she could hold over Lilith's head to get the $100 she was owed.

The day after Ollie was axed, she called Lilith Radmore-Stein at work and told her secretary that she was from the admissions office at Stratmore Prep. Of course, Lilith picked up. Ollie immediately launched into her speech, demanding her $100 and telling her former boss that if she didn't give it to her, Lilith would live to regret it. '*Ooooooooh, I'm scaaared,*' Lilith taunted. 'Ollie, you ignorant maid. I refuse to give you another second of my time.' And she slammed down the phone.

Ollie was upset about the $100. She was upset about the snake in Irving's lunchbox, the hide-and-seek fiasco, the dryer, the air-conditioning vent, and all the other abuse she and Irving had suffered at the hands of Lilith Radmore-Stein and her devil-child. So Ollie called a *New York Times* reporter and told him what she had heard.

This morning, the Justice Department had summoned her for questioning.

'So, Ollie, now that you aren't with the Radmore-Steins, where are you living?' I asked.

'We're staying at the Quaker shelter on Sixteenth Street.'

'You're homeless?' Philip asked.

'Just until I get another live-in job. It'll be harder to find, 'cuz there's me and Irving to put up, but I'm prayin' it'll happen soon.'

'Ollie,' I said excitedly, 'I know about a job that's open. Meet me at the coffee shop on Second and Seventy-third, the one where we first met, at noon tomorrow. Are you available?'

'Of course – I'm not working. Time is all I have.'

∽

The next day, Faith, Ollie, and I met at the coffee shop as planned. Irving devoured a hamburger and a milkshake in the next booth. Faith told Ollie about the closetkeeper position she was trying to fill, and Ollie said yes before Faith had finished her sentence.

'Ollie, don't you want to hear the pay before you decide?' Faith asked.

'Oh, if you're a friend of Miss Ivy's, I'm sure it'll be fair.'

'How does this sound – six hundred a week cash, plus room and board?'

'How much will the room and board cost?' Ollie asked.

'Nothing – it's part of the deal. You and Irving can stay in one of the staff suites we have downstairs. It'll have one bedroom, a living room, a kitchen, and a bathroom. Is that okay?'

'It's more than okay,' Ollie said. 'It's the answer to our prayers.' Ollie put her head in her hands and cried.

Irving looked at his mother nervously. 'What's wrong?' he asked.

'Nothing's wrong,' Ollie said to him. 'Everything's good. We just got ourselves a job and a home.' Irving smiled broadly and clapped his hands. Ollie turned to Faith. 'Don't you worry, you won't even notice Irving is there. He's quiet as a mouse and he'll stay in our room.'

'Don't be ridiculous, Ollie. We love having kids around. Mae and Lia will adore Irving. I'm hoping he'll be a real friend to my girls. In fact, when he goes to school next year, I can have my driver drop him off every day when he drops the girls. Would that work for you?'

Ollie started weeping again. Faith took that as a yes.

7. Fallout

The Baby Face affair could not have come at a worse time. With only a few weeks until schools decided who was in and who was out, the private-school-admissions process was turned on its head. As a special prosecutor investigated former FDA chairman Lyndon Pratt, the attorney general announced his intention to probe into the circumstances surrounding acceptance decisions of every big shot whose child had been admitted to a New York City private school in the last five years.

Under the leadership of Dick Nanda, president of the New York Private Headmasters Organization (NYPHO), every private school participated in the placement of a full-page ad in the *New York Times* and the *Wall Street Journal* denying that their admissions decisions were subject to outside interference.

> Every admissions department is protected by a Chinese wall to ensure that each determination made regarding an applicant is beyond reproach. There are checks and balances in

place to remove even the possibility that one individual could ever make the ultimate difference in any final admissions decision. To suggest that schools are subject to undue influence in their selection of students is to unfairly blemish the reputations of the hardworking, honorable, law-abiding admissions directors throughout NYC who are dedicated to the principle that all applicants are created equal.

Parents all over the city blew coffee out their noses when they read this.

The audacity of NYPHO's protest was highlighted by a regrettable typesetting error when their logo was printed across the bottom of the ad. *Someone* forgot to press the space bar: NYPHONYNYPHONY-NYPHONY.

Dick Nanda resigned his position as president of NYPHO. He'd finally had enough when political satirist Arthur King referred to him as 'Wrinkly Dick' in an editorial cartoon encapsulating the whole ugly affair. The scandal was the subject of nightly jokes, skits, and lists on Jay Leno and David Letterman. The highfalutin world of private schools had become a national laughingstock. The reputations of New York City's most elite schools were so battered and bruised that it would take some of America's most talented spin doctors (who were, coincidentally, private-school parents ready to volunteer for this very cause) to rehabilitate the lot of them.

This was bad for my business.

Omar's contacts told him that every trustee in town had been warned that any child they recommended would be automatically denied admission because of the mere appearance of impropriety – new NYPHO policy.

Gee, thanks, Mrs. Radmore-Stein. We had a good thing going and you ruined it for everybody.

At least Lilith got hers. She was indicted for bribery, conspiracy, and obstruction of justice. The stock in her company plummeted 70 percent, reducing her net worth by over a billion dollars. The board made her give up the corporate jet and fly commercial coach. Stockholders were calling for her head. The public lapped up every juicy detail of this arrogant woman's fall from grace as gleefully reported by her rival papers. Johnny walked out on her because, as he said, 'I don't need this kind of shit.' Soon after, he was taken into custody for shorting stock in his wife's company just before the story hit the papers. Johnny would have to disgorge the millions he'd made on insider trading. Like Lilith, he had taken a nasty fall from his high horse.

With his mother and his father fighting charges, Ransom was neglected even more than usual. Finally, Lilith's second cousin, Rowena Ratfinklestein, a yoga instructor from Niagara Falls, agreed to take the boy in. Ransom would be one of four children being raised in Rowena's modest clapboard house with a garden and clothesline in the back and an American flag in the front. He would attend the local public school. It was probably the best thing that ever happened to him.

Lilith wigged out when she realized that this was all the doing of her ignorant maid, Ollie, and could have been avoided if she'd paid her the damn $100. *For want of a nail, the kingdom was lost.*

8. Tipper Tells All

ipper chose to meet me on a Sunday evening in the back booth of a Scandinavian diner on Bayside Avenue in Queens. She came incognito, wearing a floppy straw hat and Jackie O sunglasses.

'Sorry I'm late,' I said. 'I took the wrong subway and had to walk about ten blocks.' I sat down across from her in the booth.

'Ivy, come sit next to me,' she said.

I switched sides and scooted in. She reached over and patted my stomach, then my chest.

'What are you *doing*?' I asked.

'I have to be sure you're not wearing a wire,' she whispered.

'Of course I'm not wearing a wire. I would *never* do that.'

'I'm sure you wouldn't,' she said, patting my body until she was satisfied that I was clean.

'We're not doing anything illegal. We're two friends having a few laughs over pickled herring. Don't be so paranoid,' I said, moving back to the other side of the booth. 'I think *someone's* been watching too much *Sopranos*.'

'Are you kidding? In *this* environment? The feds would like nothing better than to catch you offering me a bribe.'

'Tipper, I'm not going to offer you a bribe. I just want to get a sense of where my clients stand with you. Let's decide what to eat, then we'll talk.' We silently examined our menus, which listed various sizes of Swedish meatballs and forty varieties of herring. We both ordered the special, escolar fish Baltic-style with horseradish mirror, whatever that was.

'How are you surviving the Radmore-Stein scandal?' I asked after the waiter left.

'Ivy, don't get me started. First Cubby, now this. It's a blessing Cubby didn't live to see this day. It would have broken her heart.'

'Will you be able to put together a decent class?'

'Not really. We can't do our standard investigating into family finances. There's no way to get the real dirt on applicants from nursery-school directors – you know, the stuff they don't write in the reports but tell you confidentially over the phone? No one's talking. They've changed the rules in the middle of the game, and Mr. Van Dyke still expects me to deliver a "Who's Who" of kindergartners. It's impossible.'

'I hear you. I have no idea how to help my clients right now. But what can you do?' I said. 'Who would have thought that someone as rich and influential as Lilith would feel the need to break the law just to get her kid into school?'

'I know,' Tipper said. 'That snot-nosed brat of hers would have had five offers just for being her son.'

'Let me ask you about some of my families,' I said, lowering my voice. 'What do you think of WaShaunté Washington?'

'WaShaunté Washington. Is that the little black girl?'

'Yes.'

Tipper started wagging her finger at me. 'There's something fishy about that child. She told my evaluators that her mom had changed her skin color. First of all, she doesn't *have* a mom. Second, well, we don't know what to think about her skin-color comment. Do you have any idea what she was talking about?'

'Not a clue. As far as I know, Archie Washington's the father, there's no mom in the picture, and the child is black. Archie did tell me that WaShaunté has a very active imagination,' I said. *Dammit, I knew we couldn't trust that kid to lie*. I changed the subject. 'What about Maria Kutcher? Isn't she a pistol?'

Tipper gave me an incredulous look. '*Omar Kutcher's* your client? He *propositioned* me. He intimated that if I don't offer his daughter a place, he would *hurt* me.'

'Soooooo . . . you'll offer him a place?' I ventured.

'I don't know. On the one hand, Omar's incredibly low-class. He'd never fit into the Harvard Day community. On the other hand, I don't want him to kill me. You don't think he would, do you?'

How to answer . . . how to answer, I wondered. If I suggested he might whack her, Tipper would probably take Maria. If I said he wouldn't, her acceptance was doubtful. I did the only fair thing, which was to let Tipper come to her own conclusion. 'Supposedly he killed his own wife, so who knows what he's capable of.' That was all I said.

Tipper gulped. The waiter brought our food. It was some manner of fish indigenous to the Baltic Sea.

'How about Veronica Needleman? You interested in her?' I asked.

'I'll give you four reasons why we'd never take that kid. First, the family's essays were incoherent. Second, the parents broke up with each other *during* our interview. Third, the kid spilled her juice at snack. And fourth, she cheated on her ERB. We have a maniacal focus on ethics at Harvard Day. It's our number-one core value. There's no way we could offer her a place.'

'Right,' I said.

'Nothing personal, Ivy, but so far I'm not impressed with your client roster.'

'How about Greg McCall's son, Moses? Were you impressed with him?'

'Oh, now *him* we love. The boy's grandparents are very, very wealthy. I can practically guarantee we'll make him an offer. What do you think of the fish?'

'It's okay. I've never been a big fan of Scandinavian food. You?'

'Usually I love it, but this is kind of bland. Try it with ketchup,' she suggested.

'How about Willow Bliss and Tiny Herrera,' I said, reaching for the bottle.

'The lesbians?'

'Yes, well, their son, Jack Henry. His ERB scores indicate gifted intellect; he's reading; he plays flute; he's black.'

'We'll never take him,' she said. 'He's in a wheelchair.'

'You won't accept him because of his disability?'

'Ivy, no teacher wants a kid in a wheelchair. How do you schlep him along on field trips? Where do you park him during PE? The logistics are too complicated. Plus, it's so depressing to be around crippled people, don't you think?'

'No, I find Jack Henry inspiring to be around. I thought you'd be excited about all the diversity he represented.'

Tipper lowered her voice. 'Ivy, of course we want diversity, but it has to be *appropriate* diversity.' Tipper made those quotation marks with her fingers. 'It's fine to accept handicapped kids as long as they don't slow down the rest of the class. We're always looking for qualified black children, as long as they're right for our community. You know what I mean. Colin Powell's kid would be perfect; a maid's kid would not. And get this – we actually *had* a maid apply this year! Now, how comfortable would our Harvard Day parents be talking to *her* at a PTA potluck?' Tipper chuckled at the very idea.

'Tipper,' I said evenly, 'her name is Ollie Pou and she's also my client. And you know what? She's a fine person. She's working to give her son a better life. And correct me if I'm wrong, but didn't you once tell me that *your* mother was a maid?'

'That's right, my mother *was* a maid. And guess what? She could never have held her own with the Harvard Day parents. The only reason *I* can is because I managed to pull myself up. I went to college, got an MBA.'

'Yeah, because your mother worked two jobs to pay for your education.'

Tipper ignored my valid point. 'Was your business a nonprofit? Is that why you took blacks and gays?' she asked.

'No, these are all paying clients. And they're good, hardworking people. Tiny's an Academy Award–winning director. She'd be an asset to any parent body.'

'Yeah, but she's *too gay* for us. Don't get me wrong. We'd love to have a lesbian family, but give me one that isn't so obvious. I mean, what's with that hot-pink hair?'

'I suppose your parents wouldn't be comfortable talking to Tiny at a PTA potluck?'

'Not a chance.'

'Tipper, help me here. You promote your school's commitment to enrolling minorities. You even lead the diversity council. Is it all for show?'

'No, it's real. We're always looking for qualified candidates of color. *Of course* our regular families prefer to be with their own, but they don't want to feel like elitists, either. My job is to find diverse families who are just like our white families, except for their color or sexual preference. That's not easy.'

'I'm sure it isn't,' I said.

'Ivy, Harvard Day's a private club. We're very discriminating about the people we let in. Why would we take families who aren't like *us*? It's not just minorities who are square pegs here. Most white parents are out of our league, too. Anyone who makes it to Harvard Day is king of the hill, top of the heap, A-number-one.'

'Right. And if you can make it there, you can make it anywhere,' I said.

'Laugh if you want, but it's true.'

I looked at Tipper sadly. I'd fallen hook, line, and sinker for the official story – that schools were looking to admit kids with genuine differences, like Jack Henry. I shook my head. 'Tipper, do you hear yourself? Publicly, you say all the right things. But privately you're selling out your own people. For what? Money? A job?'

'Ivy, the Tiny Herreras and Ollie Pous of the world are *not* my people,' Tipper said with disdain. 'The families of Harvard Day, *those* are my people. *That's* where I belong. If the rest of the world can't pull themselves up like Tipper Bouquet did, well, what can I say?'

'Let them eat cake?' I suggested.

'I wouldn't go *that* far.'

'Tipper,' I said, 'are you so insecure that you think you have to pretend to be someone you're not? Your name is Tipper Bucket. *Bucket!* You're a black woman, daughter of a maid. You *work* for the people of Harvard Day. If you think they see you as one of them, well, girl, you are sadly mistaken.'

Without waiting for Tipper to reply, I scooted out of the booth and put $30 on the table. 'Thanks for the insights,' I said, walking away. Just as I reached the door, the waiter came running after me.

'Excuse me, you forgot this.' He held up my Barneys bag, which I had left by my seat.

'It's garbage. Do you mind tossing it?'

9. Buying Ivy

To my surprise, an elegant Rolls-Royce Silver Cloud was waiting for me outside the Scandinavian diner. Buck McCall. How did he *do* that? He always seemed to know where I'd be before I did. Was he intuitive, or had a team of CIA doctors implanted a chip in my brain while I was sleeping? Was he reading my mind or controlling it? *Oh, Ivy, you are being so overly dramatic. He's probably just following you.*

His bodyguard-chauffeur opened the door and I got in. Did I have a choice? Arriving right after the Four Seasons had made its evening delivery, I asked Buck if I could have some fruit from the elegantly appointed dinner tray to his side. 'By all means,' he said.

I made a plate of grapes and strawberries for myself.

'May I pour you some Chardonnay?' he offered.

'No, thanks.'

'Burger?' he suggested.

'Vegetarian?' I inquired.

'No. Beef,' he said.

'Then no, thanks. I'm watching my weight.'

'You should try Atkins,' he recommended. 'They let you eat as much meat as you want.'

'Thanks for the tip, Mr. McCall, but I'm sure you're not here to talk diets.'

'You're right, Ms. Ames. I'm not. I'm here to thank you personally for taking care of that little favor I asked of you.' He handed me an envelope stuffed with $100 bills. I was torn between the excitement of having extra money for a change and the humiliation of knowing I was doing exactly what I'd just condemned Tipper for. Irony can be so annoying. I stuffed the bills into my purse.

'Mr. McCall,' I said, 'your spying game is getting tiresome. The gifts are nice, and I thank you for them, but I could really do without being watched twenty-four hours a day.'

'Oh, I'm not spying on you, Ms. Ames. I don't need to see you to know you're doing my bidding. I'm sure you're doing everything short of parting the Red Sea to keep Moses out of the Jewish schools.'

I winced. 'Mr. McCall, do you mind? This has not been my finest hour.'

'Ah, yes, but the money wins out, doesn't it? It always does with you people.'

'You people?'

'Jews, of course.'

'What, have you made a study of this?'

He laughed, even though I hadn't meant it as a joke. 'Nothing personal, Ms. Ames, I know you're Jewish. But I've seen it with my own eyes. When Dee Dee married Greg, I offered her family a million dollars to cut her off and never speak to her or us again. Guess what? They took the money so fast, I didn't even suggest the vacation to Hawaii I'd planned to throw in to seal the deal. They've never spoken to her since.'

I couldn't believe what I was hearing. 'You mean *you're* responsible for her family sitting shiva, treating her as dead? *How could you?* You're denying Moses his grandparents and Dee Dee her family.'

'Better that than being related to more Jews, even by marriage. The point is, Ms. Ames, I knew you would take the money. I thank you for what you've done. And just to be sure you accomplish our objective here, I'd like to sweeten my offer.'

Ooooh, a bonus. This was exciting. *Maybe he'll offer me a trip to Hawaii. God knows I could use a vacation. Just hold your nose and close your eyes*, I thought, *this will all be worth it in the end . . . Wait, Ivy, look at yourself. You're doing business with a racist! You're betraying your own people! Remember Abraham, Ruth, the Maccabees, Queen Esther, the Ten Commandments, and so on and so forth?* I stared at Buck, secretly wrestling with my conscience, which had temporarily gone haywire.

Buck pulled a letter out of his jacket pocket and handed it to me. It was from Lorna Reed, head of admissions at The Balmoral School:

Dear Mr. McCall,

It was delightful meeting with you last week. As discussed, Skyler and Kate Ames will be read-mitted to The Balmoral School next September based on your pledge to pay their tuition through twelfth grade. Mr. Stanton Giles from our business office will be in touch with you shortly regarding the escrow accounts you agreed to set up.

Further, we appreciate your interest in supporting girls' basketball at The Balmoral School. Mr. Rupert Stoddard, from our development office, and Mr. Samuel Pollock, head of our architectural committee, will contact you next week to begin discussions regarding construction of the new McCall Gymnasium you are proposing.

Sincerely,
Lorna Reed

'You have *got* to be kidding me, Mr. McCall,' I said. 'This'll cost you a bloody fortune. How can it *possibly* be worth it you?' It was certainly tempting, however.

'Ms. Ames, I have more money than I can spend in fifty lifetimes. This is pocket change for me. I have *one* grandson. I would do anything to keep him from becoming more Jewish than he already is. I'm eternally grateful to you for being an instrument in preventing that from happening. And I want to show my appreciation.'

Suddenly the bodyguard-chauffeur whipped open the car door, causing my heart to beat so fast that I popped a baby aspirin, just to be safe. *Why must he always do that?*

'It has been a pleasure doing business with you, Ms. Ames,' I heard Mr. McCall say as I walked away. *Yeah, a real pleasure,* I thought.

10. Shocking News

Monday I dropped the girls at school. For some reason, I was missing my mother more than usual. If only she were here. I could tell her everything that had happened and she would give me one of those lectures that I used to ignore when she was alive. Only this time I'd listen. *C'mon, Mom, tell me what to do. At least give me a sign or something.* I headed over to the Korean nail salon at Houston and Avenue A for a manicure, thinking it might lift my spirits.

Just as I placed my freshly painted nails under the blow-dryer, my cell phone rang. Awkwardly, I balanced the receiver between my ear and shoulder and answered without messing up the polish. It was Omar. Oh boy. This was one client I didn't want to disappoint. 'Ivy, you'll never guess where I am,' he said.

'Where?'

'No, guess, really.'

'You're in Luckenbach, Texas?'

'Where the hell is that? No, I'm in Las Vegas. Sassy and I just eloped.'

'*What!*' I exclaimed. 'You've known each other, like, a month! I can't believe it.'

'Well, believe it. And it's all because of you. I'm indebted to you for life for introducing me to my *widdew pookie wookie*.'

Euuugh. *Baby talk from a mob boss.*

'Omar, would you put Sassy on? I want to congratulate her.'

'Can you believe it?' Sassy said. 'I married this biddy widdy teddy beaw.' I heard what sounded like kissing noises, which I thought was rude. '*Oooooh*, baby, lick me here, *ooooooh yes*, you nasty little horny toad,' she moaned.

Too much information . . . too much information . . .

'Sassy. SASSY. *SASSY!!*' I yelled into the phone. 'What about Philip? I thought you were going to marry him.'

'Would you give him my regrets?' she asked. 'When I met Omy Womy, I knew he was the one. He's my widdew wuv-biwd.'

I thought I was going to blow chunks right there and then.

'What about your new business?' I asked.

'Omy Womy doesn't want Pookie Wookie to decowate for anyone but *he-yum*. Omy Womy pwomised Pookie Wookie she would nevew have to wook anymore, *evew*.'

'Sassy, let me give you one small but crucial piece of advice. Don't *ever* two-time this man. If you do, you might not live to regret it.'

11. Private School Ugly

A fter hearing the news about Omar and Sassy, I was useless. Sassy and Omar? I looked up at Heaven. *Okay, Drayton, I warned her. If she dies, it's her own damn fault. Release me from my obligation. She has Omy Womy to take care of her.* I wandered through SoHo, browsing in the stores, stopping at a Starbucks for a caramel macchiato with whipped cream. SoHo used to be the center of the downtown art scene. Not anymore. Now it has some of the most expensive real estate in the city. Shops like Chanel and Yves St. Laurent have moved in. And recently, Bloomingdales opened. Bloomingdales! It was a travesty. Where have all the artists gone . . . long time pa-a-sing. *Ooooh, nice purse. Come to Mama*, I thought, stepping inside Prada.

The rest of the day was spent in a nonproductive 'No thanks, I'm just looking' haze. I retrieved the girls at 3:00, stopping only for a few minutes to discuss PTA book-committee business with Plus-Sized Mama. 'I need a snack, Mom,' Skyler said.

'Me, too,' Kate piped.

'Fine, but make it healthy,' I said.

'Aaaaw, Mom, I had a tough day. Let us have junk, please?' Skyler begged.

'Tell you what: We'll compromise and go to Kratt's.'

'Yay!' Kate shouted.

At the corner, I grabbed the *New York Times*. Then the three of us slipped into my favorite booth. Skyler was exhausted from having taken a really hard spelling test. She rested her head on the table. Michael came over to take our orders.

'I'll have a brownie sundae,' Kate said.

With Herculean effort, Skyler lifted her head. 'Me, too, but make mine a double.'

'No, just a single for Skyler. And I'll have a fruit plate with chocolate sauce on the side,' I said, nudging my daughter to sit up straight.

'Coming right up,' Michael said. He gave Skyler a meaningful wink.

I picked up the paper and scanned the front page. Nothing but distressing news from the Middle East. As I pulled out the 'Metro' section, my eyes widened. 'Holy Christmas,' I said.

'What?' Kate asked.

'Wait, let me read the story.'

A few minutes later, Michael arrived with our food. He scooted into the booth to join us.

'You brought them both doubles, didn't you?' I said, glancing up from the newspaper.

'Me? No. That's our smallest sundae,' he said. Both girls started giggling.

I shook my head. What could I do? 'There's a very upsetting piece in the paper.'

'About what?' Michael asked.

'Yeah, what?' Skyler said.

'Last Friday night, during a basketball game between Hartley and Harvard Day, Hartley fans chanted anti-Semitic slurs at a Jewish Harvard Day player. Four kids kept shouting "Jewboy" at him,' I said.

'And that surprises you?' Michael asked quietly, reaching for the front page.

'In this day and age, yeah. Those are two of the city's most elite schools. Kids who go to Hartley come from the finest, most educated families. I guess I can believe they might be anti-Semitic, but I can't imagine they felt it was acceptable to go public with it. Don't they teach them anything in those schools?' I shook my head in disgust as I took a large spoonful of Kate's ice cream and dumped it on top of my fruit. Then I poured the rest of my chocolate sauce over the whole thing.

'What does "anti-Semitic" mean?' Kate asked.

'It means people who hate Jews,' Michael explained.

'I'm Jewish,' Kate said, looking worried.

'I know you are,' he said, patting her hand.

'There are people who hate me because I'm Jewish?' Kate asked.

'People who don't know any better, yes. But you know what? I'm Jewish, too. And I won't let anyone say mean things to you about your religion,' Michael said.

'Thanks, Michael,' Kate said.

'That's the worst part about what happened here,' I added. 'There were, like, thirty students and a bunch of Hartley parents sitting with the boys who were taunting this player, but no one did anything to stop them.'

'The parents let them say those things?' Skyler asked.

'Yeah. They just sat there. Poor kid. Something like that happened to me when I was a girl. It was awful,' I said, remembering that day when Ondrea de Campo and her friends humiliated me at her Valentine's party. 'When people around you make racist remarks, you *can't* stay silent. If you're silent, that means you accept what they're saying. Let that be a lesson to you, girls.'

'Mom, if you'd been there, you would've bawled those kids out, right?'

'Your mother?' Michael said. 'Are you kidding? Your mom would never tolerate that kind of behavior. There's not a timid bone in her body.' Michael smiled at me.

'Duh-uh,' Skyler agreed. 'I can't believe you'd even ask a question like that, Kate.'

'Well, I would have said something, too,' Kate said.

Oh, God, I thought, ashamed that they had me so wrong, *I am a spineless, lily-livered, good-for-nothing hypocrite. Just call me 'Schmuck' for short.* I'd done the same thing every time Buck McCall spewed his vitriol about Jews. By keeping my mouth shut, I was complicit in his anti-Semitism. Even worse, I'd helped him in his crusade against his grandson's Jewishness. And I'd betrayed Greg and Dee Dee for the same despicable cause.

The jig was up. There would be no more lies, no more winning-at-any-cost, no more selling out for cold, hard cash. This time, I didn't ask what Ivana or Mother Teresa would do. I knew what Ivy Ames had to do.

12. To Tell the Truth, Part 2

ntering the brownstone where Shalom Day School was located, I could see why Dee Dee felt it was right for Moses. The children were neatly dressed. The boys wore yarmulkes. They were singing Hebrew songs, dancing, laughing. The walls were covered with the strained efforts of kindergartners writing their first paragraphs on the subject of 'family.' The trophy case was filled with awards for Shalom Day's baseball, basketball, and hockey teams. And people say Jews aren't athletic.

'Ms. Ames, Rabbi Jacobson will see you now,' the secretary said.

I walked into Rabbi Jacobson's office and shook her hand. She seemed too young to hold such an important position, but then again, everyone does these days. 'How can I help you?' she asked after I was seated.

'Rabbi Jacobson, what I've come to tell you today is embarrassing, but I need to make this confession to you so that *maybe* I can remedy a terrible wrong that has been done.'

'I'm listening.'

'I'm a private-school-admissions counselor. I was help-ing Greg McCall and Dee Dee Epstein apply their son, Moses, to schools.'

'I know who they are.'

'I'm sure you must. Anyway, the thing is, Greg and Dee Dee wanted this school more than any other. But Greg's father wanted Moses in a secular school. He didn't want him to grow up so Jewish. Behind Greg's back, he offered me a million dollars and promised to pay my children's tuition to private school if I would get Moses into a good non-Jewish school. I was torn about what to do. I'm a single mother and the money would have changed my life. But I'm also Jewish. I'm ashamed to say that I was willing to take Mr. McCall's bribe. Greg and Dee Dee asked me to send your school their first-choice letter. But I wrote that awful note instead. I was pretty sure you would never take Moses after getting that letter. I came to ask you if you would throw it away and make your decision about Moses knowing that Shalom Day is his parents' first choice and that there are no strings attached.'

Rabbi Jacobson's eyes widened. 'That's quite a tale, Ms. Ames. Tell me, do you think Greg's father intends to pay you the money if you do what he asked?'

'I'll never know, Rabbi. My guess is he would, but maybe I'm naïve. I suppose he could cheat me. There'd be nothing I could do about it. I mean, I don't think you can sue someone to collect on a bribe, can you?'

'I have no idea.'

'Well, if he didn't pay, it would serve me right. Frankly, I think you should string me up in the sanctuary and beat me with a menorah.'

Rabbi Jacobson laughed. 'Ms. Ames, you were tempted by evil and you almost succumbed. But in the end, you made the moral choice. What you've done today is admirable. Not many people would walk away from a million dollars and a free private-school education for their children.'

As she said that, my stomach sank. I was doing the right thing, so why did I feel like such a chump?

'Plus, I want to tell you that we *had* planned to accept Moses. But after receiving that letter, well, we couldn't. Now that you've explained it, I'm going to make sure that he's offered a space,' she said kindly.

'Thank you, rabbi. I don't deserve your forgiveness,' I said.

The rabbi smiled. 'Ms. Ames, don't you know that to forgive is divine?'

'I've heard that, yes. Anyway, you don't have to worry. You'll never get a first-choice letter like that again. I'm getting out of the business.'

'Is it really so bad? If you were an honorable adviser, you *could* make a tremendous difference in people's lives.'

'That's what I thought when I started. But I realized that the admissions world is just as cutthroat as the corporate one. And the business brought out the worst in me. I lied, I cheated, I betrayed clients – for what? I don't like the person I became doing this job. But I'm determined to change.'

The rabbi smiled. 'Ms. Ames, by doing what you did today, you've already changed.'

13. Stu Has a Bad Hair Day

tu was calling every hour on the hour. With a week to go, he was freaking out about his daughter's prospects. His nursery-school head tried to reach the directors of ongoing schools to get a read on who might want Veronica, but they weren't talking.

The traditional two-week period when nursery-school directors horse-traded for spaces with private-school-admissions directors had come to a screeching halt. NYPHO had set a new policy forbidding it. Headmasters discreetly told admissions directors to turn down applications from any family that had tried to influence them in even the *slightest* way earlier in the season.

Nobody knew anything.

Nursery-school directors couldn't clue parents in to where their child would get in if they sent a first-choice letter. There were no more of the hints, leaks, or confidential conversations that had become instrumental to the smooth operation of the admissions machine. The system was in chaos. No one was steering the ship. Admissions directors, normally at the height of their powers this time of year, found themselves *ignored* by the pillars of society, who were scared shitless of being dragged into this ugly scandal. Home sales in Rye and Greenwich hit an all-time high as families secured their backups.

Directors were floundering, forced to make admissions decisions based on official criteria like test scores, interviews, nursery-school reports, and essays. These ingredients just didn't provide enough of that nuanced, richly textured information that the decision-makers needed to suggest who would be right for their particular communities and who wouldn't.

I sat in my usual booth at Kratt's in early February, pondering what, if anything, I could do to help my clients in these radically changed times. A sun-deprived man with hair as green as asparagus walked in. He looked around. It was Stu. I stuck my face behind the menu and pretended to study it. Too late. He saw me and walked over.

'Well, if it isn't Mizzzzz Ames. What a coincidence meeting you here. No, wait. Not such a coincidence, I suppose, considering *this is where you live*,' he accused.

'Yeah, I live here. You have a problem with that, Stu?'

'When I hired you, I was under the impression that you were from Fifth Avenue. Had I known you lived in a *tenement*, I wouldn't have entrusted my daughter's education to you. You are one disappointment after another, missy.'

I rolled my eyes. 'So, I'm fired again?'

'Oh, what's the point?' Stu said, sinking into the other side of the booth, pushing my purse aside. 'The game's over. Where should I send my first-choice letter? That's all I want to know.' He looked dejected, and for a fleeting moment I felt sorry for him.

'You uncovered my secret lair just to ask me that?'

'I wanted to see you in person.'

'Stu, I have to ask. What happened to your hair? Isn't it usually red?'

'I was trying to dye it myself and the color got all messed up. Patsy used to do it for me, but now she's gone.' He looked pathetic sitting there with green hair.

'Oh, Stu, you should never try to color your own hair. Everyone knows that.'

'Thanks for the advice, Ivy. I'm getting it redone this afternoon.' He pulled a framed picture of Veronica out of his briefcase and set it on the table. With tears in his eyes, he spoke. 'I love this little girl. I expect you to do right by her. Now, which school should get the Needleman first-choice letter?'

'That depends. Which school *is* your first choice?'

'Balmoral. And if you don't think Balmoral's likely, then my first choice is the school where we have the best chance.'

'Did your director get any feedback from Balmoral on Veronica's visit there?' I asked.

'Yeah, they said her résumé was thin, her pencil grasp was immature, she chose *Moo, Baa, La, La, La!* over *Where the Wild Things Are* and then her comments weren't insightful. Also, she spilled her juice at snack.'

'*What?* Veronica spilled her juice and you're telling me now! At a social school like Balmoral . . . well, Stu, that's gonna hurt,' I said. 'I wish you'd told me before. We could have defused the incident in your thank-you letter.' I waited for Stu to blame me for Veronica's accident. He was silent.

'Which school is Patsy's first choice?' I asked.

'How am I supposed to know? Thanks to *you*, she refuses to take my calls.'

There wasn't much to say. I tried bringing some levity to the moment. 'Well, under the circumstances, let's decide by doing "rock, paper, scissors."' I held out my fists.

Oops. Stu was in no mood for humor. He made his own fist and held it up like he intended to use it. 'You think this is some kind of *joke*, Ivy?' I have to admit I was slightly scared he was going to punch me. But at the same time, it was hard to take him seriously with that hair.

Before I had a chance to respond, Michael Kratt appeared out of nowhere. 'Do you have a problem, sir?'

'Yeah, I have a problem. With *her*.' Stu shook his fist in my face.

Michael reached over and slammed Stu's arm onto the table. 'I think you'd be wise to leave right about now.'

Stu's eyes narrowed to slits. He raised his fist once more.

Michael glared right back at him. 'Go ahead, Kermit. *Make my day*.' He was brilliant, just like a nice Jewish Dirty Harry.

Stu shot me a hostile look. He snatched up the picture of Veronica and stormed out.

'Are you okay?' Michael asked me.

'I'm fine. I can't believe you threatened him.'

'I know. Someone could have been hurt.'

'No shit, Sherlock! Thank you for coming to my rescue.'

Michael sat down where Stu had been. He handed me my wallet, which must have fallen out of my purse. 'What was his problem?'

'Oh, he was frustrated.' I told Michael all about Stu and Patsy and the events that had transpired since they hired me.' There was no point telling him that it wouldn't matter where he sent his first-choice letter. No one who sees Veronica's ERB report would consider her. I've already sent a first-choice letter on the family's behalf to a downtown school where I secretly applied her. The fit would be perfect, and anyway, her parents aren't going to have any other choice.'

'I had no idea your work was so dangerous,' Michael said.

'It's fraught with risk. Every year, two or three private-school-admissions advisers are assaulted by their clients.'

'Really?'

'Nah. I just wanted to impress you,' I said, kind of flirty-like. *Ivy, let it go. He made his feelings clear.*

'Well, you've succeeded,' he said. Michael smiled sweetly, showing off those movie-star dimples of his. For a moment, I imagined what our baby might look like. *Are dimples like that hereditary? They must be. Look at Kirk and Michael Douglas.* Then I stopped myself. *You have different values, remember? He doesn't want you. Zip it.*

14. Misery Is a Thin Envelope

W hen the admissions seas changed so abruptly, I was stumped. All the strategizing I'd done on behalf of my clients was for naught. With the admissions world in disarray, I didn't know how to help them anymore. All I could do was pray.

Decision letters were mailed to families in February, on the Friday before the long Presidents' Day weekend. Private schools take that Monday and Tuesday off, so parents were left to stew in their own juice until Wednesday. The letters arrived on Saturday. As a community service, the mayor made special arrangements with the feds for Friday and Saturday overtime at the post office. He understood that parents turned into puddles of anxiety awaiting word. His children went to private school, too.

This year, every admissions office hired security in the wake of the Cubby tragedy. There would be no more appeals of decisions. You were in, you were out, or you were wait-listed, and if you had anything to say about it, say it by phone, fax, or e-mail.

That Saturday, Faith kindly offered to take my girls

along with hers to the Children's Museum as I awaited my clients' news.

Good old Ollie called before I had the chance to dial her number. When I picked up, I heard weeping and wailing on the other end. Oh, dear.

'Ollie, is that you? Are you okay?'

'Ivy, these are tears of joy. Thanks be to God, good news! Irving got into Stratmore Prep and St. David's. They both offered full scholarships, but I'm sayin' yes to Stratmore Prep.'

'Why Stratmore Prep?'

'That was the only school Mrs. Radmore-Stein wanted, so it must be the best. I'm gonna buy my Irving a blue Stratmore blazer and I'm gonna take him to Sears to get him professionally photographed. Then, I'm gonna send his picture to Mrs. Radmore-Stein in prison along with a Hallmark card and I'm gonna write, "Call me when you're paroled so we can carpool and be class parents together."' Ollie laughed so hard that she started bawling again.

༄

My phone rang immediately after Ollie and I hung up. More retching and blubbering filled my ear. Tears of joy, perhaps?

The caller composed herself, thus revealing her identity – Patsy.

'Ivy, huh-huh-huh,' she cried. 'Vero-ro-ro-ronica didn't get in anywhere. Huh-huh-huh. All we got huh-huh-huh were ten rejection letters huh-huh-huh. I'm crushed. I'm devastated huh-huh-huh-huh.'

'That's it?' I asked. 'That's all you got?'

'We got one letter of acceptance by mistake, to a school we didn't apl-pl-ply to.'

'Tell me the name of the school, Patsy.'

'The Log Cabin School in Greenwich Village. Huh-huh.'

'Patsy, Veronica *did* get into that school. I was worried she wouldn't get in anywhere after what happened with her ERB, so I mailed in a couple of last-minute applications to schools that didn't require the test. I took her there myself for interviews, and they liked her. The truth is, this would be a better school for her than any of the Baby Ivys you applied to. It's not as high-status. It's small and nurturing and I think that's what Veronica needs. Don't you?' I said all this practically in one breath.

'Ivy, I don't believe it huh-huh. You did that for Veronica?'

Yes, well I am a good person.

'Yes, I did,' I answered. 'Are you okay about it?'

'I'm grateful,' she said. 'Thank you. Thank you. Would you take me to the school next week and show it to me?'

'It would be my pleasure,' I said, relieved. 'Do you want to tell Stu about it, or should I?' *You. You. You. You. You.*

'Would you, Ivy? I don't want to talk to him.'

'Sure, Patsy, I'll do it.' Oooh, yeah, I relished the thought of telling Stu the big news of Veronica's one acceptance at a third-tier downtown school.

❧

'Ivy, you're a genius. A *genius*,' Wendy Weiner said. 'Winnie got into Nightingale, Balmoral, and Spence. Three out of ten. That's outstanding.'

Whew. I had been worried that Winnie was revealing

her true colors at every school visit. But obviously she wasn't. After Winnie spilled the beans at Harvard Day, Wendy promised her a new puppy if she'd just stick to the lie. Bribery is a powerful tool in a parent's arsenal. 'Well, that's wonderful, Wendy. I'm thrilled. Do you know which one you're choosing?'

'Hell, no,' she said. 'Archie wants to go back and visit the finalists, and then the two of us are going to sit down and decide which school would be best for Winnie. You know, he took his job as Winnie's father seriously. He has his own ideas about what's right for her, so I want to hear him out.'

'That's nice of you, Wendy. I know Archie cares about Winnie.'

'Oh, he cares, all right. Did he tell you that we're seeing each other now?'

'*What?* No.'

'Well we are, Ivy. I found my soul mate in Archie. He completes me. And I have *you* to thank.'

Words failed me. Our cockamamie plan to get Winnie into private school led to a love connection? Even with those God-awful whiny pipes of hers, Wendy had found a man. A man with a beautiful voice, no less. A voice so pleasant, people paid to hear him sing. I guess Archie did complete her.

For the next few hours, I couldn't reach any of my other clients. Did they not understand how racked with anxiety I'd be over this? Had they no consideration for my feelings after all I'd done for them? I was especially concerned about Maria Kutcher. She was such a little mobster, I mean monster, I couldn't imagine any school taking her without having been threatened or bribed, which had unfortunately been out of the question this season. Finally, I reached Omar on his cell.

'Omar, it's Ivy,' I said. Nervous sweat was pouring out at this point.

'Hi, Ivy, what's happening?' I heard no anger in his voice. That was good.

I tried to sound nonchalant. 'You know, gosh, it just hit me that admissions letters came out today and I was wondering what happened with Maria's applications. Where did she get in?' *Please, God, let her have gotten in somewhere.*

'You're gonna laugh, Ivy. And I'll tell *you* this, and only you, because I know you'll appreciate it. When I found out that none of my trustee friends could help Maria, I got a little nervous. Then I remembered you telling me that siblings get priority over other applicants. So I married Sassy. She called Balmoral and told them that Maria was Bea's stepsister and they treated her like a sibling. So now my little Maria's going to Balmoral. Ain't she a pistol?'

'Wait. Let me get this straight. You married Sassy so Maria could get into The Balmoral School under their sibling-priority policy?'

'You got it, honey.'

'But you love her, right?'

'I love fucking her,' he said. 'Don't worry, I know she's your friend. She's a nice broad. I'll treat her good.'

'You do that, Omar. You treat her real good.' We hung up.

I sat for a moment, floored, wondering which would be worse – being married to Omar or being evil Maria's stepmother. Sassy had finally gotten hers. Although she didn't know it yet, she'd met her match in Omar and Maria. The universe works in such perfect ways. I marveled at the

Zen of it all. Of course, I did genuinely hope he would never bump her off.

∾

Toward suppertime, I reached Tiny and Willow. They'd taken Jack Henry bike-riding all day. Biking? *Today?*

'Ivy, I hope you're not too disappointed, but no one took him,' Tiny said. 'He didn't even get wait-listed anywhere.'

'*What!*' I was stunned. 'His scores were so good. He's smart. He's talented. You two are great. I don't believe it.'

'We were surprised, too. But I guess the Triple Crown of diversity was more minority than any one school could handle,' she surmised. 'Don't beat yourself up about it, Ivy. We've dealt with this kind of thing our whole lives.'

'Gosh, I'm sorry, Tiny. I never imagined this would happen.' It was so unfair. Maria, the little brat, gets accepted just for being Bea's stepsister, and sweet, intelligent Jack Henry gets in nowhere.

'We're okay about it,' Tiny said. 'Disappointed, but there are *far* worse things in life than not getting into private school, don't you agree?'

'Oh yes, there are for sure.'

'The thing is,' Tiny said, 'after meeting Isaiah, we were starting to think it might not be fair to send Jack Henry to a school with mostly white kids. We don't want him to lose his black identity. We decided to put this decision in the hands of fate. If he'd gotten into a great private school, we probably would have sent him. But if not, then we believe it wasn't meant to be.'

'What'll you do now?'

'Well, we were thinking of trying to get a variance and

sending Jack Henry to a public school in a more diverse neighborhood,' Tiny explained. 'That way, he'll fit in, at least racially. And it's illegal for public schools to discriminate against kids in wheelchairs. Anyway, someone told us about an excellent charter program called School of the Basics. We're going there tomorrow to see if there's room.'

'Tiny, the bad news is that registration was three weeks ago and they're officially full. The good news is that I helped the school land a big donation last Christmas. The principal owes me one. I'll call in the favor and get Jack Henry a space.'

'Ivy, I don't know how to thank you.'

'Don't bother. School of the Basics will be lucky to have you.'

'Well, thank you anyway. And I'm looking forward to seeing you next week. You're coming, aren't you?'

'I wouldn't miss it.' Tiny had asked me to audition for the part of Marvin in her new magic wheelchair series. It was a long shot, but hey, a woman plays Bart Simpson and she gets $125,000 an episode, so I figured why not try? I'd take the job for way less than that.

I hung up with Tiny and smiled. I don't even pretend to understand the ways of the universe. But things do have a way of working out.

൭

Right after I put the phone down, Greg called. Finally.

'Ivy, Moses got into Shalom Day. We are so grateful to you for everything you did. We never could have done it without you.'

'Oh, now, go on,' I said, hoping he would continue gushing, as I really deserved it in his case.

'But you know, he also got into Harvard Day, Dalton, and Riverdale,' Greg continued. 'The thing is, and I know you're gonna think we're crazy, but now Dee Dee and I are leaning toward Harvard Day. Would it be terrible if we backed out of our first-choice letter?'

'*What*? I thought you both wanted Shalom Day!'

'Well, we did. But after Moses got into Harvard Day, we realized he'd have a better chance for the Ivy Leagues if he went there. I guess we changed our minds. But I feel like we have a moral obligation to send him to Shalom Day because we told them they were our first choice. And we don't want to do anything unethical. What do you think? Would they forgive us if we changed our minds?'

'Rabbi Jacobson is a forgiving woman. She won't like it, but she'll accept it. Call her personally and tell her you've had a change of heart. I'm sure this isn't the first time it's happened.'

'Thanks, Ivy, your advice is always so helpful. I'll call the rabbi right away.'

We hung up. I must have sat there for five minutes with my jaw hanging open. *Holy fuckity fuck fuck fuck.*

∽

'Stu, it's Ivy. Have you talked to Patsy yet?' I knew the answer to that question but wanted to ease gently into this conversation.

'Of course I haven't talked with Patsy. Thanks to *you*, she *left* me, *remember*? We talk through our lawyers now.'

'Right, right. Gosh, sorry about that,' I muttered. 'I have great news for you. Veronica got into The Log Cabin School.'

'The what?'

'The Log Cabin School. It's a warm and nurturing program downtown.'

'We didn't apply there. Where else did she get in?'

'The thing is, Veronica didn't get in anywhere else, Stu.'

'And how is that possible?' Stu said in a voice so falsely sweet that it scared me more than his usual shrieks of rage.

'It was her ERB write-up. Remember, they said she was coached.'

'Right, *your* brilliant idea. Ivy, thanks to *you*, my wife left me and my daughter's going to some two-bit gay play school in Greenwich Village. You'll pay for this, missy.'

Ugh, why does he have to call me 'missy'? 'Look, Stu, I know you had your heart set on a Baby Ivy. And I'm sorry Veronica didn't get into one. But you know what? That's not where she belongs. Veronica's a sensitive child who needs to be educated in an accepting and nurturing place. A school that's social or competitive would be the worst possible fit for her. Log Cabin is perfect for your daughter. I did you a favor by getting her in there. And one more thing, pal. I am *not* responsible for your wife leaving. Patsy left you because she was sick of being married to an asshole. I suggest you look inside *yourself* to discover why your marriage failed and not blame me.'

'Are you quite finished, Ivy?' Stu said, obviously trying to control himself.

'Yes, well, I am.'

'Good. Now may I make a suggestion for *you*?' he said.

'Sure.'

'I suggest you hire yourself a bodyguard,' Stu said and he slammed down the phone yet again.

15. Oops, We Did It Again

The next morning, I knocked on Philip's door. The girls were in school. I was at loose ends now that admissions were over.

'What's up?' he asked.

I told him all the news. How I'd confessed to Rabbi Jacobson and she accepted Moses. How, after all that, Dee Dee and Greg had decided on Harvard Day. How Omar had married Sassy just to get Maria into Balmoral. How three schools had accepted Winnie, but no one had taken Jack Henry. How the rest of my clients had fared in the end, mostly better than expected. Philip wanted to know everything.

'So you must be relieved that it's over,' he said.

'I am. And you'll be happy to know that I'm moving on to a new career,' I told him.

'You are?' he said. 'Doing what?'

'I'm exploring a few things. Tiny Herrera arranged for me to audition to be the voice of the lead character in her new animated series. She thinks I'd be perfect.'

'Hmm. You do sound a little like Betty Boop.'

'Are you making fun of me?'

'No, I love the way you talk. It's sexy,' he said.

'Really?'

Philip smiled. 'Oh, yeah. If I call you late at night, will you talk cartoony to me?'

'You *are* making fun of me.'

Philip came and sat next to me. 'Ivy, I love everything about you, especially that cute voice of yours. I love your hot body, your pretty face, your sexy eyes, your wit . . .'

I cupped my hand over his mouth. 'You can stop! I was yours at "hot body."'

Philip smiled at me. 'Do you think we can try again?'

'You want us to be more than friends?'

'I want us to be lovers.'

'I would like that,' I said, reaching over to kiss him. Mmmm, that felt delicious. Philip and I hadn't locked lips since that night last October when we fought over Buck's bribe. I hadn't realized how much I still wanted him until now.

'Why don't we go to the bedroom?' Philip suggested.

'I'll race you,' I answered.

16. Friends

Philip was seeing his editor that afternoon. I was ravenous after our carnal workout, so I went to Kratt's for lunch.

Michael was at a table of casually dressed professional types, having a lively conversation. Why bother him? I ate my egg salad on rye and was about to go when he came over. 'Were you leaving without saying hello?' he asked.

'I didn't want to interrupt you. You seemed so involved.'

'That's my reporters' lunch. They're from the *Wall Street Journal*, the *Times*, *Newsweek*, and the *Observer*. I get a table of 'em every Tuesday. It's always interesting, and they invite me to join the conversation.'

'Sounds cool,' I said.

'It is. So, what's up, Ivy? I haven't seen you since that green-haired guy almost beat you up.'

'I know. I've been busy wrapping up my clients' cases.' I told Michael what had happened, where the kids had been accepted.

'Should I invite one of my reporter friends over for an exclusive interview on this year's admissions season?'

'That's okay. I want to put the whole thing behind me.'

'So what's next?'

'I don't know. I'm exploring new careers. Maybe I can work for you. What do you think about starting a mail-order division?'

Michael looked serious. 'I'm sorry, but I make it a rule never to hire women I'm falling in love with.'

'WHAT? You're falling in love with ME? Wait a minute. I'm confused. You said you didn't want to be with me because our values were too different.'

'I know, and I believed it when I said it. But Ivy, I miss you. I think about Christmas night all the time. Don't you?'

'Well, I have to admit it's crossed my mind.'

He came over to my side of the booth and took my hand. 'Let's spend time together. Let's see where this relationship will take us. Maybe we're more alike than we know.'

'Oh, God.' I felt so guilty hearing him say this. I could still smell Philip on my body. 'Michael, I care about you a lot.'

'Those are not the words a man wants to hear,' he said.

'I know. I'm sorry. But I'm involved with someone else now.'

'Who?'

'Philip.'

'Philip from the second floor? Dammit, I knew I should have evicted him years ago.'

I laughed. 'You are funny. How about Miriam Goldofsky? Did you ever take her out? She's a doctor. *You could do woise!*'

He gave me a look that I took to mean no.

'I'm so sorry, Michael.'

'Me, too,' he said.

'Are you in love with him?' Michael asked.

'I'm not sure. I'm attracted to him.'

Michael looked down. He didn't say anything.

'Michael, I hated it when you said this to me, but please, let's stay friends,' I said. 'I'm crazy about you.'

Michael was silent for a moment. 'But only in that friend way,' he said.

'Yeah, in that friend way.'

17. Romancing the Liver

few days later, I called Faith to invite the family over. 'Skyler's birthday is two weeks from Sunday. I'm having a brunch for her. Plus, I want to celebrate the end of my business.'

'So you're really going to end it.'

'Yeah, it's time. I did so many things I'm not proud of in the name of my business. You know, after Drayton died, I made all these promises to God and myself about living life differently. Then I blew off every promise the moment anything tempted me. I've been more dishonorable this year than I ever was at Myoki. I made a complete mess of things and I'm gonna start over and get it right this time.'

'Ivy, you're too hard on yourself. You've done great. You didn't go back to that shark-infested corporate life. You became an entrepreneur. You created a new life for yourself. Most important of all, you lost weight. I'm proud of you and you should be proud of yourself,' she said. 'I mean that.'

'Thanks. I'm not sure I agree with you, but thanks just the same. So will you come to Skyler's party?'

'Sounds like fun,' Faith said. 'I'll bring champagne for mimosas. And how about on the Thursday before, I take Skyler to Toys 'Я' Us in Times Square so she can pick out her present? It's their flagship store, and they have a giant Barbie dollhouse, an enormous dinosaur, and a huge indoor Ferris wheel. My girls have been dying to see it. Bring Kate. We'll all get overstimulated together.'

∾

'So you'll come?' I asked.

'Sure. I'll bring food,' Michael said. 'Skyler's my girl. I'm gonna make her something special.'

'You don't have to do that,' I said.

'I know. But I want to. Here, taste. Tell me what you think.'

We were in Michael's kitchen. He was making a personal batch of chopped liver. 'Mmmm, that's amazing. What do you put in that?' I asked.

'Just liver, onions, hard-boiled eggs, Wesson oil, salt, and pepper.'

'You don't use chicken fat?'

'Nope, that's my secret. That's what keeps it light.' He picked up a warm morsel with his fingers and put it in my mouth.

'Mmmm, my God, this is heaven. More.'

He placed another bite on my tongue. 'Ohhh, don't stop,' I said, licking the traces off his fingers. He gave me some more.

'Ooooh, I love this,' I moaned with my eyes closed. 'Do it again, pleeeease.'

He put another large chunk in my mouth. Slowly,

I rolled it around on my tongue, relishing the flavor, smacking my lips. 'Mmmm,' I murmured.

'You should swallow,' he said.

'No, not yet. I want to savor it.'

'Okay, you have to stop. You're turning me on,' he said.

My eyes popped open. 'I am? Me eating chopped liver is a turn-on? Is that a deli-guy thing?'

'No, it's an every-guy thing,' he said. 'I'll send you home with a bowl.' He portioned out part of the mixture and placed it in a Corningware dish. It was still warm.

'You're such a nurturing guy,' I said. 'Some girl's gonna be lucky to have you.'

Michael looked up. He'd been digging through the drawer for a glass cover. 'That girl could be you,' he said.

'Tempting,' I said.

'I mean it.'

'I know. I just . . . you know how I feel about you, but Philip and I have gotten kind of serious.'

'Ah, if that's the case.' He was scrubbing the frying pan. 'What do you two have in common, anyway?'

'More than you might think,' I said.

'Such as?'

'We have fun together. The girls like him. He's a brilliant writer who can even spell.'

'Now *there's* something to base a relationship on,' he said.

'Michael . . .'

'Okay, fine, if he makes you happy . . . You broke my heart, Ivy, but I'll survive. Here, take this. Enjoy.' He handed me the bowl. 'I had hoped to sweep you off your feet with my liver, but I guess that wasn't enough.'

'Thanks,' I said, taking the dish.

Michael smiled. 'You're *sure* about Philip?'

'I am,' I said emphatically.

'Okay. I won't bring it up again. I'm moving on, starting today.'

'Good. That's what you *should* do.' But as I said it, I wasn't so sure. I've always been a sucker for a man who knows his way around a bowl of chopped liver. I just couldn't shake the feeling that letting Michael go was a terrible mistake.

18. To Tell the Truth, Part 3

I dropped by Philip's house that evening. Purportedly, I was there to invite him to Skyler's party. But secretly I was hoping for a little affection. My encounter with Michael had left me slightly shaken. I wanted to re-experience Philip's appeal. He didn't answer when I knocked, so I walked in. He leaves his door unlocked like I do. Not wise, I know.

'Philip, you home?'

'Ivy?' he yelled.

'Yes.'

'I'm in the bathroom. I'll be right out.'

I decided to check my e-mails. 'Do you mind if I use your computer?' I asked. He didn't hear. The water was running.

I went over to his computer and jiggled his mouse. His manuscript appeared on the screen. *Ooooh, I shouldn't look, I know, I know. I'm so bad.* I hoped he wouldn't think I'd invaded his privacy. But I couldn't resist taking a tiny peek. Just enough to find out what Ariana was up to.

I read quickly. My jaw dropped. There was nothing in this manuscript about Ariana, the lover of Hitler and

Churchill. Instead, I was reading a well-crafted essay describing the morning he and I spent together at the Federal Building having that informal chat with young Mr. Baker. I started scrolling up. There, in black and white, was the story of Omar and Maria, Stu and Veronica, Tiny and Willow, the Radmore-Steins, Ollie, Irving, Winnie-WaShaunté, Cubby Sedgwick. *It was all there.* A complete narrative of everything I had experienced in the last year. At the very top was his working title: *Telling Tales Out of School,* by Philip Goodman.

Philip walked through the kitchen door and saw me at the computer. He stopped like he'd been shot with a stun gun.

I felt like someone had punched me in the balls. I don't have balls, of course, but it looks excruciating when it happens to men, and my pain was just as intense, I can tell you that. 'How could you do this?' I asked, barely breaking a whisper.

'Please let me explain.'

'By all means,' I said.

'I got the idea for this book the night you had me over to dinner, when you'd gotten all that press attention and your business took off. It was before we knew each other. I thought it would be interesting to write about your experience. It was unique. I gave my agent a proposal and he pitched it to some publishers. Random House loved it and gave me a big advance. TriStar bought the movie rights. You have to understand, I hadn't been inspired to write a novel in two years, so here was a project that would get me back on the horse.'

'Oh. I'm so glad I could be of service.'

Ignoring my sarcasm, Philip continued. 'Whenever we were together, you always gave me such rich material. Your stories were so entertaining. They were *real*. You couldn't make up the characters in your life, Ivy. But then I started having feelings for you. I knew I couldn't be with you and write this book. That's when I broke it off.'

'You mean to tell me that you chose your stupid book over *me*?' I asked, refusing to entertain the idea that any living, breathing, sane man would actually do that.

'I hadn't planned to, I wanted *you*. When I told you that wild story about Ariana Nabokov von whatever-her-name-was, I intended to trash what I was really writing. Later, when we argued over that bribe you were thinking of taking, you chose *your* business over *me*,' he explained. 'Once that happened, I thought, fine, I'll write the damn book. I wasn't sure how I'd ever get material without you in my life, but then I got friendly with Sassy. She told me what good friends you were and how you always confided in her. I thought she could be my source.'

'Sassy, my confidante!' I said. 'You have *got* to be kidding.'

'Well, I was wrong, I admit it. Anyway, you and I became friends again and you started opening up to me. Your new stories were so riveting that I kept going. At that point, I was in love with you. Actually, I don't think I ever stopped loving you, even when we weren't seeing each other. But I'd hidden the truth for so long that I didn't know how to come clean. I'm sorry. I never should have lied to you like that.'

I sat on his computer chair shaking my head, staring at the flying-toasters screensaver. Then I looked at him.

'Damn you, Philip,' I said. 'You're the last person I would ever expect to lie like this. You broke up with *me* because *I* was so dishonest. And look at you; you were full of shit all along. I was falling in love with you. How could you risk what we had for *this*?'

'It was stupid. I feel like such an idiot.' He looked hopeless standing there.

I just shook my head, disgusted. Finally I stood up and walked to the door. Then I stopped and turned around. 'My father was a liar. Cad is a liar. You're a liar. I don't get it. Is God punishing me for something? Don't answer that.' I left.

19. Revenge

On Thursday, Faith picked us up in the kids' limo for our expedition to Toys 'Я' Us. Over the last few days, I'd gotten in the habit of dropping the girls at school, then climbing back into bed with Sir Elton. When I found myself listening to Joni Mitchell's *Blue* album over and over, I knew it was time to get out and try to live again. Faith promised that a trip to Toys 'Я' Us was just what the doctor ordered. I remained skeptical.

'Let's watch *Milo and Otis*,' Kate said.

'No, *Charlie and the Chocolate Factory*,' Mae insisted.

'*Yu-Gi-Oh!*' Irving said, having not a prayer for that DVD in this car full of girls. He was still new and just learning to get along.

'No way. *Yu-Gi-Oh!* isn't age-appwopwiate, I'm just thwee. *The Potty Show!*' Lia shouted.

Kate, Mae, and Skyler burst into giggles. 'You are *so* immature,' Mae told her sister. Lia burst into tears.

'Mae, for God's sake, she's three. Give her a break,' Faith warned. 'Anyway, let Skyler decide. It's her birthday.'

'*SpongeBob*,' Skyler declared.

Soon the TV was blaring. 'Are you ready, kids?' And the kids were yelling, '*Aye, Aye, Captain.*' 'I can't heeeear you,' the captain replied. '*Aye, Aye, Captain,*' they screamed even louder. 'Oh, who lives in a pineapple under the sea? *SpongeBob SquarePants!*' the children sang. 'Who's yellow and porous and squishy is he? *SpongeBob SquarePants,*' they shouted to the TV. All ten eyes were raptly focused on the screen, their voices intent on answering the captain's musical queries. You'd have to be a Communist not to love SpongeBob, that nutty fry-cook from the Crusty Crab.

Faith reached over and took my hand. 'How are you holding up?'

'Not so good, but I'll live.'

'Of course you will. This is just a setback.'

'Faith, I can't believe how I've screwed everything up. My marriage. My business. My relationships.'

'You didn't screw it up. You're just going through a difficult passage. Do you want to see Madame Lala again? This could all just be astrological.'

'No, thanks,' I said. 'What if she tells me things are about to get worse? If they are, I don't want to know. Hand me that *NYC Parent Guide*. Maybe there's something we can do with them after Toys 'Я' Us. I'll check.'

Faith gave me the paper. I flipped through it, checking out the ads for Jodi's Gym, Pee Wee Tennis, Tiger Schulmann's Karate . . . Then something familiar caught my eye. No, it couldn't be. But yes, it was. There, larger than life, was *my* picture on a two-page spread. What in the world . . .

'Faith, look.' I pointed at the paper. 'Is that *me*?'

'Holy shi – I mean, oh, my God!' she exclaimed, remembering there were minors in the car.

It *was* me – in color. Next to the picture was the headline, *NEED HELP WITH SCHOOL ADMISSIONS? DON'T HIRE IVY AMES UNLESS YOU WANT YOUR MARRIAGE DESTROYED AND YOUR CHILD IN A THIRD-TIER PLAY SCHOOL.*

'I don't believe it,' I exclaimed. 'Stu threatened to ruin me, and look what he's done.'

'Your *client* did this to you?'

'Yeah, Stu Needleman, the jerk you met in the Hamptons – you know, the one who works for Steven. My God, that's my *driver's-license picture*,' I said, digging through my wallet and not finding it. 'How did he get his hands on my driver's license?'

'What a terrible thing to say about you, Ivy,' Faith said, looking at the ad.

'Forget what he said. It's that repulsive picture. I look like an anemic biology student. I've always hated that picture, and to see it in all these newspapers, God have mercy,' I wailed.

'We've got to *do* something,' Faith said, dialing on her cell to Steven's office. She got Steven on the line and explained the problem. Then she handed me the phone. Steven said he didn't think anything could be done about the papers that had already been distributed, but he assured me that this would never happen again. I know it's not politically correct to say this, but it was such a relief to have a powerful man to lean on. Why can't I have one of my very own? *Why?*

As we shopped at Toys 'Я' Us, I kept my sunglasses and baseball cap on. If someone recognized me from that picture, I'd be devastated. Surely no one would mistake today's attractive me for that over-exposed ten-year-old photo of twenty-pounds-heavier me.

We shopped quickly, did a few turns on the Ferris wheel, saw Barbie's cool dollhouse, bought everyone a toy, and got the hell out of there.

20. The Girl from Delancey and Orchard

For Skyler's party, we squeezed new and old friends into our tiny backyard. Steven, Faith, and their children were there; Archie, Willow, Tiny, Jack Henry, Patsy, Veronica, Ollie, Irving, Wendy, Winnie, and their new dachshund puppy, Oscar Mayer – they all came. In a weak moment, I invited Omar, Sassy, and their combined brood. Plus-Sized Mama brought her husband and two kids. Even Rabbi Jacobson, from Shalom Day, made an appearance. I'd called her the day before about making a donation to the temple. I felt terrible about Greg and Dee Dee reneging on their first-choice letter after she'd bent over backward to admit them.

Michael brought food, as promised – his gift to Skyler.

'How'd you get off work?' I asked. 'That line is three blocks long.'

'My manager brought his brother in to help. I told him I was catering a private party.'

'Ooh, you are a liar. Why didn't I know that about you?'

'Hey, it's close to true. I'm helping, aren't I?'

'Yeah, you are. And don't think I haven't noticed.'

'Where's Philip? Is he coming?'

'Mmm, I don't think so. Michael, I want to introduce you to Rabbi Jacobson from Shalom Day.' Michael shook her hand.

'Ivy,' the rabbi said, 'I want to thank you for that generous pledge you made to Shalom Day. One hundred thousand dollars will make a difference to so many kids. We'd like to call it The Ivy Ames Scholarship Fund if that's okay with you.'

Michael gave me a quizzical look.

'Long story. I'll explain later,' I told him. 'You know, Rabbi, I'd prefer you call it The Buck McCall Scholarship Fund, since he's the man who gave me the money. Plus, I think it would really piss him off.'

'Well, okay, whatever you want. We always honor the wishes of the donor, whatever the motive,' she said, laughing.

To my surprise, Buck had made good on his million-dollar bribe. He was an anti-Semite and a traitor, but an anti-Semite and traitor of his word. The day after Greg and Dee Dee signed their contract with Harvard Day, $1,000,000 was deposited into my checking account. After taxes, I'd get to keep about half. I gave $100,000 to Shalom Day, $100,000 to School of the Basics, and $100,000 to a selfless New York City cabdriver's school for girls in Doobher Kishanpur, India. The rest of the money would be used to support the family until I could get a new career off the ground. If I was lucky, there might be some left over for Kate and Skyler's college. The money was dirty and I probably should have given it all away. But a girl can only be *so* good.

'Come on, just one bite,' I overheard Maria telling Bea.

'I double dog dare ya.' Maria was trying to get Bea to eat some manner of mud and pebble pie. Sassy would have her hands full with that stepdaughter of hers.

'Ivy,' Tiny said as she tapped me on the shoulder. 'I want to be the first to congratulate you. You got the part.'

'WHAT! You're kidding! I'm gonna play Marvin? This is huge!' I gave Tiny a big hug.

Tiny laughed. 'You'll need an agent. Do you want me to recommend someone?'

'I need an agent? How cool is that! Yes. Definitely. Recommend someone.'

'I'll call you tomorrow,' Tiny said, hightailing it over to her son. 'Right now I have to break up a fight.' The kids appeared to be arguing over who got to push Jack Henry next.

Patsy came over looking all contrite. 'Ivy, I heard what Stu did to you and I'm sorry. He's such a jerk. No mean thing he does surprises me, but I feel bad that he tried to hurt you after what you did for us.'

'It's okay, Patsy. It's not your fault.'

'I hope none of your clients saw it.'

'It doesn't matter. I'm going out of business.'

'How can you do that? You're the best. I've already recommended you to lots of people.'

'Thanks, Patsy, but I want to do something that suits me better.'

'Well, at least Veronica got the benefit of your advice,' she said. 'And thanks to you, I left Stu.'

'Patsy, I'm not responsible for your marriage breaking up. That was *your* choice.'

'Yes, but you were my inspiration. You're such a

successful single woman. You're always so confident. I want to be like you.'

'You want to be like me? I'm honored,' I said. I really meant that.

'Anyway, I've never been happier since I left Stu. And things are going to be even better now that he's gone.'

'He's gone?' I asked. 'Where did he go?'

'It happened suddenly. Yesterday they gave him a big promotion at work. He's gonna make a lot more money, which'll be great for my divorce settlement. Apparently, his company wants to lease oil fields north of the Arctic Circle. Steven Lord himself handpicked Stu to negotiate drilling leases from Eskimos in the region. How could he say no? It was such a good opportunity. And it must be important, because Mr. Lord sent his personal jet to fly Stu up to the assignment. He's stationed somewhere near the North Pole.'

'Well, I'll be,' I said, glancing at Steven, who looked so innocent flipping hamburgers and smoking that big cigar. 'Steven banished Stu to Siberia.'

'No, it's technically Alaska. Siberia's south of where he'll be.'

'And he's already gone?'

'He's history,' she said.

'Well, good for us.' I laughed. 'Good for all of us.'

Michael motioned for me to come inside. He opened a box and, lo and behold, there was a cinnamon-cheese coffee cake in the shape of Skyler's initials. 'Do you think she'll like it?' he asked.

'I'm sure she will.'

'You know, I renamed this on our menu. It's called Oprah Cake now.'

'Good name for it,' I said. I hadn't had any of that coffee cake since overdosing on the twenty-five thousand units we baked for Oprah's viewers. I'd never tell Michael, but the very thought of eating any more of it made me gag. I hoped no one else felt that way.

Michael lit the candles and everyone sang 'Happy Birthday.' 'I can't believe it,' Skyler announced, 'just ninety-one years until I'm a hundred.' Michael was helping Skyler cut the first piece. Then he sliced cake for everyone.

'Hey, Michael, when do you think my birthday special's gonna be on TV?' Skyler asked.

Michael looked thoughtful. I watched him, curious to see how he'd respond.

'Ivy.'

I looked behind me. Philip was in the yard. He waved me over.

'What are you doing here?' I asked him.

'I have something for Skyler,' he said, handing me a small package.

'Well, thanks,' I said, taking it and walking away.

'Wait,' he said. 'I want to apologize again. I never should have written that book. I feel terrible about it.' He looked at me with those bottomless blue eyes of his. I wished he wouldn't do that.

'Sorry, Philip. Too little, too late.'

'Ivy, I know I was wrong, but you haven't been so perfect yourself these past few months. Can't you give me another chance?'

'I may have been dishonest, but I *always* told you the truth about my lies. *You*. You were dishonest and then you lied about it.'

'We were *both* wrong,' he said.

I rolled my eyes. I suppose Philip had a point. Did I really have the right to judge him, given the way I'd conducted myself in the last year? Maybe I *should* forgive him. *It's not like he slept with another woman. He made one stupid mistake. He was young. Was I being too hard on him? But no, how could I trust him again? He's no different from Dad or Cadmon. Look at him standing there. So good-looking. Such a bright future. If I don't hook up with him, some other girl will and I'll be alone. Rabbi Jacobson did say that to forgive is divine.* 'Okay,' I said reluctantly. 'We can try again, but let's take it one day at a time.'

'Whatever you say, Ivy.' He reached down and pulled my face to his, kissing me softly, endlessly.

My jaw began to ache so I pulled away. I smiled. 'Mmm, it's nice to have you back again.'

'It's nice to be back.'

'You know what we should do?' I said. 'Let's build a fire in the backyard and burn the book you wrote. It'll be cere-monial, to symbolize our starting over. What do you think?'

Philip looked surprised. 'You think I should burn the book?'

'Yeah. You said it was a mistake and you never should have written it.'

'Right. I shouldn't have written it, but I did. And they paid me a lot for it. The publisher and studio would be furious if I didn't deliver the manuscript, and rightly so. I'd have to give the money back. I might even get sued.'

'Philip, that book is an invasion of my privacy, not to mention my clients'. I don't want my life made public like that.'

'If it's the money, I'd consider giving you twenty percent of the advance.'

I smiled sadly and shook my head. 'Philip, thank you. You've made this easy for me. I don't want your advance. And I don't want you.'

'Forty percent?' he called as I walked away.

I went over to the hydrangea bush in the back of the yard to compose myself. 'Stupid, stupid, stupid,' I said, slapping my hand to my forehead. 'What was I thinking? *Aaaaaaaah.*' I sat on the ground and put my head in my hands. Silently, I reflected on what had just happened, cursing myself for being so naïve. *When will I ever learn? Am I just cursed when it comes to men?*

'Mommy, are you okay?' I looked up. Kate was standing there.

'I'm fine, honey. Just give me a minute.'

'Mom, Sir Elton knocked the chopped liver bowl to the ground.'

I looked over at the picnic table. The dish was in the grass and liver was all over the ground. Sir Elton was gobbling it up as fast as he could. 'Sir Elton!' I shouted. 'What are you doing? You know better.' I ran over to the mess and chased the dog away. I tossed the broken pieces of the bowl in the trash. Then I used paper towels to collect the chopped liver from the grass. What a shame. Michael had worked so hard to make this and now it was ruined. Where *was* Michael, anyway? I looked around the yard. He was gone.

'Faith, have you seen Michael?' I asked. She and Steven were sitting at the picnic table eating their Oprah Cake.

'He left when you started kissing Philip. Are you two together again?' Faith asked.

'No, we're not.'

'I can't keep up with her love life,' Steven said to Faith, like I wasn't there.

Faith turned to me. 'You know,' she said, 'that Michael's a doll. I spent a lot of time talking to him today. I think he could be the real deal. Did you know that?'

'I didn't before, but I do now.'

I ran around the front of the building to the deli. The line snaked to the next block. I didn't care. I pushed my way through a crowd of sailors at the front door. It was Fleet Week in New York City.

'Hey, lady, who do you think you are, the Queen of England? Stand in line like the rest of us.'

'Oh, I work here. The faster you let me in, the faster you'll eat,' I said with a smile.

I walked inside. It was like Times Square on New Year's Eve. Michael was behind the counter serving customers.

'*Michael!*' I shouted. He didn't hear, so I waved my arms up and down and shouted his name again. Either he didn't see me or he didn't want to see me.

I had to get his attention. Climbing on top of a table, I shouted his name. He didn't look up. I was desperate. I took a deep breath, then gave the performance of my life.

> *Why do birds suddenly appear*
> *Every time . . . you are near?*
> *Just like me, they long to be*
> *Close to you-oo-oo . . .*

Whoa, what *is* it about that song? In a nanosecond, everyone shut up. I noticed out of the corner of my eye that Faith, Steven, and my other party guests had all muscled their way into the deli.

'Michael.' He finally looked at me. 'Can I talk to you in private?'

'Oh no,' a little voice said. 'Anything you have to say to him, you can say in front of me.'

I looked down at an old lady with her ancient humpbacked husband sitting at the table on which I was standing. 'Mrs. Goldofsky?'

'That's right, girlie. You're standing in my gefilte fish,' she said.

'I'm so sorry. Forgive me. I'll buy you another. Can we have a gefilte-fish platter over here?'

The crowd was getting restless. 'Lady, would you get on with it so the rest of us can eat?'

'Fine, I can do that.' I looked at Michael and took a deep breath. 'Michael, you said you were falling in love with me the other day, remember?'

Michael nodded.

'Well, I didn't know it then, but . . . I feel the same way. I was just too stupid to see it. And I'm wondering, no, I'm asking . . . would you give me another chance?'

'Don't do it, Michael. She's no damn good,' the grandma voice said.

'Mrs. Goldofsky, how can you say that? You hardly know me.'

'I know this. A nice girl doesn't stand in someone else's gefilte fish.'

'A nice girl doesn't cut in line,' a sailor shouted.

'A nice girl doesn't sing "Close to You" when people are trying to eat,' someone added. 'What was *that* about?'

'Stop it, all of you,' Patsy admonished. 'Ivy *is* a nice girl, a fine human being. The next person who insults her will have *me* to answer to. Am I making myself clear?' *Whoa, was that mousy Patsy? You go, sister girlfriend.*

I looked at Michael and prayed he would give me a second chance.

He walked around the counter and came to me. Like a knight in a dirty white apron, he offered his hand to help me down. I had to be careful not to slip with all that gefilte fish on my shoe. Michael smiled and took me in his arms. We danced in the tiny patch of real estate the crowd was willing to part with. He whispered the song he'd sung to me that night at the Knickerbocker.

> It *had to be you*
> It *had to be you*
> I *wandered around and finally found*
> The somebody who . . .

Schmaltzy, corny, sappy, call it what you like. But don't forget I'm the girl who sang the Captain and Tenille to George Clooney. A sucker for a love song, that's who I am. There had to be a hundred people in that deli, but I only saw one. Michael looked into my eyes, smiled, and stroked my hair. Then he brought his lips to mine and kissed me. It felt very sweet.

'Would somebody bring me anotha plate of gefilte-fish salad before I pass out from hunga already?' I heard Mrs. Goldofsky shout.

'Could we get the line going again?' somebody else yelled.

'Yeah, we're starved!'

'Get a room!'

Michael and I looked at each other and silently agreed to blow this joint. We turned to leave, but Mrs. Goldofsky grabbed Michael's arm. 'If this doesn't work out, don't forget my granddaughta. She's a docta.'

'Thanks, but I don't think so, Mrs. Goldofsky,' Michael said.

With friends and family, we returned to the backyard. We'd get a room soon enough. Now, it was time to celebrate Skyler's birthday.

Yikes, emergency! I ran over to Kate and pulled her thumb out of her mouth. 'Kate, stop sucking your thumb. You know what the dentist told you.'

'Can I scratch my tush instead?' she asked.

In the background, I heard Lia shouting, 'Mommy, Mae's pwaying doctow with Iwving.' I looked up and noticed Mae, stark naked, behind the new hydrangea bush.

'Everything's under control,' Irving announced. 'I'm a doctor.'

Both Ollie and Faith ran over to Mae to help her get her clothes back on.

I looked around the yard at my daughters, my friends, their children, Michael, and my dog, who was now chasing his tail. My world was just about perfect. Michael came over and put his arm around me. He pointed to his building. 'You know, someday we could turn that into one big house. What do you think?'

'Michael, I don't know what I'd do with such a big house. As you get to know me better, you'll see my needs are simple.'

Michael smiled. Would I ever tire of those dimples? 'Come on, Ivy, let's go get some of that Oprah Cake,' he said.

So we did.